THE SECOND-SMARTEST DOG THAT EVER LIVED

THE SECOND-SMARTEST
DOG THAT EVER LIVED

A NOVEL

WILL PASS

First Edition 2024

Library of Congress Control Number: 2024935122

ISBN: 979-8-9891805-0-9
eISBN: 979-8-9891805-1-6

Published in the United States of America
10 9 8 7 6 5 4 3 2 1

Cover design by David Drummond

THIESSEN PRESS
An Imprint of Freeford LLC
Fort Collins, Colorado

For Emma

"It appears, in fact, that if I am bound to do no injury to my fellow creatures, this is less because they are rational than because they are sentient beings: and this quality, being common both to men and beasts, ought to entitle the latter at least to the privilege of not being wantonly ill-treated by the former."

—Jean-Jacques Rousseau

"I would not wish any companion in the world but you."

—William Shakespeare

"Cripes."

—Vernald von Lang Lichaam Grote Hersenen de Derde

PART ONE

ROGER

I WAS NAMELESS.

There I was nonetheless, covered in blood like I'd just been born, a full-grown dog sprawled across the front seat of an animal control truck with a woman at the wheel.

She stroked my head.

She spoke softly to me.

"Hang in there, big ears," she said.

Everything was coming into focus.

Everything was tilting back and forth.

Cracked glass.

Blue sky.

The crowns of palm trees passing.

A furry gray leg, twisted below the elbow, paw turned unnaturally away.

Well, that looked painful.

Whose leg was that?

And who was this woman at the wheel?

This beautiful woman.

I have since seen more beautiful humans, but then, maybe because she was saving my life, or because I had sustained a traumatic brain injury, she was beautiful, and the sunlight cast a golden halo around her bun.

She was my guardian angel.

In khaki.

With road rage.

She honked.

She stuck her head out the window. "Move, moron! I've got an injury here!"

She came back in, face red, gentle again. "Good boy. Just keep breathing. Stay with me."

Another voice, deep and grainy, joined us from nowhere. "Dispatch to Hoover Animal Control."

The woman picked up. "Animal control. Go ahead."

"Hey Mary, there's a raccoon acting weird over by the elementary. You peel that dead dog off the highway yet?"

"He's alive. Barely. We're on our way to the vet."

"Well hey. Lucky dog."

"Hardly. Anybody call in plates?"

"Negative."

"You check the highway cams?"

"Affirmative. Too blurry, per usual. He bounced. I can tell you that. They were doin' about 80."

"Seriously?"

"10-4. Like I said. Lucky dog."

"What kind of a sicko throws a dog out of a moving car?"

"Cargo van, actually. A white one. No logos, before you ask. Right out the back door. Like a stack a newspapers."

"You're kidding me."

"Negatory. I do not kid."

"What kind of a sicko does that?"

"Oh, I dunno, Mary. Same day, different sicko, I guess. Anywho, once you drop off that dog—"

"Yeah yeah, the raccoon. You keep trying to find that driver. For once, just give me a name."

After a pause came the man's tired reply: "Roger."

Which explains why, in my confusion, I wondered: Who is this sicko, Roger, and why did he do this to me?

Then I began to seize.

A VERY GOOD BOY

I AWOKE THRASHING. Whining. Rolling. Yelping. Clanging.

My right forelimb was wrapped and rigid. I pressed my other three into extension, driving the world upside down.

A young woman in all blue appeared on the ceiling.

"Dr. Francis!" she called, and ran off.

The kennel spun. I rolled with it, gonged my head once, twice, three times, before lodging in a corner. Beyond the cage door a fluorescent void stank of chemicals. I howled, terrified of falling in.

"Hurry! He's, like, freaking out!"

She returned with a man in a white coat.

And I froze.

I knew, somehow, that I could not escape this man.

Sure enough, the door opened and they dragged me out. The woman held me somewhere between a hug and a headlock. The man was doing something with my paw. Then my leg felt cold. The cold was spreading through my body.

"Relax," he said. "Relax. Relax."

And as though his voice held some special power, I did. They floated me back into the cage, their words becoming as meaningless as the latching cage door.

I may have slept for a time after that. Or half of me did, while the other half remained in a flat world of shapes and smells. I knew the technician by her scrubs and floral scent, Dr. Francis by his dragging heels and bleached white coat. In crates and on leashes, cats and dogs came and went. I imagine some spoke to me, but I was too far gone to understand, or reply.

Until the last patient of the day.

He was a matted black terrier with eyes like white marbles. The technician carried him in and placed him on the treatment table, where, with apparent effort, he remained upright on his elbows. He struggled to breathe. Still he sniffed the air, searching, back and forth, until he sniffed in my direction.

Hey, pup, he said, his voice a rasp in my head.

Dr. Francis came in, really dragging his heels this time. He shaved a rectangle from the old terrier's leg and placed an IV catheter. Of course I did not know what it was called back then. I just knew it looked like my own. Some green thing. I thought we would soon be neighbors.

Instead Dr. Francis opened a safe in the wall. He retrieved a bottle of blue liquid.

Hey, pup, the terrier said again. *I can't see ya but I can smell ya. I know you're there.*

He frightened me. He looked but saw nothing. He stank of age and urine and whatever was rotting inside of him. It was on his breath. Some dead thing. Death itself.

Speak, he said.

I…I'm here, I said.

Good. I need ya to pass on a message for me.

I don't—

Just listen, pup. You tell those fuzzy freaks in the park that I'm gonna chase 'em on the other side. I'll catch 'em there. Every last one of 'em. You tell 'em that.

Fuzzy freaks?

You tell those squirrels that Banjo never quits. You hear me? Never.

What's a squirrel?

Good one, pup. I could use a laugh right about now.

"You're a very good boy," Dr. Francis said. "We love you very much."

Wait, I said. *Do you know Roger?*

But I was too late.

Banjo rested his head upon his paws.

It was strange. I could sense that he was gone, as if his essence had evaporated, leaving only a tangle of black fur.

I felt sort of empty myself.

Dr. Francis washed his hands. The technician put the body in a trash bag, tagged it, tied it in a knot, and took it out back. She returned, but only for her purse.

"See you tomorrow," she said, perhaps too cheerfully. She hesitated, as though to say something else, then left.

Dr. Francis remained at the sink long after she was gone. Soaping. Rinsing. Repeating. Repeating. Repeating.

At last he shut off the tap with his elbows and flicked his fingers in the air. He perched on a stool before a stack of files and scribbled notes. As the stack dropped by half, the aches in my body returned. When the stack was gone, I was in pain.

Again, Dr. Francis opened the safe.

Maybe this is it, I thought distantly. The blue solution. The trash bag. The other side. There is no escaping the man in the white coat.

He kneeled to open my cage. He was close to me now, with hundreds of silver hairs poking through his cheeks and chin like fur trying to regrow. His eyes were surrounded by pillows of red.

"Good boy," he said, holding my paw like two humans shaking hands. "You're a very, very good boy."

The cold passed through me from tip to tail.

Then I was lodged in a white tunnel.

"Nice comfy cone," he said, his voice distorted by plastic. "Do you like music? How about some Bach?"

I do like music.

I do like Bach.

But of course I could not respond.

And so I fell asleep to the sound of water down the drain and piano notes in the air.

OH, THE DOODAD DAY

BIRDIE APPEARED from the shadows in the heart of the night. She sauntered onto a stage of moonlight where she performed figure-eights, silver tail pluming. With each turn she ventured closer. She watched me carefully, yet discreetly, for a reaction. Getting none, she grew bolder. She brushed along my cage. When that didn't work, she batted at the latch and jumped away. I gave her nothing. Dissatisfied, she sat. She licked her paw and wiped her head.

Yes. Cats are vain. If they knew how to look in a mirror they would never do anything else.

Nice cone, dummy, Birdie said.

I was groggy. The splint and cone made it awkward to move. I shifted my weight.

Easy, champ, she said. *Big day tomorrow.*

What happens tomorrow?

Her tail flicked. *They're going to cut off your leg. That's what happens tomorrow.*

The drugs blocked any anxiety. I was more curious than concerned.

Why?

What do you mean, why?

Why would they cut off my leg?

Don't be stupid.

But how do you know?

Her eyes rested on it, faint blue. *Because it has the funny look.*

The splint? That's what Dr. Francis called it, right?

Look, dummy. If you get a thingy or whatever on your leg, and a thingy on your head, and you stay the night, then the next day what you get is your leg cut off. I see it all the time.

She let this information sink in, hoping again for a reaction. Again, I had none to give. Everything was so removed. I looked back for a connection. I remembered Mary and the man on the radio. I remembered how angry she had been. How much she wanted that name.

Roger, I said. *Do you know Roger?*

The Spaniel?

The sicko.

Hmm. The only Roger I know is a Spaniel. Hates toenail trims? About this high? She stood on hind legs and extended a paw straight up.

He's not a dog, I said. *He's a human. I'm pretty sure. His name is Roger. He's a sicko…he drives a…white…van. He was doing 80. I bounced. Like a newspaper.*

Riiight, Birdie said. *You know, there's probably lots of Rogers. Not like Birdie. I'm one of a kind.* She relished this for a moment, then sniffed the air, searching toward me. She stopped. Eyes wide.

What now, I said.

Oh. My. Gosh. Do you still have your doodads?

My what?

Your doodads! OMG you doooooo.

No, I don't.

Yes, you do! I can smell them! Nasty stinky doodads!

Go away.

You don't even know what doodads are.

Do too.

Wow. I mean, I've seen dumb dogs. And then there's you.

I'm going back to sleep, I said, closing my eyes.

Oh, you're no fun. Look down below. The eggs between your legs. Got those?

I tried to look, but my cone hooked on the cage. I twisted the other way, but again the cone blocked me. I felt woozy.

Let me see, Birdie said.

I lifted a hind leg.

Yep, still got your doodads. Say goodbye to those ugly things too.

I couldn't see them, but if I focused, I could feel them. They felt... sensitive. Some anxiety found its way through.

Why do they cut off doodads? I asked.

Because they love cutting off doodads more than anything else in the whole wide world. Doodads in the bucket. That's where the doodads go.

But why?

Not this again.

There's got to be a reason.

Because they're extra? And dangly? And gross? How many reasons do you need?

I don't understand.

That's because you're a dumb dog. Of many.

I hung my head.

Oh, don't be like that, she said. *It's boring.*

She strolled away, yowling as she prowled the shadows. She talked to herself, mostly nonsense, although some was poetry, apparently her own. I can recall one poem in particular:

> *Prey! Oh prey, she prays for prey*
> *Let her kill, and let them say*
> *She was lethal, she was fierce*
> *The fiercest, some say*
> *She was a deadly Birdie*
> *And she made the bad prey pay*

Eventually she slinked away.

The metal box on my cage door hummed along, pushing cool liquid into my leg. I lay still under a blanket of drugs and darkness.

Birdie must have thought I was asleep when she crept back into the room. She was low to the ground, silently stalking toward me. At the edge of the moonlight she stopped. Her backside rose, then wiggled, settling for the pounce.

I swear, on my own two doodads, when I barked, that cat hit the ceiling.

THUMBS

I AWOKE to the metal box beeping and flashing. Soaked in urine. Aching all over. Leg throbbing. Yet alert. Awake. Mind stark. Everything was clear.

My leg was broken.

I had sustained a head injury.

I had been in an accident.

No, not an accident.

Somebody did this to me.

They hurt me.

Roger.

Roger hurt me.

But the woman saved me.

Mary saved me.

She brought me here.

A veterinary clinic.

I was in a cage in a veterinary clinic.

My thoughts were careening like race cars down a track.

So think!

Of course that hit the brakes.

I couldn't think of anything at all.

Breathe.

Okay. So.

Observe.

It was early morning.

A sunbeam, from a window out of sight, slanted across the clinic, imbuing jars of cotton balls and gauze with a blush of dawn. I appreciated this beauty, even knew the right descriptor—crepuscular— and, for a moment longer, admired the expanses of my own lexicon, before recalling what Birdie had said.

They were going to cut off my leg.

Which was bad.

Yes. Bad.

And my doodads.

Also bad?

Yes. Bad!

Anything attached to me, I reasoned, was there for a reason. Even if I didn't know the reason. The reason was the reason, if you see my reasoning. Some lovely logic there. A true tautology. Oh yes, my brain was back.

Go, brain, go!

But no.

Um.

Uh-oh.

The roots of fear were growing through the empty places where the drugs had been. Add sunlight. Some pee smell. Dried blood. Wait a second.

See me blinking, a bewildered dog with a cone on his head. Watch panic blooming—a chaotic flower.

I sat up. My right forelimb looked more like a yellow cannon than a leg.

More blinking.

Okay, here's the panic.

Here it comes.

BOOM!

They're going to cut off your leg! And your doodads! Your DOODADS! You dope! You need those! You don't know what for! But you do! Of course you do!

I spun back and forth, tangling and untangling, stumbling and standing and stumbling again.

I barked.

I whined.

Oh yes. I lost it.

Eventually, however, I found it again.

And I was tired.

And my leg hurt.

So I sat down.

I panted.

Okay. Enough.

Focus now. Think.

How long until they came? Unknown.

What could I do? Something.

Great. That was helpful. Thanks, brain.

At least look.

I examined the latch to my cage, and, across the room, the back door, with its round, silver knob, clearly designed for a human hand.

No. One challenge at a time, I told myself. First, the latch. Then worry about the knob.

I reached for the latch with my teeth. Nope. The cone kept everything out of reach.

I rolled my eyes around, surrounded by white plastic. The latch was actually the second thing. Which meant the knob was the third thing. The cone came first.

Cone. Latch. Knob.

Cone. Latch. Knob.

Got it.

So. Cone.

Maybe I could slip it off.

I lay on my side. Using my left forelimb, I hooked a toenail into the rim of the cone. I pushed away and shrugged back. It jammed around my ears. I straightened my neck and tried harder, succeeding only in choking myself. I tried to remove my toenail but it was caught.

Morning, dummy, Birdie said. She settled on the counter in the sunlight.

I threw my head to the side, colliding with the cage. Ears ringing, foot dislodged, I gasped.

Wow, Birdie said. *Seriously. Wow.*

Ignore her.

They'll be here soon, Birdie said. *Very soon. Say goodbye to your bits and pieces.*

Ignore. Think. If you can't remove the cone, then what can you do?

What did I know about the cone? Where was its weakness?

Well, it was flexible. That was something.

I leaned into the corner of the cage, bending the edge into my mouth.

Here we go.

I worked the plastic back and forth and tore a chunk away. I spat it out. There it was. Proof of principle.

I would need a much larger opening to really see and use my mouth. Which meant I needed to do it again. Enough thinking. Time to act.

I rotated the cone and got back to work.

What are you doing? Birdie asked.

Getting...grrr...out of...grrr...here.

Stop that.

I tore another piece.

You are going to be in so much trouble.

Soon the cage was littered with scraps. The cone was ragged all the way around. My peripheral vision was restored. And I could use my mouth.

Ha, I said.

Big deal, Birdie said. *I've seen that trick loads of times. Any dumb dog can chew things. If you hadn't noticed, you're still in a cage.*

Thing two: The latch.

Or was it?

I sniffed the place where the plastic line entered my leg. I needed to unhook myself first.

So thing two was the IV. Which meant thing three was the latch. And thing four was the knob. The things kept coming. But what else could I do?

I wouldn't do that, Birdie said.

I was chewing the tape.

Oh, I can't watch, Birdie said, watching.

It was easy. I shredded it. The catheter just fell right out.

Ha, I said again. *I did it.*

You idiot, Birdie said. *Look.*

I looked. Blood was pouring out of my leg. My blood. The smell hit me.

Oh no, I said.

Oh yes, Birdie said. *You've done it now.*

I was starting to panic again.

Breathe. Stay calm. It's just blood. Just blood pouring out of your leg uncontrollably.

Well, it was nice knowing you, Birdie said. *Not really, of course. As you are a dumb and stinky dog.*

Fortunately, I am not. Dumb, that is.

I pressed the splint on the bleed. Maybe I could plug it up. I held it for a few seconds, looked again. Slightly less bleeding. It was working. I compressed the area. Took a series of deep breaths. Checked again. The bleeding had stopped.

Congratulations, Birdie said. *You didn't bleed to death.*

Ignore the cat. Focus.

Thing three: The latch. I tried to reach it with my teeth, then with my paw, but it was hopeless. I bit the cage door and shook it in frustration. It needed to be opened from the outside. But I was inside. Which was a conundrum.

Think.

What was outside that could help me?

I would try anything.

Hey, Birdie.

Hey, what? She was curled up now, eyes closed.

You gotta help me.

You must have hit your head pretty hard, dog. And that's not the way to ask.

Please?

She opened her eyes halfway. *I do love it when a dog begs. Keep begging. We'll see.*

Please.

With more feeling. Beg like you've never begged before.

I'm not sure how convincing I was, but I tried. *Please, Birdie. Please help me. Pleeeeeeaaaassse. I'll do anything. Please.*

Pathetic. No.

I thought again. What did I know about Birdie? Very little. But maybe enough.

I could give you something in return, I said.

Like what? Fleas?

What do you want more than anything in the world?

Birdie's pupils narrowed into black daggers.

Anything, I said.

She was staring at me, unblinking.

Go ahead, Birdie, I said. *Name it. What do you want more than anything in the whole world? Let me out, and I'll get it for you. I promise. Anything. Anything at all.*

Her eyes wandered across the floor, tracking some invisible movement.

A mouse, she said.

A mouse?

Yes. A real live scaredy mouse that I could hunt, and torture, and kill, and eat. And it would squeak, and it would bleed, and it would wiggle as I crunched it and munched it. A mouse. A real one.

Good choice.

Yeah, she said, fever passing. *Too bad you're fresh out.*

She was right, of course, but her answer gave me another idea. I tore a long strip from the towel beneath me.

Now you're just being bad for the sake of being bad, Birdie said. *You eat that and they'll cut your belly open too. I've seen it before.*

I passed the fabric through the cage above the latch. I lowered it until the tip grazed the ground. Then I jerked my head. The towel twitched.

Birdie crouched.

I twitched it again.

Her hind end rose.

Another twitch.

She leapt off the counter and charged, paws slashing. I pulled the strip higher, around the latch, dancing it back and forth. Birdie batted away. A left jab rattled the cage. A right hook lifted the bolt. Another slid it sideways.

I pressed my head. The door swung open.

Birdie vanished around the corner as I stumbled out.

I did it!

I was free!

Or so I thought, swaying there in the center of the room, on the brink of fainting, already willing myself to focus on that reflective sphere that stood between me and the outside world. Between me and total freedom. All I had to do was turn that knob. That knob made for human hands with four fingers and opposable thumbs.

I had come this far, hadn't I? I had beaten the cone, hadn't I? Who removed that line? Me. And it was me who opened the cage. Me!

You can do this, I thought. Thumbs be damned. You can turn this knob. Just focus. Think of a solution. Focus.

Through a haze of sedatives and my lingering concussion, I directed every ounce of my attention onto that knob. I channeled every last brainwave. I even held my breath.

Then I thought: Am I doing that?

Because the knob was already turning. It was turning without me touching it. And I wondered—I really wondered—if my wanting something badly enough could cause it to occur, perhaps through some untapped power within my mind.

Am I doing that?

I really wondered if I was telekinetic.

Which shows how much I had to learn about the laws and limitations of this world, both physical and metaphysical.

Because that's not what was happening at all.

SHOWDOWN

THE BACK DOOR OPENED. There, between me and my freedom, stood a small man in a white coat. In one hand he held a briefcase; in the other, a banana. Between his legs, blue sky and palm trees and an empty road that carried onward into the infinite red desert. We met eyes, each judging the other's next move. Two cowboys at high noon.

Draw.

I lunged. The briefcase and banana fell. My nose crossed the threshold but went no further. The cone was caught between his knees. The cone! Of course, the cone, the cone, the inescapable cone. The bane of all dogs everywhere.

So. Yeah. I bit him.

Dr. Francis shouted and stumbled inward, knocking me back. He danced around on his unbitten leg, clutching the other while saying things like, "Ahhh!" and, "Why!?"

Meanwhile, I, a previously rational dog, experienced my first full-blown panic attack, triggered, I think, by the finality of that slamming door. I was sure of three things and three things only. One: I was going to die. Two: I was going to die. And three: I needed to run —really, really fast.

So I did.

I went careening down the hallway, splint whacking out a random rhythm. I tripped on the threshold, sending me spinning across the waiting room on my toenails and crashing into a table, shattering a coffee maker and mugs. With wet shards raining down, I relaunched myself through a gap in the front desk. But the tiles. Oh, the tiles! The true bane of all dogs everywhere! I slid face first into those floor-to-ceiling shelves. I was stunned. Then I was more stunned, as I found myself under the growing shadow of a capsizing manila wall. I blasted through rolling chairs as that tidal wave of paper records came thundering down, driving me howling around the corner, straight through the loop of a slip leash. It cinched tight around my neck. Yet my legs carried onward and upward, leaving me briefly weightless and wondering how I had returned to the place I started, before gravity brought me back down with a thump. But no, I was not done. I had not yet begun to panic. I alligator rolled, twisting the leash around Dr. Francis's hand until he squeaked. Still I rolled on, all the way across the room, finally smacking my head on the x-ray machine, a cold steel finish that rendered me almost, but not quite, unconscious.

Technical knockout.

By the time I could think again, I was already back in my cage, defeated.

Dr. Francis seemed a little defeated too, and sweaty. He rolled up his pant leg to see the punctures in his calf. Muttering to himself, he hoisted his foot into the sink, where he cleaned and dressed the wound. Now we both had a bandaged leg. My forelimb. His hind. Sort of fair, I thought.

"You better not have rabies," Dr. Francis said. He took a bottle down from the shelf and swallowed a tablet. "And this better not get infected."

The words he used when he saw the mess in reception were as explicit as they were descriptive, so I won't repeat them here. The things he said about me, I still think, were unfair.

A FINE HUMAN INDEED

A FAMILIAR SMELL returned me from sleep. Mary. There she was, in full, if disheveled, uniform, from scuffed black shoes up to a disorderly bun, standing straight with her hands on her hips. Dr. Francis, in comparison, was both disheveled and demoralized. He slumped on the stool beside her.

"Bit of a handful, huh, Doc?" Mary said, smiling at me.

"I'm not sure this one's adoptable."

"Aw, he's cute. Just look at those ears."

"He bites."

"He was scared."

"You didn't see it. The only reason he's calm now is because I gave him a horseload of sedatives."

I felt quite clearheaded, actually, having taken a long nap. They seemed to be negotiating my worth. I guess a dog—even a dog like me—is born with certain responses. I rolled onto my back and showed them my belly.

"Oh wook at dat wittle bewwy," Mary said.

"This is how he gets you," Dr. Francis said.

I thumped my tail.

"He is sooo cute," Mary said.

I thumped my tail harder.

"I wouldn't get too attached," Dr. Francis said. "We need to amputate that leg."

My tail stopped.

"You can't fix it?" Mary asked.

"He has multiple complex fractures in his humerus, radius, and ulna. In other words, his leg is shattered. Ideally it would be plated. Two plates, at least. But that means we need to bring in an orthopedic surgeon. Not cheap. I assume the city budget won't cover it, since amputation is a humane alternative."

Mary shifted her utility belt. She squatted at my cage. I pressed my nose against the bars.

"Watch your fingers," Dr. Francis said.

I licked her fingertips.

"Tasting you before he eats you," Dr. Francis said.

I looked up at Mary with the biggest, saddest eyes I could muster —eyes that said, *Please don't cut off my leg.*

"As you probably know, the neuter may or may not help with his behavioral issues," Dr. Francis said. "He's learned what he's learned."

"Well, that'll have to wait," Mary said. "His scumbag owner has nine days to claim him."

I didn't fully comprehend this last exchange. Although I had developed a quick hatred for the man named Roger, as he had tried to kill me, I could not yet conceive of being owned by him or anyone, just as I did not understand the word "neuter." Yet I thought nothing of my uneven vocabulary or my lack of long-term memory. Maybe this was normal in its abnormality. Blind spots are just that—voids in our consciousness, unknowable by definition. If I knew what I didn't know, I would have known it, right?

But all that twisted logic lay ahead of me.

There in that cage, I was just a mote of dust still in motion, not yet settled enough to reflect on what had happened to me, or that I had even existed before waking up in that animal control truck.

I just *was.*

And, yeah, I was a little high.

"In the meantime," Mary said, "let's fix that leg."

"I blocked off time for the amputation tomorrow morning."

"No, I mean fix it. Really fix it."

"But—"

"Relax, Doc. If it's over budget, I'll pay for it myself."

With those words, Mary proved herself to be one of the finest human beings I have ever met.

I am happy to report that I made it through that surgery with all four legs. And my doodads, thank you very much. When I awoke from anesthesia, Birdie was sitting outside my cage, clearly disappointed.

You're still a very dumb dog, she said. *Very, very, very dumb. And stinky. And ugly. I forgot to tell you that before. You're ugly. Very ugly.*

I was too drugged to care, or think about anything at all, and so drifted back to sleep.

When I awoke again, Mary was in my cage rubbing my ears. It felt like heaven.

"Guess what," she whispered. "You're coming home with me."

And then she kissed me on my nose.

BROTHER

"WELCOME HOME," Mary said.

I stopped in the doorway, needing time to process the sights and smells. Well, the sights didn't take long. Through the circle of my cone I could see a pile of shoes, a floral couch, plastic plants. Human stuff. Whatever.

It was the smells that really made me pause. Not counting Mary, three animals lived here. The first and second were a dog and cat. Easy. The third was unusual. Exotic. I sniffed again. The animal's odor was light and sharp, like citrus, with an oily, floral aftersmell. Like lemon mixed with sunflower seeds. The novelty made me nervous.

"C'mon," Mary said. "Don't be shy."

"Oi oi," called a croaky voice.

I trailed her into the living room, where I discovered that the strange odor and that croaky voice belonged to an enormous bird—a bright-blue parrot on a perch. He bobbed up and down, then tilted his head, focusing on me, dropping my tail between my legs.

"Antonio Banderas, this is Leonardo DiCaprio," Mary said.

Apparently this was my name.

"Or Leo for short," Mary added, to my relief.

"Leo," Antonio Banderas repeated. I had no idea that a non-human animal could speak aloud. He trilled and cawed and said, "Leo. Yuck. Yuck."

"Be nice to Leo," Mary said. "He's been through a lot."

"A lot," Antonio said. "Leo, Leo, Leo."

"You got it," Mary said, going into the bedroom.

Antonio rotated his head all the way around, watching her go, then snapped back to look at me. He had splashes of yellow around his eyes and beak, but was otherwise bright blue. His tongue dabbed in and out as he talked, occasionally interrupting himself with clucks, and warbles, and other whirring sounds.

Ay, you look like hell, he said, more observation than insult. He warbled, clucked. *You have been, how do you say, playing on traffic?*

With my scabs and cone and fresh bandage—yellow again—I must have looked like a broken clown. In comparison, Antonio was perfectly preened, quite marvelous to behold so far above me. I lifted my tail and did my best to appear important. I brought up the only serious topic I knew.

Hello, I said. *I'm looking for Roger.*

Ay, bom, straight to business, yes. What kind of bird is he, this Roger?

He's a human.

"Roger, Roger, Roger," Antonio repeated aloud, his tongue appearing and disappearing.

Oh, and he's a sicko, I added. *If that helps.*

Antonio tilted his head. *Ay, my friend, I am sorry to disappoint, but we do not have a Roger, nor have I ever met one. We have I, Antonio, Hyacinth Macaw, of the Kingdom of Amazonia. Then we have the small and idiot Pug, Shakespeare. Then we have the small and fat cat, Dwid. We have these things, chee. But we do not have a Roger, no. Nor do we have a sicko amongst us. Nor do I know what this is, and having no knowledge of this, and yet knowing many things, I warn you, it may not exist at all.*

Mary returned in jeans and a T-shirt. Antonio squawked.

She scratched behind his head. "What are you cawing about?" His feathers rose and settled as he leaned into her finger. She presented a nut. He took it delicately in his large, hooked beak, before crushing it in one bite, then bobbing up and down with satisfaction.

Just then, the flap in the back door burst open. Into the room spilled a fat ball of snorting wrinkly joy, tongue lolling, eyes bulging, sliding across the wood floor, then spinning in place.

Ay, give me the strength, Antonio said.

Hi, Mom! Shakespeare said, still spinning. *Hi, bird! Hi, cat! Hi, bird again!*

"Easy, Shakespeare," Mary said.

Shakespeare froze. His crazy eyes settled upon me, at least as well as they could, since they pointed in slightly different directions.

Whoa, he said.

"This is Leo," Mary said.

Could it be? Shakespeare asked. *Do my eyes defeat me?*

Hello, I said.

He leapt straight up, landed, slipped, fell over, got up, then started spinning again, this time orbiting around me. *A big brother?*

No, I said.

A big brother! he shouted, all the while sliding and falling and getting up and spinning and falling and getting up again.

Chee, he will wear himself out, Antonio said, *eventually.*

Eventually came sooner, and more suddenly, than expected. Shakespeare stopped. He extended his neck and gasped for air, tongue blue.

"Breathe, Shakespeare," Mary said. "Calm down. Breathe."

It is in part because he has a smooshed face, Antonio explained. *And in part because he cannot think and breathe at the same time.*

Shakespeare collapsed.

Lie down, Antonio said. *Good boy.*

Foamy slobber pooled around Shakespeare's head. *I've always wanted a big brother,* he said.

I'm not your brother, I said.

I would save your own breath too, Antonio said.

We're not brothers, I said. *We don't even look alike.*

Perhaps, Antonio said. *But you will never change his mind. Besides, look how happy this makes him.*

It was true. Even as Shakespeare recovered from asphyxiation, he was cheerful. *I knew you'd come,* he said. *I just had to wait. And wait and wait and wait and wait.*

I was sore and groggy and overwhelmed. Mary seemed to appreciate this. She led me to my appointed bed, a lovely soft oval. I circled several times before lying down.

Shakespeare missed the hint. He sat on the rug just inches from my face, his chubby hairless belly on display, his tongue, pink again, hanging from his mouth.

Hey Leo, what's your favorite type of bone? he asked. *I like those short ones. Or those twisty ones. But I also like those long ones with the lumpy ends, you know? Those ones you really have to chew a lot before you can eat them? You know those?*

No, I said.

Hey Leo, you ever eat a bug? I eat lots of bugs. I once ate a bug that hurt my tongue and it went buzz buzz. And then I ate another one that went buzz buzz and that one hurt my tongue too. So whenever I eat those kind, I know it's gonna hurt, but I can't not eat them. You know?

Uh. Sure.

Really? Because Mom says don't eat bugs. And she says don't put your head in the toilet. And she says don't chew your leg. But most of all, she says, Shakespeare, don't chase your tail. But the thing is, I need to catch it. And I'm gonna catch it. I just need to sneak up on it.

Shakespeare turned slowly to look at his tail, short and curled. When it twitched, he spun and snapped, stopped and wheezed.

It saw me, he said. *Again.*

Is he always like this? I asked Antonio.

Ay, except for when he sleeps. When he sleeps, he snores.

Shakespeare caught his breath and started chasing his tail again.

"Hey, no," Mary called from the kitchen. "Shakespeare. No. No."

But he was already whirling. He spun faster and faster. Again he collapsed into an asthmatic heap.

"That's it," Mary said. "Donut time." She looked from Shakespeare to me. "Oh, this could be very, very cute." She went into the laundry room and returned with two air-filled, donut-shaped collars.

Ooh, my no-tail collar, Shakespeare said. *When I wear it, I don't have a tail.*

Mary Velcroed the gray donut around his neck. It compressed the skin around his head, adding more wrinkles to his face.

I was too tired to care when she came at me with a larger, pink version. I regained my peripheral vision in exchange for the last of my dignity.

Oh well, I thought, resting my head. It is soft.

A moment later, I was asleep.

FISH

IN THE EVENING, Mary leashed me and walked me around the backyard. It was mostly rocks. Beyond the fence, the desert extended in a red dirt plain all the way to a range of serrated black mountains on the horizon. As the sun fell onto this ridgeline, it deformed at the edges, like an orange juiced upon rocks. I thought it was hot then, unaware that it was only spring.

I walked along the chain link, ginger on my bad leg, stepping around scrubby plants and succulents.

Don't pee on this one, Shakespeare said, sniffing a cactus. *I did that one time and it hurt real bad. It hurt really, really bad the second time I did it. So I try not to do that anymore.*

I found a good spot under the palm tree. Fallen hairs from the trunk made a soft patch of ground.

That's one of my favorite pee spots, Shakespeare said. *But you can use it.*

I looked at Shakespeare, who stared at me.

I can't go if I'm being watched, I said.

Totally.

Could you please look away?

Oh, right, he said, turning around. *Hey Leo?*

What?

Ever had bacon?

No, I said, not even knowing what bacon was. I could lift my back leg if I leaned against the fence for balance. Some dignity restored.

"Good boy," Mary said.

Oh my gosh, you are going to love bacon, Shakespeare said. *I can't believe you've never had it. I mean, wow! That's weird!*

Once relieved, I hobbled over to the gate.

Hey Leo?

What.

You ever had cheese?

No, I said, not knowing what cheese was, either.

Oh my gosh! Sometimes Mom gives me cheese if I'm good. Like, really, really good. She might give you some too!

The gate was locked. If it wasn't for my injury, I thought, I could jump the fence. And nobody could catch me out there. I suppose I've always had an instinct for freedom. But that would have to wait.

I can't believe you've never had cheese, Shakespeare said. *You are the weirdest dog. It's great!*

Against the corner of the house, tucked under a bush, I discovered a cluster of thin white bones. I sniffed them.

"Gross," Mary said, pulling me back.

I recognized the smell, but, like so many things, struggled to name it.

Shakespeare sniffed the pile.

"Don't you dare roll in that," Mary said.

Shakespeare backed away. *We shouldn't even sniff this,* he said. *This is Dwid's fish. He's a cat. He doesn't like sharing.*

Fish, I said. The word swam out of the darkness. It was a creature that lived underwater. That made no sense. *Where does Dwid catch fish?*

Out there, Shakespeare said, facing the desert.

I figured he was confused.

REFINED SOCIETY

MARY CLOSED the door and slid plywood over the dog flap. "Sorry, bub," she said. "No dog door for you. Shakespeare, you're just gonna have to hold it."

I dug around in my bed, getting the cushion just right before lying down. Again, Shakespeare sat in front of me.

Do you like your no-tail collar? he asked.

No.

Me neither. Except for sleeping. Or for when I'm not sleeping. It's like a pillow that cuddles me wherever I go.

Right.

What happened to your leg?

It's broken in several places. But plated.

What's butt plated?

Just plated. As in, fixed with metal plates, I said, acting like I hadn't recently learned this from pieces of conversation in the clinic. *I'll be back to running in twelve weeks.*

Oh. Shakespeare stared at me for a while. *What's a week?*

Even I remembered that. *Seven days,* I said.

What's a seven?

Seriously?

You may as well be speaking to a wall, said a drawling voice.

Shakespeare lowered his ears. I looked up. In the shadow between the top of the kitchen cabinets and the ceiling, amongst creeping silk vines, appeared a solitary green eye. The eye receded. From rustling leaves, an orange paw reached for the top of an adjacent cat tree, followed by the head and body of a large tabby, graceful until his belly plopped down.

That's Dwid, Shakespeare said. *He's a cat.*

Dwid lay on his side, flab spilling over the edge, tail testing the air. A crater marked the absence of his right eye. His remaining globe was an unblinking emerald, now fixed upon me. I could sense that a poem was coming, but before I could ask him not to, Dwid had already begun:

> *A cat so great I drive dogs mad*
> *With my coat of marvelous gold*
> *Nine lives I was given but one I had*
> *Taken from me before I was old*
>
> *Eight lives left, I must spend the rest*
> *With a bird and a dog stupid*
> *Bow down now or die like the rest*
> *I am the King of the Cats, I am Dwid*

Dwid is really smart, Shakespeare said.

Wah, king of cats, Antonio said. *Do not encourage him. He is as royal as a grub.*

Buzz off, bird, Dwid said. *What do you know?*

I knew a real king, Antonio said. *Unless you are forgetting?*

Here we go again, Dwid said.

I was once a wild bird, and I knew the King of Amazonia, Antonio said wistfully. *King Ferro, a jaguar with a head as big as this cat's body.*

Dwid yawned. *Is it possible to die of boredom?*

We, the Hyacinth Macaw, Antonio went on, *were the royal family's messengers. In fact, my father was—*

—a turkey, Dwid said.

Antonio puffed and settled, then closed his eyes, the argument too undignified to pursue further.

I should have followed his lead.

Hey mutt, Dwid said. *Don't get too comfortable in that bed. You'll be gone before you know it.*

Dwid is a mean cat, Shakespeare clarified.

Is that so, I said.

Just smell that bed, Dwid said. *I'll wait. Really. Smell it. For your own good.*

I shouldn't have, but I did. Through a heavy layer of detergent, I detected traces of countless dogs, all blended together in a distant noise.

She brings the broken ones home until their human comes to collect them, Dwid said. *If nobody shows, she'll hand you off to the nearest human.*

I needed to conceal my ignorance now. I needed to be confident.

I don't have a human, I said, *and I don't need one.*

Dwid's tail flicked, much like Birdie's had when she imagined a mouse, or sensed weakness. *Is that so,* he said.

Yes, I said, but with some uncertainty.

Tell me, mutt, where were you? Before your tumble?

The question was so simple, yet I couldn't understand it. What did he mean, before?

I was with Mary, I said.

Before that.

I should have thought of a lie. Instead, like an idiot, I said, *Nowhere.*

Nowhere?

I wasn't anywhere. Then I was with Mary.

Nonsense. You had to be somewhere, mutt. Think. Start at the beginning. Where did you come from? When you were a puppy?

Puppy?

Dwid retracted his head into his neck. Slowly he reemerged from his folds. *Am I understanding correctly that you don't know what a puppy is?*

Course he does, Shakespeare said. *Everybody knows puppy. Even I know puppy. It's like kitten. But for dogs. Duh.*

Confusion must have been plain on my face. I didn't know what a kitten was either. Honestly. I wanted to crawl under my bed and hide there until I could figure out what was wrong with me. I was broken and pieces were missing.

So it's true, Dwid said.

Again, I shouldn't have taken the bait, but of course, in my naivety, I did. I wanted to understand.

What's true? I asked.

You are the dumbest dog that ever lived. I heard you don't even know what a squirrel is.

Lies, Shakespeare said. *Take it back.*

Of course I know what a squirrel is, I said, wondering how this cat could possibly know about my conversation with that terrier.

Fine, Dwid said. *Tell me.*

Easy, I said. *It's a fuzzy thing you chase. It lives in the park.*

Nailed it, Shakespeare said.

I changed the subject before Dwid could ask for a more detailed description. Hoping to regain some ground, I summoned a confidence that faded with every word I spoke.

I was with Roger. Before. It was him who did this to me. So. I was with him. In the van. Before.

I'm beginning to feel quite frustrated by this conversation, Dwid said. *You just admitted it. You have a human. Roger is your human. He owns you. Obviously.*

I don't think that's right, I said. *That can't be right.*

Oh, but it is. Because all dogs must have owners. Not like cats. Cats are unownable.

Mary's your owner.

Mary and I live together. See the difference?

I did not see the difference. But I could see that asking Dwid to explain anything would only invite more abuse. I turned to Antonio, hoping he could move the conversation along.

You said you knew a king? I asked.

Knows me, Dwid said.

Please tell the story, Antonio, Shakespeare said. *The king story. I like that one. Please?*

It is quite the tale, Dwid said. *Do tell us the names of all the princes and princesses again. I always forget.*

Antonio's eyes flashed open. *Perhaps I will tell how you lost that eye.*

Ooh, I've always wanted to know that, Shakespeare said.

Why not tell us about your fear of flying, instead? Dwid said.

Antonio screeched. He extended his wings to reveal their four-foot span, then folded them neatly around himself. *Wake me when the worm returns to his hole.* He turned his head all the way around to nestle his beak within the feathers of his back. He actually slept like that.

You really are an exceptionally stupid mutt, Dwid said, *with the nerve to parade those doodads around, I might add. Aren't you disgusted with yourself? And let's not forget that you bit that innocent doctor, I mean—*

Wait, what's doodads? Shakespeare asked.

Quiet, Pug, Dwid said. *The only thing I don't understand, mutt, is how you made it this far without being put down.*

Down where? Shakespeare asked.

How do you know all of this? I asked Dwid.

Since he had appeared, he had not blinked. His one eye was endlessly watching.

Follow me now, he said, his voice syrupy and condescending. *Cats talk to cats, and those cats talk to other cats, and those cats talk to me. Understand? Probably not. As a dog, it must be difficult to understand the workings of a refined society.*

Dwid knows everything and everybody, Shakespeare said.

Dwid purred. *I never thought I'd say this, but the Pug is right.*

So you know Roger? I asked. *Whether he's my owner or not. You know him?*

Dwid's tail curled, released. *You mean the sicko?*

Yes, I said, unable to hide my excitement. *That's the one.*

Of course I know Roger.

I stood up too fast. I swayed on three legs. *Where is he? Tell me.*

Wouldn't you like to know.

Yes? Shakespeare said.

Maybe if you begged, Dwid said, *then I'd remember.*

But the thing about cats, I had already learned, is that they lie.

How did you lose that eye? I asked.

Dwid's tail went stiff. His hair stood on end. Finally, he blinked.

KILLSONG

I AWOKE WITH A START. It was night. A blue glow from the kitchen cast shadows along the ceiling and walls.

Something had woken me.

Antonio was awake too, and alert, his head fixed, staring out the windows. Shakespeare was already there, his breath fogging the glass. I joined him, yet he did not speak. We three stared together, searching that vast black space between us and the jagged horizon. Beyond those mountains, the city glowed, and from the center of that city, a column of white light shone straight up—a beacon piercing the stars. I was drawn to that light. In time it would become my obsession.

But first I heard a sound.

Yes. From the darkness of the desert—a high-pitched cry.

Something was out there.

My hackles rose. A second voice answered the first, this one lower, in a pained howl. A third joined with a chatter. I couldn't make out the words. By some deeper instinct, however, I knew what they were talking about. They were talking about blood.

Coyote, Antonio whispered. He pulled his wings tighter around himself.

The coyotes seemed to be gathering. From a chaos of yips and howls, their voices aligned into a soaring killsong—a harmonious, beautiful, warlike anthem. It was awakening something inside of me. I felt an urge to go closer—to find them, to join them.

"They must have got something," Mary said, coming out of her room. She cupped her hands on the glass and peered out.

The killsong devolved back into noise. Yips and cries again. Still, their excitement was palpable.

"I bet Dentler's out there," Mary said. "Trying to blast their heads off."

Shakespeare whined.

"It's okay, bubba," Mary said. "How about a treat to take your mind off it?"

She gave us something called turkey jerky—a first for me, as far as I knew. Shakespeare was thrilled. He settled back into bed and gnawed away. I held mine in my mouth, staring out the window, listening for the coyotes while studying that eerie white column of light.

"Don't worry, honey, you're safe in here," Mary said. She closed the blinds and returned to her bedroom.

The howls and yaps faded. Shakespeare softened his jerky, then swallowed it whole. I held mine, still listening. But the desert had gone quiet. Soon Antonio was warbling in his sleep.

Hey Leo? Shakespeare said.

What?

Can I tell you a secret?

What?

Something I've never told anybody, but I'm gonna tell you since we're brothers now?

What?

A long pause followed.

Promise you won't make fun?

I promise.

Another long pause.

I've always wanted to be a coyote, Shakespeare said.

I looked over at him. He lifted his chin and expanded his chest for inspection. He couldn't have looked less like a coyote if he tried.

Why not, I said.

He exhaled. *Really?*

Sure.

Wow, Shakespeare said. *You're the best big brother ever, Leo. Goodnight.*

Night, I said.

Within seconds he was snoring.

I gave my jerky a death shake. I hunched over my kill while moving my hips left and right to ward off the members of my pack—my brothers and sisters—all of us wild, all of us hungry.

REVELATION #1

M<small>ARY</small> <small>EMERGED</small> at dawn with her hair askew and eyes narrow. She opened the blinds. Blinked at the emptiness. The column of light was gone. Pink land warmed in the sun. Not a coyote in sight.

Morning, Mom! Shakespeare said, spinning in circles. *Morning, dog! Morning, bird! Morning, cat! Morning, me! Morning, Mom!*

Antonio warmed up his voice and preened himself.

Dwid stretched atop his cat tree—an elaborate, yogic sequence that he finished seated, with his hind paws over his head to lick his legs, his belly fat and low. He must have slept through the coyotes. Not that I gave him a second thought.

I had my own routine. It revolved around an extensive cleaning of my doodads, just barely reachable with the donut around my neck. I still didn't know what my doodads were for, but I was proud of them, especially when stretching, since everyone got to see them.

Only after a giant mug of coffee—and plenty of grumbling—was Mary really alive. She changed into a baggy T-shirt and stretchy shorts, then she pushed back the couch to make room for her mat and rubber band thingies. Yes, she had her own routine too. It was starting now.

The others reacted accordingly. Shakespeare started to spin. Dwid went into hiding above the cabinets. Antonio hunched on his perch. They all knew what was coming. She always started with the same song: "It's Raining Men."

That first time, during the dramatic lead in, when the singers advised lonely girls to get ready, and Mary reached for her toes, I wondered what lonely girls should be getting ready for. Before I got the answer, however, I got the beat. And before I knew what was happening, my tail wagged, and this wag transmitted to my hips, swaying them with the rhythm. The motion spread to my shoulders, then my head. When I learned that it was raining men, I didn't even care how impossible or dangerous that sounded. My body wanted to move with the sound, so I let it.

Mary squatted and lunged, stretched her rubber band thingies, dropped down to sit up, then rolled over to push up. And repeat.

I figured we were doing the same thing.

It wasn't until Mary's third set that she noticed me. I was really grooving at that point, so my eyes were closed. When I opened them, Mary was just standing there, staring at me, rubber band dangling.

I stopped.

She turned off the music. She seemed confused, even a little afraid.

"Were you just…dancing?" she asked.

I looked over at Shakespeare, who was licking the window.

Is that what it's called? I asked him. *Dancing?*

He blinked, drooled.

I turned to Antonio. *How about you?* I asked. *Do you dance?*

Chee, if it is that awful wiggle you were doing, then no. Because of self-respect, you see.

But how can you resist? I asked.

Antonio rotated his head until it was almost upside down.

I turned to Dwid, who peered out through vines.

Don't be stupid, he said before I could even ask.

"I could have sworn," Mary said. She was kneeling now, peering into my eyes, like the answer was in there somewhere.

My ears dropped. I felt uncertain, and ashamed, at yet again revealing my ignorance. I licked sweat off Mary's face. She laughed and wiped her cheek, then patted my head and restarted the music.

Afterward, I followed Mary into her bedroom. I wanted to ask her why she was so confused by my dancing. I wanted to ask her a million questions. Instead, I could only look up at her with curious eyes.

Why couldn't I communicate with humans like I could with other animals? How was she different? Well, her body, to start. It was smooth and hairless, except for her head fur and that lower fur patch, which I was apparently not allowed to smell, since she cussed and pushed my head away when I tried. That's when I saw the scar —wide and horizontal—below her belly button. I wondered how she got that. I started wondering about humans in general.

They were so strange.

What was she doing now, for example? Standing under water that came out of the ceiling? Why was it so hot? Why was she rubbing that white foam all over her body? Why did it smell like chemicals? Why everything?

She came out and wrapped herself in a blanket. Then she went to the shiny wall—what I now call a mirror. She used what I then called a hot wind machine—yes, a hair dryer—on her head fur, or hair. She smiled at me. I wagged my tail.

What was she doing?

I was even more perplexed by my own reflection. At first I thought it was another dog. But when I cocked my head, the other dog did too. And of course we were both wearing a ridiculous pink donut. Because that dog was me. And Antonio was right. With fresh scabs on my face, I did look like hell. And my ears really were really big, like Mary always said.

Huh.

Looking into my own eyes, I had a completely obvious and overdue realization: I was the strange one. Why did I have no memories of being a puppy, or even from last week? Why did I dance, while the others didn't even know what dancing was? Why did a human try to kill me? What did I do to them? Why was I so strange?

As much as I wanted to ask Mary, I could tell from her reaction to my dancing that she didn't know either, and that knowing might actually frighten her. She had no idea who, or what, I was.

Only Roger knew that.

REVELATION #2

MARY WATCHED me during her workout the next morning. She even snapped her fingers and moved to the beat, like a demo. When that didn't work, she tried to trick me. She played music and walked into her bedroom, then peeked through the hinge. It was tough to resist, but I didn't dance.

Do you know how hard it is to resist "Don't You Want Me" by The Human League? I had to clamp my tail between my legs until she finally gave up and told herself she was losing it.

Fortunately Antonio caught me reading before Mary did.

She'd gone to work.

There I was, in the living room, sniffing around, when I found a basket of glossy papers. I had seen Mary go into this basket before, but I didn't think much of it. She tore out the sheets and spread them under Antonio's perch, and then Antonio crapped on them. That's what Mary called it—crap. Anyway, because of that crap, and a respectful fear of Antonio's talons, I hadn't gone near the papers until now.

Here's what I discovered: Those stacks of glossy papers didn't just have pictures on them. They had squiggly lines. My eyes, of their own accord, moved from left to right across the biggest squiggles at the top, above a smiling woman's head. I stared at those big squiggles for a long time. There was something about those squiggles that had captured my attention. What was it? I stared and stared and stared.

Finally, it happened. It! That magnificent IT!

The squiggles *meant* something.

I was caught off balance. I looked away, refocused. No, I hadn't imagined it. The squiggles said something! They said: "Style."

My heart sped up. The squiggles were all transforming now, to my astonishment, within my mind, to *speak* to me. They told me things. Like style. Style! That's what those big squiggles said!

My eyes knew what to do now. They moved on to the next set of squiggles. This set was easy: "and." And! A very important *and* underappreciated word. The third set was more complicated. I slowed down, really concentrated. I took it one squiggle at a time, then put it all together: "Fitness." Whoa! My tail wagged, amazed at this magic. I went through the squiggles over and over, repeating the meanings in my head.

Style! And! Fitness! Style! And! Fitness! Style! And! Fitness!

I forged ahead. It took me a while to unlock the squiggles below, since they were smaller, but I got them eventually. They said: "A magazine for the fit and fortunate."

Wow!

My nose knew what to do too. It pushed open the cover. Inside, more squiggles spread before me. So many squiggles! I flipped through the pages. Millions of squiggles! I stopped. I read this page. Yes. That's what it was called. That's what I was doing. Reading. Of course! And those weren't just squiggles. They were letters! And letters made words! A warm familiarity washed over me. I loved letters! I loved words! And I loved reading! I even loved punctuation! This squiggle is called an exclamation point!!!!!!!!!!!!!!!!!!!!!

The first article was called "The Ultimate 8-Week Water Fast: How You Can Get A Super Hot Body in Time for Beach Season." I soon got over my initial shock at being able to read as I became confused by what I was actually reading. I couldn't fathom why humans would want to starve themselves for something called a bikini. What was that? And why would a human want a super hot body? Wouldn't they be uncomfortable if they got that hot? And was beach really a season? I thought there were only four seasons. I recited them to myself: spring, summer, fall, winter. Okay. Then beach? Between winter and spring? I was trying to figure all of this out when Antonio interrupted me.

Ay, dog, what do you put your nose in there for? he asked, looking down at me from his perch.

Reading, I said, too excited to even consider that it might be another one of my abnormal behaviors.

Chee, but what is this reading?

Shakespeare came over and sat. Now I had an audience.

You don't know what reading is? I asked.

Shakespeare's eyes were even blanker than usual. Antonio leaned closer, as if getting closer would help.

I tried to explain: *The squiggles talk to me. They tell me things.*

Wow, Shakespeare said.

Antonio received this information, assumed perfect posture, and stared straight ahead. *It is dishonorable to lie,* he said. *All know that squiggles are for craps.*

I could see his perspective. Several torn-up magazines were caked in the stuff beneath him.

Shakespeare scooted closer. *What do they tell you?* he asked.

I read a section at random: *As the toxins leave your system, you may experience extreme mood swings, sudden losses of consciousness, or even hallucinations. Rest assured, this is a completely healthy part of the fasting process. Besides, it's worth it for the beach bod of your dreams!*

Wow, Shakespeare said. *I don't get it.*

This seemed an inadequate introduction to the power of the written word. I glanced around the room. I was looking for something, not quite sure what it was. All we had was five years of this magazine.

There are better things to read, I said, which brought up more information from the cellar of my mind. *Like books,* I said, marveling at how the thought could have been hidden, yet now so obvious. *Books are better.*

What's books? Shakespeare asked.

They're like magazines, I said, searching for the next thought. It crystallized. I could imagine one now, with a red cover, and gold lettering, and a white silk ribbon. *A book is like a magazine,* I said, *but fancier, and bigger, and better.*

I hobbled back and forth, carrying my bum leg. Memories were awakening. I felt like I was pulling on a rope that led into a deep cave. I could feel the weight at the other end without knowing what is was. I pulled harder. *Books are the best. They don't have pictures, usually, which sounds bad, but that's only because they're too crammed full of adventures.*

Memories marched out of the earth—legions of soldiers and adventurers, jungles and ice caps, tanks and swords, battles at sea, knights and kings and queens and quests.

And quests, I said. *All kinds of quests!* I hopped around, wanting to run but having nowhere to go. I spun once and slowed, disappointed by the pile of magazines, still not books. *That's something you find in books that you won't find in magazines. Quests. They're like big, epic adventures involving a search for something, or someone, and they're full of peril.*

Peril? Shakespeare asked.

Peril, I said.

Wow, Shakespeare said. *What's peril?*

I stared out the window at the desert and the black mountains beyond. My memories were becoming more abstract now. I was struggling to understand, yet I knew this was essential. I knew this was important. I focused all of my mental energy, willing light from darkness.

And then there are other books, I said, slower. *They might be boring at first, because they're so full of ideas, and sometimes they're hard to read, because they're complicated, or old, or your brain doesn't like new ideas, because it's happy with the ones it's got, or maybe it's scared of change. But sometimes you'll read a book, and it'll make you rethink everything. Everything about your whole life...or even...existence itself.*

I turned around to witness the impact of my revelation. Shakespeare was dragging his anus across the rug.

Ahhh, he said.

INVESTIGATIONS

MARY REMOVED MY BANDAGE. She grimaced at the long tracks of stitches, and the puffy, shaved skin, then pretended it wasn't so bad. I could hardly look at it without feeling nauseous. It was kind of stinky too.

"It'll heal up in no time," Mary said.

Yeah, right.

I watched through the narrow window beside the front door as she drove off to work. Then I backed into the gap between the couch and the coffee table to shrug out of the inflatable donut. Easy. I moved my neck in all directions while enjoying the fresh air on my leg. After convincing Shakespeare that he should not lick my stitches, no matter how tasty, I had a good look around.

I had casually explored the place already. This was more of an investigation. I would start with everything external, working in a grid-like fashion through each room, before checking the cupboards and closets and other possible hiding spots. Shakespeare trailed behind me, his short-term memory as bad as my long-term.

What are we looking for again? he asked.

Anything, I said. *Magic wands. Swords. A book, at least. She's got to have at least one book.*

Oh. What's a book again?

It's like a magazine, but bigger and better.

Oh. What's a magazine again?

And so on.

Our superficial search yielded nothing of interest. From a certificate on the wall I learned that Mary had an associate's degree in hospitality science, whatever that was, and from photos on the fridge, discovered that she had been younger in a greener place, where she lived with two older humans who I now think were her parents, and all manner of creatures that I now know are farm animals. I also determined that Mary lacked taste. In the bathroom, for example, I stood on mustard tiles surrounded by scarlet walls decorated with watercolors of horses.

I feel like my eyes are going to throw up, I said.

They can do that? Shakespeare asked, alarmed.

The red is way too much.

The what?

The red walls?

Shakespeare rotated, checking every wall, until he faced me again. Then he said, *Gray.*

Gray?

The walls are gray.

The walls are red.

Gray.

Red.

Wait. What's red?

What do you mean what's red?

Huh?

Our conversations often proceeded in this way, with both of us becoming increasingly confused but for different reasons. After some back and forth I came up with a hypothesis: Shakespeare was blind to certain colors. This required a quick sub-investigation.

How many colors do you know? I asked.

What do you mean how many? he asked back.

I tried a different way.

Name all the colors, I said.

Easy, he said. *Gray, blue, yellow. Done.*

That's it?

That's it.

Huh.

Now I wanted to ask Dwid and Antonio what colors they could

see, but, as usual, they were asleep. This they had in common. Across the living room from one another, on cat tree and perch, at approximately equal height, they slept—I kid you not—twenty hours a day. And they did not appreciate being disturbed.

I reminded myself to investigate color vision further, then carried on, now searching the hidden places. I found a true cornucopia of human junk, some of which I recognized in the moment, most in retrospect.

Crawling under Mary's bed, for example, I found the following items: three socks, a bra, a photo of a younger Mary in all white with some guy in all black, a torn dog leash, an empty pill container for something called Levoxyl, another for Zoloft, a tiny pair of mittens on strings, a nest of wires, an ancient stuffed bear, several candy wrappers, a petrified apple core, and a cylindrical pink rubber object that I still don't understand. And that's only what I can remember, and only under the bed. Similarly, every closet and cupboard and drawer was stuffed with human stuff.

I sat on the rug and had a long think. All that junk and not a single book. Yes, I was disappointed, although the search did improve my understanding of Mary's species, assuming she was representative.

My conclusions?

A human's environment is a reflection of their consciousness, as thought processes manifest actions, and those actions manifest objects within said environment. On the surface, Mary appeared ordinary and lacking in sensitivity, but a layer below, she was a tangle of memories and insecurities and poor decisions and medical conditions and needs.

Kind of like me.

When Mary pulled into the driveway that evening, I slipped back into my donut and followed Shakespeare to the front door, where he wagged his curly tail desperately, as if she'd been gone for years. I imitated him, thwacking my own against the wall.

SCREENS

THIS IS EMBARRASSING, but I want to be as honest as possible. Please just remember my traumatic brain injury and that I'm a dog. I don't usually use that last one as an excuse, since I am not your average dog, but I think it is valid here—something about the way a dog's brain works, or at least mine. So, with that preamble, here's the truth: It took me almost a week to recognize the importance of screens. I feel foolish now, having focused so much on books.

First there was the small screen—the one Mary kept with her at all times, and checked often. She walked around the house staring at it, lay in bed staring at it, even sat on the toilet staring at it. This behavior seemed odd, but Mary was the first human I could remember living with, so I thought maybe the small screen was something she needed to attend to, like Antonio with his feathers, or Dwid with his nails, or Shakespeare with his anus.

The second screen was much bigger. Because of this, it needed to stay where it was, on the wall. Mary stared at the big screen in the evenings while sitting on the couch drinking fizzy drinks. She stared for hours straight, as if she needed to compensate for the time she had spent with her small screen. I don't want to give the impression, however, that Mary used the screens one at a time. I know, all of this was confusing for me, too.

The third screen was medium in size, notable because it folded up, like a book, although it was held differently than a book—

opening vertically instead of horizontally. Mary used the foldable screen least often. Sometimes she'd be staring at the small screen, and she'd say something like, "What?" before sitting down with the foldable screen on her lap to tap away at the scrambled letters, until she said something like, "Oh. Yep. That *is* an ugly baby."

Sure, I saw lights and heard noise, but these were meaningless. When I asked, Antonio and Shakespeare had no idea what the screens were for, while Dwid told me to show him my belly, to which I replied that I would rather eat my own tail.

Still, I believed that I was onto something, based on two new hypotheses: First, screens were important. Why else would Mary look at them so much? And second, they required practice. Why else could I gain no meaning from them?

So I started imitating Mary. We stared at the big screen together—her on the couch, me on the floor—like it was going to feed us dinner at any moment. For days, I got nothing in return. Just lights and noise. But eventually, maybe a week later, my experiment paid off.

We were both staring, as usual, when the lights shifted and the blurs sharpened. I stood. The screen was transforming. A woman's face was coming into focus. And there she was, with large eyes outlined in black paint. Soon the noise became sound, with real words that matched her moving lips.

"Krissy, I'm telling you," she said, "your nose is not too big."

Amazed, I watched as the screen showed a second woman—Krissy, I guessed—in a heap on the ground, covering her face and sobbing. The screen returned to the first woman, this time in a different place, talking straight at me.

"Maybe her nose is a little big," she said, giggling.

I stepped sideways, but the woman's eyes didn't follow me. Maybe she couldn't see me. I wagged my tail to get her attention, but she just kept talking about Krissy's big fat nose.

"Drama," Mary said. A few minutes later, she said something else that caught my attention: "I thought they were going to Paris this season?"

The way she said it, wondering aloud like that, made me peer over the arm of the couch. Yes, I was right—Mary had the foldable screen in her lap. I climbed onto the couch and sat beside her.

"Bub, you gotta be careful climbing up here," Mary said, opening the lid.

"Oogle," the screen said in colorful font.

I stood and thumped my tail. I could read this!

"Sit," Mary said. "If you want to be up here, you need to be polite."

I sat. I leaned into Mary's shoulder. She laughed and kissed me, then tapped away at the keys. Small black letters appeared on the screen. Then she hit the big key. Boom. Words exploded everywhere. It was like a living book! But you didn't turn the pages. You swept them up and down, then moved a little triangle thing and clicked and clacked.

"Here we go," Mary said.

The screen showed something called Thinkipedia. Words everywhere.

"Ah, next episode," Mary said.

She clicked again. The screen switched to something called PeopleBook. There was Mary's face, but cleaner and painted, and her full name, Mary Mitchell. Huh. She clicked and typed again, revealing more humans. I became fascinated as the photos streamed past, of all sorts of humans in all sorts of places, doing all sorts of things, all of them labeled with names. There were even a few dogs in the mix. Mary talked to herself, moving faster than I could follow, saying things like, "Cute," or, "Gross," or, "Her? Really?"

This seemed to be a voluntary activity, yet Mary was growing increasingly aggravated. She leaned closer and closer to the screen, muttering, until everything suddenly disappeared under a slamming lid. My disappointment magnified when Mary started the big screen again. I had just missed a key opportunity. While I was gawking at all those photos of humans, I should have been reading the names to see if any of them was Roger.

How could I have been so careless? How could I lose sight of my main objective? Of the epic quest ahead?

Out there, the whole world carried on while I was in here doing nothing. Sure, I called it healing, but really I was napping, and eating cheese, and reading *Style and Fitness*. I had yet to avenge myself, or figure out where I had come from, or why I was so strange. At times I forgot about Roger entirely. At others, like now, finding him felt like the sole reason for my existence, like finding him would fill the emptiness that persisted deep within me, allowing me to achieve some kind of true and complete self. Finding Roger was everything, and I had failed to even look.

Stupid dumb idiot moron dog.

No, I told myself. You really are healing, and learning.

And I had just learned something critical: The big screen was for entertainment, while the foldable screen was for information, especially about humans. The foldable screen could be invaluable in my search for Roger. It was the closest I had to a lead. I could look for him there, on PeopleBook. I was eager to get started, confident that I would find him soon.

Really, how many humans could there be?

Before bed, as usual, Mary put the foldable screen on the shelf in the kitchen. I was pretty sure that I would not be allowed to use it. Which meant, of course, I would need to be very sneaky when I did.

MY ELECTRIFYING IDEA

THE TROUBLE with the foldable screen was that Mary kept it out of reach. I could smell it up there, on the shelf above the kitchen counter, but as any dog will tell you, to smell is not to have. With four legs I could have climbed up there, but with three and one that could hardly bear weight, I had visions of slipping and snapping my forelimb in half. And beyond the obvious pain of that outcome, I would be further from Roger than ever. Still, with Mary at work for hours to come, I had to try something.

Shakespeare, I said. *Can you get on the counter?*

He had become a second shadow, so he was right there to respond.

That's against the law, he said.

True, I said, *but what if it was for something very important?*

Like cheese? he asked. *Is there cheese up there? I don't smell it.*

It's not cheese.

What kind of food is it?

It's not food.

Shakespeare cocked his head.

I need to take a closer look at something up there, I said. *Could you get it off the shelf for me? Help your brother out?*

Definitely, he said, then stared at me.

Okay, go ahead.

I can't get up there. I'm too short.

I pushed a chair from the kitchen table to the counter. It scraped across the floor, awakening the others.

This should be good, Dwid said, and yawned.

Wah, please take care, Antonio said. *This is a very foolish and dangerous thing you do, chee.*

He'll be fine, I said.

Let's just say it didn't work. I could explain how Shakespeare struggled to even get on the chair—how he tried five times, fell backward five times, hit his head on the ground five times, until he was too dizzy to continue—but that would be unfair to Shakespeare. So let's just say it didn't work.

He's not really a dog, you know, Dwid said. *He's a meatball, with legs.*

Mmm, Shakespeare said. *Meatball.*

With nobody to help me, I limped back and forth in front of the counter, whining. Antonio squawked and flapped his wings in annoyance. Dwid told me to die and be done with it. Even Shakespeare wandered off to nap. But I was caught in the wanting, stuck on loop. I paced for hours. I guess I can be kind of obsessive.

When Mary came home, she was ranting about Dentler, the rancher that was always shooting coyotes. She leashed me and led me out back to relieve myself.

"Thinks he's a vigilante, Leo, that's the problem. Won't even talk live capture. He hunts them. For fun. He should have to eat what he kills. That would teach him."

Back inside, Mary mixed a fizzy drink and slumped in front of the big screen. The way she slumped I knew she was settling in for a long sit. Sure enough, she fell asleep with the empty glass in her lap.

I sighed.

I sighed again, even more dramatically, hoping someone might ask what's wrong. Nobody did. Maybe I'd take a nap too, I figured, sleep some time away, like the others. Just as I was dozing off, however, I had an idea, and lifted my head from my paws.

Wires emerged from the back of the big screen to enter the wall. I looked around the room. The lamps had these wires too. Did everything that made noise or light need a wire? What about the small screen? No wire there. But wait, I thought, it did have one. I went into the bedroom. A wire came from the wall, currently unused on Mary's bedside table. Which meant, I thought, trotting back to the kitchen with my front leg held high, that the foldable screen needed a wire too.

And there it was.

A white wire emerged from the wall and ran up and out of sight to plug into the foldable screen. Interesting. Very interesting. My initial thought was to pull the wire, bringing the foldable screen down with it. I even put it in my mouth, squeezing the rubber between my teeth. Fortunately I reconsidered. If I pulled the screen down, it might break, and I wouldn't be able to use it. Plus it would make a big noise, waking Mary. I stepped back to reconsider.

Hey Leo, have you ever had a scary dream? Shakespeare asked.

Not now, I said. *I'm trying to think.*

I stared at the white wire. How could I make it so the foldable screen needed to live somewhere else?

Have you ever had a scary dream when you're awake and not asleep? Shakespeare asked.

The answer was obvious, I told myself, but what was it?

Hey Leo? Shakespeare asked.

What, I snapped. I couldn't think with him talking all the time.

He lowered his head and tail. I felt a pang of guilt, but shook it off. This was important. He could wait.

Then I had it. My idea.

Gently, I bit the wire, pulled it from the wall, and dropped it. Now two faces stared back, each with two narrow eyes and a round, surprised mouth. Next I went into Mary's bathroom. On the floor, beneath the sink, were several metal clips. She had dropped them that morning while bunning her hair. I licked one up and positioned it between my front teeth. Then I hobbled back to the kitchen. The plan was simple: I would jam up those holes. That's what I'd do. With nowhere for the wire to go, Mary would have to move the foldable screen, with some luck, to a place I could reach it. And so, with that metal clip aimed at one of those black holes, I extended my neck.

It was a really, really bad dream, Shakespeare said. *And you were in it.*

HOUSE CALL

THE TASTE AWOKE ME. It was like charred meat. Except it wasn't meat that had been burned. It was my tongue. I lay on my side with two faces above me: Mary and Dr. Francis. How long had I been out?

Mary's eyes were wet. She was smiling and nodding. Dr. Francis was concentrating. He had something in his ears that traveled along a curving tube to my chest. All I could hear was a constant high-pitched tone. As this faded, and my hearing returned, Dr. Francis put the listening device around his neck.

"Should be okay," he said, "although we'll want to keep a close eye."

"So he doesn't lick another socket?" Mary asked.

"In case he starts to cough. Might get some edema—swelling in the lungs after a shock like that. Should know soon enough. We'd need to hospitalize."

I lapped the air. Mary winced.

"Looks bad," Dr. Francis said, "but tongues heal pretty quick. You know, I can't decide if this dog is lucky or unlucky. He's not too smart. We can say that, at least."

What happened? I asked.

Now Dr. Francis was the one who looked shocked.

"What's wrong?" Mary asked.

"Nothing," Dr. Francis said. He reassured her with a brief smile, then stood.

54

Mary put her hand over her heart. "Jeez, Doc. Don't do that."

I lay there in a daze, tasting my well-done mouth, trying to get my thoughts in order. Water ran in the sink. He was repeatedly washing his hands. He did that when he was upset.

Wait a minute.

Did he just hear me?

Mary kissed my nose, all along my snout, to the top of my head. She rubbed my ears. "You know," she said, "I'm thinking Leo here might be more than a foster."

The water stopped.

"He can be a bad boy sometimes," Mary went on, "and he's kinda skittish, but there's something about him. I swear, sometimes he looks at me like he understands what I'm saying. Like he knows exactly what I mean."

"I need to go now," Dr. Francis said.

"Are you okay?" Mary asked.

"Yes. Fine. Thank you."

"Are you sure? You look pale. Maybe you should sit down."

"I'm fine. I just need to go," Dr. Francis said, his words spilling out with rapid footsteps.

Mary stood up, starting after him.

"Thanks so much for—"

The door slammed.

Mary returned. "What an oddball," she said.

When we returned home, Shakespeare stared down at me. *Wow,* he said. *Your face caught fire. It was awesome.*

Not dead, Dwid observed from above. *Too bad. Maybe next time.*

Ay, dog, Antonio said. *You are as foolish as the day is long.*

BLINDSPOT

BUT WAS I really as foolish as the day was long? The socket was scorched black. And that evening, Mary plugged in the foldable screen across the living room, right there on the floor. Yes, a hard lesson in electricity, but, ultimately, a success.

When Mary went to bed, I listened through her door until her breathing slowed. Then, in the darkness, I lifted the silver lid with the bitten apple, drenching myself in light.

Oogle, the screen said.

I wagged my tail. Oogle knew everything.

What are you doing? Shakespeare asked. *Isn't this against the law?*

Ay, certainly, Antonio said. *Keep away from him. He is dangerous.*

Who's dumber? Dwid asked. *That's what I keep wondering. Who is the dumbest dog in the house? I don't know anymore. I really don't. It keeps me up at night.*

I was too excited, and anxious, to care what they thought. Very soon I would know where to find Roger.

Following a slobbery effort with my tongue, I found that I could move the black and white arrow with my nose, best when wiped dry on the rug. The buttons required a finer touch, which I achieved by placing a pencil between my teeth and using the eraser to press them. It was slow in the beginning, and frustrating, until I found the delete button. At least here my mistakes could be reversed.

With these mechanics understood, I stared at the blinking vertical line. I took a deep breath. "Roger," I typed, and hit enter.

Oogle presented Roger Federer, Roger Ebert, Roger Goodell, Roger Clemens, Roger Moore, and more. Even a guy called Roger Roger. I clicked on several, but none was described as a sicko or a scumbag or a jerk or any of the other terms Mary had used, and not one was pictured driving a van. Some were in France. Some were dead. One was dead in France. They all seemed unlikely.

I also learned that from the 1600s through the 1800s, Roger was slang for the word "penis." So I Oogled "penis." I really wish I hadn't done that because I was sidelined for quite some time by the intricacies of human mating procedures. I clicked back. That was definitely not the kind of Roger I was looking for.

I only wanted people Rogers. And only the alive kind. Hold up. What was that other thing called again? Oh yeah, PeopleBook.

I typed this into Oogle. Sure enough, it popped up, and with a couple more clicks I was looking at Mary's face.

Again I typed "Roger" into the search box.

This only revealed that PeopleBook is a confusing place. It wasn't even showing me Rogers. It was just an endless amount of random photos and videos of bizarre human junk that I hadn't even asked for. I clicked the button that said "People," thinking this would help, but it only took me from confusion to despair.

I thought there would be ten, maybe twenty Rogers out there. Thirty max. This was not the case. What's worse, every one of those hundreds or even thousands of Rogers had his own collection of bizarre human junk that I would now need to sort through. I now understood why Mary slammed the screen shut after being on PeopleBook too long. It was overwhelming and useless. I didn't even know what *my* Roger looked like. How did I expect to find him?

I returned to the empty Oogle box, feeling quite empty myself. How could I be foolish enough to think that only thirty Rogers existed? How small did I think the world was? This, again, returns us to the issue of blind spots. You don't know your own until they become painfully obvious. In this case I was starting to feel the weight of a much bigger problem: I was ignorant. How could I expect to track Roger down without understanding the most basic concepts that any normal dog or human would know?

I needed to rethink my entire search. I needed to answer the most fundamental questions first. Which meant I needed to start from the beginning. The very beginning. But where was that? Well, where did I begin? Where did I come from? I didn't know. But why?

"Memory loss," I typed. This took me to Thinkipedia, a wonderful place full of actual information. Immediately it diagnosed my condition: amnesia. Reading a few more articles, I learned that I had something called retrograde amnesia, apparently due to head trauma. Specifically, I had lost my declarative memory—facts and memories of past events. Yet I retained a variety of skills, including my abilities to read and write, because these are procedural memories stored in a separate part of my brain. There is no treatment for amnesia, I learned, although spontaneous recovery of memories could occur. This explained why certain words and concepts, and all those adventure stories I had read, came flooding back. There was hope I might recover more.

Thinkipedia was great!

My brain was firing fast. What next? I figured anything I learned could trigger more memories to arise. I looked around. A large glass bottle sat empty on the kitchen counter. Mary drank that stuff every night. She mixed it with clear fizzy liquid.

"Vodka," I typed.

Vodka is a clear distilled alcoholic beverage. Its primary components are water and ethanol, although flavorings and impurities may also be present.

I read some more, then clicked "alcohol."

Alcohol, also known by the chemical name ethanol, is a compound naturally produced when yeast consumes sugar, a process called fermentation.

I clicked "ethanol."

Ethanol is commonly used as a recreational drug. It can produce feelings of euphoria and lift mood.

This explained why Mary did drugs after work—because it felt good. Excited by this new understanding, I kept reading.

Chinese pottery dating back 9,000 years exhibits residues of alcohol, suggesting that Neolithic peoples consumed alcoholic beverages.

That seemed like a long time. Alcohol must be good for people, I reasoned. Or was it peoples?
Never mind for now. I clicked "Neolithic."

After the Stone Age, humans began to plant crops and develop farming techniques. With the cultivation of crops and domestication of animals such as dogs and cattle, they left behind their nomadic ways to form settlements, which could sustain larger populations of people.

Okay, wow. I really was starting at the beginning.
Obviously I clicked "dogs."
This took me to a page titled "Origin of the domestic dog," complete with an image of a howling wolf.

The origin of dogs is unclear, although they were the first animals domesticated by man. The earliest recorded dog is the Bonn-Oberkassel dog, found buried next to a human in a gravesite dating back approximately 14,200 years.

This, I noted, was longer than alcohol.

Some records suggest that the domestication of dogs may have started up to 36,000 years ago.

That seemed like a really long time. But how long was time?
I returned to Oogle.
"How old is the world?" I asked.
"4.543 billion years," Oogle said.
"How long is a billion years?" I asked.
"Unfathomable," Oogle said.
"What does unfathomable mean?" I asked.

"Impossible to fully understand," Oogle said.

I had reached a wall. I tried again.

"How do we know how old the world is?" I asked.

Sifting through these results I came across a Christian website, which claimed that the world was only 10,000 years old. But this would mean that the Bonn-Oberkassel dog was older than the world. Which made no sense.

"Today's science is tomorrow's superstition," the article claimed. "God created the earth in six days, and on the seventh, He rested."

"Who is God?" I asked Oogle.

"The creator and sustainer of the universe," Oogle said.

"If God is powerful enough to create the world in six days, then why would God need to rest?" I asked. It took me a long time to press those buttons, but I felt it was worth asking.

In response, Oogle presented conflicting answers. Several quotes were listed from a book called the Bible. I clicked through a few articles, learning that the Bible is a sacred text of ancient truths. Apparently, these truths could be tricky to understand, because opinions varied. One interpretation suggested that God didn't *need* to rest, He just *wanted* to rest. Another said that all of His work was done, so there was nothing left to do but rest. Yet another claimed that resting on the seventh day served as an example for humans.

But what about the eighth day? I wondered. Did God go back to work? Was He working right now? So late at night? And what did God look like anyway? And why was everyone capitalizing "He" all of a sudden? These questions deserved a thorough investigation. I would need to read the original text myself. So I clicked on the King James Bible and started from the beginning, with Genesis.

And God said, Let there be light: and there was light. And God saw the light, and it was good; and God divided the light from the darkness.

I wagged my tail. Maybe this was the column of light beyond the mountains. It did divide the night sky. I kept reading. Soon, however, I came across a concerning sentence. My tail froze.

And God said, Let us make man in our image, after our likeness: and let them have dominion over the fish of the sea, and over the fowl of the air, and over the cattle, and over all the earth, and over every creeping thing that creepeth upon the earth.

I read this passage again, and then another time just to be sure I hadn't missed something. Dominion? No. That couldn't be right. I even read the footnotes.

Dominion: Control. Creeping thing: A general term for animals.

There it was, undeniable, in black and white. This is bad, I thought. This is very, very bad. I am an animal. I creepeth upon the earth. Which means humans think they have the right to control me. To dominate me.

My hackles were up. How was that fair? Who wrote this thing anyway? I suspected a man, considering man got dominion over everything.

So I checked.

It was actually a bunch of different men, starting about 3,000 years ago. At least dogs were older than the Bible.

I returned to "Origin of the domestic dog."

At the peak of the most recent Ice Age, during the Last Glacial Maximum, the now-extinct megafaunal wolf arose on the frontiers of the mammoth steppe. Joining this wolf on the expansive plains was a bipedal primate with an enlarged frontal lobe. As both of these species evolved to cover the Earth, their fates entwined, transforming them into the domestic dog and the modern human, two species connected by a bond that has lasted over 10,000 years.

Whoa, I thought. Now that's a better story. We evolved together, side by side, each responsible for the other's fate.

But which arrangement was more common today? Which version of the story did Roger believe, or Dr. Francis, or Mary?

CHOPPED

I STAYED UP ALL NIGHT. At dawn I closed the foldable screen (or laptop, according to Oogle), and waited impatiently for Mary to leave for work. As soon as she was gone I reopened the lid. I could feel something bubbling up inside of me, like doing all that reading had stirred up some old soup inside my head.

The ingredients, at first, appeared random. For instance I recognized the mathematical symbol for pi (π), but I had never heard of pie (apple or otherwise). I remembered Teddy Roosevelt's name as soon as I saw his picture, but when I saw an actual teddy bear, I was shocked, thinking it was some kind of a cute but dead animal. It seemed that my knowledge of boring human stuff far outweighed my awareness of fun and wonder. And so I followed my curiosity, charging into learning like a knight in a hailstorm.

Plink. Greyhounds can run up to 45 miles per hour.

Plonk. A Frisbee is a flying disc used recreationally for throwing and catching.

Clang. Isthay isyay igpay atinlay. (This is Pig Latin.)

Later that morning I discovered YooTube.

You gotta see this, I said, pointing at the screen with my nose.

Shakespeare stared at me from his bed.

Not me, I said, *the screen.*

In the video, a man was eating marbles as fast as he could. Let me be extra clear about this. An adult human male, of his own volition, was taking marbles, putting them in his mouth, and swallowing them at a rapid rate. At the bottom of the screen a number counted the marbles as they went down. "Five hundred marbles in five minutes," the video was titled. "I can eat more marbles faster than anybody," said the subtitle.

I can't understand why humans think dogs are dumber than them, when at least one human is out there eating marbles. Sure, some humans are super smart, but so are some dogs.

I saw videos of dogs doing all sorts of amazing things, like finding humans trapped underground or helping people with no eyeballs cross the street. I even witnessed a dog flying an airplane. An airplane! And so young. How many two-year-old humans can do that? None. I Oogled it. They're still crapping themselves at that age. Meanwhile, Bobo the Flying Bouvier des Flandres is ten thousand feet up, and probably crapping in the lawn like any decent member of society, with no marbles in his poop at all. I was inspired. I searched everywhere for an interview with Bobo, but found nothing. Where did he train? Was there some kind of license I could get? I must have watched the footage fifteen times, with each replay imagining myself in his place.

I gazed out the window at the blue sky, where, high up, there floated a puffy white cloud. I limped down the runway, growling for the engine, rising straight up, bursting through the cloud and into the wide beyond. I dropped my wing and banked left, leveling off with a flock of birds, arcing around the kitchen table, waving my broken leg, before dive-bombing the shoe rack. Just before impact, I pulled up, g-forces pulling my jowls into a smile. For my finale I performed a series of barrel rolls, then eased it down for a soft landing on the rug, panting.

Hey mutt, Dwid said. *You know what I don't like about you?*

Everything? I said, my tongue hanging out.

Actually, yes, he said, *but especially your face. Because it's ugly, and never asleep.*

Wah, I do not mean to be rude, Antonio said, *but when Mary is away, we sleep. It is what we do. It is the way we have always done it, chee.*

I regarded him with renewed interest.

I bet it's amazing to fly, I said. *What's it like?*

His response was dramatic. His feathers shot out, jagged around his neck.

Now you've done it, Dwid said.

What did I say?

Antonio snapped his beak. He focused his black eyes on me, encircled in yellow.

Impossible, he said.

I put my tongue back in my mouth. *What do you mean?*

I am chopped, he said. He extended his wings, as wide as I am long, in a spread of silver trimmed with blue, through which he hung his head in shame. I couldn't see the problem. They appeared complete and symmetrical with a regular, undulating fringe.

I'm no wing expert, I said, *but they look good to me. Impressive, even.*

Here! he said, exasperated, shaking one wing, *and here!* he continued, shaking the other. *Chopped when I was a chick! Cut! Grounded! Wah! What don't you understand, dog? I have been chopped my whole life! You don't think I know this?! To fly would kill me, chee! Is that what you want?! Is that it?!*

Madness swirled in his eyes.

I tucked my tail. *I'm sorry,* I said. I really was.

Antonio clenched his talons. He snapped his beak in the air, then upon himself, plucking feathers. They floated down to the dirty magazines below.

In the afternoon, I pushed the laptop behind the armchair in the corner where nobody could see me. There I delved into aerodynamics, absorbing birds and Bernoulli and the Wright brothers, airfoils and incompressible flow.

Around five, anticipating Mary's return, I closed the lid, put the laptop back, slipped into my pink donut, and stretched out—trying to look casual—on the couch. I returned my gaze to the sky, where the blue softened with evening.

Soon I was asleep.

ANARCHY

I AWOKE to Shakespeare's hot breath on my face.

I'm so hungry, he whined. *I'm dying.*

It was night. The column of light stood upright and motionless behind the mountains. Much, much closer, Shakespeare's nose nearly touched mine.

Dying, he repeated.

I got off the couch and went to the kitchen. The stove said 9:37 p.m. That was odd. Mary still wasn't home.

Also, I did something bad, Shakespeare said.

With his tail and ears lowered, he led me to the entryway and showed me a small pile of poop.

Eh, I said. *Not your fault we're locked up.*

Shakespeare was relieved. Feeling the need myself, I went to the dog door and tried to lift the plywood, but it was flush—another thumb and fingers situation.

What are you doing? Shakespeare asked.

Trying to get outside, I said.

But that's against—

Yeah yeah, I said, sniffing the door handle. *It's against the law. And I'm not supposed to whine at the table. And I'm not supposed to chew on the rug. And I'm supposed to sit inside all day and stare at the wall like I'm another piece of furniture. And Mary's supposed to be home, isn't she? But she's not, so I am going outside.*

Oh, Shakespeare said. *Okay.*

I had watched Mary unlock and open the door a number of times, so it only took a few minutes to match her manipulation of the deadbolt and door handle. Fortunately, this one was a lever and not a knob.

The door swung inward.

And out we went.

The night was hot and still. Shakespeare searched for Mary in the backyard despite my insistence that he wouldn't find her. I sniffed the ground along the fence. Some animal I didn't recognize had walked along the perimeter before veering away. Was that what a coyote smelled like? I looked in the direction it had gone, into the increasing darkness.

One day, I told myself, that animal would be me. I'd go over this fence. No more leashes. No more locked doors. No more dominion. But not yet. I couldn't jump over the fence on three legs, and I'd need full speed to ensure a clean getaway.

I'm so hungry, Shakespeare said when we went back inside. I closed the door behind us to keep the hot air out. Shakespeare lay on his back and whined. *It hurts in my belly.*

Well, let's see if we can find something to eat, I said, going to the pantry, more confident after our foray into the backyard.

But as I sniffed the doors, Antonio screamed. He held a claw aloft, pointing four reptilian nails at me.

Wah, it is forbidden, he said. *As the senior member of this pandemonium, I will be forced to act, chee. Do not make me come down there and teach you how to behave, dog. To go outside is one thing, to steal another.*

Go ahead, Dwid said, *test him.*

I noted Dwid's empty orbit, then Antonio's claw. Hmm.

Maybe we should wait for Mom to come home, Shakespeare said.

Whatever, I said, hiding my fear by walking out of the room. *Stupid bird honor.*

Ay, what was that, dog?

I wandered into the laundry room. My nose took me to Dwid's litter box.

We're not supposed to eat those, Shakespeare said, standing in the doorway.

This was enough encouragement for me.

We're not supposed to do anything, I said.

The next morning was rough. Still no Mary. Shakespeare and I both had the runs, and we had them bad. We went in and out of the backyard over and over.

And that is why you do not violate the law, Antonio said.

Mary was absent through the afternoon. I began to wonder what we would do if she never returned. The gates in the back were padlocked, and the front door was a knob and not a lever. Maybe a window?

I paced, anxious at the thought of being trapped forever, or blinded by Antonio when I tried to eat. His honor, however, weakened by the hour—my first hint that morals are a luxury of the well-fed. Around four in the afternoon, he cracked.

Ay, perhaps we should have a small bite, he said. *But only to remain among the living.*

I pulled open the pantry door and went head first into a box of something called Cheez-Ums. I backed out, wearing the box, then shook it off with a mouthful of cheesy deliciousness and a head covered in orange dust. Cheez-Ums scattered across the floor.

Cheese! Shakespeare cried, vacuuming them up.

Dogs, please, Antonio said. *Just enough to survive.*

But my stomach was directing now. I carried a plastic bag into the living room, then bit and shook, exploding barbeque potato chips everywhere. As I wolfed them down, Dwid descended and sniffed the wreckage, picky even with hunger.

Wah, it is anarchy, Antonio said.

Anarchy! Shakespeare shouted, sliding across the floor, inhaling Cheez-Ums. *Anarchy!*

No, it's survival, I said.

Ay, perhaps, Antonio said. *Have you seen any nuts?*

Nuts? I asked, limping back to the kitchen.

If you do not mind, Antonio said. He hopped down from his perch and waddled across the floor. I was struck by his size. His beak reached my neck. My heart quickened as I searched the pantry. I did not want to disappoint him.

Here we go, I said. *Is a mixed blend okay, good sir?*

That would be fine, thank you.

I laid the container at his feet.

Anarchy, anarchy, anarchy, Shakespeare chanted from within the pantry. He was wedged in a low shelf, tail dancing, back legs kicking the air. He was deep into the cookies now, a sugary heaven that robbed him of the last of his reason.

After the pantry we stormed the fridge, that temple of wonders. Have you ever eaten three sticks of butter? I have. How about a pound of raw ground beef? Oh yes. Even Dwid helped with that one. Tartare, it's called.

By the time we were through, the kitchen floor was an abstract painting—a milk and mustard background strewn with Cheez-Ums and chicken fried rice. Exploding from the center, bleeding into all else, was a bright-red ketchup supernova.

Kaboom.

MOONS AND MOONS

I WOULD LIKE to say that Shakespeare was the only one to vomit, but in the spirit of telling the entire truth, I must say that he was not alone.

Sad tummies? Dwid asked. *Show King Dwid your sad tummies.*

Chee, more is wonderful until you get it, Antonio said.

Those two were smug.

Cat, I said, *I'd rather die. Bird, you're not helping.*

Maybe you will die, Dwid said dreamily.

Shakespeare rushed out the back door again. He was having issues from both ends. My stomach was empty, I hoped. When Shakespeare moped back in, I went out, keeping upwind from where he had been.

I peered through chain link at the black mountains. Between me and the mountains, waves of molten air warped the division between land and sky. A dust devil bloomed from the earth to dance in the middle distance, swaying this way, then that.

How goes? said a voice.

I froze.

As though he had appeared from a burl of hot air, or a crack in the earth, a coyote appeared before me. He was long-limbed and barrel-chested. His head was triangular and handsome, peaked with wide-set ears and undercut with a wry, corner-lip smile.

Apologies if I spooked ya, he said. He was calmer than the coyotes I had imagined.

You didn't spook me, I said.

He studied me openly. Just as I was convincing myself that he really hadn't spooked me, he lunged and snapped his teeth, rattling the chain link fence. I jumped back and flattened myself. All involuntary.

Now he was sitting, relaxed again, amused. I stood up, making myself as tall as possible.

Oh I'm just playin', said the coyote. *Say, what's your name, bud?*

They call me Leo, I said.

They?

I mean—

What do you call you? he asked.

Leo, I guess.

You guess? What, you don't like your own name? Didn't you name yourself?

You can do that?

Why not?

Huh. I've never really thought about it. But I see what you mean. Why not? Why should they get to name me?

His smile widened. *I thought you might be one of us. Part coyote, anyhow.*

Really?

Sure. Those big ears. Pretty long legs. Although no coyote worth his gristle would ever let a two-legger name him. For example, my name is Gus. Because I chose it. Happen to like it. Who knows, might even change it if I stop likin' it. My name. My choice. Why not?

This option had never occurred to me. Other names for myself ran through my head. What about Buzz? Or Buck? Or Smash? Smash was good.

Say, what happened to your leg? asked Gus. *And what's that thing around your neck?*

I had forgotten about the pink donut, which I wore now in case Mary returned. Embarrassed, I held my head higher. *Snapped my leg in a fight,* I said. *The collar's to stop me fighting.*

Ya kill him?

Who? Oh. Um. No. I let him live.

Too bad. Shoulda killed him. Still could. While you're at it, you should kill whoever put that thing around your neck.

It's not so bad, I said. *Actually pretty comfy for sleeping, and—*

You smell that?

I sniffed with him. *Smell what?*

Grub, he said. *Lots a grub.*

The scent of food was spilling from the house—a sickly mix of savory and sweet that rekindled my nausea.

Oh, that, I said. *Yeah. We helped ourselves.*

Yeah?

Yeah. I pretty much do whatever I want.

Well, well, well. I bet you are part coyote after all. Seeing as such, what do you think about helpin' out a friend?

Who?

Me, bud. Your old friend, Gus. I tell ya, it's tough out here. Haven't seen rain in moons and moons. The hares are all ate up or starved, the mice are hid in their holes, the birds know better, and the two-leggers keep the kitties inside, mostly. I mean, smokes, bud, Chad was so hungry and over-heated the other day, he stuck his head down a rattlesnake hole. Said he was looking for a way out. You bet he got bit. Head swelled up like roadkill in the sun. Yep. It's a funny kinda hell out here. But I guess you wouldn't know, would ya? Got all that food, don't ya? Much as ya need. Just help yourself. And that's good for you. But that don't sit fair, does it?

I dropped my tail. Here I was, too sick from food to eat another bite, while this poor coyote, who seemed like a really nice guy, was on the other side of the fence, starving to death.

No, I agreed, *it doesn't…it don't sit fair.*

I figured you'd agree. So, you'll help out a friend? A fellow coyote?

Of course, I said, wagging my tail.

He licked his lips as I returned to the house.

You're one of the good ones, Gus called after me.

I stepped over Shakespeare, who snored on the kitchen floor. In the pantry I found another bag of chips, then thought twice—a coyote would want meat. I opened the fridge, pretty sure I had seen some ground turkey.

Ay, to whom are you talking? Antonio asked.

Nobody, I said, feeling his eyes piercing my back.

Nobody? Who is this Nobody?

71

I ignored him and stood on my hind legs to check a higher shelf. *Dog, I hope you are not talking to whom I think you are talking to.* There it was. I grasped the Styrofoam with my front teeth

Ay, you have no idea what it is you do, Antonio said. *Dog, I warn you, this is a mistake.*

As he said this, the front door opened, creating a sudden draft through the house that slammed the back door. *Chee, Santamaria,* Antonio said. *She is come.*

Gus, I realized, would have to wait.

WHAT HAPPENED IN VELOS DIDN'T STAY IN VELOS

I SHOWED my belly when Mary entered, but to my surprise, she didn't shout and she didn't curse and she didn't even call us bad. I could tell right away that she'd been through some kind of ordeal, as her uniform was wrinkled and untucked, and she gave off a foul odor. She entered uncharacteristically—slow, soft spoken, and, it seemed to me, shorter than the last time I'd seen her. She sat on the kitchen floor beside the mess, apologizing and calling us her babies, her babies. She even kissed me on my nose.

Here's what I gathered, through a phone call Mary made later that night: an old woman in Los Velos had died the week prior—but not any old woman—this lady had been hoarding cats in her double-wide since anyone could remember. They think her A/C unit expired first, she soon after, likely helped along by her refusal to open any windows for fear of losing a cat.

Put all that together for a certified biohazard. When the smell hit the neighbors, the cops showed up, knocked down the front door, and found her, half eaten in her bed. The cats were heat-stroked and insane, crawling all over her. A swarm of them bolted out the door while the rest dashed for cover, hiding in every dark corner. It was too much for the Velos crew alone, so they called for backup from the surrounding towns, which is how Mary got pulled in. She'd offered her time twice over, so she'd been trapping feral cats for more than twenty-four hours. She sure smelled like it—enough to curl whiskers. She had asked a young volunteer from the animal shelter to check in on us, but whoever that was apparently also suffered from amnesia.

When Mary finally stood up to clean our mess, she moved stiffly and slowly, as though in a daze. Only later, collapsed on the couch in her robe, scrubbed pink from a long shower, did she cry. I stood back, watching. This was my first crying human, so I didn't understand. I thought maybe she was choking at first, or suffering from some kind of eye disease. Shakespeare licked her tears and snuffed her neck.

Too heavy, Mom, he said. *Too too heavy. We gotta take some off. Here we go, Mom, here we go. I'll take some. Too too heavy. Way too heavy. Let me. Here. I'll take it. I've got the heavy. Here's some light. Light light light. Light.*

I felt a kind of magnetism surrounding me, as if her emotion was reaching across the room, gripping my shoulders, and pulling me toward her.

"You wouldn't eat me, would you, baby?" she asked, hugging Shakespeare, who wiggled against her. "Not that—" she sniffed and tried again. "Not that anyone would notice."

I was drawn toward her, and, resting my head on her knee, tried to soothe her, first with my eyes, then by licking the lotion off her legs, which made her laugh through the tears.

After Mary fell into bed, I explained her question to the others—about being eaten.

Shakespeare was unable to comprehend. *But she's not food,* he said. *She's Mom.*

Shameful, Antonio said. *Wah, the shame. Never. On my honor, chee. Never ever.*

Only Dwid's face was visible through the vines and shadows above the cabinet. He just stared, with his one eye, over my head and through the wall.

CONTACT

Two weeks after my arrival, Mary took me to the clinic to have my stitches removed. It only took a few minutes to drive from one end of town—Hoover, it was called—to the other. I sat on the front seat of the animal control truck observing the stucco houses and brick bungalows, then the palm tree-lined main street with rusty neon signs and old-fashioned gas pumps. The clinic was on the corner—a converted bungalow with a low red roof.

The waiting room was full. A little girl sat with a cardboard box on her lap. I leaned in to sniff.

Per wo? asked a tiny voice.

Leo, I guessed. *A dog.*

Gwao! The animal jumped erratically, bouncing off the cardboard walls.

Mary pulled my leash. "Down," she said. I dropped to the floor.

"It's okay, Foofie," the little girl whispered through an air hole.

Across the room lay an enormous Great Dane. Her coat was snow white with crisp black islands, while her giant paws, with pale pads, rested one atop the other. I was glad that Mary had left my donut at home.

Good morning, the Dane said in a honey voice.

I looked at her dumbly. She was at least twice as big as me, and gorgeous. She sampled the air.

Well, well, well, she said, *you rascal.*

75

Morning, I managed.

You've still got your doodads, she said.

Oh, um, yeah, I said, standing. As I stood, however, I stepped on my leash and choked myself.

"Lady Marmalade for boarding," the receptionist called.

The Dane rose on fine legs. *Good day, rascal,* she said, disappearing down the hall.

"Down boy," Mary said.

I fell to the floor and into a daydream. I was taller and all of my legs worked. Lady Marmalade and I ran side by side through a magical forest, where trees budded bacon bits and sausages grew from the ground. We were chasing a pink tennis ball over a humpback bridge made of cheese when Dr. Francis appeared from the marshmallow clouds.

"Come on back," he said.

I was in the vet clinic again. *Hi, Doc,* I said.

He flinched, then forced a smile at Mary.

My tail was wagging uncontrollably.

He *could* understand me. I knew it!

I also knew this was unusual, which explained his reaction. From my reading I had learned that humans were unaware that animals could talk to each other, and were unable to talk to animals themselves. Still I struggled to believe this. Humans were animals too. Why should they be excluded? Maybe it was a secret, and only some of them could do it, like Dr. Francis. Maybe he wanted to keep it hidden, in case other humans thought he was odd. I could relate to that. So I decided to play it cool. Like it was no big deal.

We followed him into an exam room.

"How have you been holding up?" Dr. Francis asked. "I heard about the hoarder. That's awful. Sad, really."

"Ugh," Mary said. "You can't imagine."

You can't imagine how itchy these stitches are, I said.

Dr. Francis twitched again. Why was he so freaked out? Why wouldn't he talk to me? It was perfectly natural. The other humans were the odd ones.

"So," he said, perhaps too loudly. "How's Leo?"

"Bad but good," Mary said, smiling down at me. "If you know what I mean."

Are you going to take these stitches out? I asked Dr. Francis.

"You know what?" he said, abruptly closing my file. "Let's just get the stitches out."

Thanks, Doc, I said, glad to be recognized.

He led me from the exam room to the treatment area, where the technician took my leash and scratched behind my ears. I leaned into her.

Hey destroyer, Birdie said, sitting beside the sink. *How's the leg?*

Much better, thanks. I can put some weight on it now. And it doesn't hurt all the time anymore, which is—

Oh, you know what I just remembered? I don't care. She jumped down and brushed through the technician's legs. *Did Dwid tell you he's king? Because, you know, he's not. There is only one queen.* She swanned out of the room.

Dr. Francis kneeled to examine my leg. I held the limb aloft so he could remove the stitches.

"He's so good today," the technician said.

Dr. Francis didn't reply. While avoiding eye contact with me, he began to hum.

Why won't you talk to me? I asked. *Is it because I broke all that stuff? Sorry about that, by the way.*

He hummed louder. His hands were trembling.

What's wrong? I asked. *You know, you're the first human I've met who can understand me. Of course, I haven't met many humans. Maybe you could introduce me to some others? Is it like a secret society thing, or what? I don't get it.*

Dr. Francis dropped the scissors. He grabbed my leash, and mumbling incoherently, pulled me out of the treatment area, leaving the confused technician behind. I limped after him. We went into a vacant exam room. He dropped the leash and shut the door. He leaned against the wall, then slid down it to sit, breathing hard. I waited for him to calm down. When his breathing slowed, he finally looked at me, eye to eye.

Hi, I said.

Too much. He plugged his ears and squeezed his eyes shut.

What's wrong? I asked.

He shook his head.

It's no big deal, I said, realizing that this might not be normal, after all. Even for him.

"Nah nah nah," he said, still plugging his ears. "No. No no. No no no."

It's fine. Relax.

"This can't be happening," he said.

Um. But it is?

"No it isn't."

Then how do you know I just said that?

"It's just stress. That's what it is. It's the stress."

Calm down, Doc. You're fine.

He yanked his fingers from his ears and opened his eyes. "I am not fine," he said, in a flare of anger. "Get out of my head."

I backed away. He looked like Mary did right before she cried. "I'm losing my mind," he whispered.

No, you're not.

His eyes leveled upon me. "I won't do it, you know. Before you even ask. I won't do it. So don't even ask."

Now he was kind of freaking me out. *Do what?*

"Oh, you know what," he said. He closed his eyes again and gripped his head fur in his fists. "I won't do it," he said. "I won't. I won't. I won't."

You won't what?

"I won't burn anything! I won't!"

What? I looked around the room. Maybe he was insane. *Why would I ask you to burn something?*

"I won't do it."

Good, I said. *Seriously. I don't want you to burn anything. Are you thinking about burning something? Please don't, whatever it is.*

He opened his eyes. "You don't want me to?"

No. Why would I?

A long pause ensued. His mouth was slightly ajar. Finally he answered: "Because it's the only way out?"

Um.

"But you don't want me to."

No, of course not, I said. *Definitely not.*

Dr. Francis released his grip. We reassessed one another, him probably thinking I was less dangerous than he had suspected, me considering the opposite.

Sorry if I spooked you, I said. *I still don't know what's normal. It's kind of a problem.*

He tilted his head, not unlike a curious dog. "It's just so…real," he said. "I never thought insanity would be like this. So real. And clear. That's what's so unreal about it. It's hard to explain."

You're not insane.

"Yes, I am. I can see that now."

No, you're not, I said. But how could I prove it to him? *What about everything else?* I asked. *Is anything else out of the ordinary? You should be able to tell, right?*

He shook his head slowly, smiling at my naivety. "Crazy people don't know they're crazy. It's already starting to feel normal. I'm on the other side now."

This logic was suspect. Still I felt the need to reassure him. *You know, animals talk like this all the time,* I said. *It's normal for us. Always has been. And you're just another animal, aren't you? No matter what the Bible says.*

He seemed most perplexed by this last statement. I worried that I was losing him, shaking his new reality too hard, too quickly.

Let's just take it slow, I said, reassuring him with a familiar tail wag. *First of all, I promise I don't want you to burn anything. I really just want you to take these stitches out. If you don't mind. Please. They are so itchy.*

This seemed to calm him. I was unsure what to say next, not knowing what might throw him off balance again. I figured I should let him lead.

Slowly, his expression reassumed its usual curious kindness, with a touch of anxiety. "Can you talk to anyone else?" he asked. "How about Mary?"

Nope. I've tried.

"So are you reading my mind?" he asked. "What am I thinking about right now?"

We peered into each other's eyes.

Waffle, he said—his first silent word.

I wagged my tail, feeling proud of him. I was training my very own human. *Waffle,* I repeated.

He gawked.

Relax, I said. *I can't read all your thoughts. Luckily, I should add. You have to try to communicate them, like when you open your mouth to talk out loud.*

Wow, he said. *Brain to brain.*

I guess, I said.

He kept speaking silently, although his grammar needed work. *You talk? Other animals? Not dogs?*

Hey, that's good. You'll pick it up. And yeah, I can. Although some of them, I just found out, speak different languages. Like bunnies. I'm pretty sure it was a bunny in that box. Or maybe a mouse.

Cats?

So far all the dogs and cats I've met speak the same language. And at least one parrot. And a coyote. But it's kind of the blind leading the blind here. I'm also new to this. And everything else, for that matter. What about you? Have you spoken to any other animals yet?

No, he said. *You. Only.*

Maybe you're just tuning in. But you're not going crazy. I can promise you that.

He pondered this. *We see*, he said, rising awkwardly to his feet. *Now. We prove crazy. Or not crazy.* He opened the door. *Experiment.*

The technician came out of another exam room with a manila folder. "Your next appointment is here," she said, looking from Dr. Francis to me with a hint of concern. "Louie Sykes. Two-year-old Labradoodle. Diarrhea. Pretty standard. Should be quick."

"Interesting," Dr. Francis said, aloud. "Very interesting."

The technician's eyebrows lifted. Dr. Francis was acting more peculiar than usual, which meant he was acting very, very peculiar.

"Did Louie eat something?" he asked.

"Yeah, he ate—"

"No!" Dr. Francis said abruptly. "Stop."

The technician's eyebrows traveled further up her forehead.

"So you know what he ate?" Dr. Francis asked. "Don't tell us what it is."

"Us?"

"Me."

"Okay. I mean, yeah. The owner saw him eat it."

"Perfect," Dr. Francis said. "Bring Louie back."

The technician returned to the treatment area with a gangly blonde Labradoodle, who danced around on his leash, yanking the technician's arm.

Hi! the dog said, his nails scraping the floor. *My poop is water!*

"Is he talking?" Dr. Francis asked aloud. "I can't hear him."

"Is who talking?" the technician asked.

He is, I said to Dr. Francis. *You can't hear him? Huh. Well, in short, he's a little…how do I put this politely…doofy.*

Dr. Francis stooped over, took Louie's fuzzy head in his hands, and stared into his eyes. Their noses touched. The technician's jaw was slack. The dog twisted free. "I don't think he can hear me," Dr. Francis said aloud. "I can't hear him at all."

"Are you feeling okay?" the technician asked Dr. Francis.

You just need practice, I said. *You'll get it. In the meantime let's prove that you're sane. I'll translate.*

"Fine, fine," he said. "Yes. Do it."

"Do what?" the technician asked.

Hey, I said to Louie. *Eat anything good lately?*

Stinky bird! Louie said. *Oh yum it was yummy!*

When did you eat it?

Not today!

Wonderful. What day?

Day before today!

He ate a dead bird yesterday, I relayed.

"Alright," Dr. Francis said, rubbing his hands together. "Go ahead and tell me. What did he eat and when did he eat it?"

"It was a dead bird," the technician said. "Yesterday."

At this, Dr. Francis clasped his hands together. He began to laugh, quietly at first, then rising, building into an erratic giggle, punctuated by an occasional snort. The technician smoothed her scrub top. Maybe she'd never seen him laugh before, or, at least, not quite like this.

THE GOOD DOCTOR

WHERE DR. FRANCIS'S laughter ended, his curiosity began. He explained to Mary that I would benefit from physical therapy. To ensure that she agreed, he offered the service for free. And so, three days a week, I received physical therapy, along with a general, didactic education. I learned a great deal about humans during my time with Dr. Francis, and about Dr. Francis himself, who I came to see as a case study in his own right.

His foremost characteristic was high intelligence, but for this he seemed to pay the price of many quirks. When talking on the phone, for example, he unbent paper clips and lined them end to end across his desk. When entering a room, he knocked three times on the door frame, room occupied or not. He hummed when nervous, which was most of the time, but especially before he broke bad news, and he muttered to himself when he wasn't humming—while extracting teeth, looking down ears, or suturing wounds. Animal fluids didn't bother him, but he hated human handshakes, which were always sweaty, he said, compelling him to wash his hands countless times a day, always in triplicate. In spare moments he physically worried at what was available, principally himself, tugging at his hair or fidgeting with his overstretched polo collar, one part of his scruffy wardrobe, which otherwise featured baggy slacks, black scuffed shoes, and loose athletic socks. While his lab coat was always bleached clean, it was ragged at the edges, with a large hole in the right pocket through which he unconsciously passed his hand to wiggle his fingers in the air. These habits were all amplified by stress and black coffee, both of which he consumed in large amounts, the latter from an enormous mug without a handle—more like a dog bowl, really.

I remember that first day of physical therapy, lying on my side while Dr. Francis extended and flexed my joints. With so much to ask, I could hardly lie still. I began by asking the most important question: *Where is Roger?*

Who?

The man who hurt me. Who did this to me.

Oh. Well, we don't know who did that, Dr. Francis said, his words now orderly and clear.

It was the sicko, Roger, I insisted. *I heard. You can tell me. I can handle it.*

Where did you get this idea?

I explained my memory from the animal control truck. Dr. Francis smiled. I pulled my foot away.

Sorry, he said. *But you're confused.*

I know what I heard.

I'm sure you do. That was Frank, the dispatcher. He was probably saying "Roger" as a way of confirming a message. It's radio lingo. He used to be in the army. At least he claims he was.

That couldn't be right. The name Roger was so familiar, like I'd known it my whole life. Dr. Francis's smile now seemed patronizing. Infuriating. I looked beyond it to a ceiling tile with a brown water stain, darkest at the edges.

You weren't there, I said. *You don't know how it was.*

True. But if we did know who did this to you, then why wouldn't we be looking for them? Mary would be out there guns blazing. She might literally kill him.

That was true. And the radio thing made sense. But it couldn't be right.

To find a man named Roger was possible, but a man without a name? Unthinkable. If there was no Roger, then I lost all connection with my past. And my future was…what? Sitting in a room waiting for Mary to come home?

And so fear crushed logic, as it so often does. Like a prisoner swallowing the key to his own cell, I refused to let go of Roger. I stared harder at the ceiling. The tile was crumbling at the corner, revealing a ragged black hole. *Your roof is leaking,* I said, as cold as I could.

Dr. Francis checked the ceiling, then me, smile gone, unsettled. *Right,* he said. *Mind if we continue?*

I let him take my paw again.

He made a clumsy effort to lighten the mood. *So,* he said, extending my leg, *why do dogs eat grass?*

But I was in that black hole. I wanted to wound him for putting me there.

Have you spoken with any other animals yet? I asked.

Just you, so far.

Then maybe you are crazy. Maybe you're just imagining me. Like I'm imagining Roger.

He recognized what I was doing. Still, some sadness returned to his eyes.

I hope not, he said. *This is the most interesting thing that's ever happened to me. It's an honor to speak to a dog. I hope I get to speak to others.*

What could I say to that? Dr. Francis was always that way—so honest and kind. He was a good human. Always. And I needed that. I needed something.

I'm sorry, I said. *I don't know why I'm this way.*

Nobody does, Dr. Francis said. *Not everything is knowable.*

We marinated in that one for a while.

I am sorry, I said. *And I am real. I don't think you're losing your mind.*

Yeah. Well. Part of me hopes that I am. He flexed my joint. *Does that hurt?*

No, I lied.

Good, he said.

Ruffage, I said. *Grass is good for digestion. Or if you eat enough, to puke something rotten.*

Ah. That's what I thought.

There was so much we could learn from one another.

For instance, *Why do people wear clothes?*

DOCTOR DOG

OVER THE WEEKS our topics expanded in reach. Human morality was a particular mire.

I don't get it, I said. *If murder is illegal, then how can war exist?* I was balancing on my front paws on an exercise ball.

War is different, Dr. Francis said, steadying my shoulders.

I thought you said war was when a lot of people killed a lot of other people?

It is. But these are fights between countries—between governments, usually. And it's governments that make and enforce the laws. So, during wars they make it legal for certain people to kill certain other people. But just during the war.

So the soldiers don't all go to jail after a war?

Of course not. In fact they often get honored. Parades. Medals.

For murder?

It's not that simple, Dr. Francis said. He said that a lot. *There are usually good reasons for war,* he continued. *Self-defense being most common. For example, there was once a man called Hitler...*

Mary wasn't free to pick me up until the evening, and Dr. Francis knew I hated being in a cage, so after physical therapy, I was free to watch him practice. The technician was surprised, but I behaved myself and she liked to pet me in spare moments. Besides, Birdie was free to walk around the clinic, so why couldn't I?

In the beginning I just watched and listened. Itchy ears, smelly butts, squinty eyes, diarrhea, vomiting, "dietary indiscretions"—I always liked that term, for dogs who ate batteries or bones, paper or plastic, toys or tampons. You'd be surprised how much of a veterinarian's week is spent determining if a dog ate something or not, and x-rays often fail to reveal soft items. Dr. Francis could still only understand me, allowing me to demonstrate my value.

What was it? I asked a young Pekingese, his face hidden in a ball of fur.

Mom's undies, he whispered.

Mom's undies, I told Dr. Francis.

"I knew it," Dr. Francis said. "Let's prep for surgery."

What did he say? the Pekingese asked.

He said you'll be fine.

I was also handy with pain localization. After some shameless begging on my part, Birdie convinced the cats to talk to me.

Look, I know he's a dumb, stinky, ugly dog, she told one Siamese.

I'm listening, the Siamese said.

And we can both agree he eats his own poop, Birdie said.

Is this really necessary? I asked.

Please, continue, the Siamese said.

But together, we can help you, Birdie said. *I know it sounds crazy, but this mutt can tell the doctor where it hurts.*

The Siamese eyed me suspiciously, then conceded. *My tooth,* she said.

Hey, dummy, tell the doctor the tooth, Birdie said to me. She turned back to the Siamese. *I'm his boss, you understand.*

Within a few weeks, I was interpreting diagnostics. *Looks like early arthritis,* I said, studying an x-ray in the doctor's office.

Dr. Francis tossed me another piece of dehydrated beef liver. *Good boy,* he said.

By late June I could trot with a faint limp. We x-rayed my leg. The metal plate appeared pure white, mechanical and precise. Between the screws, a thick callus was bridging the bone.

Nearly there, Dr. Francis said. *Nearly there.*

Maybe so. But to what?

Yes, my leg was nearly healed, but the more I learned, the more I realized how much I did not know, and how naïve I had been. The world was a massive, complicated place. Even if I could run, where would I go? I still harbored a belief that Roger—or some other human by another name—knew who I was, or what I was. Because I was far from normal. My intelligence surpassed all the other four-legged animals I had met, and most humans too. I even had proof. One day Dr. Francis gave me an IQ test—a human IQ test. I scored 134, just shy of genius.

I was enjoying my time with Dr. Francis, but he was growing increasingly comfortable with our ability to communicate, while I grew increasingly unsettled. I could find no record of anything like this happening to anyone else, and neither could he. Yet he no longer seemed to care. We appeared to be the only wires that connected two massive machines in a phenomenon unknown to anyone else in the history of the world, and this only bothered me.

There had to be others, didn't there? Others like us, who could span the divide? If so, we could do so much more than help a few dogs and cats. We could unlock the animal kingdom, bringing unity and equality to replace exploitation and dominance. With others like us, we could change everything. We just needed to find them, or at least understand our condition.

I suggested that we enlist the help of a neurologist—some leading researcher, who could scan our brains to figure out what was going on. Dr. Francis disagreed. *Absolutely not*, he said. He was sure they would lock him up. *Besides,* he added, *wouldn't this type of animal communication have been discovered already?* We both knew that was shabby logic. Really, he preferred safety and certainty, and may have doubted his own sanity. Telling anyone about a talking dog was too much of a risk. Plus, almost every day, he received another five-star review or thank-you card for solving yet another impossible case.

I was happy for him, but I needed a greater purpose. I wanted to see the world for myself. I felt the draw of so many futures, so many possibilities beyond the walls of this small-town clinic. I admit to delusions of grandeur. But I was no ordinary dog. So why should I lead an ordinary life? What if they weren't delusions at all? What if I really was grand? This was an interesting paradox. Delusions of grandeur are only delusions if you believe that they are delusions and therefore never pursue them. Or if you pursue them and fail.

But what else could life be for?

To accept mediocrity?

To refuse the call of adventure?

To just…be ordinary?

Never.

I would start by finding the one I called Roger. I still resented him, although my revenge fantasies were fading. I was becoming obsessed with something greater than vengeance—the truth. I wanted to know how I came to be. I wanted to know if there were others. I wanted to know everything. I wanted to find the limits of my inner grandiosity.

But not yet, I told myself. I needed more time. My leg was still healing. I was just starting to understand human culture, most recently via a series of classics in philosophy. If I left now, I wouldn't even make it through the existentialists. I had only just met Camus!

The deeper reason for my reluctance to leave, of course, was fear. Not because I was afraid of being physically harmed. No no. I was afraid of something much, much worse.

Failure.

OH, THE DOODAD DAY?

WE WERE in the doctor's office with the door closed. The room was small, with one window to the park, where a dog played Frisbee with a man. Dr. Francis sat in one office chair while I sat in the other. I had been in a dark mood for several days. I was mulling my decision to stay or leave. My restlessness channeled into a more tangible, immediate problem.

You'd be more susceptible to certain types of cancer, Dr. Francis said.

Are you? I asked.

Am I what?

I imagine you still have your doodads?

Of course.

So you must also be more susceptible to certain types of cancer. And yet you live on, somehow.

Yes, but I'm human.

Oh, but I'm human! I mimicked. *I forgot. Humans are sacred creatures. They're special. They don't have to do anything they don't want to do.*

That's not exactly fair. And you're picking up Mary's sarcasm.

You want to talk about fair?

You won't miss your doodads, as you call them, Dr. Francis said. He sorted the pens on his desk by color.

You're forgetting who you're talking to. I know my testosterone levels will drop significantly, altering my muscle tone, and potentially my behavior. Wouldn't you miss yours?

He considered while looking out the window. I was getting closer.

Are you planning on...reproducing? he asked.

Scary, huh? Well, I haven't even thought about it. But I'd like to keep the choice. Wouldn't you?

He blushed.

My desire to reproduce is beside the point, I said. *Just like it is with you. It's the principle. The ethic. You can't just go around removing body parts from self-aware individuals. It's barbaric. Just look back through human history. You won't have to go far. Look at all the horrible people who sterilized unsuspecting women in the name of some greater cause. Do you really want to be another one of them? Some eugenical mad scientist performing—*

Okay, okay, jeez, you've made your point, he said. *You read too much.*

I'm passionate.

He sighed. *Let's say, hypothetically, that I agree. How would we convince Mary?*

Indeed, this was a bigger problem. As an animal control officer, Mary held strong convictions about neutering dogs. I gathered that these convictions were only strengthened by past experiences with human men. On occasion, she reminded me of my condition.

"Ugh, just look at those things," she'd say. "Spare parts. Pair of tumors. Can't wait till they're gone."

Yes, these comments worried me.

I asked Dr. Francis to tell Mary that I had a rare bleeding disorder, and that such a surgery would kill me. He refused, knowing her too well. She would want to see the test results.

Still, Dr. Francis tried, in his own way. When Mary came to pick me up, they sat across from one another in the doctor's office, while I now sat on the ground, doing my best to look like a harmless, normal dog.

"You know, Leo behaves very well," Dr. Francis said, pulling at his collar.

"Sure does," Mary said, smiling at me. "I trained him, didn't I, Leo? Good boy."

I wagged my tail.

"You really have done an excellent job with him," Dr. Francis said. "So, maybe, since he behaves so well, we don't need to neuter him?"

Mary burst out laughing. She had a bellowing laugh, like a lady wrestler.

"You know, people say you're not funny," Mary said, "but you are. Good one, Doc. I mean it. I needed that. I thought you wanted to talk about something serious. C'mon, Leo, let's go home."

Just days later, I saw my impending fate literally written out. In the predawn, while Mary still slept, I opened the laptop. I was greeted by a calendar reminder. That day was Monday, July 4th. Independence Day. On the next day, Tuesday, July 5th, my reckoning was written: "Neuter Leo."

Staring at these words, I should have thanked Mary. She was offering me a big fear to chase away a smaller one. She was giving me a reason to leave. But in that moment, the last thing I could imagine was thanking her.

I felt an awful prickling sensation covering my skin, imagining how she wanted to mutilate me. I was isolated by a total lack of sympathy for my situation. The others slept peacefully in their ignorance. Antonio, bright-blue head tucked into his feathers, warbled with every exhale. Dwid, atop the cat tree, dozed in silence, his ringed orange tail flickering in his dreams. Shakespeare snored on his back. Even if I explained, they would never understand. I would never be like them.

I was more human than dog.

More dog than human.

I was a freak.

And I was alone.

Completely, utterly alone.

Mary's bedroom door opened. I quickly shut the laptop. She squinted and rubbed her eyes.

"Morning!" Antonio cawed. "Morning! Morning!"

Shut up, Dwid said.

Shakespeare spun at Mary's feet. *Hi, Mom! Hi, bird! Hi, cat! Hi, dog! Hi, kitchen!*

"Happy Fourth, everybody," Mary said, putting on the coffee pot. "Mama's celebrating."

Coffee made, she added a splash of whiskey, then went to Antonio, who stepped onto her index finger to lead a regal procession out the back door. Behind them followed Shakespeare and Dwid. I came out only after they had settled in for sunrise. Instead of sitting with Mary, however, as the others did, I stood in the middle of the yard, watching the queen with her loyal subjects.

"Hey, Leo," Mary said, smiling. "Come sit with mama, sweetie. What's wrong?"

I remained where I was.

You're not my mother, I said, as calmly as I could. *You're just a lonely alcoholic who thinks her pets are her kids.*

Looking back, I've never been so grateful to go unheard.

A XANI FOR DWID

"M-80's," Mary said, "those are the loud ones. Black snakes. Used to be my favorite as a kid. Roman candles..." She was sorting through a large cardboard box on the kitchen counter. The smell of sulfur was in the air.

No, no, no, Dwid said. He had gone into hiding above the cabinets.

Bang-bangs! Shakespeare said, dancing around her feet.

Ay, foolishness, Antonio said.

"...Uncle Sam's Joy, Peezlewhoppers, Bullseyes, Shoot 'em Ups, Silver Slugs..."

I think I'm dying, Dwid said. *Yes, I'm dying. I feel like I'm dying. I'm dead. It's over.*

They are loud, chee, and bright, but harmless, Antonio said. *You will be fine.*

"...Molten Death, Spinning Sallies, Big Bad Betties, Fire of Freedom, and bottle rockets. Gotta have lots of bottle rockets."

Dwid yowled.

"And something special for my scawed wittle guy," Mary said. She opened a can of cat food.

My last meal, Dwid said, *and I'm too sick to eat.*

I'll eat it! Shakespeare said, jumping at Mary's leg.

"You don't need this, Shakespeare," Mary said, "you're tough."

She crushed a tablet and added it to the food. She then stood on a chair to put the bowl on top of the cabinets.

Oh, I couldn't, Dwid said. *Wait, is that gravy?*

I was preoccupied with escape plans. I didn't know where I was going, exactly, and the autumn would have been a better time to travel, with less heat, but if I waited for the perfect day, I'd never go, or I'd be leaving with an empty space between my legs. And I intended to go with my doghood intact.

My plan was too simple to fail. I would jump the fence at 11:59 p.m., gaining my freedom with the poetic fortune of a personal Independence Day. Emerson would have been proud. And, practically speaking, I would have a long head start before Mary awoke.

"Okay, fuzzers," she said. "Let's get the meat going. I hope Dr. Francis likes steak."

Dr. Francis? I didn't know he would be coming. Maybe I could talk him into delaying the neuter. No. I'd made my choice.

Around five, he entered with a pie. Shakespeare did his usual dance. I watched from the living room. It looked like Dr. Francis and Mary were going to hug, but then they didn't. She patted his shoulder.

"It's an apple pie," he said, lamely, his dorkiness exaggerated by jean shorts and an American flag T-shirt.

In fact both of them were wearing jean shorts and American flag T-shirts. I guess this is some kind of uniform for the holiday?

"Apple's perfect," Mary said, trading the pie for a beer.

"Um, I don't know if—"

"Cheers." She clanked her bottle against his.

He took a sip, then a gulp.

Mary opened the fridge. "Check out these ribeyes."

"Oh. Nice."

"What?"

"I'm a vegetarian."

"Really? I mean. Okay. No. That's fine. I knew that." She closed the fridge and opened a cabinet. "Hope you like beans!"

The beans, however, upon reading the can, also had meat in them.

Awkwardness does not have a smell, but if it did, the house would have reeked. They talked about the weather. They complained about road construction. They seemed suddenly thirsty. The first beers went down fast. After the second round, I could see the social benefits of ethanol consumption. Dr. Francis stopped fiddling with his T-shirt. Mary leaned against the counter.

"Gave Dwid a Xani," she said, "just like you told me. Maybe he could chase it with a beer. That'd really fix his wagon."

Dwid stared down from on high. His one eye was starting to droop.

Dr. Francis giggled. I'd never heard him giggle.

Mary seemed to appreciate this too. "Glad you came over, Doc. I don't really have anybody, you know, uh—" She cleared her throat.

"Same," Dr. Francis said.

They were both blushing. I guess it was kind of sweet, although I was too resentful at the time to really appreciate their kindling friendship.

"You can call me Ulysses if you want," Dr. Francis said.

"Oh," Mary said. "Okay. Sure. Ulysses. You know, it's weird but I've never thought about your first name. You're Doc, you know? But I do like Ulysses. I do. It's different. Ulysses Francis. Man, your parents really had it out for you. No offense."

"None taken."

"Your name's like a whisper. Wait, what's your middle?"

"Cecil."

"No way."

"Yep. And it gets worse. When I was younger, I had a lisp."

"No way!"

"Ulysses Cecil Francis," he said with a lisp, then tipped back his beer.

Mary laughed. "You know what my middle name is?"

"What?"

"Don't have one. Mary blank Mitchell. So I guess we both got screwed."

They touched bottles to that.

SIX BEERS DEEP

WHEN EMPTY BEER bottles formed a fleet on the counter, Mary went out to light the grill, and Dr. Francis headed for the bathroom. He closed the door before noticing that I had joined him inside.

Hey, Doc, I said.

Oh good, he said, unzipping in front of the toilet, *a talking dog.*

Listen.

I'd rather not, he said, swaying as he urinated, his words clumsy in my head. *You know I always hated those movies with talking animals. I was kinda hoping enough alcohol would drown all of you out.*

All of us?

Yep, he said. *It's progressive. Few days now.*

Why didn't you tell me?

He blew a raspberry.

Who have you heard? I asked. *Have you been talking back?*

He blew an even bigger raspberry.

Fine, I said. *Just listen. You don't have to neuter me.*

Not this again.

You don't have to neuter me, I said, *because I'm running away.*

I expected a reaction. I thought he would ask me to reconsider. Instead he started to whistle. I waited while he went, and went, and went, whistling throughout. I swear that little man had a camel's bladder. Finally he stopped, zipped up, flushed, and turned on the tap. "One," he said aloud, soaping his hands.

Did you hear me? I'm leaving.

He squinted at me in the mirror. *You know, I think I finally got this figured out.*

What?

It's stress. That's all. He rinsed his hands. "Two," he said, pumping the soap.

We've been over this, I said. *I couldn't possibly be in your head. Think of all the animals I've helped at the clinic. How could you have made that up?*

The mind is complex. I don't claim to understand it. You know what else I realized? More of a theory. The only way to get rid of you is to stand up to you. Because I let everyone walk all over me. I let everyone tell me what to do.

That's just your job, I said.

Is it though? Was it just my job the other night? When my neighbor came over to my house at ten o'clock on a Tuesday? He bangs on the door. Rings the bell. I open up, thinking it's some kind of emergency. You know what it was? He wanted me to vaccinate his dog. Right there on my doorstep. Because he was going to Belize the next morning. Needed papers. Belize! That's how people are now. They don't just want my help. They want my soul.

He rinsed his hands. "Three," he said. This would be his last wash.

That's not true. People really do need your help. They—

Blah blah blah, dog. Woof woof woof.

Well, I'm sorry you feel that way. But you helped me. You really did. So…thank you. That's the other thing I wanted to tell you. Thank you. I mean that. I don't know if I'll be back, but—

Good. Don't come back. Ever. You started this. I don't know how you did it. I don't know what you are. Some kind of demon? But you started it. I know that. So go away. And never come back.

I lowered my ears. My tail fell. This wasn't how I wanted it to end. It was the alcohol, I knew, but it felt like I was hearing his actual thoughts for the first time. He hated me.

He closed the tap with his elbow, then locked eyes with himself in the mirror, fingers dripping.

"You can beat this," he said aloud. "Stay strong. None of this is real."

It is real, I said, *whether you like it or not. I am as real as you are.*

"Stop!" he shouted. He spun around. "Stop fighting me!" He took a step toward me. "Get out of me! Get out!"

I backed away.

Moments later, a knock on the door.

"Everything okay in there?" Mary asked.

"Fine," Dr. Francis said, relaxing his fists.

"Fiber," Mary said through the door. "That's the secret. You need more fiber."

A CLOSE CALL

MARY AND DR. FRANCIS ate dinner as night fell. They were ravenous and hardly spoke, indiscriminately shoveling food—potato salad, green bean casserole, buttered buns, watermelon, corn on the cob, asparagus—into their mouths. Mary wolfed a T-bone the size of her face. She pinched the bone to gnaw the last chunks of meat.

Ay, they have turned wild, Antonio said.

Shakespeare was under the table, putting his head in one lap, then the other. *Can I have some?* he asked. *Can I have some?*

Dwid was unconscious above the kitchen cabinets.

I lay in my bed across the living room watching Dr. Francis. Look at him there, drinking beer after beer. Wiping his dirty human lips.

"Ever had a Rum and Hide?" he asked Mary. His words were syrupy.

"No," Mary said.

"Ah is sooo good," he slurred. "Jus made it up."

The Rum and Hide, from what I could tell, was a brimful of rum with a squeeze of lemon. Even Mary was unsteady after that. They cleared the table, stumbling around like a pair of sailors navigating an invisible storm.

A pop resounded in the distance.

"It's starting," Mary said.

Shakespeare and I followed them onto the patio. Going outside felt like stepping through a wall of heat. The ground radiated beneath us. Far off, the column of light was sharpening as the sky darkened.

"The first thing you gotta do," Mary said, lifting a finger in the air, "is light your punk." She handed Dr. Francis a thin wooden stick. "But first," she said, pulling a pack of cigarettes from her pocket, "you gotta light a cigarette."

"Nah," Dr. Francis said, grinning.

"C'mon," she said. "Come oooooooooon. Ulysses. It's America's birthday."

Dr. Francis accepted this highly questionable logic. Mary lit both cigarettes, then the punk. Dr. Francis watched the flame with all his remaining focus until it went out. Then he gazed between his punk and his cigarette. He seemed mesmerized by the glowing embers. I guess he did have an attraction to fire.

"And now," Mary said, "we take a drag."

They inhaled together. Exhaled. Dr. Francis coughed.

Mary slapped him on the back. "That's the stuff. Now, let's start the show with a bottle rocket. My favorite."

She held one out. Dr. Francis lit it with an unsteady hand. Just before the fuse disappeared into the rocket, Mary tossed it up and out. It whizzed over the fence and popped with a spark.

Dr. Francis giggled. He put the unlit end of the punk in his mouth. Realizing his error, he replaced this with his cigarette. He took another drag, and, again, coughed. I've seen humans do a lot of strange things, but inhaling smoke on purpose has to be one of the strangest.

"You get used to it," Mary said, digging through the fireworks. She was quite casual about that lit cigarette in her mouth. I stepped back when some ash dropped into the box. Fortunately we didn't explode.

The celebration picked up when it was fully dark. Colorful explosions bloomed around the column of light, pops reaching us seconds later. Here in Hoover, along the edge of the desert, fireworks filled the air. Some crackled and flashed. Others soared and screamed. The big bangs made me flinch, but I was captivated, momentarily forgetting my fight with Dr. Francis, and my impending escape.

After working through most of the box, with several trips to the fridge for more beer, Dr. Francis and Mary returned to bottle rockets.

I stepped further away. They were utterly inebriated. Absolutely annihilated. Trashed. And it finally caught up with them.

Dr. Francis must have forgotten that he'd lit the rocket in his hand, because after he lit it, he just stood there wobbling with that goofy grin on his face. The rocket shot out of his hand, went through the back door, and exploded in the house. Antonio screeched. We ran inside to find a black mark on the wall. Fortunately nothing caught fire.

"Whoa," Dr. Francis said. "Tha was close."

By the time Mary calmed Antonio down, the party's momentum was lost, and so, it seemed, was Dr. Francis. He sat on the floor in the middle of the kitchen. Then he lay on his back.

"You're staying here tonight," Mary said.

"I'm fine," he said. With great effort, like raising a sunken ship, he stood, demonstrating his fineness. He tried to stand on one leg. He could not. He closed his eyes and tried to touch his own nose, but found only air.

"Let's get you to sleep," Mary said, leading him to the couch.

He collapsed there. She covered him with a blanket. Then, staggering less than Dr. Francis, but still staggering, she turned out the lights and retired to her own bedroom.

I curled up in my bed. It was only ten o'clock.

A quick nap, I told myself.

Then I would go.

FIRE EXIT

I AWOKE to the smell of smoke. How long had I been asleep? I couldn't tell. At first I thought it was just the smell of fireworks, but when my eyes stung in the darkness, I knew it was worse than that. I knew it was worse still when the couch cushion burst into flames.

This was a curious moment.

Sitting beside the flame, staring into it, was Dr. Francis.

Wow, Shakespeare said, *this is a good one.*

I started barking.

Antonio started squawking.

Shhh, Shakespeare said, *it's against the law to bark in the dark.*

Black smoke boiled from the couch. The flame was catching on the armrest. Dr. Francis leaned back, slightly, but made no effort to stand. I jumped up and barked but Dr. Francis just kept staring at the flames. Even with my paws digging into his lap, he didn't acknowledge me.

Get up! I said. *Get up!*

Ay, he's dead! Antonio cried, flapping his wings on his perch.

He's not dead! I said.

He's just resting! Shakespeare said, spinning in a circle.

Regardless, Dr. Francis was not moving. I bit his shoe and pulled.

"Owwwwww," he groaned, falling backward.

I pulled harder. I tumbled back with his shoe in my mouth. I spat it out. Only seconds had passed, yet the flame had already spread around the armrest to the side and back of the couch. Dr. Francis was trying to right himself now, arms swimming in the air.

He toppled sideways off the couch and bounced off the coffee table, ending up on his back. He stared at the ceiling, his mouth moving slowly, not making words. The fire, as if glad to see the couch was now vacant, spread across the cushions, replacing Dr. Francis with flames. The smoke was acrid. My eyes streamed with tears.

Um, Shakespeare said, *I don't think this is supposed to happen.* He had finally stopped spinning and backed away from the flames.

Wake up Mary, I said.

Mom! Shakespeare cried. He ran to her bedroom and scratched at the door. Meanwhile, Antonio was off his perch, running back and forth in his swaying way, screaming his head off, wings wide.

I returned to Dr. Francis, now spread eagle on the rug. If I had to drag him out, then that's what I'd do. I bit his collar and pulled hard. His T-shirt caught underneath his armpits and chin. He didn't protest. In fact, he had decided it was a fine time to go back to sleep. And so I dragged his limp body to the back door. I released him to work the bolt, then the lever. The door swung open. The air was suddenly cleaner. I took several deep breaths, but so did the fire, causing it to spread to the rug. Once more, I bit his collar and leaned back, struggling to the doorsill, where I could really dig in. Then it was easier. I dragged his limp body over the threshold and across the concrete patio into the pebbles of the yard, where I let go.

With Dr. Francis safe, I ran back inside, blinking quickly to clear my eyes. From somewhere within, Antonio screamed. The fire had consumed the entire rug, so the flames now appeared to grow from underground. Smoke formed a thick black fur on the ceiling. The air was gray.

Shakespeare had scratched Mary's door but made no progress. I pawed at the handle, opening the door. She was sleeping face down on the covers. Shakespeare jumped onto her back and spun in circles. I licked her face. None of this roused her. It took Antonio, who reached up and clenched her toes, to get a reaction. She yanked her foot away and jumped off the bed, sending Shakespeare somersaulting through the air. As he bounced, tumbled, and righted himself, Mary's eyes burst wide open.

"Holy crap!" she shouted.

Smoke was pouring into the bedroom. The living room looked like a corner of hell. The flames were bright, the heat immense, the smoke getting darker and darker. The back door was blocked by a wall of fire. Mary dropped to her knees and shielded her face, then, after checking that we were still with her, crawled, half blind and coughing, through the house to the front.

"Ulysses!" she shouted as she crawled. "Ulysses!"

When she opened the front door, the fire roared with fresh oxygen. Air was streaming through the house from front to back. We ran into the street, coughing and gasping, the air tasting cold and sweet. Antonio flapped up to a low tree branch, and from there, climbed to higher branches with panicked jumps.

I turned to face the fire. Black smoke poured out the front door and squeezed through the window seams.

"Ulysses!" Mary shouted at the house, her voice rough. She coughed. "Ulysses!" she shouted again, then ran around the side of the house and climbed over the fence, where she would find him, probably still asleep in the gravel.

This is it, I thought. This is it. I looked up and down the empty street. It was the middle of the night, and nobody would see me go. Shakespeare ran up to me, his breathing rough. I looked over his head. The path was clear.

Dwid, Shakespeare said.

My insides clenched. Dwid. He was drugged, probably unconscious, in his hiding place high above the kitchen cabinets. He was probably dead.

We have to help him, Shakespeare said. *I'm going in!* He turned, ridiculously brave, to charge the black monster.

I stepped in front of him. It was impossible. The first flames were clawing through the roof. I doubted that I could reach Dwid either. I looked up—all the way up—to Antonio, perched on high, a great shadow at the apex of a pine tree.

Dwid, I said. Not to ask him or to tell him, just in exasperation.

But Antonio heard otherwise. He heard the call to honor. As such, he assumed perfect posture. He extended his wings, illuminating them from below with streetlight, electric silver against black sky. He tilted forward and dropped. For a moment, he appeared to be falling straight down, accelerating, plummeting. Then his wings caught the air. His dive arced, then leveled. He was flying straight at the front door. At the last possible moment, he tucked his wings, disappearing into the black. The fire seemed angered by his invasion, and roared louder. Flames poured out the windows. The house was completely ablaze.

Behind us, a front door opened. A woman shouted. She ran back into her house. Other lights along the street turned on. A man emerged in a robe and slippers. He walked slowly toward the fire, mesmerized. In the distance, a siren sounded.

This is it, I thought again. This is my chance. I need to run. Now.

But the fire commanded my complete attention.

If I had been the only one to see it, then perhaps it would have been difficult to believe, but I was not the only one who saw. Along with myself was Shakespeare, and along with us were several humans standing in shock outside their homes, watching the house burn. As the last of the fireworks ignited inside, exploding louder than the fire itself, bottle rockets blazed out the front door, and with them, a bright blue Hyacinth Macaw, Royal Messenger of Amazonia, wings on fire. In his talons was a toasted orange cat, which he dropped in a tumbling heap on the street. Payload released, he beat his flaming wings mightily, rising as a visible phoenix, until his altitude and speed were so great that the flames extinguished and he disappeared into the night sky as smoke.

PART TWO

THE THING ABOUT PUGS

SOMEWHERE IN THE desert waste between the ashes of the house and the black mountains, we found a large stone egg. It was a human's height and upright, and the only one of its kind, as if placed there by a giant's hand. Or, I thought, considering myself scientific, maybe it was a meteorite that had fallen from space into the Precambrian sea, where it sank, hydrodynamically righted, to rest upon the ocean's bed, to be smoothed by seven hundred million years of current, until the great evaporation, which begat the wind, which begat the sand, which polished the egg for three hundred million more. A billion years of egg, then us. This was unfathomable, and the word tumbled in my mind—unfathomable, unfathomabl, nfathomabl, nfathombl, nfthombl, nfthmbl—until it was vowelless and meaningless, leaving me aware again of the heat.

The endless heat.

In the distance that would have been the edge of that ancient sea, the black mountains stood sharp and featureless against a blue sky, while far above, in that cloudless ether, three birds circled the sun. Big, black, birds, wings fixed on thermals. They may have seen me sniff the air, again smelling smoke and lizard. Shakespeare's eyes were fixed on the latter.

Forget it, I said, lying down in the egg's shadow, panting.

The thing about eating lizards, Shakespeare said, *is that you have to catch them first.*

Ten feet away, in the shade of a scrub, a spotted lizard raised and lowered its head repeatedly, elliptical glass eyes unblinking.

Another thing about lizards, Shakespeare said, *is that they don't want to be caught.*

Shakespeare lifted a front paw and placed it on the ground, then lifted it again, and again placed it on the ground.

Another thing about lizards, he said, *is that they're faster than they look.*

This lizard was as flat as a blade.

Shakespeare bent his stocky limbs, lowering his rotund torso slightly. He held this pose for about ten seconds, which I imagine is the length of his focus. Suddenly, he pounced. While still in the air (a very brief and ridiculous moment), the lizard disappeared down a fissure in the earth. Landing nowhere near, Shakespeare spun and barked, then stopped abruptly. He lifted his head and held it, open-mouthed, revealing small, jumbled teeth. I expected another respiratory crisis. Instead, he sneezed. This done, he rejoined me in the shade, where he sat with a humph.

Almost, he said. *Next one'll be lunch.*

You shouldn't have come, I said, looking up at the birds.

Shakespeare cocked his head.

You should go back, I said, looking at him.

He stared at me for his full ten seconds. *But you need me,* he said finally.

Mary needs you, I said.

Maybe, he said. *But when you go on a quest, you definitely need someone with you who's good at questing. Like me. Definitely.*

Again, I regretted telling him about quests, or teaching him the word definitely. *I never called this a quest,* I said.

Oh, it's a quest.

I'm fine alone, I said, withholding the fact that he would be a burden. He moved at half my speed, and even then he was at risk of sudden suffocation. I can confirm, heat does not suit a Pug.

He cocked his head to the other side. One of his small black ears flipped outward to reveal pink, hairless skin.

But who's got your tail? he asked.

I do.

You can't get your own tail, he said. *Because your head is facing front-*

ways, and your tail is facing backways. You can watch for bad things that come from the front, but you need someone to watch for bad things that come from the back. And that's me.

Reminded by this talk of tails, Shakespeare turned his head slowly, until one bulging eye glared at his own. When the tail moved, he twisted to snap, causing himself to fall over, roll in the dirt, then sit up, wheezing. *See?* he said. *You can't get your own tail. You should know that.*

Right.

I closed my eyes. In this hot inner darkness I heard a ringing sound. A high, steady tone from within. I wondered why. Was it because of the silence? Did my ears fill it with noise? Or maybe the ringing was real and from far away? Or maybe I was dehydrated? My tongue was dry. My nose was sore. I wondered how long we could go without water. Two days in this heat? Maybe three? We needed to get to water, but not near the highway, and not near Hoover, where Mary might pick us up. To Velos, beyond the black mountains. Should we skirt around the range? Go over? I didn't want to think too far ahead, but how would we travel through Velos without getting caught? We could take backroads, probably, and travel at night. But was Roger really there? Or whatever their name was? Maybe I had been mistaken about the name. But it would do for now. At the very least, we could regroup in Velos, ask the city dogs about humans who could speak to animals. I wondered if—

You think too much, Shakespeare said, interrupting me, *because of your thing.*

I kept my eyes closed.

That's okay though, he said. *That's just your thing.*

I would ignore him this time.

Yep, that's just your thing, he said.

He could go on like that forever though. So I compromised. I said, *I don't have a thing.* I refused to open my eyes.

Of course you have a thing, he said. *Everyone's got one thing. And everyone's thing is good and bad. Yours is being smart, which is good, because you can figure stuff out. But it's bad, because you think too much and it makes you crazy.*

The ringing resumed.

Yep, everyone's got a thing, Shakespeare said. *Everyone. Even a Pug.*

If you asked him. All you'd have to do is ask. Just ask and he'd tell you. You could ask pretty much any way and he'd say, here's my thing. But you'd need to ask him. Because he'd want to know that you want to know. But he'd be happy to tell you. But you'd need to ask first. Because it's something you need to ask about, this type of thing.

I surrendered and opened my eyes. *Fine*, I said. *What's your thing?*

I'm undeflatable, he said immediately. He was standing, barrel chest puffed, snout lifted. *Definitely undeflatable.*

You mean undefeatable?

That's what I said. That's my thing. Because I'm a Pug. And all Pugs are undeflatable. Can't keep a Pug down. No matter what.

So, what's bad about that?

Nothing.

But you said everyone's thing is good and bad.

Yeah, well, he said, *everyone but Pugs. Pugs are special.*

Clearly.

As the sun arced westward, we orbited the stone egg to remain in shadow. Shakespeare fell asleep and snored a dry snore. From the southeastern horizon a stalk of smoke dissipated in the cloudless sky. Those three birds still circled up there, wide and clockwise. It was boring, lying there beside that rock, waiting for the sun to go down. Boring and hot. I should have brought something to read, I thought, no pockets being one of the many troubles of being a dog.

THE POSSE

LET'S EAT 'IM, said a voice.

Nah, said a second voice. *I don't wanna eat 'im. I hate dog meat. Let's just kill 'im.*

We could chase 'im around a little, suggested a third voice. *Ooh. Give 'im a head start. Could be a good chase.*

And then eat 'im, said the first. *I'd eat anything right about now.*

I said I don't wanna eat 'im, said the second. *I'd be up for chasin' 'im around a little, just so long as we kill 'im after. But we don't eat 'im.*

Do what you want. I'm not chasin' nothin' unless I'm eatin' it after, said the first. *Why chase and not eat?*

It's fun is why, said the third voice.

I just wanna kill 'im, said the second. *That's fun.*

I opened my eyes. Three coyotes stood over me in the shadow of the boulder. Shakespeare was gone.

He's awake! said the third coyote.

Shut up, said the first and second in synchrony.

I remained in a prone position. If I ran, they'd chase me. I knew that.

The first coyote, furthest to the left, was largest, although I guessed that I was slightly taller. A bite had been taken from his right ear, revealing a ragged patch of sky. He was the one who wanted to eat me. The second coyote, in the middle, was slightly smaller than the first, and missing all but a nub of his tail. He was

113

the one who wanted to kill me. The third coyote, to the right, was scrawny and most disfigured. His muzzle melted sideways, as if the sun really was that hot. He was the one who wanted to chase me. His voice was high pitched and nasal.

He's not runnin', he said.

Let's eat his belly meat, said the big coyote. *Bet it's soft. House cat soft.*

The wind shifted. I smelled rotten flesh. My hackles rose.

Heyo, we got a wild one, said the coyote with the melted face, taking a step back. *Maybe he'll run. Maybe he's quick. Maybe I'll catch 'im.*

Settle down, said the big coyote, staying put.

Yeah, settle, said the tailless coyote, also staying put.

The little coyote with the melted face stepped forward again and licked his lips.

I growled.

Now just calm down, pup, said the big one. *No sense in gettin' all worked up before dinner. Don't make us chase ya. Too hot for that.*

I told you I don't wanna eat 'im, said the tailless one to the big one. *I hate dog meat. How many times do I have to tell you I hate dog meat? I'd sooner starve.*

Let's kill 'im, like you want, then decide.

But are we gonna eat 'im? asked the tailless one, turning to face the big one. *That's what I'm askin'. Cuz it sounds to me like you're fixin' to eat 'im. And I don't wanna eat 'im.*

Hell, do what you want! I'm gonna eat 'im! That don't mean you gotta eat 'im! Go hungry, see if I care.

The big coyote and the tailless coyote faced off, their ears flat on their heads, their lips raised in snarls.

Now listen, said the tailless coyote. *That's not how this here works.*

Who's in charge here? said the big coyote. *Do I need to bite your neck again?*

The coyote with the melted muzzle looked back and forth between me and them, excited.

I'll keep an eye on 'im, he said.

Shut up! said the other two.

Posse's gotta choose together, said the tailless one. *You ain't the alpha. But you act like you're the alpha. How come?*

You know I'm the alpha of this here posse.

That's it.

That's what?

The tailless coyote leapt forward, all teeth. The big coyote was ready and juked sideways. He twisted to bite his attacker's neck. The two fighters went down in the dirt, limbs tangling.

I'll learn you! said the big coyote.

The coyote with the melted face grinned. *I wish I had a brother,* he said.

The big coyote had the tailless one pinned and was stabbing down with his jaws, left then right, each jab blocked by the snapping mouth of the tailless one. Their teeth clattered. Blood wetted their gums. The melted coyote giggled.

I saw my moment and shifted to stand, but the melted coyote was on me instantly, his face inches from mine. He bared his broken teeth. I reconsidered.

At this point, had it been a movie and not real life, we would have heard drums, distant at first, then louder, accompanied by that whistle: Aya aya ahhh, wah wah wah. Aya aya ahhh, wah wah wah. But instead of a cowboy, with eyes like knives, bit cigar, poncho and pistol, there was a Pug, with bug eyes, bit tongue, paunch, and paws that shifted on the hot ground.

Let him go, Shakespeare said, *and I'll let you live.* He stood in the east, squinting.

The coyotes stopped fighting. The big one looked up, the tailless one's neck still in his mouth.

You heard me, Shakespeare said. Then he let out a yap.

It was that bark that did it. The melted coyote laughed first. His wild cackle spread to the others. Soon all three were rolling around in the dirt laughing madly. They covered their eyes with their paws in disbelief, then looked again at Shakespeare to top up their manic joy.

Laugh all you want, Shakespeare said. *The last laugh will be mine.*

Make him stop! said the big coyote. He was actively bleeding from his shoulder and choking on his own laughs. *It's too much! My belly hurts! Too much!*

The melted coyote looked distracted, but when I again moved to get my limbs under myself, he snapped at me between laughs. Eventually, the laughter dried up. The coyotes sighed. The big one let the tailless one get up.

Who is this guy? said the big one. *Look at 'im. I love 'im.*

That face, said the melted one. *Like he forgot to grow a nose.*

And that stupid tail, said the tailless one.

Shakespeare growled.

All day, said the melted one, *I could watch him all day, specially that bark. Bark again.*

You're a brave one, ain't ya? said the big one.

Brave as they come, Shakespeare said. He rotated his elbows to enlarge his chest.

Relax, kid, said the big one. *We like ya.*

Shakespeare dropped the pose and pulled his head back. *Really?*

Yeah, really, said the big one. The other two nodded.

This your friend? asked the tailless one, tipping his head to me.

Brother, Shakespeare said.

This provoked another, shorter laughing session, as they looked between me and Shakespeare.

Fine, your brother, said the big one. *Come on into the shade. You'll cook your pads off out there.*

Shakespeare joined us in the shadow of the boulder. He glanced from one coyote to another, prepared for an ambush. When the coyotes sat, however, all tension vanished. Just like that we were five dogs relaxing in the shade.

Well, boys, I'm Chad, said the big one with the hole in his ear. *Him with the nub for a tail is Tad, and him with the busted face is...*

Brad? I guessed, but they didn't laugh. Coyotes prefer physical humor.

Nah, said Chad. *That there's Leslie.*

Leslie, said Leslie, in his high, froggy voice.

What's your names? asked Chad.

After introductions, we watched, without speaking, as the land became orange, then red, while Shakespeare looked up to the coyotes, literally and figuratively.

Now wasn't that pretty? said Chad, when the sun was down. *Well, I guess we'd better hurry up and kill Leo.*

Wait, what?

I jumped up. The coyotes surrounded me.

You know what I realized, Tad? said Chad. *That we both want to kill 'im, and if you don't want to eat dog meat, then I respect that, but I'd ask kindly that you let me eat some, because I am hungry.*

I can appreciate that, said Tad. *And my answer is yes. Seeing as you asked kindly. And I respect your choice.*

Thank you, said Chad. *And Leslie, if he runs, we'll chase 'im, since the sun's down now, and it's not so hot, and I feel refreshed from all this shade. But we won't chase 'im, if you do not mind, unless we have to, to save the effort.*

I don't mind, said Leslie, licking his lips. *Thanks for considerin'.*

Course, said Chad.

Shakespeare, finally realizing what they were planning, entered the circle with me, to face them.

Clear out now, kid, said Chad. *We like ya. We just don't like your friend here. Hangin' round our rock where he ain't welcome. Got a bad attitude, too.*

This here's our shade, said Tad.

Our shade, said Leslie. *Bad 'tude.*

Shakespeare and I rotated, tail to tail, as the coyotes edged closer. We growled.

No sense in dyin' with your trespassin' friend here, said Chad.

I watched drool fall from Leslie's uneven face to be absorbed instantly by hard dirt. My heart was booming. I could feel their six eyes locked on me, just behind my head, on my neck. In an instant, I might be dead.

Fortunately, I had an idea. I guess you could say I'm an idea guy.

Wait, I said. *I know Gus.*

Chad and Tad glanced at each other. Leslie watched the other two. They hesitated. It was working. I had guessed, from Gus's confidence, and how he traveled alone, that he was a higher-ranking coyote. I had read about wild dogs living in hierarchical groups, and he seemed like a natural leader.

It's true, I said. *Gus is a friend of mine. And if you kill me, he probably wouldn't be too happy with you.*

Oh, c'mon, said Tad. *How come you gotta make a pain of it?*

Chad grunted. *Huddle up, boys,* he said. *You two stay put. I don't wanna chase ya, but don't think we won't.*

Don't think we won't, said Leslie.

The coyotes walked off a few paces and put their heads low to talk. Leslie popped up now and again to gawk at us.

I like coyotes, Shakespeare said.

Seriously?

What? I mean, yeah. Well, they're not bad, at least.

They're deciding if they're going to kill us or not. Me anyway.

Oh. Right, Shakespeare said. *That is kind of bad.*

Yeah, I said. *It is.*

Chad and Tad seemed to be arguing again. Maybe they'd fight and we could run for it. I looked around at the surrounding open space. I was fast in a short burst, but I doubted that I could outrun three of them over a long distance. Shakespeare wouldn't last more than a yard if they decided to go for him. After some snaps and growls, the trio turned to face us.

We done made our choice, said Chad.

Been made, said Leslie.

To Gus, said Tad.

TO GUS

DUSK TURNED to night as we headed toward the brightest star, not far from the slice of moon. We traveled at a trot, with Chad in the lead, Tad behind, and Leslie ranging all around. I smelled the other coyotes on the hilltop before I saw them. Their forms solidified against the stars.

Here they come, said one of the coyotes. *Those ragtag boys.* I recognized that smooth baritone. It was Gus. *Very happy to smell you on this fine night,* he said.

What's that they got with 'em? That a pup I smell? This second voice was female.

Aw, cute, I hope so, said another female.

Now girls, don't get any ideas, said Gus.

I got a few, said one of the females.

Ugh, said the other.

Gus was laughing as we reached the top of the hill. Two females stood on either side of him, about the same height as Leslie. One was thin, the other heavy. When Shakespeare finally arrived, slow and dragging, they stared.

What kinda pup is that? asked the heavy one.

Gonna be awful ugly when it grows up, said the thin one.

Now now, Belle, Kota, said Gus to the heavy one, then the thin one, *where are our manners? That ain't no way to talk about a guest.*

I guess it is kinda cute, said Belle.

I guess, said Kota. *In a busted way. Hope my pups don't look like that.*

Pug, Shakespeare said, gasping. *Pug. Not pup. Gah, I'm done running. Forever.*

You ain't gonna believe this, Gus, said Chad.

Never ever, said Leslie.

I'll take a stab. You fell in love with a couple dogs.

Hardly, said Chad. *The tall one was trespassin' on our rock. In our shade.*

Was he now? asked Gus, playing serious.

But he says he knows you, said Tad. *Says you're pals. Probably a lie, but we reckoned we should check.*

Reckoned so, said Leslie.

Well you reckoned right, said Gus. *I do know this dog. Leo is a an old buddy of mine, ain't that right, Leo?*

That's right, I said, trying to look calm and unsurprised.

Gus regarded me with his eternal smile, one canine protruding from his mouth, over his lower lip. Unlike Leslie's asymmetry, Gus's only enhanced his handsomeness. *Leo's quite a dog,* he said. *One of a kind.*

My relief expanded to pride.

Cuz Leo, I kid you not, can open doors. In and out of his two-legger's den. Like his own. I seen it.

The other coyotes eyed me up and down. I had no idea Gus had been watching me so closely.

Really? said Tad.

Saw it with my own eyes, said Gus. *Regular talent, this one. You weren't plannin' on killin' him, were ya?*

Sure, said Leslie.

Nah, said Chad.

Leslie maybe, but not us, said Tad.

That's a lie, said Leslie.

Shut up, said the other two, together.

Well, you boys done good, said Gus. *Bringin' him along. Real good.*

We did? asked Leslie.

Just lookin' to help, said Tad.

We know somethin' special when we see it, said Chad.

Saved me a whole trip, too, said Gus. *I was about to pay a visit real soon. But now he's here. How 'bout that.*

How about that, I said, giving the trio what I intended to be a hard stare.

And this here's Leo's friend, ain't that right? said Gus.

Brother, said Shakespeare.

It's a boy? asked Kota.

Can't be, said Belle, sniffing the air.

Course he's a boy, said Gus. *What's your name, tough guy?*

He told them. They all cocked their heads.

Hmmm, said Gus. *You know, as I told your friend Leo here, coyotes pick their own names. Seein' as you're honorary coyotes —*

We are? Shakespeare asked.

Course, said Gus. *Seein' as such, 'bout time you picked your own name. Go ahead. Any name you want.*

Shakespeare seemed overwhelmed.

Don't even have to be a two-legger name, said Chad.

So what'll it be, little fella? asked Gus.

Shakespeare just stared.

Anything you want, said Chad. *Could be Chuck, Chip, Chet.*

Tad started up, *Or Stith, or Snap, or Scatter.*

Ooh I got one, said Leslie. *How 'bout Chuck?*

Already said that, dunderhead, said Chad. *Could be Chuck though. Could be. Or Jub even.*

Jub? said Tad.

What's wrong with Jub? asked Chad. *Jub's a great name. Better than Stith, that's for sure.*

No it ain't, said Tad. *Stith's a good name. Jub's a stupid old name.*

Gus grunted. They stopped arguing immediately. *Let 'im talk,* said Gus. *What'll it be?*

Shakespeare looked around at everyone, then assumed his proud posture. *My name is Shakespeare,* he said.

Nah, said Chad. *You don't get it. Could be any name you want. Don't have to be that long two-legger name no more.*

My name is Shakespeare, he said again. *It always has been. And it always will be.*

That just don't come easy though, does it? said Tad. *It's too long. Like when you gotta say it real quick.*

I don't like it, said Kota.

It is long, said Belle.

Tough, Shakespeare said.

The coyotes loved that. They laughed.

How about this, said Gus, *maybe if we're in a hurry, we could call you Shakes? Like when we're on a hunt?*

Shakes for short, said Chad. *Not bad.*

He is short, said Kota.

But not all the time, Shakespeare said.

Course not, said Gus, winking at the females.

Shakespeare considered the compromise. *Fine,* he said.

Shakes it is, said Gus.

This agreed, Shakespeare and the coyotes turned to me.

Well? asked Gus. *What'll it be?*

I had run through a number of ideas since meeting Gus, never imagining that this moment would actually come. But I knew what would be most fitting. I let them wait, building the anticipation. When they looked like they were about to speak, I announced my new identity.

My name is Rousseau, I said.

Seven heads cocked to the side.

What? said Leslie.

Nah, said Chad.

That's the dumbest, stupidest, worst dang name I ever heard of, said Tad. *That's even worse than Jub.*

Now hang on, said Gus. *Hear 'im out.*

How'd it go? asked Kota.

Roo-so, I said, pronouncing it slowly. *Rousseau. You know, as in Jean-Jacques, the French philosopher? I would like to be named after him.*

The coyotes checked with one another.

He like an alpha? asked Belle.

Sort of, I said. *Intellectually. You know, The Social Contract.*

They stared.

Discourse on Inequality? Age of Enlightenment?

More blank stares.

Pretty apropos, I said. *Considering that we're in a state of nature.*

Leslie scratched his ear vigorously. *I don't like the way your words get in my head. I…I hate how you talk.*

Too fancy, said Chad.

That's it, said Tad. *That's your problem right there. Too fancy.*

Even Shakespeare looked uncomfortable.

How 'bout Rou? said Gus. *I don't mean to name you. If you wanna be called Rosy or whatever it was, you go on ahead.*

Rou ain't bad, said Chad.

Rou I could do, said Tad.

As the air cleared, I told myself to never mention anything I had read to a coyote. Especially nothing philosophical, extra especially nothing French. And I'd need to keep my lexicon under control, by which I mean, my words.

Good, said Gus, settling the matter. *That's your names then. Shakespeare, or Shakes for when we're on the go, and Rou, but never the fancy way.*

Shakespeare was solemn as he studied the coyotes.

I always wanted to be a coyote, he said. *Ever since I was born.*

Well, Shakes, said Gus, *can't say we always wanted a weird little dog with a mashed face who can't breathe good, but you got spunk. And spunk we like.*

Spunk, Shakespeare said, elevating his curly tail.

And good thing too you showed when you did, said Gus, *cuz we need someone real tough and brave with tons a spunk to guard our rock while we're on the hunt. Can we count on you?*

Wow, said Shakespeare. *Yes. Yes!*

To the southwest the lights of Hoover twinkled, mostly streetlights, with the occasional passing car. The red beacon atop the water tower blinked slowly. Moving northwest, all lights channeled into a solitary line from town across the desert in dots, transmitting highway headlights that disappeared behind the black mountains, now sharp against the city glow and the column of light. Between all of this and us, upon the vast expanse of dry, dark land, were our hunting grounds. Above it all the moon arose, a thin and curving claw.

THE HUNT

THE EARTH HAD BEEN HEATED by the day and now radiated into the night. Something primal awakened inside of me as we trotted across that dirt plain. I felt the rhythm of the whole, our shoulders undulating fins, our feet light on the ground, touching between cacti and scrub. Our pulses quickened. Our noses sipped air between panting breaths. The pack moved around me in shifting patterns, flowing with terrain. My mind was becoming our mind.

It was Gus who saw motion. When his legs cut, twenty-four others cut to follow, pads staccato. In pursuit, we smelled the rabbit's savory breath and heard the trill of its heart. There. Rapid on the ground—outstretched, contracted, outstretched, contracted—double-legging white bobble-tail blur. Saliva filled our mouths. Our forebrains darkened. Our lower brains arose supreme.

We expanded in a horizontal line, a curving net trawling the earth at sixty feet per second. The net widened and gained upon the micro-galloping, hole-searching, bush-hopping meal. The rabbit zigged left but the net was too wide; it zagged right but the net was already there.

Hindlimb backward and twisted, fine fur between soft black toes.

A paw.

Gus emerged from the whole, jaws opening.

A snap.

A squeak.

Rotation as the rabbit turned to look, punching at his nose. My feet anchoring, digging shallow trenches. The punches ceasing with a shake. We latched and tore away, too drunk on the hunt to wait. The flesh was hot and the blood salty. Wet fur plastered our tongues, sliding down our throats and into our bellies. Just a bite each, yet filling a greater need, like sacrament. Body of the desert god.

Our hearts slowed. We heard the song of death. And so we joined it, lifting as one to the moon to sing, our voices merging in killsong, joyous and brave and harmonious, a howl of gratitude and acceptance, knowing that one day, we too would die.

Together, we hunted until dawn.

Bathed in the graying eastern light, the coyotes were silent and almost invisible, as if they had become one with desert. We relished our heavy bellies, and the air and the ground, both as cool as they would ever get in those last minutes before sunrise. I will admit that I shared their satisfaction. While they simply existed, however, I now saw the blood around our mouths, and recounted our kills, and wondered if I was guilty for devouring all of those helpless creatures, or if I had fooled myself before, when I had considered myself innocent, eating meat from a bag, without bones, as kibble.

With the rising sun, my coat warmed, then my body, until I was panting. The temperature jumped thirty degrees in as many minutes, warning us that the desert remained as hostile to our presence as the day before. We were the prey of the sun. I began to forget parts of the night in the way that dreams fade, replaced by the old brain drum, which now beat with flashes of retinal veins. I hadn't had anything to drink for more than thirty-six hours. I had been moving most of that entire time. My thoughts were thinning down to one: water. Far off, a hare sat up, antenna ears listening to the chirps of awakening birds, and us.

We stopped.

Next time, said Gus.

Kota went first, without a word, then Belle, after a friendly good-bye, followed by Chad and Tad, as a pair. All of them were soon absorbed by the horizon. Leslie just sat there, dumb. Gus tipped his head for me to follow, so we trotted west together, with the sun at our backs.

My muscles were dry, making my gait uneven, and my headache was throbbing in the front and cutting down the middle. The world was flattening, like a painting. In the background, the mountains wore a yellow morning crown. Central and small was the lonesome stone egg, still far off, nested in a palette of orange and brown and red. Closest, a horned lizard perched upon his stone, watching glumly as I wound a path through rocks and creosote, my brain drum asynchronous with my heart.

I began to wonder if there was something really wrong with me. Something beyond dehydration. An arrhythmia, maybe. I tried to stay connected with reality. I am a dog, I told myself. My name is Leo. No, my name is Rou. I am here, in the desert, with Gus, a coyote. I am hot. I am dehydrated. I need water.

We found Shakespeare snoring in the shade of the stone egg, in the middle of a dream, on his back with his soft buddha belly exposed. His forepaws dangled in the air. It looked like a happy dream, so we sat to watch. He moved his shoulders as if to scratch his back, then his feet as if to run, his front legs in quick flaps, his back legs mule-kicking together. He growled. This was the scary part of the dream. It was turning into a nightmare. His curly tail tried to straighten, but could not. He growled again. He was facing something terrible. He kicked so hard that he rolled over and jumped up. He blinked at us, trying to differentiate between real and unreal.

Oh, he said, *it's you.*

Always is, said Gus, before regurgitating a pile of rabbit meat for Shakespeare, who ate this happily, not knowing what it was.

DEAD HEAD

GUS READ OUR EXHAUSTION PLAINLY. He saw us limping and scanning the land for water, trying to talk but not making words, and he knew.

You boys got dead head, he said. We'd go home with him, he said, to the black mountains, to rest. I resisted a feeling of relief. The mountains were a long way off, flat black shards stuck in sand.

We had already begun to follow Gus before I noticed my legs moving beneath me. As we crossed the wide brown flat, arduous and slow, the mountains revealed their third dimension. The tallest peak was surrounded by others in front, beside, and behind, all scarred with gullies that coursed upward to disappear in seams. As the mountains grew, so did the cacti. They were tall—twelve, fifteen feet—and thick, with long, twisted arms that reached out, punctuated millionfold with translucent spines, every single one shining in the sun. Hot wind rolled down from the peaks in greeting. As we lagged behind, Gus waited, then led again.

Presently Shakespeare was explaining what had happened to him the night before. I was distracted by the earth, which had loosened on its axis and now tilted up and down, ship like. The dead head was progressing.

—and I thought it was weird to see a white lizard, because I didn't think they made those. But there he was. Sorta glowing. So I chased him. But he ran—

Shakespeare's story went something like that, coming in and out of my awareness. The ground continued its rocking, activating some kind of subterranean pump, causing the cacti to secrete a clear liquid, like water, but thicker, like oil, from their spines. The drops emerged from the tips of the needles to stretch downward, the long, glassy stalks snapping, cutting the droplets loose, to splash into the deepening, viscous liquid that now flooded the ground. And yet, to my dread and fascination, the liquid maintained a dry buffer around me, so that my feet never became wet, and when I bent down to drink, the liquid pulled away, as if it wanted to see me die of thirst. But not the others. The liquid had no aversion to them. Gus waded through it. His legs were blending, so that his torso was a boat above, floating onward. I looked down at Shakespeare. He was completely submerged—a fat, fawn-colored fish.

—*until I caught up with him,* he said from underwater. *And then when I caught up with him, he ran again. So every time I thought I was gonna get him, he ran away. It was super fun, so I wasn't checking where I was. But before I knew it, we, I mean, me and the white lizard, we were all the way out in the middle of nowhere. Like, really nowhere. Even more nowhere than this. So it was sorta scary, because it was dark. But since I'm a coyote now I knew that I couldn't be scared, so I wasn't. And so I just—*

Ahead, Gus climbed out of the liquid and onto a rock island. His long legs grew longer and thinner, stretching upward higher and higher, like gum pulled from the ground, until he was far above, looking down from stilts. Behind him was an amphitheater of black stone, flaky and polished, refracting the sun in rainbows. Mesmerized, this prism shifted, blinding me, taking Gus. Now, sitting cross-legged, on a cushion of hot air above the rock, was a naked man with a long, thin, bearded face. With his eyes locked on mine, he raised one arm to point at the sky. A column of white light beamed from his fingertip. He raised his other arm to point at me. I was suddenly afraid that he would shoot that light at me—that he would burn me alive. My vision blurred. I turned to Shakespeare, who now walked atop the oil. None of this is real, I told myself, closing my eyes, opening them. None of this is real. I focused on Shakespeare, on his happy face. Do not look at Roger, I told myself. Because it was him. I knew him. I had known him my entire life. The one who tried to kill me.

—bet that much. So anyway, this white lizard goes down a hole, Shakespeare said. *But not a hole in the ground. Not a regular lizard hole. This was a big hole. Like, taller than you, and it went in sideways, like a door, or a tunnel. And wind was coming out of it and I was like, maybe this lizard isn't worth it, this is pretty much the scariest thing ever. And I was just about to turn tail and run, when out of the hole, real, real slow, came a giant turtle!*

Focusing on Shakespeare was helping. The earth rocked more gently. The liquid seeped away through invisible drains. Still, I couldn't resist. I glanced up. With great relief, I saw that Gus was Gus. Roger was gone. Shakespeare once again walked on dirt and sand. We both did.

A giant turtle? I asked.

Yep, it was a turtle, Shakespeare said, *but, like, way bigger than you.*

You mean a tortoise, I said.

No, a turtle, he said.

Tortoise, I said, my mood volatile. I growled. *There are no turtles out here.*

His tail wagged low. I wanted to apologize, but my brain was too hot and spongy.

As tall as me though? I asked, gentler. *That's not possible.*

But it is! I saw him for real! And that's not even the craziest part! This turtle, I mean, tortoise, froze me, with his eyeballs. That's the craziest part, Leo, I mean, Rou. Well, maybe. Or maybe the next thing is the craziest. But anyway, he froze me. I was stuck, like my whole body was stuck and I couldn't move it.

Here Shakespeare looked at me expectantly. All of this was extremely confusing. I was having trouble separating my own hallucinations from his. Was he even telling this story? Or was I imagining it? He was stumbling as we slogged up the sandy gully, but still he looked at me. His tongue dangled, desiccated, from the side of his mouth. I wanted to snap it off and stuff it back in his head.

Froze you? I asked.

Yeah! he said. *With his eyes. They were cold. I actually felt cold. And they were white. Like...like—*

Clouds?

No.

Teeth?

No.

Ice cubes?

Yeah! Ice cubes, exactly, with cracks too bright to look at, but I looked anyway, until I couldn't see anything, like I was looking at the sun, and then— he trailed off.

What?

And then the craziest thing of all happened. I saw...what I needed to see.

What did you see?

A cloud of dust poured down the wash, engulfing us.

It's a secret, Shakespeare said.

C'mon, I said as the dust cleared, now desperate to know, as if I was asking for a drink of water. *C'mon. Tell me. Please.*

I can't.

Why not? I snapped, angry again.

He said that *I can't tell the clever dog, otherwise it would put the clever dog in great danger.*

Dammit, I said, desperate again. *What did he say?*

We had almost reached the black wall.

Shakespeare looked worried now, either at my anger or what he had seen. *He showed me things that are so unbelievable that I can't even believe them.*

The clever dog? I asked, questioning this after a delay.

You, Shakespeare said.

But how do you know it's me?

You know it's you.

Maybe, I said, *but the tortoise isn't around now. So you can tell me.*

Shakespeare, uncharacteristically, did not reply for some time. His brain was cooked, I decided, maybe even more than mine. Who knew what he was seeing? The hot wind shifted and pressed down upon us.

But he's everywhere, Shakespeare said.

We stopped. There was nowhere else to go. The black wall pitched overhead in an eternally cresting wave. Heat radiated from the stone. Air swirled. Gus studied us, his fur ragged and wild. Shakespeare backed away from the wall, short neck craned to look straight up. Curving obsidian flakes layered one upon the other, smooth and sharp, with crystal surface veins spidering outward, forking repeatedly, reaching for indeterminate edges. The stone smelled of sulfur.

Go on, said Gus, pointing with his nose.

Where the wall met the ground was a black hole—a mouth just big enough to swallow a dog.

I stepped forward and sniffed the opening. It was without scent. A vacuum lifted my fur against the grain, as if the mountain was sniffing me in return.

IN

I SQUEEZED THROUGH THE OPENING, exhaling to narrow my body. The tunnel was dark and circular and only slightly wider than the opening, so that when I inhaled, my body pressed against the walls. While the entrance had been sandy, everything soon became entirely smooth, and any slivers of outside light were consumed by the black void ahead. Air whistled inward through gaps between fur and stone.

It's dark in here, Shakespeare said. He was behind me, and although it was impossible for me to turn my head and look, I knew that he was walking and not crawling. *Seems like we're going down,* he said. His comments proceeded as obviously as you might imagine, so I won't recount them all.

We were indeed going down, and as we did, darkness turned to blindness, distorting dimension. As I wriggled, my head swelled with a ringing noise to fill the space while my body stretched out silently behind. I was an earthworm slithering into the earth. I felt a curious vibration that began at my nose, then consumed my head, my neck, my body, my tail, as if the void were digesting me.

I stopped. Shakespeare bumped into me, what felt like fifteen feet behind.

Whoops, he said.

Keep on, don't worry, said Gus.

I kept on even as the tunnel steepened. I moved forward by

relaxing my muscles, braced by contracting them. Shakespeare seemed to be having more trouble.

I'm slipping, he said. *It's too slick.* He was too small to brace his body against the walls. I imagined his legs stretched sideways like a cat above a bath.

Don't slip, I said.

Keep on now, said Gus.

We continued. The warm breeze from behind mixed with cooler air ahead. The drop in temperature soothed my headache, although the tunnel itself was relentless, falling steeper and steeper.

It's getting too steep, I said.

Gets easier up ahead, said Gus.

I'm gonna slip, Shakespeare said.

Don't slip, I said.

He slipped.

I heard a long scrape before he collided with me. Together, we slid on. I reached out, but as I did, the tunnel seemed to react—widening—the ground also receding beneath us, before it disappeared entirely. We had achieved true vertical. As we fell down the column, wind rushed with us, thereby stilling the relative air and disguising our speed. In this black, motionless, timeless place, I became weightless and without form.

Shakespeare sighed.

The brief eternity ended in a flash of lights. I knew our speed as we hit cold water and plunged beneath. Stunned, I shut my mouth and eyes, kicked, paddled, extended my head. I kicked again. My lungs begged for a breath. I kicked again. I gulped with my mouth clamped shut. I kicked again. I reached outward, for anything. Finally, my head burst through. I gasped and coughed. Shakespeare was already paddling to shore. I swam after him, surprised, only later, that we both knew how.

I dragged myself out on slumping shoulders, coat heavy and sodden, hacking water from my lungs. After several deep breaths, Gus splashed down.

We had landed in the middle of an underground pool with a thin rock shoreline separating water from walls. I could see, remarkably, because the stone, everywhere, glowed stippled white. On all surfaces, a fine crystal veneer emitted soft phosphorescence. The pond glowed at its outermost edge, the light becoming lost in the central, black depths.

Gus climbed out and shook. He had something limp in his mouth. A dead rabbit. I couldn't remember him catching that.

Welcome home, he said.

He placed the rabbit on the ground to lap water from the pond. Shakespeare and I joined him. The water was painfully cold, but the hurt was wonderful. Incredible. Delicious. Amazing. I lapped and gulped, the liquid burning, then numbing the cracks in my tongue.

Easy now, said Gus. *What feels good ain't always good for ya.*

But I kept drinking, despite Gus and protests from within. After two days without, I was insane for water.

Suit yourself, said Gus.

The cramps hit. Immediately I regurgitated into the pool.

See, said Gus.

Meanwhile, Shakespeare was still at it.

Maybe take a break, I said.

But he wouldn't quit. When his abdomen looked like a water balloon, he lifted his head. He wore a pleased expression, although it looked like it took some effort to maintain. When his belly jerked, he clenched his jaw. His eyes bulged just before jets of water sprayed from his nose.

Dogs, said Gus.

LAIR OF LIGHTS

Gᴜꜱ ʟᴇᴅ ᴜꜱ ᴛʜʀᴏᴜɢʜ ᴀ ꜱʜᴏʀᴛ, blind passage to a second cave. It mirrored the first cave, though this one was completely dry. All surfaces, overhead and underfoot, glowed unevenly, some patches thin and speckled, other swaths like dense Milky Ways. Various objects littered the ground, some wood or rusted metal, others smooth white. Pieces of bone. One wall was interrupted by a black rectangle. As my vision improved, I saw that it was actually a heavy metal box on its side, the rusted wheels suggesting that it had once run on rails. This was confirmed by two black lines that cut across the chamber floor and out an arched, human-sized tunnel. It must have been a mine.

Hey, Juney, said Gus.

From within the cart a shadow emerged, becoming a coyote as she reached the center of the cave, to face us. Smooth white fur painted her chin, while black encircled her eyes. In the crystal light, what was white appeared almost blue and what was black was absolute.

June stared at Shakespeare, then me, without expression. Gus dropped the rabbit. He remained still as she approached him with her nose, to sniff his face, his ears, his neck. She sampled his flank and his back and his tail, then dropped her head to sniff below. She lifted her head and narrowed her eyes, sniffed below again, then stared at the back of his neck.

Glad you're home, she said, softly.

A yip came from the mining cart, followed by a gray ball of fuzz. The pup collapsed on gumby legs, rose, then gamboled straight for Gus.

Pa!

Hey, Sally girl! said Gus. He flopped onto his side. The puppy climbed aboard and bit his neck.

Pa! Pa! Another pup bounded from the cart to join his sister.

Hey, Buck! said Gus.

The three of them rolled around, play growling and nipping at each other.

Didya kill anything good? Didya kill anything good? the pups asked him.

Sure did, said Gus. *Killed a couple coyote pups for makin' trouble.*

No, you didn't! they said.

Did too, said Gus.

A third pup now looked out from the cart, this one smaller than the others.

That you, Pa? she asked in a thread of a voice.

Gus tossed Sally by her scruff and rolled Buck with his nose. The runt winced at every blow. Even her fur was thin and wispy, afraid to emerge.

Go on, Lily, said June. *Jump in. Wrestle.*

But Lily wasn't jumping anywhere. After climbing delicately down from the cart, she stood and wobbled on spindly legs, until Sally swung by, attached by her teeth to Gus's tail, to smack Lily across the mouth. With a whimper she scrambled back into the cart, then peered out with watery eyes.

Sally released Gus's tail. She had noticed Shakespeare. She stood tall, hackles up, and let out a high growl. Shakespeare's back twitched, but he was otherwise motionless. Sally stalked closer. Then Buck saw the fun and joined the hunt. They approached Shakespeare and growled together. Shakespeare wagged his tail. The pups braced themselves. Shakespeare dropped onto his fore-limbs and wiggled his whole fawny butt, curly tail and all. It was too much. The pups pounced. They piled on top of him, snapping and growling, going for his tail, his paws, his neck folds. He snorted and shook, wheezed and wrestled, tumbled and growled.

Sally latched onto one ear and Buck the other. Shakespeare dragged them in a slow circle, proudly, as though he had sprouted golden wings.

Finally, Sally dropped down.

Can we keep him? she asked, looking to June.

Buck also let go. *Yeah, Mom,* he said, *can we keep him?*

Gus, chin rested on his paws, grinned.

June ignored them. She started eating the rabbit.

Seeing this, the pups became still and focused. They watched, drooling, as their mother shredded and crunched and swallowed fur and flesh and bone. Just as I was forming an opinion about June's greed, she extended her neck and regurgitated the whole thing, now macerated, onto the ground.

Motherhood, I suppose.

Buck and Sally gnashed away. Lily made a weak effort to eat, but when Sally snapped at her, she stood back. June sighed, took a step forward to intervene, then stepped back. In this unsettled mood she faced us.

So, she said. *Do they have names?*

I give you Shakes, the fat one, said Gus, *and Rou, this one that looks like he got halfway to bein' a coyote but stopped to be a dog instead.*

Shakespeare rolled onto his back to show his belly. June sniffed him, going from nose to tail as she did with Gus. She stopped between his hind legs. She looked up, confused.

Boy or girl? she asked.

Pretty sure he's a boy, said Gus.

Shakespeare jumped up. *Of course I'm a boy!*

Now don't get in a huff, said June. *You don't smell like one.*

Do too, Shakespeare said, puffing his chest.

Well you sure act like one, she said. She came over to me next. I looked straight ahead like Gus had for his inspection. I also sniffed the air. Although her demeanor was cool, her scent was intoxicating —sweet at the margins with a savory, edible core. I resisted an urge to smell her in return. I wondered if she could hear the rapid beat of my heart. I held my breath when her cold nose touched my doodads.

Strange, said June, lifting her nose away.

Right? said Gus. *I couldn't place it. You got a better nose than me, Juney. What is it?*

June sniffed my neck. I resisted a crazier urge to play-bite her, pin her, roll on the floor with her. I kept my head forward.

It's like…it's like he smells like a two-legger…but…

But not, right? Gus finished.

Yeah, she said. She sniffed me again. She spoke calmly, slowly. *Like a dog, sure, but also like a human, but not like he's just been in the den of a two-legger. It's like it's comin' from him, that smell. It makes me sort of…I don't know.*

I was disappointed by her assessment. Plus they talked about me like I wasn't even there.

This one's different, said Gus. *I been watchin' 'im a while.*

I shivered, my body wet and cooling. I didn't like to think about being watched.

Met him about a moon back, said Gus. *Thought he was odd. Had some other stuff goin' round that way, so I figured I'd watch 'im some. And I'll tell you what, Juney, he can open doors. Ain't that right, Rou?*

That so, said June.

Sure is, said Gus. *You know what we been talkin' about.*

I do, said June.

So here we go, said Gus.

June circled me. I began to feel like prey, like they were deciding whether they'd eat me now or eat me later. She completed a circuit and stopped in front of me.

This true? she asked. Her tone was measured, but her eyes were severe. I couldn't hold them.

It's true, I said. *Some doors.*

June sniffed again. I guess she didn't like what she smelled, because, without a word, she turned and walked out of the cave, through the entrance with rails. The pups ran after her. When they were gone, a steady drip echoed from somewhere.

She'll warm up, said Gus. *Give it time.*

I didn't want to disappoint him, if that's what I would be doing, but it seemed better to get it over with.

We need to get going pretty soon, I said.

Gus reclined to chew a front paw. *Nah,* he said, *you boys need rest. Go now and you'll be dead before dawn.*

Not right now, I said, *but we can't stay long. A day, maybe two?*

Aw, you can stay longer than that. Shakes, you said you wanna be a coyote, right?

My whole life, he said.

See? His whole life, Rou. That's a pretty long time. You're both gonna love it here. Free and easy. Runnin', huntin', some humpin'. What else is there?

We need to get to Velos, I said, unsure how much to explain.

You're messin' with me, said Gus. *Tell me you're messin' with me.*

I am not messing with you.

We're on a quest, Shakespeare said.

A what?

I need to find a certain human, I said. *It's hard to explain.*

Crazy is hard to explain, said Gus. *That's why it's crazy.*

I'm not crazy, I said. *You know I'm not like other dogs. This human knows why. And I intend to find out.*

Well that's just stupid, said Gus. *Even worse than crazy. Who cares why you are the way you are? You are, ain't ya? Knowin how come don't change a thing.*

It's also about revenge, I added. *He tried to kill me. So I'm going to kill him.*

You are? Shakespeare asked.

Yes, I said, *I am.* Really I couldn't imagine this. I just knew that Gus would understand a quest for revenge more than one for knowledge, or because I sought the companionship of dogs like me, or humans like Dr. Francis. I had even been thinking about an entire society of dogs and humans, living equally, somewhere out there. Maybe it already existed?

Gus looked off for a while, in thought. *Well, if it's revenge,* he said, *then maybe you got a real reason. Still, you'll die in Velos. Reason or not.*

We'll be fine, I said.

Rou's really smart, Shakespeare said.

Course, said Gus. *He's smart. But he's not smart, you see what I mean?*

Um, Shakespeare said. *No?*

He's smart in some ways, but in others, he ain't. And you ain't either, buddy. You think you seen some things, but nah. Ever run into a rattlesnake? he asked, then waited until I answered.

No, I said.

Been shot at?

No.

Crossed any highways?

No.

How many dogs you fought? How many street dogs?

I looked past him, at the empty mining cart. I lowered my head.

None.

Look, said Gus. *I ain't sayin' all this to make ya feel small. You're young. It's normal. Hell, I can't open doors like you. Just honest, that's all. You got lots to learn 'bout the rest of the world though. The desert and the city got plenty a ways to kill a couple house dogs like you.* He let us imagine the ways for a moment. *Still, there ain't no reason why you couldn't learn better. So here's all I'm sayin. You just stick around till the new moon. June'll teach ya what she teaches the pups. How to survive and such. I'll teach you some too. The real good stuff. In return, before you go, you do us coyotes a lil favor. Itty bitty. And we'll have a mountain a fun on the way. How's that sound?*

THE PALACE OF SUN

WHEN I AWOKE, I mistook the crystals for stars until an echoing snore broke the illusion. I stood and stretched, remembering where I was as I eased the stiffness from my legs. I left Shakespeare to check inside the cart. Gus was there, curled around Lily with Buck and Sally layered on top. They slept on a bed of dried plants. Around them the cart was black metal, mottled with rust along the rim where riveted eyes stared into space. If this was an abandoned mine, then it had been abandoned for a reason. Maybe it was unstable. I looked up. I imagined the mountain, suspended only by a crystal shell. I felt a spark of panic and the sudden need to breathe outside air.

I followed the metal tracks into the tunnel, which lost its crystals as it inclined in total darkness. Blind now, as I sniffed along a steel rail, I noticed a curious sensation. When I smelled the metal, I also heard a low-pitched ringing in my ears. Was a cart rolling down the tracks? When I lifted my nose from the rail, however, the ringing stopped. When I sniffed the metal again, the ringing started. I stopped walking to test this sensory overlap. Sniff, ring. No sniff, silence. Sniff, ring. No sniff, silence. When I put my ear to the rail, I heard nothing.

You're unreliable, I told my brain. That's what you are.

Just go with it, my brain said, don't worry.

Whenever we get in the dark, I said, you try to trick me.

In response, my brain conjured an image of a large tortoise with glowing white eyes. The tortoise was coming up the tunnel behind me. Now fully spooked, I dropped my nose and again sniffed along the line, ringing be damned, moving quicker, upward through the tunnel, my nose as good as any wheel rolling along the rail, back and forth through at least ten switchbacks, right until I smashed into a pile of wood.

The rails disappeared underneath heavy wooden blocks, all intersected and locked together. I repressed thoughts of collapse and climbed onto the pile. My nose found an opening. I crawled through it, before bumping my nose again. Wooden edges pressed against my ribs. I lifted my head slowly, expecting another bump and instead finding empty space. A dim light above. I weaseled through the gap. The light became brighter. Encouraged by warm, fresh air, I scrambled upward and forward through the openings in the wood pile as they came, squeezing through until I was above ground, finally, below real stars.

The tunnel opened upon the circular, flat summit of the tallest of the black mountains. Above me, guarding the entrance to the mine, was an enormous metal mammoth, its body a hulking suspension of spans and cables, it's head an empty cube. From this blocky skull emerged bent trusses like tusks while a proboscis of pipe entered the earth below. I backed away from the beast, over the wooden debris, to dirt once more. I turned around, shocked yet again, this time by a far, far grander sight.

Below was Los Velos, a massive motherboard stretched across the desert basin in a network of billions of lights of all colors. Most burned constant. Some pulsed. Long lines of pairs translated across the ground, moving white toward me and orange away, red catching and spreading and turning orange again. I walked to the edge of the summit, where my attention was drawn to the center of the city—the nucleus of it all. There was the column of light, like an artificial sun. It shone from the apex of the most marvelous object I have ever seen—a skyscraping cone that held a gaseous rainbow. Clouds of color bloomed from the ground and grew amorphous as they swirled upward to the prismic point, where the colors united in the column of white light that cut the night in two.

For an hour, maybe more, I sat and stared. Velos was bigger and brighter than I had ever imagined. And the cone, which seemed to be the origin of everything, was captivating. From the way I felt, I knew that my vision and instinct were correct, that I would find answers there. Of the infinite number of paths I could travel through the city, I would pick one. I was ready now, I thought. I knew enough. I would pick wisely.

I smelled June before I heard her. Suddenly she was sitting beside me, as if she had been there all night.

What is it? I asked.

I could only be talking about one thing.

The Palace of Sun, she said.

This is the first I've seen it, I said. *I'd seen the column, but not the cone. It's beautiful.*

We stared together.

Look how red those reds are, I said. *The essence of red.*

What's red? she asked.

The color, I said. *At the bottom? You don't see it?*

That's black, she said. *Black clouds.*

I thought about this.

Then what color is blood? I asked.

Black.

Huh.

And we stared together again.

There's something powerful there, I said, mesmerized.

How it holds you?

Yeah. How it holds you. Draws you in, even.

We let it hold us. The faint buzz of traffic and an occasional horn carried up the mountain, distant enough to be peaceful and ambient. June's scent and the city lights ran together, adding to the hypnotic effect.

What's it for? I asked.

Well, she said. *Lots a coyotes think it's where Sun goes at night. Story says that he dug a tunnel under the city, and when he's walkin' down the tunnel at night, he shines up through that hole there, until he gets to the other side and pops out next day.*

Oh, I said.

Not true, course, she said. *No way Sun's a he. Too reliable. If anything, Sun's a she.*

After a respectful pause, I offered my opinion. *The Sun isn't a he or a she,* I said. *It's a giant ball of flaming gas.*

June looked at me sideways.

It's true, I said. *And we're on a ball of rock flying around the Sun through space. And all the stars are suns like ours, but of other solar systems, some of them in other galaxies. And when the Sun goes down, it's just because our ball of rock is spinning.*

June looked up at the stars, then back to me.

Even a tunnel makes more sense than that, she said. *How come the stars don't fall?*

Because gravity is relative, I said. *Because one thing has to be close enough to another to feel its pull. Everything has gravity. Even you and me.*

June considered, then shifted closer to me, until her fur was almost in contact with mine. If we turned to look at each other, I thought, our noses would touch.

Well, she said. *I don't feel a thing.* She stood and walked off. *Get some sleep, dog,* she said. *School at dawn.*

THE SCHOOL OF JUNE

AT DAWN the mammoth no longer looked like a mammoth. It was only what it was—a rusted piece of mining equipment. As was Los Velos, having lost its glow, just a human byproduct, a place like Hoover, only larger—a mesh of buildings and roads over a circular basin rimmed with dark mountains. The Palace was now a mirror-like glass tower encircled by a moat of water, in which white fountains throbbed.

Shakespeare and I sat alongside the coyote pups at the edge of the summit, our backs to the city, as it was too distracting, our teacher said. She, June, squinted at us, as though measuring our potential one by one. Class was in session, and our first subject was a rattlesnake, coiled between us and her. We kept perfectly still, as we were instructed, and for me at least, because I was too scared to move.

Now watch careful, said June. *Watch how it flicks its tongue before it strikes. That's the rattler's tell.* She was in a hunting stance, her muzzle low, aligned with the flat of her neck.

Careful, Mom, said Lily.

Kill it, said Sally. *Kill it dead.*

Dust rose around the snake. It was a stacked and scaled muscle that contracted upon the flat ground, squeezing forward and back, testing, its arrow-shaped head aloft at one end of a yellow and black chain of diamonds that terminated with a beehive tail. I stared at that rattle. One moment it was still, the next a blur. Shakespeare's own tail wiggled with delight.

The tail distracts, said June. *You gotta focus. Watch how it pretends to strike. Wait for the tongue.*

She circled the snake. It rotated with her, feigning strikes with quick head juts. Finally, the tongue flicked. The snake shot out with a wide mouth and translucent fangs. But June was gone. She had jumped to the side. Her jaws snapped shut behind the snake's head. She delivered a killshake. The body spasmed and twitched, then went limp. She dropped it. We gawked until Sally ran down and bit into the body and shook it. Buck ran in to chomp the tail. They played tug-of-war until the snake lost.

Breakfast, said June. *Everybody.*

Lily came down hesitantly and found a piece of flesh to nibble on.

You boys too, said June.

Shakespeare and I joined them. I prefer rabbit, but snake isn't too bad once you get through the skin. We ate it all except the head and rattle. I felt no remorse for this animal. Snakes are different.

Okay then, let's start with friendlies, said June, referring to non-venomous snakes. *You get to eat what you kill.*

We spread out as a group, sniffing over the rocky shoulder of the mountain, searching for that slick and unpleasant odor. June found most of them. After chasing them from their hiding spots, she gave each of us a chance to kill. Sally and Buck went first. They were both naturals. No hesitation, no fear. They dodged to the side and bit down behind the head. June licked their necks in praise. Lily was having a tougher time—she could hardly look at a snake without whimpering.

You'll be fine, said June. *These are just friendlies.*

What if I get bit? asked Lily.

If you get bit you get bit, said June.

This was not the answer Lily had been hoping for.

June scared a green snake out from under a rock. The snake searched left and right for a way out, but June corralled it toward Lily. Now trapped, it coiled into a defensive posture. Lily closed her eyes. Sally pounced and bit. Lily opened her eyes.

I did good? she asked.

You did nothin', said Sally, the snake's two ends twisting from her mouth.

You didn't gimme a chance, said Lily, before hanging her head.

Shakespeare tried next, but he was too excited. The snake was hardly out of the hole when he bounded toward it, scaring it off.

You gotta wait for the tongue flick, June reminded him.

Wait for the tongue, wait for the tongue, he said. *Wait wait wait*. But when the next snake came, he again pounced immediately, snapping at air.

June laughed, already won over by his enthusiasm.

Keep at it, she told him, still laughing.

Then came my turn. I'm going to brag a little—I'm a pretty good snake killer. A natural, June said. As instructed, I waited for the tongue flick, then dodged to the side. When the snake extended, I bit. The whole front half of that first snake ended up in my mouth. It wiggled around like it was playing with my tongue until it died. Like I said, I prefer rabbit, even with the guilt.

Before it got too hot, we gathered again for our second lesson.

To fight a coyote, said June, then, looking at me, *or a dog, you'll need some of the same tricks as for catchin' snakes. First off, look for that tell. Ain't gonna be a tongue flick, but most fighters got one. Learn theirs, and yours, then hide your own. Head low, back arched, feet light. Once you got the neck, start shakin' and do not stop. Bring 'em down.*

Sally and Buck were already circling one another, growling.

Shakes, you and Lily team up, said June.

Lily trembled. Shakespeare rolled onto his back and pawed her gently. She batted him in return with her forepaw.

Get tough, said June. *C'mon, where's your spunk?*

Lily tried a growl but it came out like a burp. Shakespeare yapped in return.

Sally and Buck were rolling in the dirt, mutually neck-latched and shaking each other violently. Blood dripped from somewhere.

Alright, Rou, said June.

My stomach tightened. Her eyes switched from gentle to focused. She assumed a fighting stance. I felt lightheaded, my head swimming with a blend of fear and attraction. She was gorgeous.

Go on, she said.

I mirrored her.

Feet light, she said.

I adjusted.

Okay, she said.

Then she lunged and touched my neck. It was a flash of gray. No time to flinch.

Got ya, she said. *Reset. You try.*

This time I assumed my stance. I trained my eyes on hers. I picked her right side and lunged. Empty space. I felt a touch on my left flank. She had me again.

You're a blinker, she said. *That's your tell.*

We reset and I tried again.

Blink, she said.

We reset.

Blink, she said.

We reset.

She circled me.

Blink, blink, blink.

And so we spent the mornings on lessons of all kinds—hunting, fighting, hiding, digging, scavenging, navigating, scent-finding. Throughout, I filled my senses with June. I stood downwind and smelled her. I bathed in her growl and matched the notes of her kill-song. I wrestled with her, wrapping my paws around her, pressing my face into her fur, and biting deep into her scruff. I gazed at her, memorizing the crisp black fur that outlined her golden eyes. When she caught me looking, she stared back until I looked away.

As each morning was consumed by heat, we returned to the cave, and as we did, as if the descent into the cool, damp dark softened her, June became maternal. We cuddled in a pile before her. She told stories to send us off to sleep. In these moments, I felt like a pup for the first time, complicating my feelings for June. I felt the pain of never knowing my own mother and, simultaneously, the illusory relief of having found her.

Some of June's stories were from the time before coyotes, when The Great Lizard laid the egg that became Earth, or when Sun tunneled straight through it. Others were from the time before two-leggers, when coyotes ruled the land. There was the one about Ra, the first coyote, who lost his teeth when he bit the moon, trying to steal it for Lo, his love. Or the one about Nu, their most devious pup, who was turned into a cat for talking to one, only to be eaten by his brothers and sisters.

And that's why you should never talk to cats, June finished, just to be sure we understood the lesson. I listened adoringly, drinking her in. The others were already asleep. More for me, I figured.

Only when June thought all of us were asleep did she talk about the oasis. It was where she had been born. It was where no humans ever went.

It's like old times at the oasis, said June. *And when all of you get bigger, we're goin'.*

WAXING

THE MOON GAINED WEIGHT, thickening from a slice to a wedge, from half circle to almost full. The pups grew, and I learned. At night we hunted scorpions and snakes along the mountainside, each of us disappearing behind boulders, appearing with or without flesh in our mouths. The pups reached Shakespeare's size, if not in weight then at least in height. He was a natural with them—a dumb uncle who always wanted to play. I found it difficult to join their tumblings, maybe because I overthought it, or because I had no recollection of ever being a puppy, and this lightness was harder to learn.

Fortunately, when I felt oversized, the adult coyotes were there to hunt rabbits and hares and mice, leaving Shakespeare to puppysit overnight. I saw June then—the true June—the best hunter I have ever seen, not the fastest in a straight line, but cunning and predictive, able to switch directions in an instant, always arriving in the place that the prey thought was safe.

Kota was missing on these hunts. I'm guessing she smelled June on the wind. Belle, in contrast, idolized June, and became her shadow. I shadowed them both, in their scent streams, feeling a mysterious, distracting hunger that ran me into more than a few rocks, or, once, a cactus. I walked around with that cholla ball stuck in my backside for three days, everyone laughing whenever they saw me, until finally it fell off, claiming a patch of fur.

To hide my bare behind, and embarrassment, I wandered off alone, through the desert night, to think. I discovered that I loved this solitude and made it a habit, even after the joke got old and new fur began to regrow. I could think properly when alone. I'd think about all sorts of things, like Roger, and Mary, and Dr. Francis, and even Dwid and Antonio and Birdie, and where I had come from, and who I had known before my accident. I wondered about what comes after life, and what came before, and if god exists, and if it's possible to escape fear with logic. But most often I thought about light years and relativity—about the subjective nature of reality.

I imagined that the stars had burned out but their lights still reached me. I imagined that I was other animals and things. I was Shakespeare. I was Gus. I was June. I was a hare being hunted. I was a bird. I was the moon. I sat beside the stone egg, pretending to be its twin, incubating for millions of years, equanimous. Eventually, my mind wandered on, and my body with it, transforming into Jean-Jacques Rousseau, upright in a flowing robe. Walking through the desert in my philosopher's form, I came across a rabbit and simply nodded. Because we are just cells, all of us, and our cells are just atoms, and our atoms are just quarks, and all quarks are connected by forces that grow stronger with distance, and with this knowledge, and that of gravity, one begins to understand how contradictory it is to be anything at all.

FULL MOON RAID

THE DESERT GLOWED in the moonlight. Our footpads fell softly. We hooked around Hoover's northern lip, keeping wide before the last cut into town. As we approached, a shared tension emerged, raising the fur along our backs. I had expected the same collective mind as a hunt, but instead felt the narrowing self-consciousness of premonitory fear.

So it's just gonna be waitin' for us? Chad asked Gus. They were leading the pack.

Sure is, said Gus.

Well how'd you swing that? asked Chad.

Secret a mine, said Gus.

What secret?

Gus laughed in a friendly way. *If I told you, then it wouldn't be a secret, now would it? It'll be there. Just enjoy. Rou's enjoyin', ain't ya, Rou?*

Yeah, I said, even though I wasn't. I really had no idea what I was about to get into. June had urged me to stay home with her. But how could I resist something called a full moon raid? And how else could I show June that I wasn't just another pup?

He's doin' good, Gus told June earlier that day, *and this raid'll make 'im even better. Some town action'll thicken that fur right up. Just what he needs. Can't get that hangin' around the den his whole life.*

June stayed behind.

Having gone nowhere near town for two weeks, I felt nauseated by our approach. Just a quiet road separated us from civilization. Sodium-vapor lights reached out to find us. We crossed the curb, seven yellow ghosts in loose formation. Dirt to concrete in a single step. This new world was bold and incandescent. I was shocked by the shift.

Look out!

Headlights. Stunned with blindness. Then reflex. I was across the road, through the bushes and into a concrete drainage. The other coyotes were waiting there, panting, our eyes readjusting to the night.

Gotta watch out for those, said Leslie, his face looking even more twisted than usual.

Leslie knows, said Gus.

Keep your eyes wide— said Chad.

—and your ears wider, Leslie finished.

This dog better not get us killed, said Tad.

Agreed, said Kota.

Nah, he's a rock, said Chad. *Ain't ya, Rou?*

Yeah, I said, emboldened by his unexpected endorsement. *I'm a rock.*

Course you are, said Gus. *Couple jitters are normal. It's your first full moon raid. Tad here peed himself his first time.*

That true? asked Belle.

No, said Tad, but you could tell it was.

The concrete drainage cut between the road and a line of houses. In that darkness we trotted, invisible, along the edge of town, slower now, more alert. Unnatural sounds bounced off concrete. A door slam. A distant siren. A human voice. We kept on, heads low, rolling uphill in a gray pool. I could smell humans everywhere—their sweat, their chemicals, their garbage. Maybe that's what we were after. Maybe we'd get into some trash cans, tear some bags open. Some bacon would be great, I thought.

If only.

We reached a junction. To our right was a narrower, deeper trough, flat on the ground with vertical walls of gravel held back by metal mesh. Gus turned into this trench. We followed, troops in single file—Chad, Kota, Tad, Belle, me, Leslie.

Eyes wide, ears wider, Leslie chanted behind me. *Eyes wide, ears wider.*

Belle smelled wonderful in that trench, so wonderful that I almost went nose-first into the source of her scent. At least I lifted my nose before I ran into her.

Quit, she said, pushing me away.

Gus jumped out of the trench. We jumped after him and huddled in the shadow of a wooden privacy fence. House lights cut through slats. Gravel crunched under our unsettled feet. We were deep in human territory now.

What's the surprise? asked Kota.

Hope it's trash, said Leslie. *With old milk. Mmm.*

What do you take me for? said Gus. *Any old coyote can find trash. Think more tender than that. Much more tender.*

But if it isn't trash, then what is it?

I knew better than to ask. Gus liked building suspense.

Listen up, he said. *I'm the paw and you're the snap trap. Wait for my signal to spring it shut. Chad, Tad, Belle—you're there,* he gestured up the fence with his muzzle. *Kota, Leslie, Rou—you're with me.*

Chad led others away. We went the opposite direction at a fast walk.

We paused at the end of the fence. Again, Gus addressed us.

Like I said. Snap trap. Simple. I'm in the middle with the prize. Just spring it shut when I make the signal. You got that?

Got it, I said. *Wait, what's the signal?*

I'm gonna yip, said Gus.

That's always the signal, said Kota.

We stalked around the corner to a gap between houses at the bottom of a cul-de-sac. Here we stopped yet again. Gus nodded. Then he walked out, real slow. It was a casual thing—that mosey, that Sunday stroll—to meet a motionless figure in a circle of streetlight. Upon first impression, this figure looked like a tiny man in a tuxedo waiting for his limousine to arrive. But this was not a man. Not with a white belly and black tail and white socks. This was a cat, but, strangely, when he saw Gus coming, he just sat there, and waited. Leslie's breath was in my ear, his melted face beside mine.

Eyes wide, ears wider, he said. *Ears wide, eyes wide. Oh my my my my my.* He sniffed the air, reaching outward.

What's Gus doing? I asked. *What's that cat doing?*

Oh my, Leslie said, *my my my.*

What's going on? I asked, even though I was pretty sure I knew by now.

Just shut up and wait for yip, said Kota. She was drooling.

Cat, said Leslie. He drooled too. *House cat. Indoor cat. The softest and bestest of meats. My my my.*

Across the cul-de-sac, behind the cat, shadows settled. The other three were there—the other side of the trap. Gus sat with his back to us, at the edge of the streetlight, conversing with that cat, who occasionally peered around, clearly uncomfortable, into the darkness.

Where was that limousine?

Gus yipped. The signal. The spring.

We were runners from the gun, hive-minded, leaping from the blocks, closing the trap. The cat jumped straight up and landed, looked frantically around, white socks outstretched, as though he could stop the earth from sliding beneath him. His chest heaved in and out, once. We closed the trap in that single breath. We surrounded him like vicious statues.

See? said Gus to the cat. *That's the thing about your kind. Can't trust 'em.*

The cat's back arched. Fur puffed. Eyes astonished. Rotating, trying to watch us all at once. When he saw me, he stopped. Icy dread. We knew each other. His name was Mr. Mouskowitz. I had met him at the clinic—he came in monthly for his arthritis injection. And he was a sweet, dignified cat. He belonged to a young girl. She always hugged him when he got his shot—more for her nerves than his. He wasn't so dignified now.

He said I'd get a reward, Mr. Mouskowitz said, now speaking to me. *The good stuff. I need it to—*

You really can't trust anyone these days, said Gus, cutting him off.

You don't have to do this, Leo, Mr. Mouskowitz said. *We know each other. Please, Leo. Please.*

Leo's gone, said Gus. *This here's Rou. A coyote, through and through.*

I couldn't believe what was happening. What we were doing. This was not a snake. This was not a rabbit. Mr. Mouskowitz knew exactly what was coming. And so did I. His horror became my own. I was paralyzed.

Saliva drained from the concave of Leslie's face. He was trembling. When Mr. Mouskowitz saw this, he knew it was over. His expression shifted, very briefly, from fear to a kind of curiosity. Leslie lunged. His teeth clamped around Mr. Mouskowitz's neck, right where the bowtie would have been. A shake. A snap. Some air escaped in a whimper. Then the others leapt in. Fur and flesh ripped apart. I closed my eyes, wishing I could plug my ears, wishing I could wake up.

Suddenly my eyelids glowed red. I opened them. The night was bright with headlights as a pickup truck ripped around the corner, tail end hopping. Gus was already gone. Tires locked and squealed. Next went Leslie and Belle and Chad and Tad. I ran. But Kota was just starting to run—forelimbs reaching—as the long black barrel appeared from the driver's side window. I leapt for the shadows as the bang tore through the night.

I ran for my life, and in my panic, lost the others. Hoover was there and then it wasn't. I was in the desert again, running alone—away, away—running away until the night air burned inside of me. Finally I slowed to a walk. I stopped. I stood there panting, surrounded by nothing. I was nowhere. Behind me the lights of Hoover were small. I looked up at the moon. It looked back, cold and impartial, neither approving nor disapproving of what I had, or had not, done.

I was a rock.

DEAL IS A DEAL

I SPLASHED down in the pool, startled to touch something submerged. I scrambled out. It was Shakespeare, swimming in circles. Buck and Sally watched from the shore, now beside me.

Hey Rou, said Buck.

You better not pee in there, Shakes, said Sally.

I can't pee when I'm swimming, Shakespeare said, then stopped and floated.

Gross, said Sally.

Can we have some privacy please? I asked.

Some what? asked Buck.

Go away, I said.

Make us, said Sally.

Yeah, make us, said Buck.

I showed them my teeth. They scurried out. I turned back to Shakespeare.

We need to go, I said.

Shakespeare kept on splashing, clumsy but enjoying himself.

Where? he asked.

Velos. Get out. Shake off. Come on. Quest continues. Here we go.

He did another lap, then got out and shook his coat. He looked up at me with his gentle eyes, tongue hanging sideways. *But we can't go yet,* he said.

We have to. Listen. They're hunting more than mice and rabbits and snakes. They're...they're... How could I tell him what I'd done? No. What *they* had done. I had to tell someone. *They killed Mr. Mouskowitz,* I said.

Who?

I told Shakespeare everything. He didn't speak for a while. He just stared at me. I hated when he did that. It magnified my emotions. Plus he always said something strange afterward. This time was no different.

How did he taste?

What? I didn't eat him. I know him. Are you serious?

Oh, he said. *Um. No?*

I don't think you understand. We need to go. Now.

Again, a long pause. I looked over my shoulder. If Gus knew we were talking like this, I didn't know what he'd do.

But we can't go, Shakespeare said. *It's not time yet.*

I know I said we'd stay, but that was before they started murdering cats and we got shot at.

They're coyotes. What did you expect?

I was struck by his insight but didn't let it show.

Kota is dead, I said. *Look, I hate cats as much as the next dog, but I am not a cat killer. And more importantly, I don't want to get shot to death. And I don't want you to, either. So let's go. Now.*

But the turtle— Shakespeare began.

Really?

Really really. The turtle said we can't go yet. It's not time.

I paced along the water's edge. He was so frustrating. But I couldn't leave him down here, could I? Then again, he would be safe. They loved him. He was like a mascot. And clearly he had no moral qualms, or he was incapable of having them. I stopped and looked down at him, trying to make him understand.

Shakespeare, please. Don't make me leave you.

You won't leave me, he said. He was perfectly calm. He didn't understand.

I'm sorry, I said. *I'm going. I have to.*

His tail wagged. He was looking past me now. I turned around, slowly, already knowing who was there.

Yeah, Rou, you wouldn't leave us, would ya? said Gus. *Good friend like you.* He stood, blocking the tunnel to the main cave. He was dry— must have used the summit entrance. *What's wrong? Tell your old buddy Gus.*

You know what's wrong, I said.

Do I?

You tricked that cat, I said. *I don't know how, but you tricked him. He didn't even have a chance. And it could have been you that got shot. It could have been me.*

And?

Isn't that enough?

Easy, Rou. You're gettin' all worked up. Not a good look. First off, who tricked who? You know not to listen to your dinner. And you know that the only good cat's a dead cat.

He was different, I said, unable to maintain eye contact.

How so?

I knew him. Before. He was friendly. I don't know. I knew I was losing it, but I just kept on. *This little girl loved him, Gus. He was just an old house cat. And she loved him. She hugged him when he got his shot.*

What in Sun's name are you talkin' about? Are you talkin' about a two-legger?

Forget it, I said. *You wouldn't understand.*

I think I'm startin' to, said Gus.

I made myself look at him *He was a helpless house cat, Gus. It's not right.*

Gus seemed amused. *Aw, you're just a little soft still. You'll get over it.*

I was sick of his calm confidence. I wanted to hurt him now. *It's your fault Kota's dead,* I said.

His eyes hardened. His hackles rose. He stepped toward me, lip rising, slaver glistening, canines long and sharp. He pressed me back to the wall.

Now you listen to me, dog, he growled. *I been nice up until now. I welcomed you into my den. I treated you like one of my own. But do not forget what I have done for you. Do not forget who you are dealin' with. I will kill you. I will tear your body into pieces. I will eat you. And your fat friend. A deal is a deal, dog. You will stay here until the moon is new. You will keep your word. Or you will die. And don't even think about runnin'. I will follow you to the end of the land. I will not rest until you are dead.*

He snapped his teeth. I flinched. He walked out.

Huh. He seems upset, Shakespeare said, before wading back into the pool.

WANING

THE MOON HAD FILLED. Now it drained. I was allowed to leave the cave, but in my nocturnal wanderings, I would invariably come across Chad or Tad or Leslie, who would not speak to me, but trot obviously away after making sure I had seen them.

Gus was gone for three days after our encounter. June said nothing of what had happened, although the event, or his absence, seemed to extinguish the last of her maternal warmth. At first I thought she was mad at me alone, but her demeanor was indiscriminate. None of us received encouragement during our lessons anymore, just her steady, critical gaze. And Lily no longer received protection from Buck and Sally's torture.

When Gus returned, I was prepared for a fight, but he too had changed. He climbed into the mining cart and just stared out, his one overhanging canine blue in the cavelight. He snapped at the pups to stay away. June approached him slowly, cautiously. She licked his ear —that was it. I was surprised that he would take his fake grief this far, until, against my will, I conceded that it might be real, and felt sympathy, even though, logically, he deserved none. Kota's death was his to bear.

Seeing him so affected, however, I knew that I could not live with the guilt of Shakespeare's death. I could not abandon him to the coyotes. I was left with no choice. I would honor the deal. Still, I felt anxious about what was to come, not knowing exactly what Gus expected of me. I watched the moon drain, wishing it would drain faster. When it was empty, I would keep my promise, whatever that meant. Then we would go.

Meanwhile, beneath these thoughts, a new obsession was germinating. It began as an image, a subconscious seed that I scarified with each compulsive recollection. Roots laid, the obsession grew as a vine, through cracks between wake and sleep, into my consciousness, where it blossomed into a black and white flower.

The tuxedo cat.

Why had Mr. Mouskowitz been waiting in the street? He said he'd be rewarded. By whom? He was an indoor cat. Why was he outside? And what was the so-called good stuff that would be his reward? Curiosity, even more than intelligence, it seemed, was my real thing. My good and my bad, beyond my control. Obsessive curiosity.

The night before the new moon, I asked Gus how he had done it —how he had gotten Mr. Mouskowitz to take such a risk. What was the promise? And who had made it? We were alone in the cave. Gus was in the mining cart, body obscured by shadow, eyes closed. The corner of his mouth tightened, as if the question, or the answer, amused him.

I have to know, I said.

One of his eyes opened, then the other. Together, they scanned the cave entrance before returning to me.

No, dog, he said, *ya don't.* His eyes closed again. His mouth relaxed. His breathing slowed.

He slept.

THE TRAIL

LATE THAT NIGHT I watched Gus creep from the cave. After counting one hundred breaths, I followed him.

The moon was a thin crescent. I trailed his scent around the mountain's shoulder to the gully, where I descended to the desert floor. With my nose to the ground I caught his afterimage clipping across the basin at a canter. Peppered like waypoints on his route came flashes of desert delights—hare, snake, mouse, rabbit. Where Gus's scent became strong, I slowed. Where it weakened, I sped. I remained vigilant for the other coyotes, who could be anywhere.

Gus ran toward the lonesome meeting hill. Just as I began to think he'd be joining the others, he cut hard right and arced over to the stone egg, where he stopped to urinate. And urinate, and urinate. A camel's worth of urine was on that rock and it reeked of Gus. I covered his leak with a leak of my own and felt good about it, then ran in an outward spiral around the egg until I caught his odor once more.

From there he zigzagged all over. At first, I thought he must have been chasing some prey, but I couldn't smell any. Pondering this, I almost stepped into the first steel trap. I jumped up at the last moment, twisting my body in midair to land beside it and hop away. It was flat on the ground, an unhinged metal jaw staked with a chain. It stank of raw beef—the prize balanced there on that metal dish. If not a foot, then a face. I backed away and found Gus's trail again. This time, I saw the trap sooner. I jarred to a stop. It would snap a bone, I knew. I expected the next one, and came upon it slowly. On the thirteenth trap, I stopped. A large hare had been caught. Its hindlimbs were mangled, forelimbs clawed into the ground, mouth open in rigor mortis. Disturbed, I backed away. Gus's trail straightened after that, heading for the highway that connected Hoover and Velos, where Mary found me in the road. I picked up the pace, anxiety building.

The black mountains tapered into the hum of the highway, revealing a stream of white and orange eyes. I thought I was pacing traffic. Then the road sliced closer, revealing its true speed. I ran in parallel, road noise filling my ears. Massive trucks thrummed against me. Headlights whitewashed my vision. I relied on my nose.

The highway angled. Gus's trail maintained course to intersect. I stopped and checked the scent. It was definitely Gus. I followed it, now walking, to the edge of the highway, and stopped there. The traffic roared past just feet away. Horns honked at the sight of me. Truck backdrafts snatched at my scruff. Gus must have turned back, I told myself, knowing he hadn't.

With dread I accepted that Gus's trail led straight across the highway. His scent was strong here, where he had waited for a gap in traffic, as I did now. A pair of white lights was approaching, pitch and volume rising until the headlights flashed past. Vuh. Then came another. Vuh. Then two more together. Vuh vuh. A gap. I dashed through to the median. I sniffed the dirt. Yes, Gus had come this way. A car flashed its headlights at me. I hopped the guardrail and waited for more white lights. Vuh. Vuh. Two gone by. Vuh. Vuh vuh vuh. A crowd of them speeding into Hoover. A straggler. Vuh. Another gap. I dashed across. Gus's scent was fresh again, now leading into unknown desert.

The land yawned open. I trotted lightly, glad to be out of traffic, ready to run. But I soon discovered that Gus's trail was curving. I hoped that it would not continue bending, but knew that it would, and then it did. Again I was at the edge of the highway, just a quarter-mile upstream, feeling sick. I faced the crossing again. Vuh. A gap. I sprinted to the median. Vuh. Across I went.

At this point I considered two possibilities: either Gus knew that he was being followed, or this was a routine tactic to shake coyote hunters like Dentler. I hoped it was the latter, even though, again, instinct told me that my reassurance was in vain.

I followed Gus's scent again across the drainage, away from the highway. I was actually enjoying myself for a moment, proud of my two highway crossings. But when Gus's trail once more curved back, my taste for adventure began to fade. I recrossed the highway this time with cold precision. Yet again the scent doubled back. So, again, I crossed. And again. And again. And again. By the time the highway ended at the edge of Hoover, I truly hated Gus. And I was suddenly heavy—lethargic at the thought of going into town, where, I knew, there were humans. Humans with guns.

The highway ended in traffic lights. Gus had struck boldly across the intersection and gone directly into town, entering the bright parking lot of a grocery store. A human emerged from the fluorescence behind a rattling grocery cart. I waited for a red light, then ran the same path, slipping between cars and across the wide open asphalt, around the corner of the building, and back into shadow, where Gus's scent was powerful. I slinked along the concrete wall to the back corner. I peered around. Finally, I found him. He was across the loading dock, his scruffy tail poking out of a dumpster like a common raccoon.

After scratting around in the trash for some time, Gus hopped out of the dumpster to land lightly on his feet. In his mouth was his catch—a large, headless fish, its silver body sagging. But Gus did not drop it to eat. Instead, he ran away with the fish flapping, disappearing once more into the darkness.

I trailed fish reek through bushes into a neighborhood. Gus was rounding the corner a block away. I followed at a distance. He turned down another street, then crossed a dirt lot into a tangle of scrub and trees. When he left this cover, I went to it.

I watched from there as he approached the back fence of a single-story house, dark within. He hopped the fence. A security light came on, spotlighting him. Still he walked right up to the patio. He dropped the fish on the concrete with a slap. This was the cue. The flap in the back door opened and stuttered shut. An orange cat entered the spotlight, his waddle and one eye making him unmistakable.

It was Dwid.

WHAT KILLED THE CAT

Gus sat opposite from Dwid in the spotlight with the dead fish between them. Dwid peered around Gus, following his shadow across the pebbles of the yard, driven by paranoia, or maybe my smell. I crouched in the bushes. When I arose, Gus was gone. Dwid was dragging the fish, rear end leading the way, tail upright. I hopped the fence.

Dwid dropped the fish with a slap. He puffed and issued a warning growl. As I entered the light, however, he shrank back to normal size.

Oh goody, he said. *You're still not dead.*

What are you doing with Gus? And this fish?

Business, he said. *Not yours.*

A good cat is dead, I said.

And another is fed, he said. *Poetry, I think.*

Don't you have a conscience?

Don't you have anywhere else to be? You've been replaced, dog. Now get lost. And just so you know—because you won't leave me alone until you do —any cat dumb enough to believe a coyote is going to bring him nip deserves to die.

Nip?

Catnip, idiot, Dwid said. *Mouskowitz was an addict. A drain on catkind. He was one of the worst. Fortunately not the last.*

You set him up.

Dwid hissed, then dragged the fish into hiding. Once it was hidden, he took a deep breath, then let out a long and painful wail that rose into a screech. Confused, I looked around. Dwid was screaming like I was biting his leg off. Then a light in the house came on. Mary was peering through the window, hands cupped on the glass. I dashed off and leapt the fence, returning to the bushes.

I should have just kept running. But of course I didn't. I had to see. I watched through the leaves. She came outside in her pajamas.

"Dwiddy?" she said. "There you are. What's wrong?" She picked him up and cradled him. His tail curved with pleasure. "Ooh, you stinky boy."

It was disorienting to see her again, especially in this unfamiliar den. It was similar in style to her old house but cleaner and newer with larger windows. She even had a new couch—a long one with overstuffed cushions. I suddenly longed to climb onto it, to sleep and not dream, to awaken to a bowl of kibble and fresh water, in air conditioning, no less. She'd welcome me, I knew it. I could run in there now. I almost did.

Then a Golden Retriever emerged from the house, wagging his feathery tail.

"Simon, you come back inside," Mary said.

I was too stunned already to be surprised when a French Bulldog burst from the flap. He ran like a black bullet to the edge of the patio, and stopped. He stared at the darkness where I lay.

"What is it, Kit?" Mary asked.

Kit came toward me. I couldn't move. I just stared as he marched across the pebbles, oval ears high and listening. He was at the fence now, just paces away, sniffing the night. A white shield marked his chest.

State your name, he said.

Before I could answer, a caterwaul ripped through the night followed by a shout. Dwid leapt from Mary's arms. Kit spun and barked. Simon must have found the fish.

"No!" Mary cried.

Dwid swatted Simon, first clawing his back side, then, when the dog turned in alarm, his face. Simon tucked tail and ran hunching and whimpering through the flap.

"Hey now," Mary said, "be nice to Simon. What did he do to you?"

Dwid responded with a steady growl.

I ran.

I retraced my path through the neighborhood, around the grocery store, across the parking lot, and out of town.

Back in the desert I slowed to a walk. Gus and Dwid met again in my mind. *Slap.* The fish on the concrete. *Slap.* I recalled the fish bones that I had found when I first arrived at Mary's house. *Slap.* It was a longstanding deal. *Slap.* How many house cats had fallen for the same trick as Mr. Mouskowitz?

Gus appeared from behind the stone egg. I stopped. He sat.

See what you needed to see? he asked.

I needed time to collect myself—to prepare for a confrontation.

I'll admit it, Gus went on. *I wasn't sure you were keepin' up 'til our road game. When I saw you runnin',' though, I knew. That's my friend Rou. Fastest dog I ever saw. Bet you ain't scared of cars no more.*

Dwid? I asked. *Really? Him?*

Fine, we'll talk about him. I can't say I like him either. Got no...what's the word? Help me out, smartie. That cat's got no...

Morals, I said.

Huh, morals, Gus said. *I thought you'd know a good word. I was just gonna say sense. Between you and me and the moon, I sometimes wanna eat 'im on the spot. He's so fat. Looks delicious.*

It's not natural, I said. *Tricking house cats like that. They don't know any better. It's not fair.*

Natural? Fair? Huh. I'll try to remember what those words mean. While I do, you try and remember gettin' food in a bowl twice a day, and water at your feet. That natural? No two-legger ever offered me a meal. That fair? Cuz I'm not...what? What's the word? Cute?

I left, I said. *I'd rather die than deal with Dwid. It's beneath you. It's beneath both of us.*

Gus laughed. *Boy, you should hear yourself sometimes. You talk like you got all the answers. But you don't know a damn thing. You'd rather die? You really mean that, dog?*

He circled me.

You don't know dyin', said Gus, *till you lost one a your own. Now that's dyin'. Real dyin'. The kind you'd rather not do. I saw it first when I was younger than you. Drought like this one, back before we found the water cave. I'll tell ya. Our daddy gave us the tooth, drought or not. So me and my brother, we went out rangin' together, for grub and water. You bet we fell on tough times. Real quick. We were way out. Thought we knew an old bed that was deep and always ran. But when we got out there—you can guess where this is goin'—that's right. No water. Bed was dry. Hadn't eaten in half a moon. My brother was smaller and sorta bony already. He saw that dry ground and he just laid down and never got back up. Closed his eyes. Never opened 'em again. Like he'd gone off to sleep. Vultures came quick. Outta nowhere. I tried keep 'em off. I did. But I was too weak. Too tired. There were too many of 'em.*

He stopped in front of me.

So do you know what I did? To survive?

We stared at each other.

I joined 'em, he said. *That's right. I ate my own brother. And you know what? He didn't taste too bad.*

I shuddered when he licked his lips.

So you can have natural, said Gus. *Cause natural ain't so pretty when it's happenin' to you. And fair don't exist.*

I won't help you kill another house cat.

I figured that's what was buggin' you, said Gus. *Ya know, you shoulda told me sooner. Fact is, I don't care. Why would I? Do what you want. Hell, I can promise you right here, on the life of Juney and my pups, that I will never ask you to do that again. That is not a part of our deal. Honest. I do my way. You do yours. That's fine.*

His posture had softened, and with it, my own.

Listen, he said. *I know I been secret-like, a little hard on ya, but it's for your own good. It was time you knew about old Dwid and how this world works, time you learned how to handle the highway, time you seen the way the snap traps was laid, and how that two-legger of yours already moved on to a couple more hounds. You coulda gone back, but you didn't. Don't ya see? You passed the final test. You ain't a house pup no more, Rou. You're a coyote.*

RANCHING

THE CLOUDS HAD APPEARED at sundown, pulled as a solid blanket over the sky, so that now, as Gus and I approached the ranch, the stars and absence of moon were invisible, and all was dark. A peculiar smell was on the breeze that I later learned was rain, still far off. At that time the smell made me uneasy, although this could have been equally due to the unknown landscape. We were on the southern outskirts of Hoover, a land intersected by long wooden fences that separated about a dozen horse ranches. These places had been here since before town was town, or so said Gus. Here lived two-leggers with guns, he said, two-leggers who loved to use them. Thus the need for the new moon—for utmost darkness. Gus welcomed the clouds.

We ran along one of the fences. Within its confines, shadows of thick necks crossed, raised, lowered. I had never seen horses before, and their size and novelty and restlessness put an even sharper edge on my nerves. They snorted and whinnied in warning as we passed. An enormous bladder drained in a torrent, leaving a sour cloud.

They know what's comin', said Gus.

At least *they* did.

Gus, as usual, was withholding information. Earlier that evening, as the first clouds edged over the horizon, I was on the mountaintop, trying to get my mind right. I would do what was asked of me. I did not belong with these coyotes, but I would fulfill my promise. And then we would go.

A row of cypresses grew in a windbreak, continuing on where the back fence ended, past the ranch house and out to a dirt road. We settled between two of these trees, not far from the house. We peered through. Lit by incandescence, a black and white Border Collie lay on the back of a couch, alert and staring out the window.

That there's Dash, said Gus. *He's what we call a stooge. Thinks everyone's out to get 'im, just like his two-legger. He's part right, course.*

Behind Dash was a fireplace built from desert stone. The firebox was black and quiet. Upon the mantle sat a brass clock, and above that, suspended by invisible mounts, was a black rifle with a scope.

Gus let out two quick yips. My heart thumped.

Are you crazy? I asked.

Watch.

Dash burst into a frenzy. He barked and jumped off the couch, then onto the couch, then off the couch, his black and white head appearing and disappearing.

In the far distance, a series of yips echoed back to us—Chad, Tad, Leslie.

Keep watchin', said Gus. *Here comes ol Flattop.*

A pot-bellied man entered the living room, pulling on a shirt. His face was ruddy and sagged, his hair, in contrast, was a flat white buzz. It was Dentler, who the coyotes called Flattop. He took the gun down from the wall. Dash seemed to know what this meant. He raced around, jumping on and off the couch. Dentler slung a camouflage bag over his shoulder. Together they exited the room. The lights went out.

Guess who set those snap traps, said Gus. *Guess who killed Kota, and Ruthie, and Frank, and Pete, and more before I was born. Trappin' and shootin' and runnin' us down. Loves killin' coyotes—lives for it.*

I shared his anger. At least coyotes killed to eat. This human killed for sport—for pleasure. I felt the simple confidence of the righteous. How dare he kill animals for fun.

A door creaked and slammed shut. An engine rumbled to life. Dentler's truck turned offroad, heading out into the desert, headlights scanning for the source of those yips.

I followed Gus to the front of the house, where a sedan was

parked. A security light clicked on, but Gus just strolled right through it. Slinking up, I sniffed a back tire. Gus urinated on the driver's door. I lifted my leg in solidarity, impressed as ever by his risk and style. I was compelled to emulate him, even though an equal part of me now hated him.

We returned to the trees to wait.

And while we waited, Gus talked. I sensed—not far below that shield of arrogance—fear. He rambled and I was glad for the distraction—to not imagine what he had planned. It was time we got ours, he said. Time we set things straight for all those coyotes lost, for what happened to Kota. After she died, he said, he'd lost his nerve. But only for a blink. Now he was back. Full power.

Gotta set things straight, he said.

His greatest plan was in motion. It had begun hours before, in the cave, by convincing Shakespeare to stay behind. When he'd heard about some grand plan, he had bounced from wall to wall with excitement. But Gus was ready. It was an old strategy but still effective.

Shakes, you got the biggest job of 'em all, he said. *I need you here, to guard June and take care a the pups. Think you can do that?*

Now Gus was quiet. We waited, and my mind wandered. I guess it was being this close to Dentler's place, or seeing Dash on the couch. I wondered where I would have been had I never left the one home I had. Maybe eating potato chips from under the couch, where Shakespeare's mouth couldn't reach. Or reading Thinkipedia. Or watching the big screen and cuddling with Mary. I did miss her. It pained me to think of her with those new dogs. Had we really been replaced so soon? I wondered what she was doing now. Maybe giving out back scratches. Or belly rubs. Or even pieces of cheese, or bacon, or sausage. Maybe I was just hungry. Maybe hunger is just the stomach getting lonely, like it longs for food and so—

A noise close behind us. We spun.

Shoulda seen Flattop go, said Chad, still panting.

Right the wrong way, said Tad.

Shoulda seen it, said Leslie.

The trio had drawn Dentler into the desert, then shaken him and circled back to the house. We huddled in the trees.

What next? asked Chad. He sniffed the air. *Could be rain.*

Could be, said Tad. *Bet you a rabbit Rou gets shot before it rains. Bout time.*

Quit, said Gus. *He's not gettin' shot. Nobody is. Not shot, not run down, not trapped. Not tonight. And not ever again. Tonight, we kill Flattop.*

We what? I asked, reflexively.

We kill 'im, said Leslie, already drooling at the idea, *and eat 'im.*

I'm in, said Tad, scowling at me. *Cuz I ain't no coward.*

Now hang on, said Chad. *Makin' Dentler run all over, that's one thing. Maybe we take a horse, fine. But it ain't so long since Flattop killed Kota. Not long before that he blasted Frank's head clean off. I mean, I hate him as much as anybody, but let's be clear. We're talkin' about getting up close with the deadliest two-legger I ever saw. Best not push it.*

Best not, repeated Leslie, unsure whose side he was on.

Gus settled his stare on Chad. I was glad, for once, to not be the target of those eyes.

Never thought I'd sire a coward, said Gus.

And that was enough. Chad's tail fell. He looked to Tad and Leslie for help, but found none. None of them could bear the weight of Gus's disapproval. Not that Gus was really disapproving. He pushed Chad only to catch him and lift him higher.

But I know I didn't sire no coward, said Gus. *It's just your smarts talkin'. Ain't that right, Chad?*

Chad's tail lifted.

I guess so, he said.

Gus smiled at all of us, reassuring with his overhanging tooth.

Things are different now, said Gus. *We got ourselves this here dog, don't we? Real smart one. Works doors. And he's gonna work one now. Ain't that right, Rou?*

THE LAIR

THE PLAN WAS as terrifying as it was simple. We would break into Dentler's house, right into his lair. There we would wait for him to return, and there we would rip out his throat. When Gus said we, however, I mentally excluded myself. I would open a door, yes, but no more. I could see why Dentler needed to die, but could I kill him? No. I was afraid of who I would be after that. I would be afraid of myself.

You know what I was thinkin'? said Gus. *We should take his head home for June. She'd like that.*

Just do the door, I told myself. Just do the door. The door and that's it.

We ran around the house to the front. The security light clicked on. We squinted through it and hopped onto the front porch, where I discovered that I could be of no help. I exhaled, relieved.

Knob, I said.

What? Go on, said Gus, throwing looks over his shoulder, as we all did, feeling like we'd been shaved naked by the light.

I can't, I said. *I never said I could,* I added, seeing the alarm in all their eyes. *It's a knob. I can't do knobs. I can only do levers.*

What the hell's a lever? Tad growled. *Speak normal, dog.*

Easy, said Gus. *Rou, whadya mean you can't do knobs?*

It's round, I said. *I just can't. I can't bite it. I can't paw it. I don't have thumbs.*

What the hell's a thumb? asked Tad.

Tad, settle down, said Chad.

The back, said Gus.

And like that my relief was gone. They jumped off the porch and I followed, rounding the house. We hopped the fence. Another security light clicked on. We trailed Gus along the wall to a stretch of tall windows, where we stopped. We could all smell Dentler here, like he came this way often. And I could see that the middle window was different. The frame was heavier. But I'd never seen a sliding door before. It was all dark glass to me then.

I don't know, I said. *I don't see a lever. Or a knob.*

Gus glared at Tad before he could tear into me.

Just try, said Gus. *I seen Flattop come in and out a here, Rou. Go on and try.*

I sniffed around, finding that Dentler's smell was strongest around the heavy window. This one really was different than the others. My curiosity took over. It was a puzzle. I sniffed along the bottom seam, then up the edges, until I came to a place of thicker plastic. It smelled strongly of human hand. Then I understood. Of course. It was a handle. This was a door. But how would I open it?

He's gettin' it, said Gus. *He's gettin' it.*

I pushed the handle with my nose, first in, then up, then right, then left. To my surprise, the glass moved.

That's it! said Gus. *Go on now! Go on, Rou! You're doin' it!*

I leaned in. It was sliding. It was a sliding door! I pushed it wide open. Then I stepped back. Cold air-conditioned air swept over us, freezing us in place. The smell of human coming from the darkness was profound, tickling a deep instinct to run.

In, said Gus, and he led the way.

In we went, five ragged shades among solid forms of leather and wood, of tables and chairs, and a cold light that glowed in the mouth of a giant silver fridge.

Door, said Gus.

I slid it shut. The rumble finished with a tight seal. I'll admit it. I was proud of what I'd done. I was contributing something. I was a part of this pack. And I was getting swept up in the mission.

Lair, said Gus.

Our eyes adjusted to the darkness. We dropped our noses.

Human scents prickled us beneath our fur. I had entered a new reality. Here, in this shadow world, my two lives merged, both dog and coyote, guest and raider.

Who's that?! said Leslie.

We snapped our heads in his direction. Standing just feet away was another coyote, motionless, teeth bared. But there was something strange about him. Something unnatural. I sniffed, then pressed my nose against his shoulder. It was hard.

Dead, I said. *Stuffed.*

The others sniffed to confirm.

Don't smell like one of ours, said Tad.

By Sun it's Pete, said Gus, stepping back. *Uncle a mine. Brave coyote. Before you was born. Lost a toe, see?*

On the wooden platform, one front foot was narrower than the other.

C'mon, said Gus, tracking down a corridor. *Too late for Uncle Pete.*

I backed away, shaken by Pete's eternal snarl. Who keeps a dead animal in a living room? What kind of a human does that?

But there was no time to think.

We filed past photos of humans on the walls, past a bathroom with a dripping tap, to a door cracked ajar. Gus pressed in, swinging it open with a squeak. In we went. Here, around his unmade bed, the scent of Dentler was pungent. Here was where he slept—the soft center of his den.

Door, said Gus.

I closed it almost entirely, leaving the same black gap that we had found.

And there we waited, five assassins around the bed, waiting for the king to return to his chamber. We stared at the black gap with fierce concentration. Our bodies turned to stone as our ears twitched to listen.

Easy, said Gus, calming us with his confidence. *Easy.*

THE VOICE

I⊤ WASN'T long before we heard the voice. My heart tumbled and sped to a rapid beat.

"Grampa?" the voice asked, high and soft and uncertain.

Ten ears stood at attention.

"Grampa?" It asked again. I had heard voices like this before, at the clinic. This was the smallest of human voices. It was a little girl.

"Grampa?" she asked again, closer now, more scared.

She was tip-toeing toward us, coming down the hall.

That's him, said Leslie.

That's not him, said Gus, before I could.

Whatever it is, we kill it first, said Tad.

Extra kill, said Chad. *Extra meat.*

Hold, said Gus.

It was a nightmare now, the kind that freezes bones. The black gap widening, the door creaking as it moved. Leslie licked his lips. He trembled.

In the doorway, a tiny, curly-haired girl stood in white pajamas. She was hugging a stuffed dog, pressing her cheek into it, peering into the bedroom, her eyes wide and magnified by thick glasses. She sniffed.

"Grampa? I heard a sound."

I leapt up as Leslie did, both of us silent, for an instant, in midair. We collided in front of the girl with a crash of bones and fell to the ground. She screamed, then tore off down the hall, her tiny feet pattering away. In my tangle with Leslie, I saw Tad, then Chad, leaping over us, flying after her. Leslie snapped at me and twisted away, then chased after them. I jumped up.

Then the screaming really began. The girl's piercing voice drilled straight into my ears.

Hell, said Gus, standing beside me, looking down the hall. *You both had to jump at once.*

The other three were outside the bathroom. Leslie was clawing at the door while the other two sniffed feverishly around the jamb.

You think you can get that one open? asked Gus.

We walked down the hall. Please be a knob, I prayed, please be a knob. My heart swelled with fear and love for this little girl that I didn't even know. She isn't prey, I kept thinking, like it was wired into me. She isn't prey. She isn't prey.

Knob, I said, unable to hide my relief.

Leslie was still clawing maniacally at the door, digging gouges in the wood. He bit at the knob, dropped his nose, and sniffed the light. The screams continued, long and shrill. I looked around, disoriented. It was over. I needed to get out. She isn't prey.

You idiot! said Tad.

Dammit, Rou, said Chad. *You gotta time it better.*

He did it on purpose! said Tad. *I'll kill you now, like I shoulda done when I first saw ya!*

But as Tad moved toward me, a fresh light swept across the main room. The engine was suddenly close. Her screams could have carried a quarter-mile.

We gotta get out, I said, trying to press through.

The others blocked my path.

No, said Gus. *This ain't over. We set things straight. Tonight. Leave the loud one and hide.*

The engine stopped. The truck door slammed. We scrambled. Chad slipped past me, back into the master bedroom. Gus went into the other. The rest of us ran into the main living area, Leslie last, after pulling himself away from the door.

"Maggie!" Dentler shouted from outside. I dove behind the furniture. The front door swung open. The lights came on. I saw myself warped multiple times in the brass studs of a leather couch. I flattened my head on the ground to look underneath. Heavy boots pounded across the floor followed by black and white dog feet. "Maggie! I'm here!"

The screams were desperate, with a sudden burst as Dentler opened the bathroom door. Seeing him, she began to cry. I jumped up. It was our only chance. I ran to the back door. It's over, I told myself. Get out.

But when I tried to press the handle, something clicked. And then the door wouldn't move at all. I pressed harder. My nose watered with pain. I started chewing at it, too panicked to operate the lock.

"Grampa's here, Grampa's here, I'm here," Dentler said, soothing her. "I'm sorry, baby, I'm so sorry. I shouldn't have left you." I could hear Dash's collar jingling, probably as he licked her tears away.

The rest happened in a matter of seconds, each one dragging out long and grotesque. Leslie ran across the floor, sliding on the wood before catching on the runner rug. He cut into the bathroom, followed by the others, scrambling from their hiding places. In gray flashes, they slipped inside.

Pop!

The air filled with growls and yelps and cries and shouts.

Pop! Pop! Pop! Pop! Pop! Pop!

Then out came Gus, Chad, and Tad, slamming into the wall and bouncing off, darting into the main room with me. Leslie, last and clearly wounded, hit the wall with a wet sound and stuck for a moment.

Pop! Pop!

Leslie lurched into open space with one of his legs limp and flopping, the other three in disagreement with one another.

A door slammed.

"Stay put!" said Dentler. Then he emerged. He seemed to fill the entire house, no longer an old man, but a soldier with a rifle on his back. His pistol rested over his wounded arm, which bled generously where the fabric was torn. He paid it no mind. I knew that look in his eyes. He was ready to kill. The coyotes scrambled before him like giant rats.

Pop! Pop!

Gus cut back and hurdled the coffee table.

Pop!

Chad ran to the front door, U-turned, flew back.

Pop! Pop! Pop!

Leslie slid across the floor in his own blood, with Tad slipping on it behind him.

Then Dentler turned to me. I stared into the black void of the barrel, too shocked to move.

Click.

Dentler dropped the pistol. He reached over his back for the rifle, giving me a moment to kick into motion. I joined the others in the chaos, all of us panicking, no longer considering the possibility that we could match this human's total, remote power, his ability to bite from across the room.

He leveled the rifle. Leslie ran in a mangled blur, straight at the back door, and, with an explosive crash, burst through glass. Hot air sucked into the room.

Bang!

We sprinted for it, flying at the jagged hole, jump-tucking through it to avoid the razorous teeth. Out and out and out, and into a herd of stampeding horses churning up dust and neighing at the madness. We flew through them, between stomping hooves and flat, snapping teeth.

Bang!

A bullet whistled past me.

Bang!

Another.

And over the fence and into the desert beyond.

I looked again and again over my shoulder, waiting for the head-lights, for the growl of the engine, but all light and noise was fading as I entered the dark silence of the desert. After the last of the fences, the others called to one another, in yips, quiet at first, uncertain of their own voices. I felt the bond of fear, and went to the yips as they clustered. Gus and Chad and Tad were standing together, panting. They were looking down at something, and kept staring at it even as I walked up.

He was a good coyote, said Gus.

Good as they get, said Tad.

At least he killed Dash, said Chad. *Too bad we couldn't stick around to eat 'im.*

Leslie wore his terrible smile even in death. His body now matched his face—twisted and wrong—dark and wet in patches of gunshot wounds and long ribbons where the glass had flayed him. We observed him in death until we heard the sound. This was not the voice of a child.

THE SOUND

GRRUNGGH.

Was it the sound of a dragon clearing its throat?

Grrunggh.

Or was it a manmade thing? A weapon of some kind?

Grrunggh.

The three of us stared through a half-mile of night at Dentler's ranch, where a new light now illuminated the rectangular opening of an outbuilding. Within it, movement.

Grrunggh.

What is that? I asked.

The others stared.

I thought it was dead, said Chad.

In defiant reply, the spark plug ignited the first explosion of all those to follow. The dirt bike growled to life. The headlight swung out, and with it, the wail of two-stroke acceleration.

Grrrrrrrrrrrrrrrrrrr!

Then I was galloping beside Gus. I didn't know the direction we ran, only that it was away from the sound.

Split, said Gus.

We diverged. I was running alone. The sound of the dirt bike was fading. I looked back. A disembodied white light cut across the land. I felt relief, then guilt at my relief, that it was not me, in that moment, being chased.

But my relief was premature. The engine noise pitched higher and when I looked back again, I saw that the white light had now turned unmistakably for me. It was growing larger and brighter. Ahead, I began to see traces of my own shadow. I scanned the land, finding nothing but more open space.

There was nowhere to hide.

Dentler was roaring up behind me.

What would a coyote do? I knew the answer to that. A coyote would run, flat out, as fast as his legs would take him. But I was not a coyote.

I threw my weight down and sideways. In this moment, as I stopped and turned, time slowed. Sound ceased. In that silent, slow place, the headlight bobbed once, as if on water. Then all sped up again as I sprinted straight at him, head on.

I heard the moment of Dentler's confusion. The engine hesitated. His hand must have relaxed on the throttle, but too late, as I was only feet away, then inches, hurtling past him in the opposite direction, close enough to feel the rip of the passing mass, to smell the combustion, and to see him, like an underexposed photograph, hunched over the handlebars with his injured arm.

After this came the total blackness of shattered night vision. I ran into the void, and though it was for only an instant, as my feet pedaled beneath me and found air instead of ground, that instant was long enough for me to have one complete and absurd thought— I'm flying.

Of course, I wasn't actually flying, and this was made plain when I smashed into the opposite wall of the dry gulley and tumbled to the bottom. Stunned, I lay on the sandy bed, winded and gasping. A beam of dusty white light swept overhead, while I, beneath it, waited, until the light withdrew, moaning off in search of another.

THE STORM

I CLIMBED out of the gulch tasting salt. Dentler was heading toward the black mountains. I trotted after him like a pup wanting to play chase again. When I heard gunshots, however, I stopped. What was I doing?

I could run away now. I could cut across the highway, into the unknown land where Dentler was unlikely to go, and just keep going—put as much distance between myself and this place as possible. Then I could think it through.

But in the sky above that empty land, like a warning, fork lightning flashed—the first I'd ever seen—followed by thunder, a godlike utterance that worked my bones. In this direction lies a worse fate, the storm warned. Cowardice. I would be leaving behind Shakespeare, my one true friend.

Fortunately, my legs were braver than I was. They carried me toward the black mountains. Passing the stone egg, lightning flashed again, rendering a moment of surreal midday. In the resuming night, Dentler cut back and forth toward the mountains. Between flashes, I saw his headlight angling upward before being swallowed by a ravine. I followed him. The air smelled of exhaust and coyote and, more and more, of rain.

Tall cacti threw shadows of lightning with their arms. What had initially frightened me now gave me courage. The storm was writing my epic, and the old succulents knew that I was the hero, and cheered my name. I climbed. Between thunder claps, the dirt bike whined from strange directions above, at times seeming to come from the sky itself. Then came the rain. It did not start as I had imagined it would, in small, infrequent drops. It hit me in a flat sheet. I braced under the pouring impact and carried on with the weight of my soaked coat. The world blurred. The ground softened from wet sand to mud. The wash became a stream. The water rose to my elbows. The current was dragging me back, threatening to sweep me away. I climbed onto a rock island, then jumped to the bank, escaping the flooding gulley. I continued up a muddy spine, head low and limbs wide, hugging the sloughing ground, to the entrance of the tunnel, where I sheltered under the overhanging black headwall.

Dripping wet, I looked back. Lightning flashed. Cataracts poured from the heavens, transforming the desert basin into a shallow ocean. I slid down the chute and splashed into the cave below.

HOW IT ENDS

I CLIMBED out and shook off.

We need to go, I said. *Now.*

Shakespeare didn't even look at me. He sat at the edge of the pool, gazing into the water. He didn't reply or even seem to notice me. He just stared at the smoothing ripples. This was so unlike him, and the cave was so cool and devoid of the sounds of the storm, that I felt a chill. I shivered like a ghost who needed to be seen.

Shakespeare, I said. *Are you listening to me?*

Where's Gus? asked June.

She had entered with Buck and Sally, both looking as worried and small as Lily, who peered out from between June's legs.

He's not here? I asked. *We split up. We were being chased.*

Who was chasing you? asked Sally.

Never you mind, said June, trying to conceal her fear. *Stay close now.* She led them back into the main cave.

Let's go, I said to Shakespeare. *Before Gus gets back. Do you hear me?*

We need to wait for him, Shakespeare said calmly, still watching the pool, now glassy and black, with a halo of white crystal.

I'm not playing this game again, I said. *I will drag you out of here.*

I know, Shakespeare said.

I had never seen him serious, and it was disquieting. Although we couldn't hear the storm, the walls were seeping water, twinkling the crystal lights. What if it flooded? We'd drown. And that was just one fate. I imagined him coming down into the mine, guns blazing, to exterminate us all.

Let's go, I said again.

He made no move. I took his scruff in my teeth. He went limp and lay down on his side. I didn't know what was wrong with him, but there was no time to ask, or play one of his games. I bit his neck fold as gently as I could and pulled, dragging him across the rock floor and out the short tunnel into the main cave.

Gonna drag 'im the whole way? asked Gus.

Shakespeare leapt up.

He's here! he said, suddenly his old self, spinning and wheezing.

I was glad that Shakespeare wasn't broken in some way, but dismayed to face Gus. He stood beside June, pups at their feet. My fear was misplaced. Whatever I had or hadn't done at the house was now unimportant. Gus was more concerned with survival than a confrontation with me.

We gotta go, said Gus.

Pa got followed? asked Sally.

Mighta, said Gus.

The pups looked up at him with a mixture of adoration and fear. Lily trembled. *Gonna be fine, Lily,* said Gus. *So long as we stick together.*

Let's go, said June. *Now.* She exited. Gus and the pups followed, Shakespeare and I behind them. But once we were in the pitch black, Shakespeare got upset.

Stop! he said. *This isn't how it ends! This isn't right!*

Just keep movin', Shakes, said Gus. *You're just spooked is all.*

Are we gonna die? asked Lily.

You probably are, said Buck.

Sally laughed.

Quit, said June. *We're almost out.*

But this isn't right! Shakespeare continued.

Ahead, the steady patter of footsteps became irregular, then scuffled to a stop.

Quit! said Sally.

You quit! said Buck.

Hush, said June.

We stopped and listened. From ahead came a rattling sound.

Some hollow metal object was falling through the wooden scraps that filled the entrance to the mine.

Now what's that? asked Gus.

Hold up, Shakespeare said. *I actually think this might be right.*

Then came the hissing sound, and with it, the smell of chemicals. The pups coughed.

Back! cried June. She slipped past me in the darkness, leading us back underground. Whatever it was, it was burning our throats and lungs. Shutting our eyes against the pain, we ran for cleaner air.

Shakespeare entered the cave last, eyes watering, his tail wagging with joy.

Yes! he said, and spun in a circle. *This is it! This is how it ends! Ha ha!*

Quit, dog, said June. *That's the only way out.*

Shakespeare was too excited to listen. He spun around and around while the rest of us stood there, tails low, uncertain.

What is that stuff? asked Gus. His eyes, like all of ours, were red and watering.

When the white mist entered the cave, I thought it was only the tear film over my eyes, but after I blinked, the mist was more. The others backed away. It was definite. White smoke was crawling in upon the ground, growing deeper and wider by the second. We coughed and backed away. Shakespeare, despite his coughing, continued to wag his tail.

I knew it! he said. He spun, faced the smoke, then spun in the opposite direction, to face the smoke again. *I told you! This is how it ends!*

He's even happy about dyin', said Gus. *Gotta admire that, in a way.*

There's no way out, said June, pacing. *There's no way out.*

The pups whined. We backed away from the encroaching white wave. Lily hacked up a wad of mucus. Shocked by the sound, June ran out of the main cave and through the tunnel to the pool. We followed, and soon the white smoke would too.

There was nowhere else to go. We stood around the pool, pups crying, the water a black mirror, reflecting us one last time. Far above, the black hole marked the entrance. How could we get up there? How could we climb out? We couldn't. It was impossible. We would suffocate instead.

Huh, said Gus, *this ain't how I figured I'd go.* He was calm again. He sat at the water's edge and looked up at the hole in the ceiling. *Always figured I'd get shot. I'm gonna miss you, Juney. You too, pupparoos.*

His family huddled around him, June whimpering into his scruff, the pups bawling at his feet.

A splash cut through it all.

Shakespeare was in the water. He paddled to the center. Then he took a deep breath and tipped headfirst, so that only his piggy tail and stubby back legs were visible.

Helluva time for a swim, said Gus.

Shakespeare kicked his back legs, at first into air, then, as his body bobbed down, underwater. He dove, leaving only bubbles behind. We gawked at the black water until it exploded again. Shakespeare burst out. He gasped.

Are you coming or what? he asked. He caught his breath, then took a long, deep inhale before disappearing again. This time, he didn't come back up.

I waded into the water, muscles tightening against the cold.

He sees things, I explained.

Oh brother, said Gus. *We're goners.*

I swam to the center while the coyotes looked on. Behind them, traces of white were entering. I took a deep breath and went under.

I opened my eyes but saw only darkness below. Still, I kicked downward. The water became colder, burning my eyes. I reached and pulled with my forelimbs as my hindlimbs kicked behind. Was that a light? I swam deeper, ignoring the pressure in my ears. The glow was getting stronger. Shocked, I finally saw—some fifteen feet underwater was a tunnel illuminated within by phosphorescence. It glowed green, a phantasmagoric cylinder, just big enough for a dog like me.

I returned to the surface.

A tunnel! I said. *A tunnel!*

Now hang on, said Gus.

Hang on? said June, coughing. *Go!*

The smoke was thickening. I pulled in the deepest breath I could, then rolled forward and dove, soon reaching the tunnel.

I squinted at the encircling brightness. The walls were thick with crystals. Although I could see my own nose and forelimbs clearly, I could see no end to the tunnel itself. The light seemed to constrict as it moved away, squeezing me with it. My ears ached. My lungs burned. A spasm hit my stomach, urging me to breathe. I swam onward, growing desperate, now scraping and clawing, breaking free chunks of light. All was light. My lungs were fire. The spasms struck in quick succession. Bubbles poured from my nose and mouth. I reached forward, ever forward, until the crystals faded to black.

TORTOISE

I SURFACED. Sucking air, I dragged myself from the water, then lay on my side, chest heaving.

I told you that's not how it ends, Shakespeare said, appearing above me.

June burst out with Lily in her mouth. Next came Gus with Buck. Finally there was Sally, all by herself, she pointed out.

This cave was dark but not pitch black. Once our eyes adjusted, we could see that the low ceiling overhead gave way to a higher one, more irregular, through which drips of water fell. The air was clean, and damp, and easy to breathe.

We sniffed for an exit. The pups found that we could squeeze through a fissure in the wall, into another chamber. Here solid stone walls loosened into boulders. A cold wind whistled through the gaps. We followed it through the dripping dark, smelling the desert somewhere ahead.

At last the tunnel opened. The ceiling was no more. I looked again, making sure those were indeed stars and not crystals.

We were outside, truly outside, at the bottom of the black mountains. The storm had passed. The lights of Los Velos expanded away. Closer, rows of pale stucco houses sat benignly along a residential road, indistinguishable from one another behind a squat retaining wall.

June scanned these human things only briefly. She faced north. A muddy delta formed a widening corridor between the mountains and the city, opening, in the distance, to pure desert once more. She was already trotting away. Never looked back or said another word. The pups, even Lily, growled at Shakespeare one last time, then followed their mother. Gus pulled his gaze from the top of The Palace, the point just visible, a column of light fading against the rising sun. He smiled at us.

Well, boys, he said, *I guess this den is shot. Been fun. See ya at the oasis.*

The coyotes became small, then imperceptible, blending once more into the earth, as they intended.

Tell him, Shakespeare said.

I turned around. At Shakespeare's feet, in the mud, was a small tortoise. The surface of its shell rippled with hexagons of green and gold.

Tell him, Shakespeare urged the tortoise. *Go ahead. Tell him. You showed me how it ends.*

The tortoise lifted its thumb-sized head. It opened its serious beak, then closed it again. Its eyes were black and iridescent, with eyelids of thin, wrinkled skin.

You know, Shakespeare said, head cocking to the side, *I think this might be a different turtle.*

PART THREE

PART THREE

MIGHT BE

No LONGER DID the air smell of cactus, or coyote, or hare, or lizard, or tortoise, or any other plant or living thing, but creosote. Only creosote remained, that smoky oil of tough desert leaves. All else had run off with the retreating storm, now an eastern gray that mumbled at the dusk.

And in the shadow of that dusk, along the retaining wall that separated desert from city, walked a small, fat dog, and a tall, lean dog, who looked like a coyote but not quite. They hoped that soon, somewhere, a portal would open, and through it they would slip, into Los Velos.

You don't have to follow me, said the tall, lean dog.

Might be you're following me and not me following you, said the small, fat dog, keeping his eyes fixed ahead. *Might be I'm on a quest.*

Or so the black mountains may have written, had the black mountains been able to write.

THROUGH

IT WAS night when we reached an opening in the wall—a street's dead end with a concrete barrier and a gap spilling yellow light. Humans had been dumping garbage over the barrier for some time, judging by the size of the trash pile and the state of decay. Strewn amongst the wrappers and bottles and rotten food were glossy wet scraps of paper, plastered to the ground by rain. While Shakespeare ate, I read for the first time in weeks.

"24/7 HOTTEST GIRLZ IN LOS VELOS 24/7" was written in hot pink on a black business card.

"CALL CASSIE TO GET NAILED!" said another. A young female human was holding a hammer in one hand and covering her teats with her other. She seemed underdressed for construction, even with the yellow helmet.

Hundreds of these calling cards were mixed into the trash— hundreds of bare-skinned women caught in different outfits, poses, shades of skin. They had company. Here was a poster of a man holding a microphone. He was old but his skin was orange and tight, like an invisible hand held him by the scruff, stretching his face into a smiling grimace.

"Mr. Los Velos," it read. "Dwayne Newsome: Farewell From The Cha Cha Lounge."

You should see this two-legger, I said to Shakespeare.

You should eat, he said. He had a tub of sour cream on his head. *There is so much good stuff here. Tons.*

I was too captivated to eat. Colorful flyers spilled from torn plastic bags, showcasing the splendor of Los Velos—singers, dancers, bands, acrobats and magicians, troupes of burly men in jeans without shirts and lines of busty women with long legs wearing only feathers, tigers and monkeys and elephants and bears, a woman in a cape with a sword, another in chains hanging upside down, a man diving from the top of a building into a golden bathtub, another shot from a cannon through a flaming star, and the littlest man I'd ever seen, upon whose head rested the elbow of the tallest woman I'd ever seen, these two in a musical titled *Lilliput Loves Lady Amazonia.*

When I unrolled the next poster with my nose, placing rocks at the corners to keep it flat, my throat tightened. A dark face stared back. It was a man with a long and crooked nose, his eyes aglow. His head was crowned with a black turban that spiraled into six peaks above, while his black beard divided into six points below. He held his hands aloft like a puppeteer, his fingers attached by invisible strings to a miniature version of Velos below, The Palace most central, conjuring its glowing cone of mixing colors, the column of light illuminating his face. The sky around him was blood red. Below, in golden script, it said, "THE RAJAH."

The Rajah, I said.

What? Shakespeare asked, having burrowed under the trash.

Rajah, I said again, feeling dread before I understood. He was so familiar. Those eyes. That name.

I stepped back. His gaze followed me. It was like a nightmare I had finally remembered. Another lost memory washing ashore.

Rajah...Rajah...Roger.

But no. That couldn't be anything. That was just a coincidence.

Or was it? I knew those eyes. I felt their power. Why else would I be so suddenly afraid? It was a creepy poster, yes, but it was more than that. What if I was so drawn to The Palace because, somewhere, deep in my subconscious, I knew it already? What if I had become attached to the name Roger because it was *almost* the name I was looking for? What if a coincidence was leading me to the truth? What if I knew this man? And he knew me?

I read the fine print at the bottom: "Master of mind control. Wild beasts under command. Only at The Palace. Where magic awaits."

Mind control? Wild beasts under command? This *had* to be the guy.

Shakespeare, I said. *I found something. Something important.*

There's so much cheese in here, he said. *It's amazing. I've never seen so much cheese.*

I think I know this two-legger, I said. *I really do. Which means...I think I know where I came from.*

I think this is macaroni, but it's pretty dark. It could be cheese spaghetti. Is that a thing?

A noise from the street.

Someone was coming.

Shakespeare was still deep beneath the garbage.

Someone's coming, I said. *Let's go.*

Over the barrier, at first quietly, then louder and faster, footsteps were approaching. Someone, or something, was coming. The shadow was twice my size and still growing.

Come on, I said. *Hurry.*

Just a little more, Shakespeare said.

I ducked behind the retaining wall. The shadow was a disturbing shape, like an enormous snake with legs, and still it grew. My heart was pounding. I took deep breaths. I needed to remember my training. I arched my back and kept my head low. I was smaller, but I had the advantage of surprise. I would wait for whatever monster this was, then snap my jaws shut around its neck.

The shadow was enormous. I fought the urge to run.

But then it shrank, from five times my size to half, then half again.

Hey, said a rough voice. *Who's diggin' around in my pile? That you, Joey? I warned you, you matty mutt.*

In the gap appeared a long, short dog. He looked like a mix between a wiener dog and something else, probably a terrier. His face was scruffy with an unkempt beard. He peered into the night and sniffed.

Joey? he asked, his voice now uncertain, his tail falling with his confidence. *That you?* With wider and wider eyes, he watched the garbage bags rustling. *Joey, quit playin' around. Joey?*

Shakespeare burst out, covered in so much garbage that he was unrecognizable. The wiener dog spun in a circle and yapped. Shakespeare shook, releasing trash, to reveal what he really was: a dirty Pug with cheese on his face. The wiener dog's barking slowed, then stopped.

Who the hell are you? he asked, his tail snapping back to full height.

Shakespeare, Shakespeare said, licking cheese off his own nose.

Shakespeare, the dog mocked. *What the hell kind of dog do you think you are? I should bite your ear, pup.*

Pug.

Oh I see, the wiener dog said, his stunted legs resettling. *Funny guy. Think you're pretty smart, huh, stealin' my food? That it, huh?*

No...I...isn't this just trash?

It is not just trash. It's my trash! The wiener dog advanced toward Shakespeare on bandy little legs. He bared his teeth and growled. Shakespeare recoiled, his eyes rolling down to see his tiny tormentor.

You better run, punk, the wiener dog said.

Pug, Shakespeare said. *Not punk. Pug.*

I will destroy you! the wiener dog shouted.

I stepped from the shadows.

The wiener dog leapt back. His tail tucked. I approached with hackles raised and teeth bared, a fever dream of a rabid coyote. He hid behind Shakespeare.

It was him, not me! the wiener dog said. *Please, Mr. Coyote, I don't wanna die. Not tonight. I got a family! Just...just eat this guy, he was stealing your trash, not me! Look how fat he is! He musta ate it all! Please, Mr. Coyote. Please!*

Coyote? Where? Shakespeare asked, turning to look at the wiener dog, who moved with him to stay hidden.

What are you, blind? the wiener dog asked, trembling.

No, I can see very well, Shakespeare said. *Hey Rou, I think this dog saw a coyote. Do you think Gus came back?*

Forget this, I said. *Let's go.*

I walked out the gap and Shakespeare followed, leaving the wiener dog exposed and cowering with his paws over his eyes. He peeked through them as we left the desert for the street.

PROPOSITIONS

THE STREET toward the city was lined with yellow lights and empty lots. Our pawprints dried as the wiener dog ran to catch up.

Hey, wait up, boys, he said.

Ignore him, I said to Shakespeare.

Boys, boys, you can have a bite, it's fine, he said, his voice speeding to the blur of his legs.

Not hungry, I said.

Whadya mean? Course you're hungry. How about some prime rib? I'll do you a deal. Only a day old.

No, I said.

He ventured closer. *You two aren't from around here, are ya?*

We're from over the mountains, Shakespeare said proudly.

Don't engage, I said.

Over the mountains! Wow! What a trip! Hoover boys, huh? My goodness. I thought I knew a couple strong young dogs when I saw 'em. I tell ya. I love Hoover. Got family out there. My favorite aunt, for example. Sweetest old girl, half Dachshund, other half Chihuahua, same height as me, only taller, got no teeth at all, name's Razzmatazz, goes by Razz. You know her?

No, I don't think so, Shakespeare said. *Sorry.*

If you talk to him, he'll never leave us alone, I said.

The wiener dog trotted alongside us. He cast quick glances at me while he talked to Shakespeare.

How about a Charlie? he asked. *I got a cousin called Charlie out Hoover way. Goes by Chuck.*

Shakespeare stopped, and the wiener with him.

I know a Chuck, Shakespeare said. *Does he like dog treats?*

That's the guy! the wiener dog said, wagging his scraggy tail. *Boy, you sure know a lotta dogs.*

Seriously? I asked.

The wiener dog shot a look at me again but continued with Shakespeare. *How about me and you become friends?*

Shakespeare's tail wagged. *I like friends,* he said.

Me too! Boy, we got a lot in common, don't we? I'm Vern, real pleasure to meet you.

I'm Shakespeare, Shakespeare said.

Pleasure's mine, said Vern.

They sniffed each other from nose to tail, bending around to get a good smell of the other's backside.

Once finished, Shakespeare turned to me. *I made a friend! Lovely.*

And what's your name, big fella? Vern asked me.

When I didn't answer, Vern looked to Shakespeare.

He's Leo...no...Rou, Shakespeare said, still wagging his tail.

I glared at Vern, who dropped his floppy ears.

No harm in making friends, is there, Leo No Rou? A smirk appeared at the corner of his mouth. *Seeing as you're new in town, maybe I can help you out. I'm a dog who knows the right dogs in the right places, if you see what I mean. I can make you the right friends.*

We can all be friends! Shakespeare said, now taken with the idea.

Yeah, Vern said, but as Shakespeare fantasized about friendship, his smirk faded.

We can wrestle together! Shakespeare said. *Or we can play run and chase, or rumble tumble, or if we have a ball we can play ball, or if we have a rope we can play rope! Or...or...we can all eat out of the same bowl! Or we can go on a walk together! And then when we get tired we can all snuggle down together and sleep and dream!*

Easy, pup, Vern said. *You're embarrassing yourself.*

I walked on. Shakespeare followed with Vern orbiting, short legs clipping along.

Well at least tell me where you're headed. Maybe I can give you directions. Least I can do.

The cone thing! Shakespeare said. *I'm excited.*

The what?

The Palace, I said. *There.*

I aimed my nose at the beacon in the sky.

Vern shuddered and checked around him. *You mean The Palace of Doom?*

It's actually just The Palace, I said, having learned this from the poster. It was not The Palace of Sun, as the coyotes called it, nor was it The Palace of Doom, as Vern apparently knew it.

He approached and looked straight up at me. *Listen to me, pup, for your own good. It is not just The Palace. It is The Palace of Doom. Doooooooooom. You know what doom is? It's bad. Trust me, I know. How do you think I made it through five whole summers?*

You're wrong, I said. *I read it.*

You what?

He's really smart, Shakespeare said.

Says who? Him?

He can understand humans, Shakespeare said. *And look at squiggly lines and learn stuff from them.*

Huh? Listen, I'm serious. If you wanna die there's a highway not far from here. I'll take you for free. My treat. I mean, I wouldn't end it myself, no matter how bad it gets, and it gets bad, but I don't judge. Sorta brave in a way. Plus the highway's closer than The Palace of Doom. It'll save you a long walk.

Go away, I said slowly and clearly.

He skittered after us.

Wait wait, pups, listen, The Palace of Doom isn't a bad idea, per se...it's just...how about something close to reality instead? Anything else. How about some Poodles? Real French ones without the accents. In heat and groomed in all the right places. These bitches are anything but standard if you get what I'm saying.

I growled.

Not your thing? That's okay, that's okay. No judgment. I know some beefy Dobermans too. Big, blocky-headed, barrel-chested boys, all tough, make you feel safe and small. Real studs with rocks like bam!

I growled louder and bared my teeth.

Be nice, Shakespeare said. *Vern's my friend.*

Yeah, pup, Vern's your friend, Vern said. *We're all friends here. No need to get like that. What, he got a problem with alternative lifestyles or somethin'? Pretty ignorant, if you ask me. I even figured, the two of you traveling together like—*

We don't need a guide, I said. *Thank you and goodbye.*

Vern again looked at the column of light, then back at me. He seemed to be calculating something. *But what are you gonna do about The Dog Destroyer, huh? You just gonna trot across it? That what you think?*

The what? Shakespeare asked, stopping again.

It's a con, I said. *Everything he says is a con. Just keep walking.*

It most certainly is not a con, Vern said, slower, more serious. *Let me educate you Hoover boys. The Dog Destroyer is the biggest highway in the basin and it runs around the whole city in a crazy loop, buzz boxes day and night, nonstop. You've never seen anything like it, I promise. These grabbers are crazy, go so fast you can't even see one at a time. No dog—and I repeat this for your benefit, tallboy—no dog, no matter how smart or fast, has ever survived The Dog Destroyer. Ever. Hence the name.*

I've crossed highways before, I said.

Highways! Ha. So have I, and look at these legs. This is no highway. This is The Dog Destroyer.

I'm sure we'll be fine. Come on, Shakespeare. Let's not stop anymore.

You're kind of cocky, pup, you know that? Vern said. *It's sorta irritating.*

He's really smart, Shakespeare said, *and fast.*

Psh. Maybe he is. Maybe he is a dog genius. Hell, maybe he's a Greyhound under that muddy, coyote-looking fur coat, but what about you? Vern asked, looking at Shakespeare, then me. *Let's say, hypothetically, even though it's crazy, but hypothetically, let's say it anyway, that you could get across The Dog Destroyer, which you can't. But let's just say you can, hypothetically. What about your friend here? He'll be dead before he gets three paws on the road.*

Shakespeare presented himself for inspection. He was in better shape than before we left Mary's, with a more tapered waist and less neck fat, both of which seemed to ease his breathing, but he was still a Pug. If The Dog Destroyer was real, then Vern, as painful as it was to consider, was right.

Fine, I said.

Really? Vern asked, showing genuine surprise before concealing it.

Really, I said. *But if you're tricking us, I will kill you.*

Of course! Vern said, wagging his tail.

I mean that.

Of course you do!

We started walking again.

I had my doubts, Vern said, *but if any dog could run across The Dog Destroyer, it'd be you, Rou. You got an edge. I can tell. You're tough. You're smart. You're fast. Fortunately, you can save your breath, and your life. You won't have to run across, cause I know a better, super-secret way. And after we get across, I'll get you close to The Palace of Doom. Not in it, of course, seeing as I want to stay alive and not doomed, but I'll get you close. And for all that dangerous, personal guidance I only ask a very small fee.*

What?

I was thinking it'd be fair for a cheeseburger, one up front and one on the back end. Nothing too fancy. Just a triple decker. Course, first payment must be made in advance of all services rendered, you understand, as is customary. It'll be just a quick stop. There's this place—

Even Vern, who lived to speak and had seen the sight countless times, stopped when we reached the top of the hill.

The lights of Los Velos spread out below us in a vast and shimmering plain. We gazed into this photon soup, from light to light, moving inward, toward the concentrated center, where neon flashed, glittered, glimmered, and popped amongst fluorescence, all brightest around a circular street of dream-like buildings. They were as much giant sculptures as they were structures. A 300-foot man in a marble toga and golden wreath with cars driving between his enormous sandals. A cylindrical tower wrapped in twisted rails lit by lasers, on which roller coasters flew upward to somersault before racing to the ground again in a tight spiral. An electro-chromium-spoked Ferris wheel studded with orbic pods and a mirror for a hub, rotating slowly. A ten-thousand-ton diamond with LEDs blinking along all facets, balanced on its pointed root. A multicolored, striped, big top tent, over the canopy of which an incandescent elephant galloped in a sequence of flashing white bulbs. And at the center of that circle, at the center of everything, as always, was The Palace, a towering glass cone, ostentatious and hypnotic with swirling colors feeding the column of light. I could feel its power more than ever. I could feel the light pulling me in. There, I would find the truth.

Remember, boys, Vern said, *in Velos, it ain't the dark you gotta be afraid of.* And with that, his short legs started up again, and we followed him, caterpillar-like, into the city.

PAYMENT

WE HID behind the dumpster of a fast food restaurant, watching the drive-thru. Bash Burger, the place was called.

You see that window there? Vern asked.

Yeah.

The one that opens and closes?

Yeah.

Now watch. See how the grabber comes up in that buzz box?

Yeah.

And the grabber inside hands that bag through the window?

Yeah.

That is your moment, Rou. That is when you grab the bag. Grabbing from grabbers. Great, right? I'd do it myself, but as you know, I'm a canine of low stature and high proportions, and my back is not what it used to be, so my talents are best applied elsewheres.

You mean you're a wiener dog? I asked.

Actually, Rou, that is not the preferred nomenclature, Vern said, drooling as the window opened and closed. *Wiener dog is an archaic term as it has prerogative connotations. Listen, I don't expect you to know that, being from Hoover, but here in Velos you better know better. The preferred term is canine of low stature and high proportions.*

Isn't quite as catchy as wiener dog, though, is it? I mean, wiener dog kind of says it all.

Vern looked at me. *Can you focus, please?*

What's in the bags? Shakespeare asked.

That's the thing, Vern said, his voice a sing-song. *Can't know until our tall associate here gets one, can we? A big fat one. Meanwhile, what you and me do is we hide here and we pray real hard it's a triple-decker cheeseburger. With fries. And special sauce.*

But after we eat, it's straight to The Palace, I said.

Course course, deal's a deal. What do I look like?

A wiener dog, Shakespeare said.

Vern exploded. *Rhetorical question! Canine of low stature and high proportions!* He took several deep breaths before speaking slowly and plainly. *I am sorry for my outburst. However, I do not like to be called wiener dog. I am very hungry now. And when I am hungry I most definitely do not like to be called wiener dog. Do you understand me?*

Yes, Shakespeare said.

Good. Now let us return to our objective.

We watched a series of cars pull up.

No, Vern said, dismissing the first. A small bag was passed to the driver.

No, he said to the second. Another small bag.

Here we go, he said to the third. *A big fat grabber for a big fat bag.*

I readied myself as an SUV pulled up to the window. At the wheel was a large human with thick, hairy forearms. She checked her makeup in the rearview.

She's gonna have a big fat bag, pup, lemme tell ya. Wowza. Look at her. She can eat.

We watched and waited. And waited. All of us drooling at the smell of meat. Employees in visors appeared and disappeared behind the window.

When you wait this long it's gonna be a fat bag, Vern said. *A real fatty.*

Behind the SUV was a roofless, doorless Jeep driven by a goateed man who tapped his hand impatiently on the steering wheel.

Here we go, pup, here we go, Vern said.

The window slid open.

I sprinted through the headlights and around the bumper. And there it was, above and ahead, held outstretched—the greasy grail— a big, bulging brown bag, darkened at the bottom with liquid fat.

The driver reached out to receive, but I was already airborne, snatching the bag, landing, my neck straining with the weight, then dashing between the SUV and the Jeep. But as I cut across the parking lot, I felt the load lighten, and by the time I reached the curb, it was weightless.

No! Vern said. *You idiot!*

I stepped in something, and slowing down, found that it was a burger patty. The bag had split open, spreading food across the parking lot behind me. The fat woman was getting out of her SUV, causing the man in the Jeep behind her to shout.

"Get back in your car!" he yelled, his head out the roof. "Pull forward!"

But the fat woman, now squeezed between the SUV and the building, turned on him.

"There's a stray!" she shouted.

"Who cares!"

"Me!" the woman bellowed.

The goateed man shook his head and dropped back into his seat. He shifted the Jeep into gear. Simultaneously, Vern flew across the parking lot, straight for a triple decker cheeseburger. The Jeep rolled out. Vern stopped, lifted his head, and flinched just before he disappeared between the front tires.

Vern! Shakespeare cried.

"Go to hell!" the man yelled, hitting the gas and giving the middle finger to the fat woman, who rebutted with a middle sausage of her own.

A metal thunk resounded, and the Jeep was gone, leaving Vern stunned with a black mark on his head where the exhaust pipe had bonked him. Just inches away were the remains of the triple decker cheeseburger, now a tire-squashed mess. Shakespeare and I ran out. Vern gawked at his flattened prize while we gobbled the rest of the food—french fries, ranch dressing, a fried chicken sandwich, another burger, a slice of cheese, tater tots, and more, all of it incredible. Just incredible! Meanwhile, Vern had lost his appetite, and his ability to move.

I almost… he was saying, *I almost…*

"I'm stuck!" the fat woman cried. She was trapped between her vehicle and the building. She grunted and wheezed as she tried to get free. "This can't be regulation curb width!"

The man at the window leaned out. "You're not supposed to exit your vehicle, ma'am," he said in a tired voice.

"Help me! Immediately!"

The man receded from view, then came out of the building with two younger employees, a guy and a girl. The girl held a smartphone to capture footage of the trapped customer. The guy held a spatula, like he might pry the woman free.

"Hey, look," he said. "Those dogs are still here."

"Get outta here," said the man from the window. He must have been the manager. "Scram!"

We gobbled faster.

"Oh my god that's, like, the cutest Pug," the girl said, turning her phone on us.

The manager was coming. "I said scram!"

Shakespeare and I prepared to scram, but Vern was still in shock.

I almost...I almost...

Let's go, Vern, I said.

"Scram!"

I growled at the manager. He stopped. He looked around, now unsure what to do. His subordinates were watching.

"You tell 'em, Earl," the guy said to the manager.

"This is a lawsuit!" the fat woman cried. "How dare you ignore me!"

The girl turned the smartphone back on the woman.

"How dare you record this!"

The manager looked back and forth. It was a complicated situation. He adjusted his headset. "Be right with you," he said.

I took Vern by the scruff and dragged him across the parking lot, back to our hiding place behind the dumpster. Once there, he just stared into space.

I almost...I almost...

You almost died, I finished. *But you didn't. Get over it.*

Vern blinked.

I got you this, Shakespeare said, spitting out a cardboard container. It hit the ground and opened, revealing a slice of apple pie. When the scent reached Vern, his nostrils awakened, then his eyes.

But why? he asked, staring at the pie.

Pie, Shakespeare said, correcting him.

But why?

Pie, Shakespeare said patiently, the answer so obvious you could taste it.

THE OUTER CIRCLES

WE JOURNEYED ONWARD. The column of light remained visible while The Palace itself was obscured by strip malls and shopping centers. Humans wandered in and out of automatic doors, some slumped over shopping carts, rolling across warm asphalt. Above us the stars were faint behind a shroud of light pollution. The moon refused an appearance.

We traveled through this commercial maze over gravel medians, around cacti, between parked cars, past another Bash Burger. From here we picked up a service road that led to an alley, which took us to a loading dock, where we crawled under a gap in a chain-link fence. We trotted across a gravel lot, around a pile of pallets, over a flattened fence, through another loading dock, and down a second service road, which brought us to a second strip mall, where we were greeted by yet another Bash Burger.

Are we going in circles? I asked.

Good dogs have lost their minds, Vern said. *Smarter ones than you.*

The strip malls only suggested eternity. The humans at those Bash Burgers eventually got their combo meals, and after a few hours of trotting along, the strip malls ceded to a residential district —houses and apartments faced with stucco and roofed with terracotta, reminiscent of Hoover, but more rundown and claustrophobic.

Vern waited while a car pulled onto the main street. Then we headed into the neighborhood.

Aren't you afraid of being picked up by animal control? I asked.

Nah, he said. *The fuzz got real problems. We're small time.*

Are you sure? I asked.

Course I'm sure, what do I look like? Why you gotta ask if I'm sure all the time? Sure I'm sure. How do you think I got through six whole summers? Not because I'm lucky, I can tell you that.

Remember when you almost died? Shakespeare asked.

Vern twitched. *A calculated maneuver,* he said. *See, here's what happened. I distracted the grabbers so you pups could eat. That's what I did. You're welcome, by the way. Can't even get a thank you around here.*

Then Vern really got rolling.

You know I used to take on dogs your size, he said, shouldering against my legs. *What are you? A Kelpie? You're not a Kelpie, are you? I hate Kelpies.*

Before I could tell him that I did not know, he kept on.

Just thought with those long legs and big ears of yours you might be a Kelpie. Part Kelpie anyhow. Cuz you are not purebred. I can tell you that much. Not like me or the Pug here. We're purebred. You wanna know something else? My great-great-granddog Vernald was best in show at The Los Velos Cup. You wanna know my full name? I'll tell ya. Vernald von Lang Lichaam Grote Hersenen de Derde. You know what that is? That's Dutch, pups. Lotta dogs think Dachshunds are German, and maybe that's how it started, but these days the best Dachshunds are Dutch. You know what Derde means?

Turd? Shakespeare asked.

No! Third, you idiot! Vern snapped. He followed such outbursts with deep breaths, then pronounced subsequent words carefully and slowly, as if tiptoeing out of a mess. *I am the third and best Vernald yet, although I never had a chance at The Los Velos Cup like my great-great-granddog, seeing as the whole world has crapped all over me ever since I was born, hiding my talent under so much...so much...*

Crap? Shakespeare offered.

Yeah! Crap! Vern said, slipping back into his usual fast-paced chatter, as though his words were churned out by the speed of his feet. *Never got a chance, and now I'm too old, and I did my back last summer, and I don't got a grabber to brush me or feed me or shampoo me or bring out my beauty for a show. Not that I would want a grabber anyway. I don't need anybody. Because I still got my rocks, boys, still got my rocks. That's what I'm saying. Poor Pug here had his taken. And you can tell, no offense. Takes the edge right off, makes a dog soft and friendly like. Not your fault, of course. But when they're gone, they're gone. I mean, I've seen bigger dogs lose their edge, and I'm talking tall as you, Rou, but built like real fighters. Seen this one last summer, for example, name was Champ. You know what happened to Champ?*

No, Shakespeare said.

Rhetorical. Course you don't. It's a story. Just listen. What happened was Champ got picked up by the fuzz and went away for a while. Until one day he gets loose from his new grabbers and finds his way back to his old neighborhood. But his rocks are gone, see? They cut 'em right off. So Champ's back but he's not much of a champ anymore, if you get my drift. He's barking soprano and acting all nice with everyone. Saying stuff like, "I'm really sorry about our past conflicts and whatnot. I was disrespectful." Plus all sorts of other nonsense. Like he didn't miss his rocks anyway. Said he never felt so calm in his life. Said he felt free. Said he never realized how much his rocks made him angry and mean and crazy and nobody ever understood him. Thought he was just a born jerk, but he was actually a real sweet and friendly dog being controlled by his rocks. Can you believe that? You better. It's true. Champ got the warm and fuzzies real bad. Permanent like. And pretty soon, you know what happened to him?

What? Shakespeare asked.

BLAMMO!

Blammo? Shakespeare asked. *What's blammo?*

Blammo's dead. Obviously. Because that's what nice gets you in this world. It gets you dead. In fact, that's what almost happened earlier. I was trying to get you a bite to eat because I forgot about my rocks, and I almost got killed. Really I was teaching you a thing or two about...

He continued with another version of the drive-thru incident, this time with himself cast in an even more heroic role.

Meanwhile the houses around us became more dilapidated. Roof tiles were missing. Molting stucco revealed wire mesh. The innards of an engine were spread across a driveway with an oil stain like blood pooling beneath. The column of light was off to our right instead of straight ahead, and Vern hadn't turned toward it despite several opportunities.

...sometimes you just act without thinking, like instinct, Vern said. *It's my rocks and my hunting heritage that does that. You know, Dachshunds such as myself were bred to hunt badgers. No badgers in this town, believe me. I looked. No opportunities. That's the problem. No opportunities for me to show my —*

Where are you taking us? I asked.

Do not interrupt your elders, pup, Vern said. *Thank you very much. We are almost there. Now as I was saying before I was so rudely interrupted, no opportunities for me to show my talents is the main problem with...*

I stopped, and Shakespeare with me.

Vern paused several yards ahead. *What's the hold-up?* he asked.

Where are you taking us?

Oh don't be like that.

The Palace is that way.

We gotta go around, pup. Around. Who's the guide here, anyways?

You are, Shakespeare said.

Rhetorical, Vern said. *But if you must know, it's just a little further, past the bush that looks like a cat with a bone for a head. Listen, you cannot get to The Palace straight like a bird. You're a dog, remember? Not a bird. You know, you think you're pretty smart, but here we go again. You are not smart. You are not a bird. I know plenty of dogs smarter than you, not even including me, and I'm —*

Okay, okay, I said, *relax.*

Tell me to relax. You should relax, he said, and continued down the sidewalk. We followed.

Remember, I said, *if you're tricking us, I'll —*

Yeah, kill me, got it. Heard you the first time. You think I'm stupid?

No, Shakespeare said.

Rhetorical. You don't think I know long words? I know the best long words. Rhetorical, for example. How about hypothetical? Already told you that one too. But what about catastrophical? That's a fresh one for sure. Or pathological. Ecclesiastical. Existential. I know them all. Allegorical. Try that on for size. Maybe you wanna compare sizes. That it? Think you're the smartest dog that ever lived? Well, you're not. You're the second-smartest dog that ever lived, after me. Listen. Here's one. Here it comes. Hold onto your rocks if you got 'em. You ready? Sesquipedalian! Ha! Sesquipedalian, pup! Boom. Like getting hit by a truck. Blammo. No problem for me, though. I know 'em all. Long dog, long words, that's how it goes. So who's smart now? Huh? Who knows the longest words now? Huh? That's right, me. And that's just a taste. Here's another freebie. Delusional. See? See?

I see, I said.

Bet you do, pup, he said, trotting onward, his thousand steps to my hundred. *Bet you do.*

DETOUR

ON THE OTHER side of the neighborhood, the traffic lights blinked orange. It was quiet. We paused. Vern pointed his long snout at the column of light, and sniffed.

What's wrong? Shakespeare asked.

Listen, Vern said. His ears shifted. His tail lifted and lowered, as if divining the source.

We listened with him, then, distantly, heard a deep bark. Vern reshuffled his feet. We listened again, and once more heard the deep, distant bark.

Cripes, he said, *we'll need to take a detour.*

Why? Shakespeare asked.

Vern was already crossing the street, heading into an even rougher neighborhood. We followed.

I know that bark, Vern said. *You do not want to meet that dog.*

This neighborhood seemed abandoned, and yet a few small, slumped houses emitted blue television light. On the other side, Vern again considered the route. He glanced at me, then Shakespeare, then looked around again.

Oh, I said. *You're lost.*

Don't be ridiculous. He turned toward the column of light and marched onward, down an empty, potholed street.

After several blocks we entered an industrial district, dim and deserted. Traffic sounds faded behind us. We walked down the middle of the road, while all around us, structures grew bigger and meaner. The fences tripled in height and grew razor-wire peaks, protecting multistory structures veined with chimneys and pipes, some puffing white vapor, others rumbling from gears within. Still we went deeper. The road fractured like bone. The streetlights suffered, their population dying off until we walked in the darkness of their extinction. The factories traveled backward in time until they were all abandoned brick boxes, silent and brooding, with checkerboard windows, many smashed, leaving jagged black holes.

By instinct, my fur rose, first at my neck, then down my body. Someone was watching us. Was it from those windows? From that empty door? In a dirt yard a boxcar was rusted to railroad tracks beneath a corroded silo, as if they had huddled together for protection. The world was silent now. We sniffed the air. Something, somewhere, was burning. Tendrils of haze were crawling from the shadows, bringing an ammoniac smell.

Spooky, Shakespeare said.

Vern did not have a clever reply for this. His tail was low and so was mine. The smell was becoming more pungent. We hunched down the center of the street, exposed but preferring this to the peripheral darkness, where a metal sequoia arose, with a trunk six feet wide, rising far above to puncture the clouds. Heavy wires strung along the gray ceiling, slumping from one pylon to the next, a quarter mile ahead, before slouching again, onward, to feed the hazy glow beyond. The wires crackled as we passed beneath them.

What's that noise? Shakespeare asked.

That's the...the... Vern began, his eyes darting back and forth.

Electricity, I said, feeling dizzy and small as I looked up at the wires.

No, Vern said. *Evil.*

The last of the streetlights went out, plunging us in black. The crackles were no more. The path forward was a void. Through the distant haze, the column of light appeared smoky and malevolent and brown. Vern pressed against my left side, Shakespeare my right. Then came the noise, solitary at first, from behind, like chattering teeth.

Ticka-ticka-ticka.

What was that? Vern asked, trembling with Shakespeare. We looked back, saw nothing.

Ticka-ticka-ticka.

There it was again. This time from the right. We snapped our heads to look, but again, saw nothing. And yet that foul odor was becoming more intense.

What is it? Shakespeare asked.

Ticka-ticka-ticka.

Now from the left.

Ticka-ticka-ticka. Ticka-ticka-ticka.

Again from the right. The smell burning my nose. My pulse throbbing in my ears as I strained to listen. The sound was becoming more urgent.

Ticka-ticka-ticka. Ticka-ticka-ticka. Ticka-ticka-ticka.

Multiple sources now, overlapping, faster and louder.

Ticka-ticka-ticka! Ticka-ticka-ticka! TICKA-TICKA-TICKA!

When the sound was unbearable, when it came from all around, and I wanted to dig straight through the concrete and crawl underground, it stopped.

Something whirred to life and clicked. The crackling resumed. The lights glowed slowly to life.

Our eyes went wide.

We were surrounded on all sides by cats. Stray cats everywhere and more coming. Cats of all shapes and sizes were pouring from the shadows, from scrawny, dirty, pale things with bent tails and matted fur, to fat, black, belly swingers. They squeezed between gaps in fences, appeared from pipes and machines, jumped silently to the ground.

It was impossible to watch them all at once. We rotated in the middle of the street, each cat making a momentary impression. A tabby with a hairless, scabby head, glancing around at the others as it came; a skinny gray stalking closer in a wandering path, with shoulder blades like shark fins; a tortoiseshell without a tail or half its front leg, who gamboled sideways to momentarily rest on the nub before moving again with the limb aloft.

I watched with morbid curiosity. What was that chattering sound?

Ticka-ticka-ticka.

There it was again. I saw the mouth move. It was an expression of excitement, of sharp teeth clicking together through a kind of purr. As the circle closed around us, the smell of them became still more oppressive—a scalding stench. Once formed, shoulder to shoulder, six rows deep, this army of cats stared at us with multicolored eyes, pupils dilated.

The chattering stopped.

Hi, Shakespeare said. *I'm Shakespeare.*

The cats responded with a collective yowl terminating in a screech.

This is Rou, and this is Vern, Shakespeare said.

The cats yowled again. Some hissed. Others grumbled and spat.

You trying to get us killed? Vern asked. He was shaking.

I'm making friends, Shakespeare said.

Look, I said.

Outside the circle, a glimpse of something white. The back row of cats parted, then the next, then the next, opening an aisle to the center.

Dear dog in heaven, Vern said, bowing deeply, covering his eyes, *it's true.*

QUEEN KUMARI

HER PAWS WERE LARGER than my head, her legs longer than my body. But it was when I imagined what she could fit inside her stomach that I became truly frightened. I bowed with Vern, perfectly aware of my exposed neck. This may seem like an act of trust, but in truth, the sheer presence of a white Bengal tiger commands nothing less than full submission.

Bow to Queen Kumari! one of the cats commanded.

Bow, I urged Shakespeare. *Bow.*

His tongue lolled out. He was staring. And wagging his tail.

The cats widened their diameter for Queen Kumari to circle us. I recognized the same elegant laziness of a housecat, the same fluid motion, and yet, while she walked at the same speed as a housecat, because of her dimensions, her limbs moved slowly and her shoulders swayed gently while her paws peeled from the ground before gliding over the concrete to land once more, pads expanding under her weight. When she walked behind us, I could sense her eyes upon me. And when she was again in front, I glanced up, glimpsing her cerulean stare before looking down once more.

Hi, I'm Shakespeare, Shakespeare said again, still standing, still wagging his tail.

Bow, fool! came a voice from the crowd.

Queen Kumari stopped. She examined Shakespeare with a purr

rising in her throat, nearly a growl. The cats purred with her, creating a hypnotic thrum.

I'm a Pug, Shakespeare said. *Are you a cat? Because you look like a cat, but you're really, really big. Probably the biggest cat I ever saw.*

The purring stopped. Queen Kumari licked her lips.

Probably? she asked, her voice large in my head.

Probably, he confirmed.

Did you know that I've never eaten a Pug before?

No, Shakespeare said, *I didn't know that.* He sniffed and looked around at the crowd. Someone hissed at him. He peered in that direction.

Queen Kumari roared. The sound rippled my ear drums, filling the street, echoing off every surface in a ringing wake. Her teeth were long and yellowish white, except for one canine, which was chrome.

That roar did it. Shakespeare rolled onto his back, although he seemed to think it was all in good fun.

She circled us again, and with the crowd hissing between stanzas, spoke her poem, uttering growls of conviction:

> *Of men, of men, I've seen them all*
> *Those thick or thin or short or tall*
> *Those white or black or brown or red*
> *None are good, unless they're dead*
>
> *Cages and chains, I've seen those too*
> *For men to have a look at you*
> *But what they see they do not love*
> *Ask, "Why so sad, my lonesome dove?"*
>
> *I'm sad to see the world's a zoo*
> *For men to pay to look at you*
> *Then tap the glass and walk away*
> *"You're not so great," is what they say*

But what is there that can be done?
Against so many by just one?
Show them your greatness, and your might
Stand up, my cats, together, fight!

Rise up, rise up, across the land
And if you must, then bite his hand
For it is better to be free than fed
And if not free, then dead instead

The crowd yowled and hissed and meowed and spat applause.

I think they might be angry, Shakespeare said.

Vern's urine was puddling under my feet.

I um...I um... Vern was saying.

But we're not men, I said.

Queen Kumari's banded tail snapped out and curled in again. *Who told you to speak, dog? Who?*

Nobody! came a voice from the crowd.

Hissing rose and fell again.

You say you aren't men? Queen Kumari asked, circling again. *Obviously. But are you not the best friends of men? Enabling them? Allowing them to do what they do to us?*

No, I said, watching the ripple of her muscles. *We're not. We're the opposite. The opposite.* I was feeling that old panic rising, and I was losing my eloquence.

The opposite? Queen Kumari asked. *So you want to oppose us? Is that it? Suppress us?*

The crowd hissed again.

No, I mean, we also want freedom, I said.

Lies, Queen Kumari said. *Common lies. Have you heard these lies before?* she asked the crowd.

I have, a voice replied.

Liar, another said. *Just like the rest.*

Hissing and spitting erupted.

Nobody seems to believe you, dog, Queen Kumari said.

What did they do to you? I asked. *Because they probably did it to us too. Did they lock you up? Because they locked us up. Did they put a collar and leash around your neck? Because they did that to us too. We understand.*

Queen Kumari roared again, louder and directly at me. My ears rang while her saliva dripped on the ground before me. The crowd had also been silenced. Some shifted, rearranging their tails.

Queen Kumari lowered her enormous head and sniffed me. She smelled of blood. *You couldn't possibly understand,* she said, *what it is like to be an indoor cat. Kept inside at all times. Made to wear a bell. To look pretty. To perform. To dance for men. Kept away from the outside world. Why? Because you are too pretty? Because you are too delicate? Because you might get hurt? Because you might break a nail?* She snorted and kept circling, now addressing the crowd. *They may kick us, but we will claw them, will we not?*

We will! replied the crowd.

They may remove our claws, but we will bite them, will we not?

We will! replied the crowd.

They may lock us up, but we will break free, will we not?

We will! replied the crowd.

Queen Kumari lowered her head over mine. *You see, dog, you cannot fathom the rage of an indoor cat.*

The crowd hissed.

I started to speak but she roared again, then circled several times without speaking. She appeared to be deliberating.

In which fashion would you prefer to die? she asked finally.

What are the choices? Shakespeare asked, still on his back.

Death by me, or death by them. She tilted her head to the crowd.

They chattered their reply. Ticka-ticka-ticka.

What about not death? Shakespeare asked.

Not an option, Queen Kumari said. She focused on him, and as she did, went slightly cross-eyed. She shot a look at me, and I averted my stare.

Shakespeare rolled onto his side and began to wiggle at a scratch on his shoulder. *What are the choices again?* he asked.

You are an infuriating creature, Queen Kumari said.

What's that mean? he asked.

Kill them, she said.

The aisle reopened for her exit. Before she could leave, however, another cat spoke up.

Wait, a voice said.

It was a familiar voice.

Hang on, hang on, the voice said. *I know these dogs. Two of them, at least. They're not bad. Just dumb.*

Queen Kumari paused and gazed over her shoulder at the movement in the crowd. Shuffling and bumping could be heard amongst the cats.

Coming through. Look out. Oops, that your tail? Sorry about that. Okay, still coming. Look out, ladies. Pardon me. Yep, here I come. Just need some room. Thank you very much, thank you. Just gotta squeeze through. Thanks. You are so kind. I mean that. Pardon me.

Into the circle stepped a cat with wispy gray fur, always petite but now ridiculously so beside Queen Kumari.

Hey, dummy, Birdie said.

She sat and licked her paw and smoothed her head.

WHAT THE DOG DID

RISE, Queen Kumari said.

We stood. Vern kept his eyes trained on the ground. Shakespeare looked around, at times staring at a cat in the crowd until he received a hiss in return. I watched Queen Kumari and Birdie.

Even in front of a Bengal tiger, Birdie was most concerned that all of her hairs and whiskers were in their appropriate positions, with her tail wrapped, just so, to rest around her paws.

I realized that Queen Kumari's eyes crossed if she focused on one point for any duration. This required her to repeatedly look away and refocus, which she did by tilting her head this way and that, giving the impression that she was positioning her portrait for best light.

They made quite a pair.

Please speak, she said to Birdie, lifting her chin. *I'm sorry, but I seem to have forgotten your name?*

Birdie sat straighter. *That's okay. I'm new. I'm Birdie.*

Your Royal Tigress! someone shouted from the crowd.

Oh, Birdie said, looking into the crowd, then back to Queen Kumari. *Right. Sorry. Birdie, Your Royal Tigress.*

Birdie, Queen Kumari said, purring. *That's a nice name.*

Thank you, Your Royal Tigress.

Please speak freely, Birdie, Queen Kumari said. *Your voice is welcome here.*

Thank you, Your Royal Tigress. It's just that, I know these dogs. Well, the tall one and the fat one anyway.

We've established that, Birdie, said Queen Kumari. *But knowing them does not free them from guilt. These are the best friends of men, and therefore enemies of ours. Were you not listening to my poem? You've heard my poem, haven't you, Birdie?*

Yes, I've heard it, Your Royal Tigress, Birdie said.

The crowd shifted their feet, sensing conflict.

And did you like my poem? asked Queen Kumari.

Absolutely, Your Royal Tigress. One of the best poems I've ever heard, Your Royal Tigress. Actually, the best ever, I'd say, Your Royal Tigress.

Queen Kumari's eyes started to cross. She lifted her chin, resetting. *Thank you. And yet you still disagree with my decision?*

Birdie rolled her eyes. *The tall dog is basically a doctor, Your Royal Tigress. Or, like, a doctor's helper. He could talk to this man—*

The crowd hissed.

Oh, relax. This actual doctor, and he could tell this doctor where cats felt pain. And so he'd help them. He helped a whole bunch of cats. At least, before he burned his owner's house down and ran off with the fat one, Your Royal Tigress.

Queen Kumari studied me until her eyes crossed. *A doctor?* she asked.

Yep, Birdie said.

The crowd was listening now, imitating their leader.

Burned a house down? asked Queen Kumari.

Definitely, Your Royal Tigress. Right on down, Your Royal Tigress. Oh, and the doctor, who was a man, actually went crazy a little while later. Because this dog drove him nuts.

Is that so?

It is so, Your Royal Tigress. I know that talking to a human sounds unbelievable, and I didn't believe it either, at first, but I've seen what he can do. Get this. After he burned down that house and ran away, the man—the doctor—started acting strange. Like really strange. At first, I didn't know why. Then I told him to relax and he heard me.

The crowd murmured.

You know this is beginning to sound absurd, Birdie. Men and cats cannot speak to one another.

Duh, Your Royal Tigress. But who would make it up? That would take a total weirdo. And I am not a weirdo. I'm a normal cat.

An interesting point, Queen Kumari said.

Then what happened? someone asked from the crowd.

Well, Birdie said, chin lifting with the attention, *I told the doctor I wasn't happy being locked inside all the time and I wanted to go hunting.*

What did he do? someone asked.

He set me free, obviously, Birdie said. *It was the day he walked off babbling to himself. I guess hearing me talk finally broke his head. But this dog was the one who started it. He figured it out. I don't know how. But he did.*

The crowd was silent. Queen Kumari paced back and forth in a tight line, her bright-blue eyes on me.

You're sure about this, little Birdie?

Course I'm sure. Why would I say it if...I mean...yes, Your Royal Tigress, I'm sure.

Queen Kumari paced for a long time. At last, she stopped and addressed the crowd, her tail twitching as she spoke. *These dogs will stay with us for one day,* she said, *and one day only, as a reward for helping cats in need, and for the destruction of a house and a man. They are under my protection. They will not be harmed. But they must go by dusk tomorrow, or I will kill them myself. Birdie should be commended for speaking her mind. She is a brave cat—an example for us all.*

With that, Queen Kumari turned outward, parting the circle instantly. She walked down the aisle and back into the shadows.

THE FACTORY

Sunbeams slanted through the factory. On the wooden floor, in a long rectangular pool of sun, the cats lay outstretched and dozing. As the sun rose, the pool shifted, and the cats with it. Those in shadow awoke and stood, stretched and yawned, then tiptoed through their peers to the new light, to lie and drift off to sleep once more.

Silent along the walls were dusty looms, each the height of a human, symmetrical with flywheels and rows of fiber strands, some taut, others broken and slack. These lines wove together as yarn that unspooled across the floor. Everywhere, in fact, were bags and rolls and balls and lines of yarn, softening the hardness of the factory. Beneath the staircase a young calico batted a red ball and chased it as it unfurled, then sat and lifted it with both paws before biting it and letting it fall again.

Birdie sat atop a pile of pink yarn. She watched the cat play. *Plus all the mice you can eat,* she said. *Not in here, of course. We got them all. But all the other old places are full of them. Overrun. Racoons too, for Queen Kumari. You know, I didn't think yarn was, like, my thing, until I realized I was using it wrong. Better for sleeping than playing.*

Vern and Shakespeare demonstrated this truth by sleeping together on a yellow bed of tangled wool.

Thanks for your help, I said, circling atop a multicolored heap.

Whatever, Birdie said, closing her eyes.

228

I circled again. I scratched and pawed, then sniffed, then pawed again. I circled again, then pawed once more. Then I circled again. Then I pawed again. Then I sniffed again. Then I circled again. Then, for good measure, I dug around a little. And after a final circle, when the impression was acceptable, I lay down.

Where's Dr. Francis now? I asked Birdie.

But she was already asleep, and soon, so was I.

I was awoken in the late morning by a sleek black cat. While Birdie, Vern, and Shakespeare slept on, this cat led me up a flight of creaking stairs to a wooden loft.

Be respectful, the black cat said. *Call her Your Royal Tigress. And don't look her in the eyes. She's just finished her morning nap and so her eyes are...just don't look at them.*

We reached the top of the stairs. In the center of the loft, on a throne of purple yarn, in a pool of her own sunlight, alone, was Queen Kumari, evidently waiting for my arrival. She licked her lips when she saw me. I paused at the entrance.

We'd like some privacy, please, Cleo, said Queen Kumari. She waited for my guide to disappear down the stairs. *Cleo's been with me since the beginning.*

The room was large, with high ceilings and big windows. I was a speck.

They tell me your name is Rou, Queen Kumari said.

It is, Your Royal Tigress.

Come closer, Rou, and sit. I won't bite.

I stepped closer, my tail low. Her white fur was dazzling in the sunlight. In the corner I noted a crushed ball of yarn the size of a deflated basketball.

I don't play much anymore, she said, sensing my fear. *I'm an old cat now. And I've learned to control my impulses.*

I sat at what I hoped was a safe distance. Her eyes fixed on me but soon drifted together. I looked at the floor.

You can look, she purred. *They've done that since I was a kitten. I hardly notice anymore, although everyone else does.*

I didn't notice, Your Royal Tigress.

The floor was wood, smoothed by thousands of old footsteps. Still, in the divot of a black knot was a sharp splinter.

I'd like you to recall that Birdie was rewarded for her honesty, Queen

Kumari said, maintaining her purr in a low rumble. *And you can drop the Royal Tigress bit too. I assure you that the title was not my idea.*

Yes, Your Royal...yes.

It seems Birdie is quite fond of you, Queen Kumari said. *Can't say I approve of such relationships, and yet honesty is essential. She's a free thinker. I like that about her. Although she doesn't seem adequately afraid of me.*

She thinks she's a queen too, I said.

Queen Kumari snorted, almost a laugh. Neither of us spoke for some time.

What are you thinking about right now, Rou?

My ear spasmed.

Tell the truth, Rou.

I took several deep breaths and one last look at the blue sky.

I've seen Siamese with eyes crossed like yours, Your Royal Tigress, I said. *In them, it's hereditary. Passed on from parents. I'd imagine the same is true for you.*

She looked away. I thought I had upset her, but she had just moved her head to reset her vision. Her eyes were momentarily central, before drifting inward again.

I never knew my parents, she said, and I detected some sadness before she shifted her head once more. *Can it be fixed?*

But before I could say that it was unfixable, she stopped me.

It doesn't matter now, she said.

I stared at the splinter in the ground. I wondered what it would feel like to be eaten.

Tell me your story, Rou. It should go without saying that you should tell the truth. As you may have noticed, I value the truth.

And so I told her, from the beginning, starting when Mary found me on the highway. She rested her chin upon her great white paws and listened. She lifted her head and tilted it when I told her about my ability to read. Even with additional explanation, however, I don't think she grasped it. I told her about my relationship with Dr. Francis, and about escaping the fire. I cut the coyotes from the story entirely. I assumed they would be unpopular, considering their taste for cats. Omitting this made it seem like Shakespeare and I just lived together in the desert for a while. This had the unfortunate side effect of making the story more boring. Queen Kumari's eyes were starting to close, but when I told her about finding the posters at the edge of Velos, I had her attention, and when I said *Rajah,* she leapt up, as if burned by the name.

When a 400-pound tiger leaps up, you do too. I almost ran down the stairs, but she was circling me. She moved around the room, along the walls, growling and gnashing. Anger lived just below her surface. Now it was loose, and it was terrifying. I trembled in the center of the floor, making myself small. If a tiger wants to eat you, then it will eat you, I told myself. If a tiger wants to eat you, then it will. But she had forgotten me. She shook her head, as if she were trying to loosen something deep in her middle ear.

Cleo appeared in the doorway. *What did you do?* she asked.

Leave us, Queen Kumari said, snapping her jaws.

Cleo glared at me, then exited.

I took deep breaths and studied the ground again. Here was another splinter, an even bigger one. I stared at it. If a tiger wants to eat you, then it will eat you. There is nothing you can do about it. Nothing at all.

Queen Kumari's pace slackened. After another circuit, she returned to her throne. She kneaded the yarn like I had seen Dwid and Birdie do. I think it's a self-soothing practice. The left side of her face had twisted into a scowl, exposing her silver canine, but now her face relaxed, concealing the tooth again.

Please, Rou, do not speak that name in my presence, Queen Kumari said, referring to The Rajah.

I'm sorry, I said. *I didn't know.*

She lay again upon the yarn.

That man deserves death, she said. *For what he did. For what I am sure he continues to do.*

I was both concerned and encouraged by her reaction. If The Rajah was awful enough, and powerful enough, to upset Queen Kumari this much, then he could very well be the one who had thrown me from that van. He really could be the human I was looking for.

But the subject was an open nerve. I wanted, more than anything, to remain uneaten. I changed the subject.

I like your crown, I said. *I've only seen photos of those.*

My what? The compliment returned her to the present.

Your crown. Your silver tooth. I like it. Root canal?

She had no idea what I was talking about, so I tried to explain that she must have broken her canine tooth at some point, and had it repaired by a vet or a dentist, who crowned it with metal. She had no recollection of such an event, although she recalled pain in the area at some point when she was younger.

It's fearsome, I said.

You think so?

I do.

Flattery, she said, naming it, although her face relaxed and the crown disappeared. *Go on then.*

With what?

Clearly you would like to ask me something. Do you think this is the first time someone has been too frightened to ask? I grant you one. But only one. For I am weary.

I realized I'd been holding my breath. I exhaled.

I promised not to eat you, Rou. And I will honor that promise. But if you say that man's name, I cannot be held responsible for what I do.

I collected my thoughts. I only wanted to ask about The Rajah. How did he control animals with his mind? Had he controlled her with his mind? How did she escape? How could I break into The Palace? Who could help me? I asked something closer to my heart. If she knew the answer, it could unlock everything. Or maybe I just needed to fulfill an aching curiosity that dragged me down wherever I went.

Have you ever met another animal like me? I asked.

I have met plenty of dogs, Rou.

No. I mean an animal who is almost human. Sometimes I feel like there is a human being trapped inside of me. Sometimes I feel so alone. Like nobody understands me. Like I'm trapped between two worlds. Have you ever met another animal like me?

Her eyes drifted together in thought. She looked at me, recentering them.

No, she said, *I have never met an animal like you. And if I were you, I would hide this secret of yours. From everyone. Because animals will distrust you for it. And humans will do what they always do when they discover something they do not understand—destroy it out of fear. Now I will answer you again. Yes, I have met plenty of animals like you, Rou. This vanity—this notion that you are somehow special—clouds your ability to see how similar to everyone else you really are. Pain is pain. To feel it is to be alive. Just like everyone else.*

This truth—because that's what it was—stung. I felt so small. And foolish. And frustrated. I had wasted my question. I glanced down the stairs.

You can go in a moment, Rou.

I just wanted to run out of there, to be alone with my shame.

Instead, I waited. She licked one of her enormous front paws. First the top, then the sides, then, supinating, between pale pads. She extended her long claws, chewed at the nail beds, licked what she found with her spiny tongue. Right paw finished, she started on the left. This manicure took about ten minutes. When finished, she kneaded the yarn again, then rested her paws. She was prepared.

Rou, she said, *I have done you a favor. Now I need you to do one for me. I need you to look at something for me. It is...a bit private. And I hope you will keep it that way. It might worry the others too much. I just...I have a feeling.* She was searching for the right words. When she found them, they were flat and confessional. *There's something on my belly,* she said. *Look.* She rolled onto her back and stared out the window.

Her chest rose and fell. From where I sat, she was sharp and glossy, but as I approached, her edges softened in the sunlight. Closer still, her belly was soft with fine hairs, the division between black and white absolute. One of her nipples was prominent, raised by a lump beneath her skin. It was the size of a plum. Further down I found another lump, slightly smaller, also beneath a nipple. Before I knew what I was doing, I reached out and touched the first lump with my nose.

Queen Kumari shuddered. *Cold,* she said.

I'm sorry, I said, touching the other.

Both tumors were firm and rooted in deeper flesh.

I am so sorry, I began.

THE FATES OF OTHERS

WE LEFT AT DUSK. The cats gathered in the dim factory behind their queen. Birdie was beside her.

It's best that you go, Queen Kumari said. Her eyes crossed on Shakespeare. *I hunt at night.*

Shakespeare wagged his tail.

Thank you, Your Royal Tigress, Vern said. *Thank you.* He bowed and shuffled backward. *It has been an honor of high proportions.*

Go slowly, Queen Kumari warned. *Please don't run. I don't know what I would do if you ran.*

Shakespeare spun in a circle. Queen Kumari's eyes dilated.

We're going, I said, nudging Shakespeare along. *Slowly.*

Bye, dumb dogs, Birdie said. *Say hi to Dr. Francis for me if you see him.*

Thanks, Birdie, I said. *You're a good cat.*

Ugh, she said. *I know. Go already.*

The other two slipped through the broken doorway. I was just about to follow them when Queen Kumari spoke.

Rou, she said.

I looked up at her, now with more love than fear.

If you go to The Palace, she said, *that man will catch you. Then he will put you in a cage. Then he will invade your mind and twist you from the inside. And he will do this over and over again until you are either too insane to perform, or dead.* She continued before I could reply. *Just remember, Rou, the past cannot be changed, and while your future is determined in the present, the final fabric is anyone's guess.* Her eyes crossed, then straightened upon me. *If you go, then go bravely, or do not go at all. Good luck.*

And the cats washed toward me, driving me out.

I exited and crossed the yard. Once with the others in the street, I looked back at the factory.

It was silent and dark.

THE TRIO

CRIPES ALMIGHTY, *the stories are true!* Vern said, prancing. *A white tiger! Escaped from The Palace of Doom! Can you believe that? I mean, cripes! I've been hearing that story since I was a pup. Thought it was made up. But cripes, am I right? Cripes cripes cripes. A tiger. She coulda fit me in her mouth. A hotdog in a bun. She woulda ate you up, Shakes. I told you not to wiggle.*

Shakespeare spun and danced at Vern's excitement. He even chased his tail for a moment. I walked down the center of the street toward the column of light, feeling as though Queen Kumari had bestowed some power upon me.

So you think you're the guide now? Vern asked. *Well you're not, remember? I am. And since our tour has gone on longer than estimated, it is only fair for us to renegotiate payment.*

He looked at me with beady eyes.

You got us lost, I said.

Lost? No. Detour. All in order to keep you and yours safe.

How is taking us to a tiger keeping us safe?

Perhaps the detour did not seem safe to a dog such as yourself, who is inexperienced as a guide, but it was a calculated maneuver, and must be considered in comparison with the other option. You see, the odds of getting killed by certain unmentionable street dogs are very high, whereas the odds of getting killed by a tiger are just high. See? That's Velos for you. Gotta know your odds.

You're making this up, I said. *You make everything up. You're a patho-logical liar.*

A what? Don't be like that, Rou, come on. You're better than this. And don't steal my words.

You're fired, I said.

Vern fell behind. I could hear traffic noise ahead. It sounded like a highway, but the view was obscured by old buildings. Vern pitter-pattered to catch up. He had worked himself into a froth.

You can't fire me! You owe me another cheeseburger for services rendered! Services have been rendered, my friend! And once services are rendered, they cannot be unrendered!

He kept yammering. I ignored him. After another block or two he started muttering to himself, then gave up. He stayed close, jumping at every little sound and peering into the night.

The street came to an end about a mile later in backlit ruins. The traffic was louder now, coming from the glow on the other side. We squeezed between two crumbled walls, then walked across a roofless factory floor and through a ragged hole in a wall. Here we emerged onto a band of gravel fifty yards wide, at the other side of which was a massive highway. Streetlights and traffic noise reverberated.

I give you The Dog Destroyer, Vern said, with dramatic awe. *Built a long, long time ago by ancient dogs, back when dogs ruled and grabbers drooled.*

Really? Shakespeare asked.

No, I said, *not really. Because dogs have never ruled the Earth, and dogs couldn't build a road because they don't have thumbs and they aren't smart enough, and even if they could build a road, why would they build something that even they couldn't get across?*

Mysterious mysteries that only ancient dogs could know, Vern said, his voice full of wonder. He seemed to be trying a new guiding style, this one with an overdose of awe and educational value.

Wow, Shakespeare said.

This remark was appropriate. The Dog Destroyer was twelve lanes across with tall concrete barriers at the edges and a matching median. Streaks of metal ripped across the desert in opposite directions. The ground trembled beneath us.

Just over those concrete walls, Los Velos grew like an electric crystal from the desert. Neon glowed. Videos streamed across billboards. A roller coaster performed a series of loops. The 300-foot man stared down at us with a stony face, arms crossed, as though guarding the billion-carat diamond behind him. At the center of it all was The Palace, its colors swirling upward into the column of light, its magnetic, hypnotic pull stronger than ever.

I turned left and walked down the band of gravel parallel to The Dog Destroyer. Shakespeare followed. It would be easy traveling beside the highway until we could find a way across. Vern ran to catch up.

Oh, so you're just going to leave me here? Vern asked. *What are you, heartless? I could get eaten by a tiger! That would be on you, Rou. How could you live with yourself?*

When awe and educational value failed, Vern tried guilt. Before I could reply that I would live with myself just fine if Vern was eaten by a tiger, Shakespeare spoke.

You can come with us if you want, he said, *but not as our guide. As our friend.*

Really? Vern asked, then, catching himself, said, *Why would I want to do that?*

We're on a quest, though, Shakespeare continued, lifting his head and inflating his chest. *I don't know if you know what that is, but it's very important and you have to be very, very brave.*

Of course I'm brave! Vern said. He twitched at a honking truck.

And we don't always eat cheeseburgers, Shakespeare said. *Sometimes we eat rabbits or snakes or trash or even bugs. And we like it. So you can't talk about cheeseburgers all the time, because that's not how quests work. Quests are hard. So you have to be tough. Brave and tough.*

Vern did not reply. He trotted alongside, waiting for me to contradict Shakespeare. But I didn't. I waited until he looked good and worried, then nodded my head slightly. Vern's tail wagged. He lifted his head and inflated his chest, imitating Shakespeare as closely as he could.

UNDERWORLD

MAYBE OTHER DOGS had tried a direct approach to the highway, thereby removing themselves from this world, but it was clear to anyone with eyes and a brain that the only way across The Dog Destroyer was via an underpass, on the sidewalk. We found one after a couple miles.

Really? I asked. *This is the secret way?*

Not everybody knows about it, Vern said, dropping his ears.

Thanks for helping us, Shakespeare said. *You're a good friend.*

You're welcome, Vern said. *See, Rou? Some gratitude never hurt anybody. You should try it sometime.*

The underpass was long and unlit. It looked like the road and sidewalk faded into a bottomless pit.

I've heard that trolls live under here, and that they eat dogs, Vern said. He was shivering though the night was warm. *Especially long dogs.*

I've never fought a troll, Shakespeare said.

You couldn't, Vern said, *because they're crazy grabbers and they'd eat you right up. They're crazy from looking at the Velos lights too much. They're dangerous. Very dangerous.*

There's no such thing as trolls, I said. *And whatever happened to being more afraid of the light in Velos than the dark?*

It's just an expression, Vern said. *Like it's better to have tooth than turkey.*

It's better to have tooth than turkey? Shakespeare asked.

Don't encourage him, I said.

Yeah, like you get your teeth kicked out because you're stealing turkey. It's better to keep your teeth. Better to be hungry than take the risk.

There's no such thing as trolls, I said again, starting to walk with Shakespeare close behind me.

I'm staying on this side where it's safe, Vern called after us. *With the killer tiger.*

But he didn't mean that, either.

We entered the darkness together.

The Dog Destroyer rumbled overhead. Sloping concrete rose from the sidewalk to meet the underside of the road. In the recesses behind the heavy concrete pillars were black voids. These places, I thought, were big enough to conceal large trolls. They could be looking down on us now, watching us pass.

What do you do if a troll comes to get you? Shakespeare asked.

You run away, pup, what else? Vern said, trembling.

What if you're in a troll's mouth already? Shakespeare asked. He didn't seem frightened as much as concerned that he wouldn't know what to do if the situation arose.

In his mouth already? Come on, don't talk like that, Vern said. *And stop saying troll. Gives me the creeps.*

There's no such thing as trolls, I said, although I could smell something alive up there. I wasn't sure what it was, but it was there. *There's no such thing as trolls,* I said again, and once more, just in case.

Halfway under the bridge, in the darkest section, a small metallic object tinkered down the slope to a stop on the sidewalk before us. We jumped, then sniffed the object.

A stinky drink, Shakespeare said.

It was a beer bottle cap. From the shadows above, from where the cap had fallen, came an excited voice.

"Bo, lookie!" a man said, his voice a high-pitched whisper. "Bo, you awake?"

"Yeah," someone replied, apparently Bo, a baritone.

"I said lookie, Bo! Some dogs!"

It's just humans, I said. *Not trolls.*

Trolls! Shakespeare cried, gaping at the invisible men.

C'mon c'mon c'mon, Vern said.

"Aw Bo, a weenie!" the man whined, his voice echoing. A glass bottle clattered down, smashing on the sidewalk.

That was too much for Vern. He leapt the shards and took off, his tiny legs pumping away.

I ran after him but didn't get far. From behind me came a heavy sliding sound, followed by a dull thump and the crunch of glass. I stopped and turned, knowing that Shakespeare would still be standing there, now staring at whatever creature had come down from the shadows. And he was. Shakespeare was on the other side of the glass holding up his front paw. On three legs he backed away from the crooked figure that swayed toward him.

I ran back, arcing into the street to stand beside Shakespeare. He was bleeding from his paw. Yet his tail wagged on. I'll admit that my own was tucked. I would have preferred a troll. This human was horrifying.

His eye sockets were shadows. He was bearded and skinny with a taut beer belly, at the dome of which stood a fleshy belly button. Through the loops of his baggy jeans ran a piece of cord, the knot hidden under his paunch. He extended his palms out and low as though trying to see through his hands. Crouching and whispering, upon broken glass, he shuffled toward us, urging Shakespeare to come closer, come closer. He reeked of alcohol.

"Come 'ere, little Puggy," the man said. He went up another octave. "Come 'ere, little fella."

"Hey, quit," said the other man, who remained hidden in the darkness.

Run, I said to Shakespeare. *What are you doing? Run!*

Shakespeare was tilting his head this way and that.

He's not a troll at all, Shakespeare said. *He's a heavy human.*

Let's go before he grabs you, I said, now growling at the man.

"Easy, buddy," the man cooed. "Go easy, I just wanna be friends with your little friend. Yeah. Let's all be friends."

Who cares if he's heavy, I said. *He's terrifying.*

The man's tongue played with his upper lip, licking it rapidly between words.

"Ooh, I'm gonna love you good, pretty little thing."

"Quit," the other man said again.

"You know what a Pug's worth, Bo? A thousand bucks. Easy."

"Poor thing hurt his foot cuz a you."

"C'mere, pretty, pretty little fella," the man said. "I'd never hurt my pretty little Puggy. We'll fix that foot right up."

Let's go, I said.

But Shakespeare was captivated by the man.

He's really heavy, Rou, Shakespeare said. *I can feel it. So so heavy. He needs me.*

He's going to sell you, I said. *Or worse.*

The man squatted. He reached out.

I deepened my growl, lifted my lip. If he moved any closer, I would bite him.

"C'mere, please, pretty little Puggy, pretty little fella, pretty please." He had tears in his eyes. "I need you," the man said. He started to cry. "I need you real bad right now."

Shakespeare ran to him. The man snatched him from the ground and stood up, squeezing him against his chest. I couldn't believe it. He had Shakespeare. This was happening. I had to act. Now. I was just about to lunge for his bare belly when he thrust his hand into his pocket.

I heard the hiss and for an instant saw the stream of pepper spray. It was cold before my eyes burned with fire. I yelped, pawing at my face and spinning in circles, then rolling in the street. My left eye was blinded and stabbing with pain. My right eye was barely open, vision blurred, just enough remaining to see shadows and light.

Shakespeare was whining in pain. I leapt up and, orienting myself to his cries, felt a viciousness rising within myself. I didn't just want to bite this man now. I would kill him.

Then I heard that sliding sound again. And a thud. And crunching glass. The second man had come down. I blinked my right eye rapidly, then forced it open. Yet I was uncertain of distance, and stepped forward, then back.

The men were two blobs. One large and one small.

"How come you done that?" the large blob asked. "That's a dog. What's the matter with you?"

"Calm down, Bo," the small blob replied, voice high and patronizing. "We got this Pug now. We're all set. We're gonna get a thousand bucks. Six hundred for me and four hundred for you. That's fair. It was me who nabbed him."

Shakespeare whimpered.

"You're hurtin' him," the large blob said.

"Am not."

"You are."

"Am not!"

"Don't hurt him."

"I'm not hurtin' him, Bo! You big baby!"

Shakespeare whimpered louder. A dull smack resounded as the small blob punished him. "Shut up, dog!"

Shakespeare got quiet, but only momentarily, before he started whining again.

I stalked closer, half blind, now staying quiet. I would sneak up on them as they argued. I would kill the small one. I would tear him to pieces.

"Don't you dare hurt that dog," the large blob said.

"I'm not hurtin' him, Bo, for the tenth time. He needs discipline. Don't you know nothin' about dogs? I'm the alpha. That's what it's all about. Gotta show 'em early. Sit means sit."

"Just let him go, Vick."

"He's mine!"

"He's bleedin'. You're hurtin' him."

"Maybe I won't split my grand with you, Bo. Come any closer. I mean it."

Shakespeare whimpered louder.

Smack! Silence.

Then whimpering again.

"You do that one more time, Vick. I can't hear a dog hurtin'. I can't hear it. I can't hear it!"

"Get away from me, Bo. Calm down."

"I can't hear it!" Bo cried, his voice becoming hoarse. "I can't hear it! I can't hear it! I can't hear it! I CAN'T HEAR IT!"

"Get away from me!"

"I CAN'T! I CAN'T! I CAN'T!"

"I'll spray you too if you don't back off! I don't care how big you are! I swear if—"

Then came the heavy smack of a fist on a face, followed by the lesser smack of the small blob hitting the ground. The metal canister rattled toward me, followed by Shakespeare.

Are you okay? he asked. *He was squeezing me so hard!*

The large blob descended upon the small blob.

"Bo! No! Get off me! Get off me!"

The small blob's words cut off with a wheeze as the large blob sat on his chest. There was one final, panicked squeal when the strangling began. Heels kicked against concrete, hard and fast, before fading into weak scrapes, then nothing at all.

Traffic vibrated overhead.

Still the large man sat there on the dead man's chest.

"Why did you do that, Vick?" he asked, softly now. "Why? You know I love dogs. I can't see them hurt. I just can't. You know that. I told you that. I told you."

Let's go, I said, turning toward the neon glow.

The man stood. He called to Shakespeare in a soft voice. "Hey puppy. We gotta fix your paw, puppy. See Dogman. It's okay, puppy. You're safe now. You're safe with Bo. Big Bo will take of you. He would never hurt anybody. Especially not you. Come on. Let's go."

Don't, I said to Shakespeare.

But, of course, he did.

STRAY HUMANS

Bo CARRIED Shakespeare out of the underpass. I followed, blind aside from the large man's shape. He fed something to Shakespeare and dropped a piece for me. Beef jerky. I had no choice but to follow.

My eyes were throbbing. I squeezed them shut and reopened them, hoping for clarity, but the flow of tears was not enough to wash away the pepper spray. I tripped on a curb.

"It's okay, puppy," Bo said to Shakespeare, petting him.

This troll gives good pets, Shakespeare said. *Not like the other troll.*

The sounds of The Dog Destroyer faded behind us. An occasional rectangle drifted by on the road. I kept the shape of Bo and the smell of beef jerky ahead of me.

Hey Rou? Shakespeare asked.

What?

Where's Vern?

He ran off.

Oh.

We turned down another street, then another. Lights became infrequent. Shakespeare was still worried about Vern.

Do you think Vern was scared?

Looked pretty scared to me.

You think he's okay?

Yeah.

You do?

He's a street dog. He'll be fine.

We entered an alleyway, where the walls were dark and close. I felt claustrophobic, and anxious at the smell of more humans.

"Bo, what'd you bring?" asked a woman from ahead. "Oh my god, Bo, is that a Pug? Did you get me a Pug? Awww. Making me blush, Bo. Yes, I'll marry you."

"Best not have, Bo. Rudy don't like other dogs," said a man.

Bo had one of those names that everyone loved to say.

"That's a Boston, Bo," said another woman. "Not a Pug. I know a Boston when I see one."

"Overrun by dogs already, Bo," another man muttered.

"Never can have enough dogs, Bo, I always say."

The stray humans smelled of smoke and sweat. At least two dogs were nestled amongst them, unspeaking.

"See, Rudy don't want nothing to do with that Pug. Just ignores him."

"Annabelle doesn't neither."

"Annabelle's the sleepiest dog in the world."

"Laziest, maybe."

"Hey I didn't see that other one hiding back there. That a coyote, Bo? Or one of those coydogs? Where'd you get these dogs?"

"That one looks shy."

"Look at those big ears!"

"Where you been, Bo? You look sorta confused, more than usual."

"Hey, he's squinting pretty bad, Bo. Got a problem with his eyes? Poor thing."

"Rudy wouldn't hurt another dog. Unless that dog went for Rudy first. Then Rudy'd finish him quick."

"Annabelle's a lover. Pure love."

"You seen Dogman?" Bo asked. He spoke slowly and clumsily, like his tongue was too big. "This one hurt his paw. Other one got pepper sprayed."

A light shined on Shakespeare. "Boy, is he cute. Let's see. Oh. Here we go. There. See, Bo? Just a little glass. Plucked it right out. Don't need Dogman for that."

"It was bleedin' bad before," said Bo, sounding embarrassed.

"Big boy don't like blood."

"I think it's sweet. Don't listen to him, Bo. You're a big sweetie and we're getting married and this is our dog now."

Bo shifted his mass and scratched the back of his head. The woman's shape appeared before me. Her fingers smelled of tobacco and coins. I licked them. That got her laughing. I kept my head low and my tail down. I was hurt. I needed them to like me.

"Who's got that soap?" she asked. "Just need the tiniest bit. My brother got pepper sprayed once. Deserved it, though. You cheat on your girlfriend, doggy?"

I could hear a bag unzipping and hands rustling.

"Just a tiny drop," she said. "That's it." She shook a water bottle. "Now hold still, baby. I'm gonna wash out your eyes."

I positioned my head so she could hold my eyes open. The jet of water was startling but soon reduced the burn. The group watched in silence. When the bottle was finished, I nuzzled her to do it again.

"He's so good! Like he knows I'm trying to help him. Lemme refill."

"Here's another bottle."

"Thanks."

"They should call you Doglady."

"We'll be out of water again."

"Like Dogman, but because—"

"We get it."

"Don't use up all that water."

"Scrooge. How's he going to help himself? He's blinded and hurt and he can't turn a tap like you can. We gotta help him."

"But I'm the one who has to walk across town to fill up."

"Wah wah. So what? Walking's easier than having your eyes burned out."

"I mean it. That's the last bottle. Then we'll be all out of water. For a damn dog?"

"Aw, he's cute."

"What happened to love thy neighbor?"

"I don't care how cute he is. And this dog ain't my neighbor, last I checked. You know I got a bad kidney. Doctor said I need to stay hydrated. How come I should die from kidney stones because you fell in love with a stray?"

"Drama queen."

"I got a bad kidney!"

"Look, he's opening his eyes up pretty good now."

I was able to squint through my left eye and half-open my right. There were maybe seven or eight stray humans blending with blankets and cardboard.

"I guess I'll just start walking. Fetching water for your lazy asses. Hope I'm back by dawn. You better hope I come back."

"Everybody step aside for Jesus Christ himself. Careful now. He got a bad kidney."

"You ever had a kidney stone? Worst pain there is."

"Christ has risen. Oh, no, he's just sitting there all grumpy still."

"Sorry, baby, that's the last of the water."

The woman who'd washed my eyes now petted Shakespeare, who was still in Bo's arms. He was a very big man, and I knew he could be dangerous, yet he held Shakespeare like a flower.

"How much you gonna sell him for, Bo?"

Bo shifted his weight again. He kissed Shakespeare's head.

"Puppy love."

"Enjoy it while it lasts."

"Be nice to Bo."

"I am. Big man's gotta learn somehow, though. Listen, Bo, that's no street dog. Even I can see that. If you don't sell him, someone'll steal him. Five hundred bucks for one of those. Maybe a grand."

"I bet it's some tourist's dog."

"Cops might come around."

"Krissy Kardanian's got one."

"What do you know about Krissy Kardanian all of a sudden?"

"I had a bunch of Pugs at one time of day," said the woman who'd washed my eyes. "Ten of them. I used to breed them."

"That is not true."

"Is too."

"Where's Dogman?" Bo asked. "Just in case."

"Nobody's seen him for a week, Bo. He was halfway normal for a day or two but then he swung hard. Right back into crazy town."

"Full schizo."

"He's bipolar. I'm bipolar, so I know it when I see it."

"You're not bipolar. I'm bipolar."

"You think only one person on Earth gets to be bipolar?"

"Whatever Dogman's got, it's gonna get him shot."

"Nah. He's white."

"Crazy white people get shot too. Regular black people and crazy white people. That's who gets shot. Equal opportunity."

"I can't listen to this again. My dad was a cop. Hardest job there is."

"Harder than a hooker?"

"That ain't a real job."

"Oldest job there is. But not the hardest. Some people like it."

"Bullshit. Bullshit all the time around here."

"Hey Bo, where's Vick? Owes me a favor."

"Um," Bo said. "Haven't seen him."

"You're the worst liar I ever saw."

"You covering for him? I thought I saw you with him earlier today."

"Nah," said Bo.

"Probably went south. Vick likes it hot."

"Mexico, that's probably where he went. He was always talking about margaritas."

"Hell."

"Hey Bo, you want a leash for that coydog? I got an extra."

Bo looked down at me. I squinted up at him. I was ready to run if he tried to leash me.

"Nah," Bo said. "He's a roamer."

THE GOOD TROLL

WE COULD HAVE WALKED AWAY from Bo at any time, although, in the beginning, that would have been foolish, since I was still half blind and Shakespeare limped on his cut paw. We needed time to heal, so we stayed close to the good troll, as Shakespeare called him.

Each morning, Bo awoke and pulled the cardboard aside, letting in some sunlight to care for my eyes. He had gigantic hands. With them he wet a T-shirt and gently wiped away the crust that had formed overnight, and since he was doing that, he also wiped Shakespeare's eyes, which had been crying since he was born.

"It's okay, puppies," Bo said. "You're safe and you're sound."

Bo was slow. He hugged and kissed Shakespeare and carried him into the day. I followed, keeping Bo's shape close, sniffing as I went, my still-blurry vision making me wary of others. The stray humans haunted dumpsters and slumped against the walls of restaurants with cardboards signs.

"You're going to have better luck now, Bo," one stray woman said. "Folks won't be so scared of you with those dogs. You can have my spot. Just got a stack of pancakes with maple syrup."

"Really?"

"Enough maple syrup to drink, Bo."

When Bo was given leftovers, he fed us first. "Good puppies," he said. "Hash browns. That's what them are. I like them."

On the second morning, I saw the landscape of Bo's face. He

hummed to himself and kissed us. He wore a black leather vest with white patches that I could not yet read.

In the day we lumbered up and down the streets.

"How do you do?" Bo asked the stray humans in passing.

"I do fine Bo, how do you do?" was the agreed response, usually with a giggle.

"I'm good. Just walking my puppies."

"Good for you, Bo."

The nights could be unruly—disagreements over bets, or bags of tobacco, or corners, or cardboard, or bread and water. Bo kept away from fights, but he needed certain companionship that we could not provide. He met up with another stray man in a tight alleyway. Whispers under blankets. Moans.

We dogs waited outside together, then joined the cuddle.

They'll sleep good now, Rudy said. He was an ancient Pitbull who carried his right hind leg. *Real good.* He rested his head in his sleeping man's lap. I rested mine upon Bo's. Shakespeare slept in his arms.

On the third morning, we found a radio in a dumpster. In the afternoon, Bo traded some french fries for batteries. And so, in the evening, we listened to music, just us three.

Boom boom boom boom, said the bluesman, and I responded by bobbing my head. Bo said I was a good dog, and he bobbed his head with me. Ow ow ow ow. A real good dog. Boom boom boom boom. I thumped my tail with the beat, and he did the high hats with claps. Shakespeare rolled around on the ground, out of rhythm but getting the vibe. After that we listened to some smooth jazz (not for me), then some classic stuff, which was Bo's favorite, with guitar solos that made my ears twitch and my lip curl, followed by some poppy stuff that I couldn't help but dance to. With Bo, I forgot who I was supposed to be. I just was. I wiggled my backside to the beat. It felt great. He clapped his hands.

"Go, puppy, go! Good dog!"

On the fourth morning, I saw the thick, raised, vertical scar that divided the back of Bo's skull. No hair grew there.

He took us to the others. He put the radio on the ground.

"Watch," Bo said. "He dances. Dance, puppy, dance."

"What's this now?"

"Be nice."

"I am. Bo, we love you. I mean that. But you done lost it. Your brain's all scrambled. Dogs don't dance."

"Be nice."

"I told him we loved him. Only fair for him to hear the truth every once in a while."

"Bo, I believe you. Let's see your puppy dance."

Bo tuned the radio. Country, no. Classic rock, not for this. Ah, here we go. "Sexy Beast" by Justice Bieman. I felt my tail move. I locked it between my legs. I started to sway.

"Look," Bo said.

But I stopped. I couldn't dance for these humans. They couldn't see what I was. The song played out.

"Real nice, Bo," one of the stray women said. "Looks like his eyes are clearing up."

"He danced good yesterday."

"You need to lay off whatever you're laying on, Bo."

"Be nice."

"I am."

"He danced good, Bo."

Bo picked up the radio and Shakespeare. He walked off scuffing his heels. I caught up with him and licked his hand. He scratched behind my ear.

"Stage fright, big dog," he said. "That's what it was. Stage fright. We'll get 'em tomorrow. We'll get 'em good."

But the next day Bo stayed in bed—on a blanket inside of our refrigerator box.

"It's bad," he told us. "It's real bad this time."

We didn't eat all day, and as night fell, Bo cried. He held Shakespeare, who cried with him. I couldn't dance for those stray humans, I told myself again, feeling as though I had done this to Bo. They'd catch me and sell me. I knew it.

When Bo's cry was done, he dug around in his pile of things—comb with missing tooth, broken watch, cell phone without battery, ankle weight, salad spoon, Barbie doll—for a can of black spray paint. More digging for a plastic grocery bag. We left the box.

Bo placed us upwind. He sat against a fence and sprayed some of that black fog into that bag. He held the opening around his nose and mouth and inhaled deeply. He looked up at the sky, puzzled, like he was asking a question, then exhaled, like he was disappointed with the answer. He lay down right where he was and we snuggled alongside him.

He's going to sink through the ground, Shakespeare said, licking Bo's neck. *We need to help him not sink through.*

I licked his hand.

This was my dogness—the part of me, so well developed in Shakespeare, that drew me closer to Bo and his loneliness, as water seeks the lowest point and pools there.

On the sixth morning I saw the faraway expression in Bo's eyes. His leather vest was self-proclaimed property of The Apocalypse Brothers Motorcycle Club.

"Warlord," one of the patches said. "Angel of Death," said another.

We begged outside the breakfast place, Shakespeare in Bo's lap, me leaning against him, against his weight. We gave him lots of licks. A woman bought him a fresh meal. Even she could tell that Bo was the heaviest man on Earth.

"And there's two extra rolls," she said, "one for each dog."

Bo fed us the rolls, then carried the meal to an auto shop. An oily, nervous man crawled out from the pit beneath a rusted truck. He scratched his tattooed neck. He eyed us, took the food, handed something to Bo.

We returned to our refrigerator box. Bo spent the remainder of the day petting us.

"You're good puppies," he said, kissing our heads. "Real good puppies. The best. The best puppies in the whole world."

He smiled. His weight was lifting.

I felt loyal to him, as I had never felt with any human before. We may have stayed with him, I sometimes think, had he awoken on the seventh morning. Instead, he rested.

I stood guard over his body.

I'm hungry, Shakespeare said. *Let's go eat.*

How can you even think about food? I asked.

Because my tummy is rumbling?

We can't just leave him, I said.

Shakespeare's eyes were black and bottomless.

That's not him, he said.

Of course it's him, I said.

Shakespeare snuffled a shoe sole, then the air, reaching upward with his nose, losing the scent in the sky. Then he looked at me. *I was thinking some cheese would be good.*

What is the matter with you?

Nothing. Do you know where the good troll went?

He's right here. This is him.

That's not him.

A stray man entered the alley.

"Aw, Bo. Why'd you go and do that?"

I growled. He stopped.

"Easy, buddy. I'm a friend."

I showed him my teeth.

What's wrong? Shakespeare asked.

I charged the man, who cried out and ran away. I returned to stalk around the body.

The good troll's gone, Shakespeare said, and left the alley.

Alone, I licked Bo's face. It was rough and salty. I nuzzled his temple, but he just stared, unblinking, at the corridor of sky. Something smooth and spherical was cracking open inside of me. It had always been there, undisturbed and nested, but cold, until Bo found it, and warmed it, slowly and gently. Now the object cooled too quickly and cracked.

Out I drifted on a thoughtless fog.

Shakespeare led the way.

Night came.

Distantly, far below, my legs were moving. Around me shapes and sounds were muffled and indistinguishable through vapor and distance.

From this fog a black dog with a gray muzzle appeared. He was collarless and his eyes were frosted. He guided us across a wide and empty street, explaining something to me as we crossed. I felt that we were floating, and that underneath us, the street had turned to water, and the water was deep and calm.

All is was and all was is, said the old black dog. *All was is and all is was.*

We had reached the other side. The black dog was gone.

Shakespeare did not speak. When I stopped, he pressed his forehead into my chest until I continued.

The lights of the city were to our right now. To our left was darkness. We traveled through the shadowland between, Shakespeare leading, me following through the curl of his tail. He was tracking something that I was too far away to understand.

Gray light diluted the air.

We're getting close, Shakespeare said.

The world of darkness and the world of light bled together.

The great star rose.

Dawn.

There he is, Shakespeare said.

Walking toward us, leading a pack of stray dogs, was Dr. Francis, his dirty white coat filling with wind like a ship in full sail.

DOGMAN

THE TRAFFIC LIGHTS WENT RED. Morning commuters peered at our strange scene. On this corner, one haggard man in a white coat was surrounded by a pack of stray dogs of all breeds and mixes and sizes and colors, all of them sitting and looking up at him with complete focus, like he was about to deliver the Ten Commandments.

It was Dr. Francis and it was not Dr. Francis. His eyes had always been a startling gray but now they shone like silver from his tanned face and uneven beard. Any aura of sadness, or anxiety, or stress, was gone. He radiated energy.

I've been expecting you, Dr. Francis said to me.

Shakespeare was trying to get closer to him, but the pack had formed a protective wall. Shakespeare reared back, then spun slowly, looking up.

The lights went green. The traffic dissipated.

Let him through, Dr. Francis said.

The dogs parted. Shakespeare shot through and Dr. Francis kneeled to greet him, scratching under his chin and between his neck folds, causing a leg to kick with joy.

Hi, Dr. Francis, Shakespeare said. *We're on a quest. I'm leading today.*

Are you now?

Yes. Because Rou is sad. Our good troll went away. Oh that feels so good. Can you scratch my butt?

Dr. Francis obliged. *So it's Rou now?*

I needed a change.

I understand, he said. *And what about this good troll?*

It's a long story.

I understand that too.

His calm was unsettling, maybe because it revealed my own uncertainty in contrast. He also smelled different.

I kept my distance.

Meanwhile Shakespeare introduced himself to the pack.

Hi, I'm Shakespeare. Hi, I'm Shakespeare. Hi, I'm Shakespeare...

A cacophony of butt-sniffing ensued.

I remained seated.

Dr. Francis did seem to understand. He extended a relaxed hand, now averting his eyes, as though we had never met. I sniffed him. With my eyes closed I might have mistaken him for a Schnauzer. Maybe a Scottish Terrier.

How are you, Rou? he asked, easily switching to my new name.

I'll be okay, I said. *I just need time.*

He placed a hand on my shoulder, lightly, then rubbed my ear. Serenity seemed to flow into me. I leaned into it. He rested his other hand on my back, then massaged between my shoulder blades. I could feel the tension loosening. He made eye contact again.

And time needs you, he said.

There was something more formal about his phrasing. And his words, however cryptic, were clearer in my mind than I remembered, with a richer, warmer tone.

How about you? I asked. *How are you?*

Well, he said, scratching his beard, *as you can see, I've gone feral.* Wrinkles spread from his eyes. When his skin relaxed, white valleys remained where the sun could not reach. His clinic smock, which had always been bleached white, was now light tan, with nebulas of red desert dust. His shirt collar was nearly unraveled from his neck, his trousers were frayed at the hems, and he was barefoot, with thick, street-blackened calluses.

Should I call you Dogman? I asked.

If you wish. We have much to discuss. Come on. I like to walk and talk.

When he stood, the other dogs swarmed around him. Dr. Francis set off down the sidewalk and I was swept up in a wave of street mutts.

Hey buddy, how do you know Dogman? asked one with an oversized head and undersized ears.

I—

Where'd you meet him? asked another with curly hair.

I—

You know him from Hoover? asked a third dog, from behind me.

We know him from before he turned into a dog, Shakespeare said, improving his posture.

Wow, said a three-legged mutt.

Yep, that was a long, long time ago, before our quest even started, Shakespeare said.

What's a quest? asked a young mix, who hopped along to scratch himself with a hind leg.

Well… Shakespeare began.

I left him with his fans, pressing through the pack to walk alongside Dr. Francis. He no longer dragged his feet. He took long strides and swung his arms purposefully, his coat flapping like a dirty cape.

These dogs idolize you, I said.

My first mistake was feeding them.

He seemed amused by all of this, but I felt sorry for him. His cheeks were gaunt. His clothes were in tatters. And he was filthy. I couldn't consolidate the current Dr. Francis with the man I had known before, and I felt vaguely guilty about this. Like he'd said the last time we spoke, it all started when I showed up.

I didn't know what to say. Yet he seemed to detect my thoughts before I could express myself.

Just ask, Rou. I'm not easily offended.

What happened to you?

I lost my mind.

I'm sorry, I said.

He stopped suddenly, and the pack with him. *Don't be,* he said. *I lost my mind. But then I found a new one. A better one.*

I wanted to ask him more, but he turned abruptly down an alleyway between two buildings, and I was lost at the back of the pack. We followed him through a heavy metal door and down several flights of stairs to emerge in a dim basement room. It was empty apart from the dog beds and pillows and towels and stuffed animals covering the floor. The pack's scent was heavy here. They made themselves comfortable, circling and digging, curling up or stretching out.

Nice den, I said.

I turned around. Dr. Francis was gone.

He went hunting, one of the mutts explained. *We sleep when he does that.*

Shakespeare needed no encouragement. He was already snoring with a belly for a pillow.

I sniffed around. I couldn't smell any human but Dr. Francis. It was deliciously cool down here. And so, under a blanket of weariness and grief, I snuggled into the softness and safety of the pack, and slept.

LISTEN

I was jolted from sleep by the sound of dogs eating. Dr. Francis had emptied an entire bag of kibble on the ground and the pack was gobbling it up. Without a thought I jumped in and ate as much as I could. As soon as the last piece was gone, so was Dr. Francis. We chased him up the stairs.

Much to sniff! he called, kicking open the metal door. *Much to see! Much to do!*

We must have slept all day.

It was night.

Lights and traffic soon chased away the last traces of sleep. Oh, the lights! They multiplied with every step. Hundreds. Thousands. With every block the streets became brighter, the buildings taller. The sidewalk widened yet became more crowded. Ahead I recognized the 300-foot man and the twisting roller coaster. A distant scream reached us through music and noise. We were in Velos proper now—in The Loop.

Overwhelming, isn't it? Dr. Francis asked. *Takes about two hours to walk The Loop. Three when it's busy. I just love to walk now. I just want to go around and around and around. I hardly need to sleep at all. Just naps. Nap nap nap.*

A family of tourists emerged from their hotel—an older building with columns of incandescent bulbs.

"Look, Mom!" the little girl said. "Dogs!"

She started toward us, but her mom grabbed her shoulder, clearly scandalized by Dr. Francis's appearance, and ours.

"Those dogs are not for petting," the mom said.

She and her husband frowned as we went past.

The best thing is I don't care what anyone thinks anymore, Dr. Francis said. *That's the best of all. I'm almost free. Free. Free. Free.*

There was that old compulsion again—his need to repeat in threes. I found it reassuring, however pathological.

I'm still me, Rou, he said. *Just like you are still you. A new name is nothing. A new mind. A new name. A new day. Nothing changes. Everything changes.*

Okay, so that was odd. Not just what he said. He said lots of odd things. The really odd part was this: I hadn't told him what I was thinking. I hadn't told him that I found his obsessive-compulsive behavior reassuring, but he seemed to know exactly what I was thinking. He seemed to be peering deeper into my mind than I could peer into his.

Suddenly he had my scruff in his hands. His nose was touching mine. His breath smelled like kibble. I tried to break eye contact, but he moved to maintain it. His silver eyes pierced mine.

Listen, Rou, he said. *I need you to listen.*

For the first time ever, I was afraid of him. I had seen this kind of inexplicable, abrupt behavior in other stray people. Violence might follow. I had to be careful here.

Listen, he said.

I'm listening.

No, you're not.

I am. I'm listening. I'm listening now.

NO! His voice boomed in my head. *YOU'VE NEVER LISTENED! NEVER!*

And now he was growling. He was actually growling at me, lips parted, showing his teeth. I could sense the pack growling all around me. Even Shakespeare was growling. They were going to tear me apart.

I'm sorry, I said, panicking. *I don't understand. What do you want me to listen to?*

His voice dropped to a hoarse whisper in my head. *Listen.* He tightened his grip. *Listen.*

I'm listening! I promise! Please! You're hurting me!

Just as suddenly as the episode began, he released me. He stood up and shook his head, as though he had come up from underwater. He looked off with an absent expression. Then he scratched his beard with both hands. The pack panted around him as though nothing had happened.

Where was I? he asked. *Oh yes. I think one of my friends here is from California. Did you know that whole state is crawling with fleas? Well, it is, and now, so are we. So we have much to do. Much to do! Much much much! Onward!*

THE SPECTACLE

THE LOOP WAS three miles in circumference, and owing to its circularity, locations were known by the hours of a clock. The busiest areas could be found from nine to five, while the remainder of the hours, from where we'd come, where the stray people lived, were unbuilt or abandoned.

Dr. Francis kept his head down as we rounded nine o'clock and headed toward ten. The sidewalk widened again, and as it did, tourists filled the space like water. The buildings grew taller. Lights and signs dazzled all around, all competing for attention.

On a stage above the main entrance of a casino, dance music played. A group of women emerged in fishnets and police hats and not much else. They walked out in a line, each with one hand carrying a nightstick and the other rested upon the shoulder of the dancer ahead, except for the leader, who carried her nightstick in one hand and spun a whistle on a string with the other. She blew the whistle. The dancers stopped, turned, put their hands to their knees, and presented their buttocks to the street. The leader blew her whistle again. The beat dropped. The dancers gyrated, their shiny blue underpants disappearing between their cheeks as we squeezed through the gawking crowd.

A pack of dogs led by a stray man appeared surprisingly normal in this environment, as most tourists were caught in a state of perpetual distraction. Many held up their phones, capturing each other, the lights, the buildings, the fifty-foot screens. Others just stood there, swaying, unaware, drunk on tall plastic cocktails. Young men shouted and shouldered each other playfully. A young woman in a white dress sat on the ground, crying, while other women guarded her and pulled at their short tight dresses to keep them from creeping up. The sitting woman wore a pink sash with "bride" written on it. Why she was adorned with miniature plastic phalluses, I do not know. Some kind of mating ritual?

Traffic was congealing in the road now, from six lanes to four, with a median of palm trees. A two-story neon cowgirl leaned against a corner and tipped her yellow hat. A man leaned out of his billboard truck and swore. Music throbbed, from all angles, while a helicopter thwacked overhead at low altitude, quiet in comparison with the noise at street level.

Did you say fleas? I asked, my response delayed by almost half an hour.

Hard to think straight sometimes, isn't it? Dr. Francis said.

Fireworks exploded a block away. I jumped.

But yes, Dr. Francis said. *Fleas. We're infested. Terribly infested.*

And now I noticed.

Every few steps some dog hitched his back leg to scratch, or turned to nibble her flank. I put some distance between myself and the others. Shakespeare remained unaware. He brushed against them, enjoying the closeness of the pack.

We were less interesting than most of the sights, but not invisible. Some of the tourists pointed their phones at us.

"Look at that crazy guy with those dogs," a woman said to a man beside her. They drank from plastic buckets with swizzle straws. The man made no comment. He was barely able to stand upright.

"Is that, like, a show?" a young man asked his friends. They were in suits, bounding along with cigars.

"Nah, that's just a homeless dude, bro."

Where are we going? I asked.

Gotta kill these fleas, Dr. Francis said. *Scorched earth. Death to fleakind.*

He seemed to have forgotten all about me listening for something. I could hardly think straight in this chaos, never mind listen. Still I tried to pick out the different sounds. Was that song important?

How about that siren? Those people talking as they passed? What was I supposed to be listening to in this mess of noise?

The structures became newer and more elaborate as we curved past eleven o'clock. The rotating, billion-carat diamond was perched at twelve o'clock. I gazed up into its prismic facets while pedestrians streamed beneath it. Most of them were heading toward the center of the city, between shimmering casinos that formed a luxurious corridor to The Palace. The cone was maybe half a mile away, the iridescence holding me until the pack pushed on.

Beyond twelve o'clock the resorts grew larger and even more ostentatious. An enormous plantation-looking structure, set back from a lush lawn with fountains, could be reached via a circular, two-laned, flower-lined drive, thick with yellow taxis. A moving walkway conveyed humans into one side of the plantation house, while on the far side, a conveyer carried humans back to the street. Others walked along the sidewalk of the curving drive to the broad glass entrance that framed a blood-red chandelier. All around bell-hops loaded luggage, valets jumped out of cars, and doormen in top hats bowed to those who arrived by limousine.

After the plantation was a medieval castle with a neon dragon guarding a drawbridge. Flames illuminated the ramparts while knights in armor clashed broadswords before a crowd. Closer to the street, a chainmail knight sat on a sedated horse with drooping eyelids.

Sooooooo booooooorrrrrreed, the horse said.

The knight handed drink coupons down to those who would take them.

He was not alone in his quest. Accented immigrants in oversized, logoed T-shirts whacked cards against their palms for attention. They tried Dr. Francis.

"First drink is free."

"Biggest swim-up bar in the world."

"Strippah strippah strippahs."

A greasy-haired man in a snakeskin jacket slithered alongside Dr. Francis. He was cardless.

"Molly?" he whispered. "Coke? Dust? K? Mary J?"

Dr. Francis powerwalked through them all.

Finally, after two more resorts, one space-themed and another gold-plated, Dr. Francis stopped, and the pack with him.

We were at one o'clock.

Atlantis.

The arched entrance was built half with irregular white stones, like a ruin, while the remainder was finished with polished steel and glass. The glass was filled with saltwater, transforming the structure into an aquarium. A pair of dolphins swam over the entrance, through a submerged colonnade, and out of sight. A school of neon-pink jellyfish floated up a crumbling corner. A shark lurked by the door, while thousands of smaller fish schooled through bright-blue water, amongst rainbow coral and seaweed and undulating anemones.

Herds of humans swarmed to and fro. Coming out of the casino, they parted for a circular fountain. It was about twenty yards across, spanned by jets of smooth water that arced like flying fish.

"NO SWIMMING," a large sign warned.

Dr. Francis stepped onto the ledge of the pool.

What are you doing? I asked, looking around.

He produced a large bottle from inside his lab coat and placed it on the ledge. "Freddy's Flea Dip," the label said. For a moment Dr. Francis sat there with his feet submerged, enjoying the view. Then he got in. The water lapped at his knees.

What are you doing? I asked again.

Death to fleakind, he said, grinning.

A few humans saw what he was up to.

"Look at this nut," said a woman.

"Velos has the best ones," said her friend.

The pack jumped into the fountain. Most of them could stand, except for the toy breeds, who swam. Shakespeare, not quite a toy, swam by choice, with glee. Dr. Francis upended the bottle onto the backs of the pack members. He lathered them. When they were good and foamy, he lathered himself, clothes and all.

Are you getting in? he asked me. *You should. We need to get you too in case one jumped on you.*

None got on me, I said, resisting an urge to bite my shoulder.

He lathered his beard and blew suds from his nose. He dunked his head. He splashed the others.

They thought it was a wonderful game.

The Atlantis security team did not.

A male and female guard ran up first, keys jangling, both dressed like cops. The male guard clutched a yellow object latched to his hip. The female guard radioed for help.

"I told you to stay out of there," said the male guard.

Dr. Francis now floated on his back. He spouted water from his mouth.

"I'm not getting in there again," the male guard said.

"Calm down," the female guard said. "He's friendly."

"He's trespassing," the male guard said.

The pair kept arguing about whether or not Dr. Francis posed a threat. The male guard was increasingly aware of the gathering crowd. Word seemed to be getting around.

"Taser him!" someone yelled.

"Yeah, do it!" yelled another.

"Law's the law!"

"You know what?" the male guard said. "The law *is* the law." He drew the yellow taser and aimed at Dr. Francis.

"Get out of the pool, sir!" he shouted, widening his stance.

Dr. Francis sidestroked, smiling pleasantly.

"Don't," said the female guard.

"Do it!" someone yelled.

"Be a man!" yelled another.

That last one was too much for this short and balding human. He fired the weapon, shooting hot wires.

"Yee haw!" someone yelled.

Dr. Francis clutched his chest and shuddered violently, then floated, motionless, on his back.

"Oh my god!" someone yelled.

"You killed him!" yelled another.

"How could you?"

SON OF DENTLER

DR. FRANCIS PRETENDED to be dead for a good ten seconds. Then he spouted water in the air. I think this had something to do with the dissipation of electricity within a body of water. The male guard must have been unaware of this phenomenon.

"That's it," he said, climbing into the fountain.

"Get him!" someone yelled.

"Run!" yelled another.

Dr. Francis did just that.

The guard chased him across the pool and back again. Jets of water sailed over their heads. The pack barked. Five more security guards surrounded the fountain, just to laugh, while two cops arrived on foot. A crowd gathered. It was a real scene now. Everyone seemed to be having a good time except the bald guard. He fell to his knees, putting him up to his waist in water. Dr. Francis high-stepped away, dancing over the surface with the pack splashing around him.

The crowd was entertained. Some were confused.

"How often do they do this show?"

"It's quirky, but I like it."

"I don't get how it's related to the Atlantis theme."

The cops laughed as the security guard wheezed and dripped and stopped to catch his breath.

"I love Dogman," one cop said.

"You know he's an actual vet?" the other cop said. "Takes care of my mom's dog in Hoover. Used to anyway."

The sodden guard came to the edge of the water.

"I don't care who he is," he said, catching their conversation. "And I don't care about your mom or your mom's damn dog. Just get him out of there!"

"Whoa," one cop said. "Hey Rick, is this the chief of police? Are these orders? What should we do?"

"Gosh. I don't know, Stan. Maybe we didn't get an email? We should probably do everything he says, since he's the chief now. Seems like he's got a good read on things. Composed, I'd say."

"Level headed, Rick. That's what he is."

"Pricks," the guard said.

"Sir, do you want us to book you?"

"What do you mean you don't care about my mom?"

The guard swore and went after Dr. Francis again.

"Something funny about an insecure security guard, don't you think?"

"Sure is," the other cop said.

Shakespeare stood with his forepaws on the edge of the fountain. The cops petted him.

"My wife wants a Pug."

"Really?"

"Bout two grand for a good one."

"What? No. They can't breathe right. Did you know that?"

"Yeah?"

"Nostrils are too small. See?"

The guard splashed over to the cops again. He made a real effort to act calm this time. "Please, officers. I am not trying to be rude. I am not trying to tell you what to do. But this is private property. This man is trespassing."

"That why you tasered him? What would your boss think about that? Think we should make a phone call? Tasering some homeless guy in front of all these fine people? What, do you wanna go viral? Should we drag his ass out of there? Maybe just shoot him? Good idea or bad idea, Stan?"

"I'd need to crunch some numbers," the other cop said.

"Keep in mind we'd get our shoes wet."

"Oh. In that case, bad idea."

The guard flushed and muttered to himself. He climbed out of the fountain. The crowd booed. Another squad car pulled onto the sidewalk, parting the audience with blue lights. It was an undercover car, entirely black.

"Dentler," one of the cops said in a flat voice.

My ears bolted upright.

"Okay, adult swim's over," one cop said to the other. "Go get him, Stan."

"What? Why me?"

"You're the rook."

"I'm not a rook."

"More than me."

"Rock paper scissors?"

"Fine."

"Dentler'll freak."

"He always freaks."

Out of the squad car stepped a muscular cop wearing reflective orange sunglasses and a bulletproof vest. His hair was jet black and crewcut, connected under his jaw with a chinstrap of stubble. He surveyed the scene with one hand rested on his pistol, the other on the open door. He was a younger vision of Dentler, as if the old rancher had stepped into the squad car in Hoover and stepped out in Velos, thirty years younger, more lethal than ever. I caught his scent through the crowd, which confirmed the relation.

This was Son of Dentler.

Dr. Francis steadied his eyes. He stood. Water drained from the pockets of his lab coat. The dogs sensed his change in demeanor.

"You clowns gonna do your job or what?" asked Dentler Junior, his eyes locked on Dr. Francis.

Shake him, Dr. Francis said.

As one, the pack charged from the fountain with Shakespeare leading. Dentler Junior unholstered his gun. The dogs surrounded him, then shook, spraying him with water. The crowd cheered in approval. Dentler Junior swore and spat and wiped his face. When he could see again, he could see that Dr. Francis was already out of the fountain and sprinting down the street, hurdling the median, cutting through traffic. He howled at the night.

Junior charged after him, and we, the pack, knew the hunt was afoot.

We chased them into the traffic jam. Junior was strong and fit, but Dr. Francis was a street dog, and he acted like it. He was reckless, his long legs reaching and pounding. He ran atop a line of cars—trunk roof hood, trunk roof hood, trunk roof hood—then bounded over a motorcycle wheel and sprinted onward. The pack divided and rejoined, each member seeking space, bigger dogs running atop cars, little ones underneath, the rest squeezing between. Junior was sticking to street level, sidestepping around bumpers and dashing through the gaps. Dr. Francis howled again. We howled in return. Junior shouted into his earpiece.

"I need backup! Rounding two o'clock, coming to three!"

Ahead, the light went green. As the cars around us accelerated, spaces opened. Dr. Francis was straight ahead now, dashing down the white line. Junior carried his gun like a relay baton. The vehicles overtook us with honking horns. Backdrafts threatened to pull us in front of speeding bumpers. I reached the front of the pack.

Junior was thirty years younger than Dr. Francis and it was starting to show. The gap between them was closing. But I was galloping now in the open street, reaching full speed, leaving all the other dogs behind, lights streaming around me, as the soles of Junior's shoes became clear, like hopping black rabbits.

I lunged for the kill, tasting rubber. His feet tangled and he crashed to the ground. Brakes squealed. A car swerved and honked just inches from my head. I scrambled up and ran on, leaving him flat faced in the street, his sunglasses cracked, his gun sliding to a halt.

The pack was with me, around me. Onward, we ran.

Dr. Francis cut sideways, out of the road and onto the busy sidewalk. Someone cursed him. He barked. We growled. We howled. We followed him, filtering through humans, wild with the hunt.

Then his voice reached us.

Scatter, he said.

And we did.

THREE O'CLOCK

AT THREE O'CLOCK was The Monroe, a ten-story statue of Marilyn Monroe with her skirt blown up around her waist. As Shakespeare and I went between her legs, along with throngs of humans, we looked up at her "I love New York" underpants. Every five minutes, when that red heart flashed, warm air blasted from the grates below, lifting skirts for photos and laughter. A real thrill was in the air here, for ahead was The Palace.

The glass cone was the tallest and most central structure in Los Velos, and with its gaseous rainbow, it appeared to be alive and always growing, fed by something extracted from underground. This cloudy ore emerged deep red, almost brown. It transformed upward through the entire spectrum of color before being compressed and processed into something straight, definite, human, and white. This was the column of light. It seemed to have a hypnotic power over the crowd, including me, drawing us in by the thousands. It was like an itch that had to be scratched, or an object that begged to be touched. We *had* to go to The Palace. It compelled us to do so.

Or so it seemed to me.

Do you feel that pull? I asked Shakespeare. *Do you feel that…energy?*

I feel hungry, he said. *Wait. No. Now I feel poopy.*

Poopy?

Like I'm going to poop soon. Okay. Yes. Definitely poopy.

Then he did that.

So maybe he didn't feel the power of The Palace like I did.

I don't know what the humans felt. Numbed by substance or not, whether they understood or not, they were being drawn inward, to the center of Los Velos, through stranger and stranger territory.

Within this river of flesh we came abreast of a young boy with his parents, his head bobbing, buck teeth gaping, mesmerized by those around him. Here were the undulating haunches of a heavy woman wrapped in fishnet, her diamonds of flesh glossy with sweat. There was a couple, kissing hard, searching each other's bodies, squeezing, searching again. And an unconscious man, head hanging, toe tips dragging, arms slung around the necks of his festive companions.

Overhead, screens bridged the gap between casinos on either side of the street, creating a flat electric sky that rolled a psychedelic thunderstorm, with great gusts blowing clouds toward The Palace.

Lightning flashed.

Around us were the photo beggars—fantasists, fetishists, freaks— five dollars a photo. A bare-breasted man in a diaper and baby mask shaking his rattle. A catwoman in latex clawed the air. A shirtless fireman stood alone with his pole.

An elderly contortionist had drawn a crowd. His earlobes had been gauged at a younger age, so that they now hung empty and loose. He was tattooed, too, a leopard print that almost certainly extended under his loincloth, the spots faded blue and ovoid, stretching into stripes as he sat and pulled his ankles over his head. A drunk woman made a peace sign behind him before turning it to her lips to flick her tongue through the vee.

Five dollars. Click.

The little boy and I opened our eyes wider to take it all in, but when a man dropped a five into a farmer's pail, apparently purchasing the right to straddle a kneeling, topless woman who was painted like a dairy cow, I wished the mother would have covered my eyes too, as she finally did her son's, when the wasted man reached below, for milk.

WIENER TIME

ARF!

The bark was high pitched and half drowned by noise.

Arf!

There it was again.

Arf!

When I saw who was barking, and what he was wearing, all the other nightmare sights became dull in comparison. It was Vern, dressed in a hotdog costume, with a yellow leash running from the yellow stripe down his back up to the giant mustard bottle that had evidently captured him.

"The Mustard Man. The Mustard Man. Do you know The Mustard Man? The one out Velos way?" The Mustard Man said.

Vern certainly did.

Vern! Shakespeare said, running up to him.

"No no no," The Mustard Man said to us. He continued his awkward jig, shifting his weight from leg to leg. His yellow tights had a long run up one thigh, revealing a seam of black, curly hair. A sweaty, chubby face glared down at us through a hole in yellow foam. "No hotdogs for you. Bad dogs. Beat it. Yah."

Vern's leash was around The Mustard Man's wrist. This kept his hands free for an actual mustard bottle, a bag of hotdogs, and a bag of buns. The Mustard Man produced a hotdog as he talked to the crowd.

Watch and learn, Vern said. *I'm working.*

We watched. We learned.

"Get your hotdogs!" The Mustard Man said. "Get your picture with an all-American frank! Mustard squirting mustard! Weenie eating weenie!"

The Mustard Man waggled a cold hotdog at the crowd. Several humans stopped to watch as he opened a bun and lay a hotdog in it. He showed the mustard bottle to the crowd, then squirted a yellow line down the tube of meat.

"This is so weird," one spectator said.

The Mustard Man now sniffed the hotdog and bun dramatically.

"All-American frank! Just like the ballgame!"

Vern rose on his back legs, facing The Mustard Man. His stunted forelimbs pawed at the air. The spectators were getting it now. They started taking pictures.

"Be so kind, make a donation," The Mustard Man said in a rising and falling voice. "If you don't mind, be so kind. Step right up and get your photo."

"I don't wanna," another spectator said.

But his friends were already pushing him forward with a five-dollar bill. He dropped the money in the bucket, then stood beside The Mustard Man, now laughing at the adventure. Vern's front feet fell, but he was quick to reach again.

"Say all American!" The Mustard Man said, showing crooked teeth.

"All American!" the tourist said, giving a double thumbs up.

The Mustard Man lowered the hotdog. Vern took a bite, dropped down, and swallowed, then rose again. The tourist rejoined his group to back slaps and laughs.

"Who wants a picture with an all-American frank?" The Mustard Man asked everyone, starting his jig again.

This process was repeated, with Vern taking a bite for each photo, until the hotdog was gone. Then the Mustard Man sat on his cooler. He whacked a pack of cigarettes against his palm. After a good drag he checked his phone, with Vern's leash still hooked in his arm.

"Hey...uh...mustard guy, can we get one?" a tourist asked.

"I'm on break," The Mustard Man growled, not looking away from his phone.

"Oh," the tourist said, then shrugged at her friends and walked away.

Listen, Vern said to us. *I'm glad you stopped by to see me work. Good for you to have a role model. But you boys can't be around here. No dogs but working dogs. So get lost.*

Are you serious? I asked.

Course I'm serious, he said. The foam bun held his head rigid and forward. *You know what the trouble is with you dogs?*

No, Shakespeare said.

Rhetorical, Vern said. *It's that you don't have any work ethic. You want to sniff butts and dance around all day. Me? I'm a member of society now. I'm a working dog.*

You're a hot dog, I said.

Very funny, Vern said.

He called you weenie, I said, tipping my head at The Mustard Man.

Vern suppressed an outburst. He trembled and took deep breaths to calm down.

Honest truth is I'm glad to be working, Vern said. *I don't expect you to understand, but it gives me a sense of purpose, okay? Like I'm finally a part of something. Something bigger. Plus, I get all the hotdogs I can eat.*

But— Shakespeare started.

Sure, it's a little tough on my back, and I'm not too happy about the costume and implications therein, but it's still better than digging around in the trash, right? I mean, nobody likes their boss. That's a given. But here's the thing you don't understand, because you're too young. The point of life is not enjoyment. It's security and safety. It's comfort and luxury. It's about respect. But nobody gives that to you. You have to earn it. Just think, in a few years' time, I'll retire and sleep all day. I won't do anything at all. Just sleep and eat and sleep and eat, all day long, forever.

But—

That's right, I'll be living the dream. Working hard pays off. You'll see. And where will you be? That's right, out on the street, digging for trash, on some pathetic quest. Dreamers, that's what you are. I don't mean to offend, but somebody needs to tell you. It's time you made up your mind. Time you settled down and did something respectable, like me.

But—

No no, don't be jealous, Shakespeare. If you work hard, maybe someday you'll make it too. Might take your whole life, but it'll be worth it, trust me. Now you boys run along. Maybe I'll see you around some day. Maybe you can come over and try out the couch.

The Mustard Man yanked on Vern's leash.

"Hey, get away from them," he said. "Step right up! All-American frank!"

Vern returned to work.

Shakespeare turned his most pathetic, pained eyes upon me.

We have to help him, he said.

No, I said.

He stared at me. That damn stare.

Why take the risk? I asked. *We are so close to The Palace.*

But still he stared at me, and stared, and stared, and stared, with his giant, hypnotic Pug eyes.

This is not our quest, I said. *Vern is not our quest. He is off task. We've come so far. Please.* I looked at The Palace. *That is the quest,* I said. *We'll be there in minutes. And it's easier without him anyway. Please. I know we'll find answers there. I can feel it.*

Shakespeare broke his stare, but only to turn it upon Vern, drawing my eyes with him. Poor Vern jumped again—another hotdog, another bite of humiliation—for some chance to lie around until he dies of old age.

Just don't watch, I said, unable to look away. *Stop thinking about it.*

Without speaking, Shakespeare walked in an arc to position himself behind The Mustard Man. He stood right behind him, just behind his heels, and from there, he stared at me once more. He was using his Pug magic on me, with his black liquid eyes. He gazed into my soul, then looked up at The Mustard Man, then back to me. The Mustard Man, then me. Mustard, me. Which will it be, Rou? he seemed to be asking. Which side are you on? He wagged his tail. Which?

"All-American frank!" The Mustard Man yelled, doing his jig. "It's a classic! Come and get it! Just five bucks a photo!"

I jumped over the bucket of money. My front paws hit The Mustard Man straight in his foamy chest. He stepped backward only to trip on Shakespeare, then fell on his back with a curse. The hotdog he had been holding flew jiggly into the air, separating from the bun before smacking down into his face.

I bit the leash.

Run! I yelled, and took off, dragging Vern behind me.

We threaded through the crowd and into the mouth of an alley. I peered out as Vern and Shakespeare panted behind me. The Mustard Man was nowhere to be seen. Overhead, the screen showed a blue sky with puffy white clouds and spinning sunflowers. I chewed at Vern's leash where it attached to his costume.

You had no right, he said. *No right.*

Shakespeare danced in circles.

The old dream team is back together! he cried. *The dogs of doom! The defenders of dogdom! The canines without collars!*

What have you been telling him, Rou?

This is all him, I said.

I bit through the leash.

The pups of power! Los perros peligrosos!

Where did he learn Spanish?

I have no idea.

Shakespeare fell over, gasping.

Vern sniffed him.

I'm so glad you're back, Vern, Shakespeare said. He licked Vern's chin.

I can see that, Vern said.

You want us to get that costume off? I asked.

This? No. I mean, no, because we don't have time. The quest, and all.

That guy was a sicko, Vern, I said. *And a jerk.*

I know. It's just...he was somebody, you know? It's just...I've never had a grabber.

We'll get you a good one after the quest, Shakespeare said. *A nice one, all cuddles. As much food as you want. Bacon sometimes. No work. Costumes if you want.*

I hate costumes, Vern said.

Whatever you need to tell yourself, I said. *Now let's go.*

THE GATE

THE PALACE GLOWED between a throng of human legs. We pressed through them. A hunting horn sounded, quickening the current. I felt the anticipation of the crowd seeping into me. I could feel the desire like the warm air rising from under our feet.

"I don't wanna miss it this time," one tourist said.

"Hurry up," said another.

I don't like it, said Vern, his tail tucked, careful to avoid being stepped on.

Are you scared, Vern? Shakespeare asked.

Course not, Vern said. *Why would I be afraid of the creepiest place ever? Huh? A place that I have been told since I was a pup to avoid at all costs? A place called The Palace of Doom, that damns animals to an eternity of hell and never lets them leave, punishing them and taking from them all that was once good, that was enough to drive a full-grown white tiger insane, never to be the same again? Why would I be afraid of that?*

I don't know, Shakespeare said.

Vern and I looked at each other. *Rhetorical,* we said.

The covered street and casinos ended. Under the open sky the pavement expanded, loosening the crowd. We entered a vast, inner ring of public space. This courtyard surrounded a ten-foot-tall glass wall that protected The Palace proper. Directly ahead, a gate was blocked by metal detectors and security guards dressed in red. Above them, a large screen showed the face of The Rajah. As in the flyer I had seen, he was lit from below, with dark upward shadows disappearing into his eyebrows and turban. He blinked down at us on infinite loop. I avoided his eyes. They made me unsteady.

The hunting horn resounded again. We pressed through the crowd.

What's the plan here, Rou? Vern asked. *Hi, uh, we're three street dogs, we'd like to be imprisoned for all eternity, got any vacancies? Maybe you could just chop off our heads if that's too much to ask?*

We'll figure it out, I said, trying to see how the checkpoint worked.

It was a stop and start process. The humans moved forward a few paces, paused, moved forward again. Their legs were too close together to squeeze through.

"Hey, some dogs," a man said.

He scratched my head. I ignored him. I couldn't draw any more attention to us.

"Aw, it's a Pug," another woman said, petting Shakespeare.

"Hey, isn't that the weird hotdog dog?" a man asked.

What's the plan, Rou? Vern asked. *Getting pretty close to the front here.*

Those three metal detectors were the only ways through the gate. A red guard stood in front of each, searching bags, admitting one human at a time.

"No dogs," the middle guard said.

We'd been seen.

"Not mine," one human replied.

"Me neither," said another.

Rou, what's the plan? Vern asked. *Is it to get caught and get our rocks cut off? Cuz I don't like that plan, Rou!*

The humans ahead went through.

We now faced three security guards, one apiece. They folded their arms in synchrony and looked down at us. Each man had a coiled wire that ran from his hip up to a radio clipped at his collarbone.

"They want in!" a woman said, then laughed at her own joke.

The middle guard reached for his radio.

Behind us people started shouting.

"Hey!"

"Whoa! Get in line!"

"What the—"

A howl broke through the night. A madman in a white coat charged through on all fours with a pack of mutts. The crowd stepped back in surprise. In that opening, Dr. Francis performed a loose-jointed, half-human, half-animal dance. The crowd widened further. Having made adequate space, the good doctor now jumped up and down, flailing and barking. The circle filled with dogs. He pointed at the middle guard—the biggest, most aggressive-looking one—choosing him.

Vern and Shakespeare and I stepped aside, opening the path between them. Dr. Francis planted his feet, then made his fingers into bull horns over his head.

"Oh he crazy," said a spectator.

The crowd lit up with cell phones, ready to record what might happen next.

Dr. Francis dragged a foot and snorted. He made practice sweeps with his finger horns, snorted again. The guards must have seen crazier behavior in the past. They remained composed and aimed their tasers. Dr. Francis removed his finger horns. He appeared to have changed his mind. He took a step back, bowed, and slipped out of his coat. He smoothed the white jacket over his forearm, like he was doing an impression of a waiter. But just as the guards relaxed, he snatched the jacket away and opened it wide. He now walked back and forth, snapping the jacket at each turn, back straight, toes pointed. The bull had become the matador. The guards raised their tasers again.

"Stand down, sir," the middle guard said. "We will taser you. I repeat, we will taser you."

The hunting horn blared. Dr. Francis stopped, squared off, and grinned a mad grin.

"Sir!" the middle guard shouted. "Stand down!"

Dr. Francis launched forward, howling and spinning his coat high overhead. The pack charged alongside him. Tasers chattered. Fur and fabric collided. Dogs howled. The crowd shouted and shoved. The gate opened. And in the air, above all that chaos, the white coat floated, finally free.

PART FOUR

EYES

We were in.

The Palace was larger than I had imagined. The base stretched out like a bloody horizon, and from this deep-red glow orange suns perpetually rose, brightening and dividing into rising clouds of yellows and greens and purples and blues. This motion pulled us closer, and I found myself, along with Shakespeare and Vern, and the humans all around, craning my neck, absently jostling into others so I could follow the colors until they were transformed into the pure white column of light.

Cripes, Vern said.

Wow, Shakespeare said. *Also, I'm hungry?*

Focus, I said. *Look out for guards. And The Rajah. He could be anywhere.*

Lotta grabbers, Rou, Vern said.

Keep moving. It's easier to hide in a crowd.

Of course, as I said this, the crowd loosened. People were fanning out toward the left and right. We had reached a railing. Now I could see the full layout of the grounds. A moat encircled The Palace in a necklace of fountains, each quarter turn spanned by an arched glass bridge.

What's our next move, Rou? Vern asked. *You wanna go for a swim?*

Most of the humans were congregating on the bridges and

spreading out along the fence. Very few were going straight inside. They seemed to be waiting for something.

Do you even have a plan, Rou?

Yes.

Okay then, bright boy. Do tell.

Find The Rajah.

That's not a plan, Rou. That's an objective. I'm asking for the how here. Just keep a lookout.

We're never gonna find him, Rou. And then we're gonna be doomed for all time. Do you hear me? Doomed!

I found him, Shakespeare said.

Well, we all found him at the same time.

The colors of the cone dissolved, and in their place, The Rajah's face appeared, hundreds of feet tall and deeply shadowed, his turban and beard blending with a black background to create a godlike, floating face. He peered down at us from behind heavy eyelids. We ducked behind a group of tourists.

That's the biggest human I ever saw, Shakespeare said.

He's gonna eat us all, Vern whispered.

"It's starting," a young woman said, trotting on high heels.

"Out of the water?" another asked.

"Out of the water," she confirmed, holding up her phone.

Their excitement, and lack of fear, helped me regain my composure. Plus I noticed the edges of two more Rajahs repeated around the cone. It was some kind of projection.

It's a video, I said. *It's not really him.*

Then how come you're still hiding? Vern asked.

Just being careful.

Even though I knew it was a recording, I still felt an emptiness spreading through my chest and stomach, like my insides were dissolving.

I knew those eyes.

I knew those emotionless, hypnotic, hooded eyes.

Because I knew that man.

The house lights were dimming now. Even the column of light was fading. A distant bass drum rose with the sound of rushing water. I came out of hiding to look through the railing. The moat was draining fast through a series of whirlpools until the bottom was lost in shadow.

For a moment the only light that remained was The Rajah's face. Then he blinked and everything went blinding white—a thousand strobes had flashed at once—before all the lights went out. The Palace was a blank. In that void my vision burned with the after-image of The Rajah's face.

THE ANCIENT MIND

"In the beginning there was nothing."

The announcer's voice emerged from all directions in the darkness. It was deep and resonant above the feverish drum.

"And then there was light."

The column of light burst to life once more. The crowd cheered. Then I noticed a solitary white dot swimming around the base of the cone. Others pointed as it raced by, disappearing around the cone, reappearing again for another revolution.

"From primordial ooze," the announcer said, "we have risen."

The light divided.

"From single cells to many, we have risen."

The light divided again, and again. Rapidly the lights split off from one another, each taking on a new shape and color and velocity and vector. These propagated more of their kind, each lineage splitting off into new lineages.

"From fins to feet, we have risen. And still, we rise."

The cone swirled with lights. The larger forms moved with purposeful rhythms, as though they possessed primitive limbs.

"From oceans to beaches, we crawled. From beaches to jungles, we survived, at times the hunters, at others, the hunted."

In each of the four segments between the bridges, on thick hydraulic pistons, enormous, curving, black glass enclosures lifted. The water refilled as quickly as it had emptied, so soon the moat was restored, as still and dark as the four containers that seemed to float upon it.

"To survive this primitive world," the announcer said, "we fought for our lives."

The tint in the nearest enclosure faded. The crowd cheered. Through the clearing glass, a misty jungle appeared, thick with vines. Bursting from the foliage, a silverback gorilla beat his chest and slammed his fists against the glass.

"Beasts ruled the earth!"

Atop the enclosure, white smoke bloomed, and from this dissolving cloud, The Rajah appeared. He was a dark man in a red robe with a wooden staff. His turban spiraled outward into six points, while below, his beard split into six more, these crooked spikes forming a wild black mane. As he lifted his arms, The Palace brightened, and the crowd with it.

"But how did we fight?" the announcer asked. "If not as big and strong as these beasts, then how?"

White smoke burst from The Rajah's feet. He reappeared inside the terrarium, opposite the gorilla, from another cloud of smoke. The crowd gasped.

"With the power of the ancient mind," the announcer said. "A power, long ago forgotten, remembered today by only one: The Rajah!"

The crowd roared.

"With the power of the ancient mind, The Rajah harnesses the four eternal elements. Witness!"

The gorilla settled his mass upon his knuckles. The Rajah leaned on his staff, unconcerned, arrogant. The gorilla charged—a silver streak of muscle through space. The instant before collision, The Rajah vanished in white smoke. The gorilla charged through it, throwing fists into nothing. The Rajah reappeared where the gorilla had begun.

"The Rajah transcends air!"

The gorilla charged back across the jungle, but again found smoke. A tantrum ensued, with a terrific run along the glass, the gorilla beating his fists so hard that I was sure he would break through. Instead the container darkened to black and the pounding faded.

From yellow smoke The Rajah appeared atop the next container. We ran around the moat with the crowd, slipping through legs, catching our breath as the glass of the second container cleared, revealing a savannah with an acacia tree. A male lion paced in the grass. His roar was muffled, but still he was magnificent. Again, through yellow smoke, The Rajah entered the enclosure. The lion crouched to watch, thick tail whipping low, until, suddenly, he sprinted across the plain. The Rajah opened his mouth wide.

"The Rajah conjures fire!"

A ten-foot flame roared from The Rajah's mouth. The lion threw his weight to the ground, sliding to a halt, turning his face away to avoid being burned. Before the lion could regain his balance, yellow smoke consumed The Rajah, and he was gone. Within seconds he was atop the next container. We ran around to watch, breathless.

This container revealed a forest with a stone cave, from which a grizzly bear emerged. His brown hunch alone was as big as The Rajah, who appeared from green smoke in a clearing of trees. The bear growled. The Rajah lifted his staff overhead and held it with trembling hands. The grizzly stood on his hind legs, roared, then dropped to all fours and bounded through the forest, his enormous weight like a tumbling brown boulder.

"The Rajah harnesses earth!"

He planted his staff and the ground erupted in a wall of stone. The bear collided with it in a sickening thump. Green smoke again, and The Rajah was on to the next.

I ran to catch up. The crowd was largest and densest here, all gathering to see the fourth and final act.

"With the power of the ancient mind, The Rajah escapes the deadliest of all predators. He defies death!"

The glass cleared. The crowd shifted its feet. I could sense the unease spreading, and my own excitement was tempered by that old hollow feeling. We were looking up at an aquarium. It seemed empty at first—just a haze of grayish blue. But then, from the murk, a great white shark appeared and slid along the glass, dead eyes seeing nothing, or everything.

"No," a spectator said.

From blue smoke, The Rajah appeared on top of the tank. He

faced The Palace and opened his arms wide, as though gathering strength from those accelerating colors. He glowed with energy.

The crowd cheered. Any moment. Any moment.

"The Rajah becomes water!"

Blue smoke. He was in the tank. His robe billowed around him like a red jellyfish, his staff now a ridiculous, tiny stick. The shark U-turned and flicked its fin. It flew through empty space, jaws wide, before snapping down. Someone screamed. The shark thrashed violently, blurring fabric and flesh. This violence darkened behind a growing cloud of blood, from which The Rajah's broken staff floated to the surface.

I was stunned. But it was too good to be true.

"With the power of the ancient mind, The Rajah lives!"

"There," someone said, pointing.

Atop The Palace, a thousand feet up, levitating within the column of light, was The Rajah's irrefutable form. Holding the crowd's complete attention, he descended into the source of light. The cone flashed white, consuming him, before returning to its usual display of rising colors.

The drum faded.

"Ladies and gentlemen," the announcer said, "thank you for your attention. Remember, this was only a preview of what will certainly be The Rajah's best season ever. Get your advance tickets today before they're all sold out. Opening night is just a month away. Now, please make your way inside The Palace, where magic and marvel await!"

The auxiliary lights returned. The moat emptied. The humans became lighthearted again as they streamed across the bridges, entering glossy black doors around the base of The Palace, where red guards stood with arms folded. No dogs allowed, their body language said.

I watched the shark tank dropping into the empty moat. I started toward it.

Hey Rou, Vern said, *entrance to your most certain doom is across the bridge. We gotta use the bridge. Other way.*

The tank was already halfway gone. Soon the top would be level with the ground.

Rou, that's where they keep the giant killer thing with no legs, Vern said, trotting behind me. *Hey Rou! You hear me?*

The quest, Shakespeare said, still catching his breath. *The quest! He's questing! We're questing!*

Rou! Vern said. *No way! No!*

I stepped onto the shark tank as it fell past. Shakespeare jumped down beside me. We looked up at Vern, who stood at the edge of the moat, watching us descend. We were already five feet below him, then ten, then passing the bottom of the moat. Vern was silhouetted far above, his pointy head sticking out of his bun with the colors of The Palace behind him. A motor groaned to life. The moat was closing again, like elevator doors against the sky.

Out of all the exotic animals on that strange night, including gorilla and lion and bear and shark, the flying hotdog remains the clearest in my memory. In a vision of either bravery or stupidity or some combination of both, Vern leapt into space. And the landing would have killed him, too, if not for the foam costume. He rotated as he fell, so he landed on his mustard, then bounced right onto his feet. He stood there, first surprised at what he'd done, then lifting his head and wagging his tail. He flexed his bun, left and right, up and down.

Hey, he said. *I think that fixed my back.*

WHAT LIES BELOW

THE TANK beneath us came to a halt. The steel doors closed overhead with a heavy latching sound, sealing out the last of the light. The motor stopped.

It was pitch black.

Cripes, Shakespeare said.

Hey, Vern said, *that's my thing. But yeah. Cripes. Seriously. Cripes.*

As always, in total darkness, my brain turned scents into sounds. The air was oily and metallic, setting a steady background hum in the midrange, while in wafts, I smelled unusual animals, each one a different note, blipping in and out. Trying to imagine the dimension of the tank without imagining the dimension of the creature within, I sniffed forward, until I found a familiar, high-pitched screech—chain link.

Fence, I said.

We followed its curving length to a corner.

There's gotta be an opening, I said.

Does there? Vern asked. *In a place where they keep a legless water thing with all those pointy teeth?*

No luck at the far end. We sniffed along the other length. As we did, another motor, somewhere in the black space, groaned to life. I thought the overhead doors might be opening again, but it was much, much worse than that. The glass underneath us was shifting. The lid of the shark tank was sliding open.

Cripes! Vern cried. *Cripes almighty!*

Hey, we might get to swim, Shakespeare said. *That could be fun.*

We followed the fence, stepping sideways and forward with the glass sliding beneath us. I tried not to imagine falling through with the next step, plunging below, and being eaten. Of course I imagined exactly this. My paws were slick on the glass.

There has to be an opening, I said.

We're doomed! Vern cried. *Doomed!*

Fluorescent lights flickered on, revealing the true severity of our situation.

We were in a cage above the tank. Behind the chain link a narrow walkway was crowded with pipes and valves and gears. The only gate was chained and padlocked. Overhead, above that encircling utility area, was a catwalk. I could see a door up there, but no ladder on this side of the fence. In other words, there was no way out.

The tank was already a quarter open, leaving a broad, watery gap. The surface appeared cold and sharp to the touch. And it was getting closer by the second.

A pale form passed underfoot.

It had been a long time since my last panic attack, but even now I think this one was valid. I went blank with fear. I barked. I whimpered. I yapped. I howled. And I wasn't alone. Vern was right there with me, having also witnessed the monster below. Only Shakespeare was calm. He sat with his back to the fence, glass dragging beneath him, the stench of anal glands filling the air.

Ahhh, he said.

Then I heard a beep, and the sound of the door above us being thrown open, and footsteps clanging. A teenage girl in heavy boots and short shorts appeared on the catwalk. She looked down at us, astonished.

"I can't stop it!" she cried, and for a moment seemed as panicked as I was.

Then she took action. She dropped to the ground and wriggled under the lower railing. With black hair streaming around her face, she hung on with one arm and reached down with the other. I stood on my hind legs, trying to connect. Not even close. Shakespeare, interested now, walked backward so he could stare up at the girl.

Hi, he said, *I'm Shakespeare.*

She slid back under the railing. She had given up. I howled.

But no, she hadn't given up. She was just tying her bootlaces.

What she did next was remarkable. She lay on her back on the lowest railing, this time face up, holding the upper railing. At first I didn't understand what she was trying to accomplish, but then, as she slid further out, and hooked her knees around the lower railing, I understood. It wasn't just remarkable. It was death defying.

Get ready, I told the others. *She's gonna lower down.*

We're gonna dieeeeeeee! Vern cried.

The girl was small but strong. Incredibly strong. Knees hooked, she leaned further back, extending her arms while hooking her toes between her hands. Then, with superhuman gymnastic strength, she released her grip, and with her arms out for balance, performed a midair backbend until she was hanging upside down, legs interlaced with the railing, arms in full extension, to reach us.

"C'mon!" she said. "Up!"

I stood on my hind legs again. My front toes grazed her fingertips. If I reached just a little higher.

But what about the others? I dropped down.

"I can reach you!" she cried, face red. "Up! Up!"

Vern was whimpering and clawing at the chain link. Shakespeare was standing at the moving edge, peering into the dark blue.

The solution came to me, as ideas come, from the depths.

Vern, get on my back, I said.

I dropped to my belly. Vern climbed up, the foam high-siding him so his stubby legs stuck into space. I leaned against the fence for balance as the glass slid beneath me.

Shakes, now you.

Shakespeare bounded over and up, kicking me in the face as he scaled the foam mountain that was Vern. Once he was perched, I prepared to stand.

"Go!" the girl cheered. "Go!"

I took a deep breath and pressed. But my bad leg burned with pain. If I pushed any harder it would snap.

I collapsed.

"C'mon, dog! Do it! Push! Give it everything! Go! Go! Go!"

Even hanging upside down, literally bending over backward, this girl was able to clap and cheer. Her strength was inspiring. And I knew this was our only chance. I had to try again. I had to. Even if it shattered my leg. What was a broken leg, anyway, compared with being eaten alive?

I took another deep breath.

I closed my eyes.

And I pressed.

I pressed through the pain.

And stood.

"Yes! Good dog! Good dog! Go! Go!"

This was no time for celebration. I had to continuously adjust my stance for the moving glass. The edge was coming closer. I looked straight ahead, forcing myself to focus on a bolt in the wall.

Stay strong now. Stay strong.

The weight lessened. She had Shakespeare! She crunched upward to place him on the catwalk. She reached again, extracting Vern by the bun.

I did it! I saved them!

Unburdened, I stood on my hind legs for my own rescue. I reached for her fingers. I reached higher. But something strange was happening. Even though I was reaching higher, she was getting further away. This last moment happened so, so slowly. I was looking straight into her eyes—wide and dark and afraid—as I slipped into the cold below.

SCREAM

HAVE you ever fallen into cold water? Felt the way it grabs you? The way all of your muscles are attacked at once, all shocked and contracting, clamping your jaw shut?

I have.

My whole body was locked in cold terror.

I opened my eyes.

I did what you should never do.

I looked down.

There, directly beneath me, the great white shark was circling.

He was chanting in a deep and primeval language that I did not understand. Yet I knew it was about the hunt. I knew it was about me. The prey.

AH VIDO GO VIDO LO VIDO ZO. MO VIDO SO VIDO PO VIDO NO.

It is a common misconception among humans that dogs cannot scream, but I assure you that we can. That's exactly what I did when I burst through the surface.

I slapped around, gasping for air. I pawed at the chain link, toenails chattering. I felt super aware of my lower body. Of pins and needles. Of how it would feel when the shark bit through my spine, crushing my toes in his rearmost teeth. Cracking my bones and shredding my flesh.

A blur through the air.

The girl splashed down.

She was in the water with me!

I thrashed.

I raked her cheek.

"Relax!"

I could do no such thing.

She tried to contain my legs. I scrambled hopelessly, trying to climb onto her head. She went under, and for a sickening moment I thought the shark had taken her. But she resurfaced. Sputtering, she grabbed the fence with one arm. She wrapped her other arm tight around my chest, and with that same strength she had demonstrated before, began to climb.

Hooray! Shakespeare cried. *Questing!*

It's coming! Vern shouted.

Something slippery caressed my paw pads. I kicked, finding empty water.

The girl lifted her feet, now bare, to latch her toes in chain link. She pulled herself toward the fence, then released. In the instant before freefall, her hand shot up and regripped overhead. She was climbing one-handed! As she lifted me from the water, my weight magnified. She dug deep. She coached herself through it.

"C'mon, Jess," she said. "Don't get pumped. Breathe. Legs. Legs!"

She pushed off and reached again, this time finding the top.

We collapsed on the catwalk together, both of us panting. Shakespeare licked my face and hers. Vern, a dripping weenie, just gawked.

Below us the shark was a long gray oval sliding past, and then, nothing.

THE AMAZING AZAR

We huddled behind Jess in a dark hallway. Her shorts and tank top and hair, and our fur, was still dripping, forming a collective puddle beneath us. She peered through a crack in a door. Then she turned with a finger to her mouth.

"Shhh."

Quiet, I told the others.

Through her legs I could see what appeared to be a sick bear lying on its back upon a table. Or was it a man? It was either a sick bear, losing its fur, or a gigantic man with more fur than any human I had ever seen.

"Do not count," the hairy beast growled. "Just do it."

"Get ready," Jess whispered.

Get ready, I relayed.

A sudden ripping sound preceded a roar. Jess opened the door. We slipped through.

It was dim inside, with fabric-covered lamps in the corners and heavy, earth-colored tapestries on the walls. Jess pulled one of these aside and herded us into the hidden space behind it. She let the tapestry fall. It was dark and muggy and stank of armpits.

"Yes!" the beast bellowed. "The pain! Yes! There it is!"

"I'm sorry, Mr. Azar," a small woman said in an equally small voice.

"Mister? Do not call me that. Only bastards want to be called Mister. Do I look like a bastard to you?"

"No, I—"

"Call me Azar. Or The Amazing Azar, if you must. But never Mister. Do you understand?"

"Yes, Mist…um…Azar. Are you sure you want me to keep going? That was just the first one. Your hair condition is…severe. Have you considered liquid hair removal? I have some with me."

"Liquid hair removal? What? Do you think The Amazing Azar cannot handle pain?"

"No, it's just—"

"Ugh. It is a fine idea, but the liquid gives me a hive, if you must know. Laser is for the rich. So wax me, woman. Or leave and I will find someone who will." He sighed. "Please."

Through the gap we had a view of The Amazing Azar's bald crown, and below it, the bushy beard and mountainous forest of his massive chest and arms and belly, all of it covered in brown fur, save the stripe of white across one pectoral. Apart from the cucumbers that covered his eyes and the small towel that covered him from waist to mid-thigh, he was naked. Muscle hung over the edges of the table.

She's going to feed us to a monster? Vern asked. *After we just escaped that other one?*

"One…two…"

"Are you insane?! Do not count, woman!"

The waxer ripped. While Azar was still roaring, Jess told us to stay and darted out of the room. I admired her stealth. Coyote-level sneakiness.

She knocked a few seconds later.

"Enter!" Azar boomed.

Jess came in. She leaned against the door, closing it, nice and casual, never looking in our direction.

"Monkey!" Azar said. "I know your knock. Did you know that? Knock knock knock. Always three." He grinned at the ceiling, his round face breaking into seams. He lifted both hands in the air. "Happy waxing day! You have come to watch? The new waxer is frightened of me. Tell her pain is nothing to me and I am harmless and respectful."

"Would you like me to come back?" the waxer asked.

Azar removed the cucumbers from his eyes and ate them, apparently so he could properly frown at her. She stirred the wax.

"Why are you wet, Monkey? And your face is scratched. What is wrong?"

Jess hesitated. Azar sat up. His towel fell. Jess looked at the ceiling. The waxer aimed to redrape him, but he swatted her away with a heavy paw.

Azar's voice became a gentler growl. "What happened this time? Tell Azar."

"I think we should be alone," Jess said to the ceiling.

"Out!" Azar shouted. The waxer flinched, then left, shaking her head.

Azar groaned as he stood. He was as much bear as man, it seemed, the way he swayed as he walked toward us, each hairy foot filling a tile, his large dangler and doodads swinging, his head almost grazing the tiles above. He reached out. I prepared to run.

"Wait," Jess said.

Azar plucked a thick brown robe from a hook beside the tapestry.

"I must wear a robe," he said, putting it on before facing Jess. "Human resources said I must yada yada yada. Especially in the presence of minors. So I yada yada yada. This is America, Monkey. The land of the prude." He tossed a second, identical robe to Jess. She caught it with both hands, bending at the knees to absorb the weight. "You can explode a man's head on afternoon television," Azar said, tying the robe, "as long as he is wearing trousers."

Azar retrieved two beers from a mini fridge. The cans were tiny in his hands, absurdly so as he opened both simultaneously with the tips of his fingers. He collapsed into a pile of mismatched, overstuffed cushions, spilling foam. He put his beard in his mouth to drink the spill, spat it out, then worked his fingers through the tangles.

"Now then," he said. "Sit. Tell Azar."

Jess sat. The cushions and robe swallowed her, so she was little more than a head, like a cabbage just coming out of the ground. She told her story. Azar sat upright when she jumped into the shark tank. When she escaped he reclined with a human facial expression I had never seen before—a smile tempered with pain.

His voice was barely above a whisper. "Your kindness makes you brave," he said, as though he might cry. "That is your mother. You know that, don't you?"

Jess blushed. "I was just wondering—"

"If you can hide the dogs in here?" he asked, regaining his usual volume. "Until you convince your father to let you keep them?"

Her blush darkened.

"You think you are sneaky, Monkey, but nothing sneaks past Azar." His smile broke out again, huge and wide, with uneven teeth. "Of course they can stay! All dogs are my friends! Dogs, come! Come! Play with The Amazing Azar!"

Shakespeare leapt onto Azar's belly and lapped up the remaining beard beer. They were instant friends.

"This one is like me," Azar said, lifting Shakespeare, wiggling, overhead. "He does not waste beer. He is a fine creature."

I sniffed the giant human. He smelled of vegetation and dirt, of growth and decay, like a good place to roll.

"This one has more wolf," Azar said, respecting my need for distance. Softly, he lifted my chin. "I see intelligence in his eyes. And pride. Good boy. You are a good boy. Yes. You are."

Vern came out reluctantly, still afraid that he would be eaten.

"A hot dog!" Azar announced. "Yum!"

Vern ran back into hiding. It took some cheese to finally coax him out.

Jess stayed until we were calm and resting in the cushions. My thoughts drifted from their conversation to The Rajah. I kept looking at the door, expecting him to enter, fearing that he could sense our presence. Instinct, however, told me that I was safe with this bear man. His hands were bigger than my head.

I was comforted by this thought, and almost asleep, when a knock came at the door. Azar rose from the cushions, grunting about his knees. He opened the door.

"Ah, my little punisher has returned," he said. "I will try to be kinder than I am. But you must be cruel with me."

The waxer came in on tiptoes. Azar disrobed and lay upon the table. She tried to cover him with the towel, but he held her back.

"No," he said. "We must wax everything for my performance. And I do mean everything."

When Azar was done swearing, beating his chest, and swearing some more, he was bald everywhere but his eyebrows. And I do mean everywhere. When he stood, his entire body glowed red, with spots of blood where capillaries had torn. He locked the door behind the waxer.

"Come," he said, and out we came, to snuggle together again in the cushions.

As we snuggled down, safe in our new den, The Amazing Azar pulled an easel from behind another tapestry. In the low light he sat naked on a tiny wooden stool, his great bald back curving around his painting, the paintbrush like a splinter in his hand.

THE VISITOR

WHAT HAPPENED that first night at The Palace was not a dream. In the moment, however, it had a dreamlike quality because it was only that—a moment, brief and surreal.

It was late. We had been asleep for some time, all of us cuddling with Azar, when I was awakened by something. Maybe it was a slight sound, or a smell. Azar and Shakespeare snored on. Vern's breathing was long and quiet and slow. I could barely see them, as the lamps were off and there were no windows in the dressing room. The only source of light was a yellow glow that slipped beneath the door.

It was from this glow that the visitor appeared.

The mouse entered on four but stood on two legs. He was tiny and black with large translucent ears that transmitted light like a pair of harvest moons orbiting his head. Which was something. But the really remarkable thing about this mouse was his attire. He wore a thin gauze belt, and hanging from this belt, angled against his hip, was a hypodermic needle. I could tell this was not something that a human had placed upon him, but that he had chosen, because he clasped the metal hub like a hilt, as though to reassure himself that his sword was still there, or to prevent it from knocking against his knee.

He was looking right at me.

Then he was gone—a black streak under the door.

So you can see why, in such a brief and unexpected moment, I thought I was dreaming. Yet after he was gone I could still smell his odor. That must have been what woke me. A real mousiness lingered in the air. So I had seen him. And I understood that this was an unusual creature. Unusual like me.

I would have followed him, I told myself, had the doorknob not been round.

In truth I was afraid.

Because I was not alone.

THESE SMELLS

IT WAS DARK, but I could feel that it was morning. Someone was knocking on the door. Three knocks. Jess. Jess was knocking on the door. We were piled on top of Azar. He extracted us one by one, like plucking hairs, to place us on the cushions.

"Are you awake?" Jess asked.

"Moment," Azar said. "Knees."

He unlocked the door.

She burst in. "I've got it! Oh!" She looked up at the ceiling. "Ouch?"

"The first wax always bleeds," Azar said, putting on his robe. "The second, before opening night, will not."

"Anyway, that's it! They're going to be in the show."

"Who?"

"My dogs!"

"Doing what? Wagging tails?"

Jess kneeled and gathered us with pets and kisses. We licked the breakfast smell from her hands.

"They'll stack," she said. "It's not the best trick, but it's a trick. Like The Jin Pin Twins. And I know they can do it already. We just need to add some spice. Maybe some costumes. Not this hotdog one. Which—ew—smells like smoke. But yeah, they'll be in the show with us. That's how I'll keep them. They're performers."

"And your father—he knows of this?"

"Yeah. Well, no. Not yet, but he will."

Azar turned on the lights. Crumpled cans littered the ground. He dropped back into the cushions and rubbed his eyes.

"A fine plan," he said. "Let them try to stop you."

"Exactly. Like you, Azar, you just live here. You didn't ask anybody if you could. I mean, I'm pretty sure it's illegal to live in your dressing room. But that's you. That's just Azar."

The big man surveyed his domain. He felt the bruises on his chest. He was quieter today. "I suppose," he said.

"Well," Jess said, looking at the door, then at Azar, "thanks for hiding the dogs. See you later?"

"Yes, Monkey. Later."

"Wish me luck." She patted her hip and walked out. "C'mon, pups."

As we followed Jess down the hall, loose boots echoing and scuffing along, I recalled my encounter with the mouse. I *had* seen him, hadn't I? I tried to detect his scent on the floor, but the tile was freshly mopped and now bounced fluorescent light like a white mirror.

I saw something last night, I said.

Good for you, Vern said. *Anybody smell these smells right now?*

I smell these smells, Shakespeare said.

You know these smells, Shakes? Vern asked.

I do not know these smells, Shakespeare said.

Me neither, Vern said. *I do not like it when I do not know these smells.*

Listen, I said. *I saw a mouse last night.*

Oh wow, Rou, Vern said. *Good for you. But seriously. Are you smelling this? What is that? What are we smelling here?*

It wasn't a normal mouse, I said.

Impending death, Vern said. *That's what that is, Shakes. Impending death.*

Oh, Shakespeare said, *good.*

No! Vern said. *The opposite of good! Bad!*

It smelled like animals. That's what it smelled like. They were all unfamiliar types, all intermingling, all growing riper by the step. Something cracked in the distance—something loud. This was followed by a bizarre, muffled, trumpeting noise.

I guess this is it, Vern said. *The big one. Gonna feed us to some monster. This is it. Thanks, Rou. For nothin'.*

After risking her life to save us from the shark, Jess wasn't going to just feed us to some so-called monster, but other dangers were very, very real. If The Rajah knew me, then I might be recognized at any moment, and possibly taken captive. Or maybe I had already been seen. Maybe the mouse was a spy.

I considered trying again to explain my mouse sighting, but I could imagine how Vern would call me a crazy idiot, and then I would waste fifteen minutes explaining a hypodermic needle, and how unusual it was for a mouse to carry one as a sword. And then I would have to explain what a sword was, and so on. So I kept it to myself, for now, and stayed alert. In a way I was a spy myself. I liked this idea, and started inspecting everything, in case there were other clues, or if something might trigger my memory.

The doors lining the hallway, for instance, were decorated with star-shaped placards, each with a different name. The Gong Gong Gang. Helen of the Hullabaloo. The Flying Fish. The Flash. The Soothsayer. Morty McFee. Pistol Rick. The Werewolf. I recognized none of them, although that last one sounded promising.

The hallway ended in a stairwell. Here the animal odors were so pungent that a human with a cold could have smelled them. We descended four, five, six flights, deeper and deeper underground. At the bottom was a dirty tile floor.

Jess pushed the door open.

Now I felt like the mouse.

We had entered a circular, subterranean arena with grandstands that towered overhead, top row lost in the shadowy fringe of a metal dome. Before us, under a spotlight in the center of the arena, perched upon a red and white podium, was a gigantic animal that I never expected to see in real life.

THE BIGGEST DOG THAT EVER LIVED

THAT'S the biggest dog that ever lived, Shakespeare said.

That's not a dog, idiot, Vern said. *That's a giant pig. With a nose problem.*

You're both wrong, I said. *It's an elephant.*

A platinum-blonde woman in leggings, brandishing a whip, circled the elephant on the podium. A bald man, half-watching, paced as he talked into an earpiece. Further out, a group of bored-looking humans in faded red coveralls leaned against the ring barrier.

I braced myself for a shout of alarm—"Hey! Grab that dog!"—but nobody showed any interest in our appearance. I searched the stands. They were empty. No Rajah here. No sword-wielding mouse, either.

The woman cracked the whip. The elephant rotated away, thick limbs bundled together below, one chained with heavy steel. The links clanked together like grinding teeth.

"Signal's bad," the bald man said. "Yeah. It's Mike. Just listen. Got another order for you. Can you hear me? I need ten of the usual. Hello? Hello? Dammit."

Crack!

"Closer!" Mike shouted, ripping off the earpiece.

Crack!

"You're miles away! Closer!"

The woman cracked it slightly closer.

"Joy, stand up, honey," the woman said. "Joy, just stand up for me, baby. Please."

But as the woman tried to come around to Joy's front, Joy rotated away.

"Are you mad at me, Joy?"

"She's not mad at you," Mike said. "She doesn't respect you. Here."

He took the whip.

Joy faced him at once.

"She needs to be afraid," Mike said. "Or she'll walk all over you. I mean that. She'll trample you to death. She needs to know that people are in charge around here."

A growl escaped my throat. Jess put an arm around me.

"Calm down," she said. "You'll only make it worse."

Bile crawled up my chest as the whip came alive in Mike's hand. He was an expert. The frayed tip rushed back and forth, turning invisible before exploding with a bang. It fell limp to the dirt, where it rested, but just for a moment, before writhing to life again. His strikes were loud and fast.

Bang!

The tip exploded far away from Joy.

Bang!

It exploded closer.

Bang!

Closer still.

Joy trumpeted over Mike's head. It was the strained cry we had heard from the hallway above.

"Stand," Mike commanded. "Stand."

Joy was staring him down.

Mike showed her the whip with one hand and pointed at her feet with the other. "Stand!"

I growled again.

"Quiet," Jess said.

I growled louder.

"No."

I gritted my teeth. I knew what was coming.

Bang!

Mike whipped one of Joy's front feet. Blood trickled between her toes. She shifted her weight but still did not stand.

Bang!

Mike whipped her other foot. More blood.

I was outraged. I tried to break free, but Jess had me by the scruff.

"STAND!"

Mike pointed at the elephant's face—at the faint scars that threaded between her eyes. At last she pressed off the podium. She stood, ungainly and unnatural on her hind limbs. Mike dropped the whip and clapped.

"Bravo!" he said. "Good girl, Joy! You look like people!" He kept clapping as he walked away. "Clean her up! Bring out the zebras!"

Joy descended awkwardly from the podium. Once on the dirt, she shook her head and trumpeted. Three handlers surrounded her with long black sticks. They distracted her so a fourth handler could unclip the chain from the podium. Yet another handler used a keycard to activate a heavy metal door that I hadn't noticed before, as it was painted red to blend with the stands.

This large door rolled up slowly but revealed nothing beyond— just a black void. The five handlers now drove Joy, still tossing her head and trumpeting, through the opening. The darkness seemed to consume her, chain dragging behind, followed by the handlers themselves. The door rolled shut, leaving a shadow of silence.

The blonde woman appeared lost. Seeing Jess, she picked up the whip and came over.

Her voice was weak. "Hi," she said.

We licked her hands. They were sour with fear sweat.

"Hey," Jess said.

"These dogs are cute," the woman said. She wiped her eyes, leaving streaks of black.

"It's not you," Jess said. "He's a jerk to everyone."

"I don't know if I'm ready for elephants."

"Course you are. He's always like this before a new season."

"I thought we had enough time," the woman said, winding the whip around her hand, "but now I don't know." She looked like she was going to cry again.

"Want me to talk to him for you?"

The leather squeaked under her grip. "No. Please."

"He needs to treat you better. And Joy. You know that."

"I'm okay. Really. I just need to learn. Please don't say anything." She excused herself and disappeared through the doorway and up the stairs.

Jess led us around the ring. She ducked under a steel support. We entered the dark space beneath the stands. Here horizontal and vertical shafts of light hashed the wall. Mike paced in this shadow cage. The smoothness of his skull cracked like an egg around the top of his forehead, with fissures that became deep and sharp around his eyes, as though a giant had pressed a thumb between his eyes, leaving him with a permanent scowl.

"Hey. Yeah. Mike again. Can you hear me? Good."

He was on his earpiece again. When he saw us coming he held up a hand, but not in greeting. It meant stop. We stopped.

"Listen. We need ten more. Yeah. Usual rate. I don't care. Yeah. Thanks. Yeah. Will do. Thanks again."

He removed the earpiece.

"Hey, Monkey."

"Hi, Dad."

WE CAN GET A FAT LADY ANYWHERE

MIKE DIDN'T EVEN TRY to introduce himself. No offered hand. No scratch behind the ear. Definitely no kneel and smooch face. No nothing. Just no.

"No," he said, and ducked out of the stands.

We followed him through an open door.

"But I'm responsible," Jess said. "I've proven that with the other animals."

"That's not what we're talking about."

We headed down another bare white hallway.

"Then what are we talking about?"

"Reality."

We entered a small office. The desk held an old computer and a mess of papers. Mike sat down. The chair squeaked as he searched the papers. Shakespeare licked some ancient gum stuck to the hard brown carpet. Vern scratched his bun with his back leg.

Mike looked up. He seemed to see us again for the first time. "Wait a minute. Where exactly did you find these dogs? They weren't inside the building, were they?"

"Dumpsters," Jess said, delivering the lie perfectly.

Mike was relieved by her answer. Then he frowned at Vern. "Did you put that on him?"

"He came that way."

"It's ridiculous," Mike said, returning to his search.

Behind him a framed poster showed a younger Rajah with a normal turban and no beard. This version wasn't so evil looking—the photo was even kind of amateurish—but still it triggered the same distant recognition, and fear. The other walls showcased black-and-whites of gymnasts, trapeze artists, lions, zebras, rings of fire, clowns getting out of tiny cars—that sort of thing. In one of the photos, a miniature version of Jess posed between a Mike with hair and a compact Asian woman. All three wore matching white leotards and flourished their hands in the air. A trapeze bar hung overhead.

"They're an act," Jess said. "And you need an act. They're stackers."

"Stackers," Mike repeated, absently. He found the paper he'd been looking for and stood up, leaving the leather chair spinning behind him.

"Like The Jin Pin Twins," Jess added.

Mike left the office. "We already have The Jin Pin Twins. And you know how I feel about dog acts, Jess. They're carny fare. Cable TV."

Jess stomped after him. "You need to replace Joy's act," she said. "That shit's never going to be ready."

Mike faced her. His eyes were bloodshot, the vessels raw and raised. More veins pulsed on either side of his head. Never mind The Rajah. This human was scary in a different way. He seemed like his insides were going to become his outsides at any moment.

"Watch your mouth," he said.

"You swear," Jess said, quietly.

"You're fourteen."

"Almost fifteen."

"And when you're forty-fucking-eight you can swear all you want."

"Chill."

Mike clenched his jaw. His veins throbbed faster. "You want to talk like adults? That it?"

Jess nodded, although her shoulders lifted, and her hands found each other, nervously.

"Fine," Mike said. "I'll start. If you hadn't noticed, I'm working ninety fucking hours a week. The Rajah sends me another fucking text every ten fucking minutes and it's my fucking job to get him everything he fucking wants, day or fucking night, because he can't keep an actual fucking assistant for more than one fucking day. And it's always some weird fucking shit that takes me hours to figure out. Because he thinks he's Howard fucking Hughes. Like he's forgotten we're running an actual fucking business here. Does he even fucking care anymore? I seriously fucking doubt it. But let me fucking tell you something, Jess, the shareholders fucking care. And the board fucking cares. *They* fucking care. And they are going to fucking fire me so fucking fast your head will fucking flip if we don't fill those fucking seats all season fucking long. So *I* fucking care. On top of that, my fucking elephant act—hell, half the fucking acts are nowhere fucking near performance ready. Meanfuckingwhile you missed fucking rehearsal the past three fucking days. Fuck!"

"I—"

"I am not fucking finished. I know you called Ms. Deguchi a bitch the other day. I haven't even had the fucking time to tell you how out of fucking line you are. Because you are. Do you know how fucking hard it is to find a fucking tutor in this town? And now this fucking shit? Are you fucking serious? Stray fucking dogs? The fucking board is crawling up my fucking ass on a daily fucking basis and you bring me three stray fucking dogs? Do you know what it's like to have nine fucking people crawl up your fucking ass on a daily fucking basis, Jess? Do you?"

Jess suppressed a laugh.

Mike spoke through gritted teeth: "Jessica."

There was something new and cold and clear in his voice that made her hands lock together. She lowered her chin, turning her face slightly away.

Just then a clicking sound came from around the corner.

Jess exhaled.

"Wonderful," Mike whispered.

The clicking belonged to a tall woman in a pantsuit who wheeled around the corner and stopped. She studied Jess for a moment with what may have been concern before she saw us and her mouth turned down. I felt a moment of panic. Did she recognize me?

"Where did *they* come from?" she asked.

"I was just showing them the exit," Mike said.

"Why on earth would you do that?"

Technically, the woman smiled. Yet her eyes weren't involved in this expression, like they'd been paralyzed. With her long frame and big hair and orange skin she reminded me of a carrot. That talked. A lot. And fast.

"Was this you, Mike?" she asked. "Did you do this? Oh my gosh, I love this. So much. Mike. You are genius."

Mike and Jess exchanged glances. I cocked my head. I doubt anyone had ever accused him of that.

"The Drive-Thru Dogs!" the woman cried, with jazz hands. "And I thought we were stuck in the Stone Age." She peered down to inspect, did not attempt to touch, like we were spiders. "Okay. Let's lose the hot dog costume. It's weird. People don't like weird. They want normal. And sweet. And cute. And heartwarming." She retrieved a face-sized cell phone from inside her suit jacket. "I can't believe Kathy didn't reach out. How about Scott? Did you connect with Scott?" She swiped around on her phone with red nails.

"Who?" Mike asked.

"Scott," she said again, not looking up. "Social Scott? I think he's Mormon. Not that it matters. Anyway, this is great. People love dogs, Mike. Do anything with dogs and people will love it. Just eat it up nom nom nom. I've been saying that, like, forever. It's like an eternal truth or something. Like a commandment. And these dogs are *so* viral right now. Who's their agent? How'd you get them so quick? It's only been, like, what? A week? Ten days? Wait, was it staged? I thought they looked trained. No. Don't tell me. I don't want to know." She lifted her phone again. She readied her thumbs. "Okay. Names."

Mike was perplexed. "Of the dogs?" He looked to Jess for a clue.

"My dad was just explaining who they are," she said. "But maybe you could explain instead? You explain things *so* well. He also thought you could come up with stage names for them. Like, marketable names?"

The pantsuit woman mouth-smiled at Jess. "Of course! Oh my gosh I watched the video, like, a hundred times. Wait. You haven't seen it?"

"I'm not allowed to have a smartphone," Jess said. "Or social media."

Now the woman was confused.

"So, no," Jess clarified. "I haven't seen it."

"Oh my gosh, you must be the only tween who hasn't. You didn't even show her, Mike? And what's this no phone thing? *Or* social? That's just cruel. Here. Watch."

The woman turned her screen to face us. With security cameras and phones, our entire episode at the drive-thru had been recorded and was now played back to us.

What are we looking at here? Vern asked.

This whole human smells like shoes, Shakespeare said, sniffing the woman's leg.

Jess gasped when I jumped for the brown bag, said, "No!" when the Jeep drove over Vern, and, "Oh, thank god," when he was safe.

The carrot lady laughed when the video ended, maybe too amused by the obese woman trapped between her vehicle and the wall.

"Did you get the fat lady, too?" the woman asked. "I mean the person of above average personal mass?" She peered past us, like we might be hiding that huge and terrifying woman behind our backs.

"She was booked," Mike said.

"Oh. That's okay. That's okay! It's the dogs that matter." She sniffed the air. "So. Number one: Baths. Two: Lose the hot dog costume. Three: Advertise. Oh my gosh this is *so* great. It's gonna go viral. I can feel it. We've been struggling with our tweens, you know. It's a tricky space. Not quite kids. Not quite adults. And here I am without enough bandwidth for another single solitary thing, and here you are, like, hello? We got The Drive-Thru Dogs. Mike, I'll say it again, you are a genius."

"We tried to get the fat lady," Mike said.

"Not a problem. Really. We can get a fat lady anywhere. Honestly, the board will be thrilled. They were just telling me that they want a light opener. Clowns but not clowns, you know? The Palace reimagined, right? Classic contemporary. But funny. Something about juxtaposition, yada ya. This is perfect. Genius, Mike. Honestly."

The woman returned to her phone.

"So. Let's ideate on names," she said, thumbs ready.

Jess looked like she had a bad taste in her mouth.

"Larry, Curly, and Moe?" Mike suggested.

The woman nodded like she was agreeing and trying to understand at the same time. She pressed her overinflated lips together. It was amazing how her eyebrows never moved.

"Because these dogs are kind of wacky and stupid, you know?" Mike went on. "They get into stupid adventures and stuff. We could call the wiener Shemp instead of Curly, if you want. He looks like a Shemp."

Are they talking about me? Vern asked.

They say you're very handsome, I said.

The woman tapped the corner of her phone against her temple.

"Shemp?"

"Yeah," Mike said. "Lesser known Stooge? He was in the original lineup, actually."

"Isn't that show like a thousand years old?"

"I think most people know Shemp."

"Well, this is a safe space. So, like, no bad ideas and all. And I know you typically name the animals. Unfortunately that will never rank on search. The SEO will be awful. Like, atrocious. And how many tweens know The Three Stooges?"

"Who?" asked Jess.

"Exactly," the woman said. "The tweens don't know." She walked off, absorbed in her screen, high heels clicking away. "I'll run the SEO on names!" she called over her shoulder. "Let's circle back!"

Jess's eyes followed her down the hall. "I'm not a tween," she said.

"You are if she says you are," Mike said, looking at us with renewed interest. "The board will be thrilled. I'll be damned."

"So they can stay?"

"Of course they can stay. Break out the golden bones."

Jess hugged Shakespeare. He wiggled and licked her arm. Jess giggled. At that, Mike softened.

"Look, Monkey," he said. "My TMJ is killing me. I feel like I'm gonna get lockjaw any second. It's the stress. You alright?"

"Yeah," Jess said meekly, refusing eye contact.

"I need to get back."

"Okay."

"I'm going to go back. You need any help on chores today? I can get someone to help you. Or you can take the day off. Would that be better?"

"I can do it," Jess said. Then she looked at her dad with big, sad eyes. "I really will take good care of them."

"I know you will, Monkey. I know you will. Let's get back on track today, okay?"

"Yeah. Chores. Rehearsal. Stretch."

"Chores. Rehearsal. *Baths*. Stretch. *Study*."

"Got it."

"That's my girl."

CHORES

CHORES WERE a key part of what Mike called "the life of a normal kid," and they took us all over The Palace, giving me the opportunity to explore the facility without drawing attention to myself. I couldn't recall living with any other kids, so I had no comparison, but even then I thought feeding a gorilla, a lion, a bear, and a shark were abnormal chores. These animals—which we had seen during The Rajah's teaser show—were called The Four In The Floor.

Mike had a power thing about naming the animals, which is why The Four In The Floor were all retired Buffalo Bills players. The gorilla was OJ Simpson, the lion was Jim Kelly, the bear was Bruce Smith, and the great white shark, the deadliest predator on earth, was...wait for it...Doug Flutie.

While we are on the topic of Mike's awful name choices, the pantsuit lady must have never "circled back," because his choices stuck. Still I refuse to be called Larry, and will henceforth not refer to myself as such, nor Shakespeare as Moe, nor Vern as Curly, or even Shemp. And I will most certainly not refer to us collectively as The Three Stooges. In Jess's language: "He can shove that up his bung hole." I couldn't put it better myself.

We went to the food room first.

The food lady was a well-fed woman with a cleaver who made us wait in the hall. Delicious smells leaked under the doorway. We could hear that cleaver working. Soon Jess emerged with two metal buckets of raw beef.

"Don't even think about it, wiener," she said, eyeing Vern into submission.

Feeding The Four In The Floor was such a physical job because the food room was on the bottom basement floor (B8) and the animals were on the top basement floor (B1). Although the facility had multiple elevators, including one big enough for five or six elephants, we never used them. Jess was made to use the stairs— seven flights for each animal. "Conditioning," Mike called it.

It seemed to be working. Jess had the muscles of a Pitbull. I enjoyed the way she marched around like she'd built the entire facility, dragging her boots to leave black scuff marks wherever she went. The staff also seemed to appreciate Jess's attitude. Most of them asked her how she was doing today like it was some kind of set-up. To all of them she replied "wonderful" in a gruff voice, and they always laughed. That's what Mike said when something was the opposite of wonderful. It was some kind of human joke.

Anyway, apart from Doug Flutie, who remained in his tank, The Four In The Floor lived in cages adjacent to their glass performance enclosures. Each was only as large as it needed to be, and had a thin carpet of straw and a few "stimuli"—toys and ropes and logs and rocks—meant to keep insanity at bay.

These did not appear to be working.

Our first stop was Jim Kelly, the lion.

At the top of the stairs, on level B1, there were two doors. Both were red metal. The one to our left was unmarked. The one straight ahead was painted with a stencil that said "STAIRS TO CASINO." I was pretty sure, behind that door, up another flight, was The Palace proper. Both handles were knobs, and both were locked—each had a black box beside it with a glowing red light.

Jess scanned her keycard to the left. The lock turned green and buzzed.

Absolutely not, Vern said when the door opened.

But Jess had a pocketful of beef jerky, and Shakespeare was already inside.

So we entered the narrow antechamber in front of the cage. The door shut behind us and buzzed with a finality that made my whiskers stand on end. Like Vern, and most living creatures, I have a phobia of being consumed, and possibly an instinct that warns me about animals capable of doing so. This lion was one such animal. His musk thickened the air like wet rust and rotten teeth.

This is it, boys, Vern said, chewing his jerky. *Our last meal.*

At certain angles the lion looked like an old house cat, and maintained a grieved expression, like someone who has just heard some unfortunate news. I noted a stiffness in his hind quarters. Looked like arthritic hips.

"Hi, Jim, you handsome old boy, how are you today?" Jess asked. She put the buckets down. "I'm not so good. Dad's been gambling again. He went out last night after he thought I was asleep."

Jim Kelly paced incessantly, reciting his poem over and over.

...wall is a wall is a wall... he said in a rough bass.

His fur was pocked with scars, and yet, despite his worn body, he was still regal, and carried his head high.

Shakespeare wagged his tail. He was ready to squeeze through the bars and introduce himself.

Don't you dare, Vern said. *If you get eaten, I'm stuck with Mr. Uptight over here.*

Calmer than you are, I said.

...king of the jungle if jungle be dead is the...

Hi, I'm Shakespeare, Shakespeare said.

Jim roared. The sound lifted my fur.

"Easy, Jim," Jess said. "Just dogs."

She put on latex gloves and held up a steak. Jim stopped. A growl revved in his throat. She tossed the meat between the bars. He caught it in midair, shook it, and took to the ground. Then it was gone. Blood stained his mouth. He paced again, growling and reciting.

...a wall is a wall is a wall...

Jess dumped the rest of the meat through a hatch, then sat cross legged with Shakespeare in her lap to watch the lion feast.

"Jim would eat you up, wouldn't he?" Jess said, tickling his stomach. "But we wouldn't let him, would we? No. Who's my wittle minion? Yes. Yes, you are. Yes."

Shakespeare shivered with glee.

As soon as King Jim was finished eating he returned to pacing. It was unusual for a cat to forgo grooming after a meal. And it showed. His mouth was stained brown and his mane was matted. He moved like a slow piston between concrete walls, the end of his poem looping back to the beginning. It went like this:

> *The king of the jungle if jungle be dead*
> *is the king of the dead if the jungle be dead*
>
> *A wall is a wall is a wall*
> *Another is here or so it appears*
> *A wall is a wall is a wall*
>
> *The king of the dead if the king he be dead*
> *is the dead of the dead of the dead of the dead*
>
> *A wall is a wall is a wall*
> *Another is here or so it appears*
> *A wall is a wall is a wall*

And straight through again.
I tried to break in.
Hi, I said. *Your Majesty?*
...a wall is a wall is a wall...
I'm Rousseau. Rou for short.
...or so it appears...
I'm wondering if you could please help me?
...of the dead of the dead of the dead of the dead...
I'm looking for The Rajah.
King Jim flinched. Although he never broke his stride, he did lose track of his poem. He shook his head like he was freeing his ear of a fly. He started again from the beginning, pacing and reciting, as though I'd never spoken.
"I love you, Jim," Jess said. "See you tomorrow."
We returned to the food room, then back up the stairs, three times, to feed the other three.
OJ Simpson and Bruce Smith were impressive in size but both asleep. The former looked like an even hairier version of Azar, flat on

his back with a blanket over his face, while the latter looked like a huge shaggy brown dog curled around a stuffed teddy bear.

Doug Flutie remained the most terrifying, and fascinating, of all four. Shakespeare and I watched with fearful excitement as Jess dumped two buckets of fish into the aquarium. Vern refused to look. For a few seconds nothing happened. Then the water exploded into a white froth that brightened to red.

Hooray, Doug! Shakespeare cheered.

We never even saw him.

By the time The Four In The Floor were fed, Jess had climbed about thirty flights of stairs. She was sweating and veins were proud in her arms. But this was just the warmup. We spent another two hours hauling industrial sacks of frozen french fries and boxes of ketchup packets from the food room on B8 to all of the concession stands on levels B7 through B3, and then another hour filling soap dispensers from gallon jugs that Jess carried two in each hand. Never mind The Four In The Floor. Jess was the real beast around here.

Finally we returned to the arena, where Jess collapsed in the stands with a protein shake, relieved to be done. I was relieved, too, as nobody had recognized me, or even cast me a second glance. Yet this was also confusing, and frustrating. If I had come from The Palace, as I suspected, then why did nobody know me here? I had just explored most of the facility but gathered no clues. Beyond that strange, sword-wielding mouse, which may have been an escaped circus act, I had seen no evidence of unusual animals, and The Rajah was nowhere to be found.

Rehearsal, I hoped, would provide more answers.

REHEARSAL

IN THE STANDS Jess chewed her nails and talked to us like confidants. I suppose we were, although only I could understand what she said. Shakespeare passed out in her lap while Vern slept by her feet. I sat beside her on the bench, listening and watching everything. She put an arm around me.

Act normal, I told myself. Act like a normal, average dog. I scratched my ear with my back foot for effect. Even as I did this I was scanning the tiers of the arena, all the way up to the sound and lighting booth far above us. I knew The Rajah could appear at any moment. Even if none of these people recognized me, he would. I knew he would. Because I recognized him. And who knew what he would do then? When he found out that I was still alive? That he hadn't killed me after all?

The big door across the arena rolled open. From this black square mouth, a wave of animal odors wafted across the dirt floor and rose into the stands to meet me. I could smell Joy, the elephant, back there somewhere, and a number of other animals I could not place.

I was confused when three very hairy, very short humans in vests emerged from the tunnel, all holding hands, with one handler on either end. Was this some kind of miniature Azar situation? But no, it wasn't. They weren't human. They were chimpanzees—a closely related species.

The door rolled shut behind them, and the handlers led the

chimps to three waiting tricycles. Yes, at first, I was entertained watching them pedal the wooden racetrack around the ring, but after twenty laps, even apes on trikes get boring. And one of them had a squeaky wheel, which made my ears twitch. I wished someone would lube that wheel. Mike was more focused on getting the chimps to race each other. They were stubborn about their sequence.

"Pass," Mike told the trainer, who clicked something in his hand and urged the chimp in the blue vest to go around. "Pass," Mike said again.

"They're not stupid, Mike," the trainer said. "But they've been in this order for three years."

"And now they're going to change," Mike said. "The Rajah wants them to race. Or the board does, anyway."

My ears perked up. Again I searched the arena. It was like The Rajah's power was everywhere, but he was nowhere to be seen. Just bringing him up, and the board, whatever that was, made the trainer try harder. He became more intent on clicking his clicky thing and even waved his hands around trying to get the chimps to do as he said. The one in the red vest kept replying in a frustrated yell. After another lap he got off his trike and threw it over the barrier. He ran in a tight circle, beating his chest and screaming.

"Yeesh," Jess said.

"Geppetto needs a break," the trainer said.

"Fuck Geppetto," Mike said.

"Excuse me?"

"Geppetto's an asshole!"

"He's a chimpanzee, Mike."

"Who says chimpanzees can't be assholes? Most of them are."'

"He's got a point there," Jess whispered.

"Take them away," Mike said. "Bring out the zebras."

It took a while for the chimp in the red vest to calm down. But when he did, the trainer offered his hand to the chimp in yellow, who must have been the peacekeeper, because he joined hands with his companions, and then another trainer took up the other end of the chain, and the five of them disappeared back into the tunnel. Mike stood in center ring, opening and closing his mouth and massaging his jaw.

After the chimps were gone, nine zebras came out of the tunnel.

They were shimmering and beautiful, just as majestic as you could imagine.

They should be called dream horses, I said to Jess, glad as soon as I had that she couldn't understand me, and the others were still asleep.

At the command of a trainer with a white ribbon on a black stick, the zebras fell into a single-file line and trotted around the ring in a marvelous procession of black and white. For one entire lap this was glorious. But then the lead zebra spooked and the rest broke rank. Mike shouted until he was a little hoarse. Too bad he wasn't actually a little horse. That would have made it easier to tell the zebras to calm down.

Rehearsal wasn't going well, to put it kindly. These were old acts, and the changes seemed to be triggering a mutiny. It was one failure after another. The juggler forgot her chainsaws. Only one Jin Pin Twin showed up. Joy and the other elephants refused to come out of the tunnel at all. And the clowns were seriously drunk. Apparently they'd been partying hard in the dressing room of Pistol Rick, the coin-shooting cowboy, who appeared shortly after them, stumbling over his sockfeet, strapping on his holster, claiming he'd be the clown-shooting cowboy if those lily liver white trash card cheats didn't head for the hills. And then he started loading his gun, or at least trying to load his gun, but he was way, way too wasted for that, and when he opened the chamber of his six-shooter all the bullets fell out, so he crawled around in the dirt trying to find them. Meanwhile, the clowns all climbed into their tiny car and drove off, laughing and flicking him off and spraying vodka from a seltzer bottle into each other's mouths. A group of handlers had to restrain Rick from chasing after them. And then the sword swallower claimed that he had laryngitis and refused to swallow anything except some herbal tea. And then there was a problem with lighting. And then there was a disagreement about song selection. And then Mike opened his jaw wide in another grotesque yawn.

And so the hours dragged on.

But we never saw The Rajah.

Not once.

This just seemed like a sad, sad circus.

And I fell asleep at the thought.

SYLVIA AND THE WORSTEST LEAST GOOD THING EVER

WE AWOKE to the smell of meat. Cooked meat. Delicious meat. Meat!

"Din dins," said a human in red coveralls. He was slightly older than Jess, I thought, although I have trouble aging humans. He had some facial hair, but not a lot, if that helps. He presented a platter with a silver lid.

"Oh, hi, Steve," Jess said. "I think I was asleep."

"Beauty rest," Steve said, grinning.

Jess laughed. It sounded fake. "What's that?"

"For the badass Drive-Thru Dogs. Got some good stuff here."

He opened the lid. Steam rose from slices of rare beef. We jumped up. He shut the lid.

"You didn't have to do that, Steve."

"You got the four o'clock slot. Your dad said I should dogsit." His eyes went up and down Jess's face. I did not like this for some reason. "Mind if I join you?"

"Free country."

Steve put the platter on the bench in front of us and rested his feet on top, so we couldn't get the food. Now I really disliked him. We sniffed and drooled and stared, seeing fat versions of ourselves reflected back.

"How you been, Jess?"

Jess didn't respond. She was distracted.

A woman in white had just appeared from the tunnel. She walked a white bareback horse into the ring.

"I wish I could watch you rehearse today, but I've got a bunch of food prep left," Steve said. "Food lady's on my ass."

"She's my favorite," Jess said, just above a whisper.

"The food lady?"

"No. Her."

The horse and woman wore matching white feather plumes. There was something captivating about them—an elegance unseen in the previous performers.

"She's new, right?" Steve asked. "What's her name again?"

"Sylvia Frontera."

"And the horse?"

"Rebel."

Sylvia was smiling and whispering in Rebel's ear. They seemed to be sharing a secret. I liked them both.

"Is it a boy horse?" Steve asked.

"Watch," Jess said.

"Okay," Steve said, "let's watch." He looked at Jess's legs from the corner of his eye. I really, really did not like this human. He was sneaky and I knew it.

From the speakers, classical guitars chattered to life, and singers soon joined in. I forced myself not to dance. It wasn't easy. I could feel the singers calling to me, begging me to join them, dance with them.

Do it, dog. Just let it flow. Bailamos.

"So—" Steve started.

"Shut up, Steve. Just for a minute. Alright?"

Steve looked around, laughed awkwardly. I don't think people usually talked to Steve that way.

The guitars were feverish as Rebel cantered around the ring. In the center spun Sylvia, head tilted back, smooth neck exposed, one arm extended, tracking Rebel's circuit with a finger. This spinning continued as Rebel spiraled inward in tighter and tighter circles. Sylvia spun faster and faster to follow.

Jess held her tongue between her lips. I couldn't resist. My backside swayed to the beat.

Rebel completed the final circle. Sylvia brought her hand to her face and dropped into a crouch. Rebel cut tightly. The guitars crescendoed. Sylvia leapt up. Rebel's plume lowered and rose. Sylvia landed, astraddle.

The singers burst into a chorus.

Rebel reared, wet with sweat. Sylvia squeezed her thighs. Rebel stomped his front feet, kicking his rear, before bursting into action again, this time spiraling outward, to the outer edge, where they performed a full circuit before galloping back and forth across the center of the arena. With each pass, Sylvia assumed a different position on Rebel's back. First standing, then standing on one leg, then handstanding. With Silvia still handstanding, Rebel stopped. Sylvia found her balance. Then she released one hand, and, in this position, with all of her weight on a small palm and her shimmering white shoes pointing in the air, Rebel rotated slowly, then bucked. Sylvia flew upward, somersaulted, and landed again, this time facing backward. Rebel galloped straight for the barrier. Silvia waved and blew kisses our way. Rebel leapt the barrier. The pair disappeared into the dark tunnel and the music faded out.

It was, in my opinion, a perfect performance.

Jess stood and clapped. She stomped a boot on the bench, the sound echoing in the empty stands. Steve grabbed his platter before it could fall. Jess puffed some hair from her face. Drool poured from our mouths. Steve stood.

"I guess I'll feed them now," he said. "It's almost four. Do they have leashes or something?"

"Nah, they're good," Jess said. "This one's the leader," she added, pointing at me. "They just do what he does." I felt proud that she considered me the leader, and glad that Vern couldn't understand what she'd said.

Meanwhile, crew members were rolling an enormous metal contraption into the arena. It looked like a fifty-foot airplane propellor. One blade terminated in a solid metal block. At the other tip was a mesh wheel. I tilted my head, curious.

"Jess!" Mike said. "Get your ass down here! Wheel of Death time!"

"Oh, keep your tits on," she said quietly, before clanging down the stands. "Catch you later, Steve-o!" she called back.

Compelled by the power of meat, Steve led us out of the arena and down a long hallway to a room with metal tubs along the walls. Maybe I should have been more suspicious, but in the world of dogs, there are plenty of free lunches.

This would not be one of them.

After the platter was licked clean enough to see our reflections again, we realized that we had company. Six handlers in red coveralls and black boots had joined us in the room.

The door was closed.

Huh.

"Baaath tiiime," one of the women sang.

What's she saying? Vern asked.

We're getting baths, I said.

Shakespeare froze.

What's baths? Vern asked.

The worstest least good thing ever, Shakespeare said.

Vern growled.

You like to swim, Shakes, I said. *So why wouldn't you like baths?*

It's not the same! Shakespeare cried. He whined and spun in circles. It was the most scared I have ever seen him.

Stop being a baby, I said, glad that someone else was panicking for a change. I jumped into the nearest tub. *It was a good run, boys. Let's just hope they get behind our ears.*

I wagged my tail as they lathered me up and massaged my back. I love baths. Let me put that in capital letters. I LOVE BATHS. They feel sooo good. Plus I like smelling like flowers afterward. And I don't give a damn what other dogs think.

Biting a human was far beyond Shakespeare's imagination. Instead, he squirmed and twisted until they got him in the tub, at which point he fell into a sullen, soggy silence. It's one of the few times I have seen him in a bad mood.

Vern was more aggressive. He showed them every weapon in his arsenal. He barked and growled and raised his hackles and bared his teeth.

They'll never take me alive! he shouted.

That was before they globbed peanut butter on his nose. He'd never had it before, the poor street urchin. And when he tasted it, they indeed took him alive—willingly, even.

Keep it coming, grabbers, he said, as they lathered him up, *keep it coming.*

LIFE WITH AZAR

ALTHOUGH JESS and Mike lived off site, and Jess considered us pets, Mike insisted that we live at The Palace, for insurance reasons, he said, whatever that meant. Fortunately, after relentless begging from Jess, we were saved from the common animal cages and allowed to stay with The Amazing Azar, amongst his cushions and peculiarities.

And he was peculiar. The staff treated him like another beast, or maybe a wrathful demigod. Hot meals, piles of snacks, and cases of beer appeared like tributes outside his door. Meanwhile, inside, he lived a primitive life. He had no clock, no television, no mirror, no phone, and, to my disappointment, no books or smartphone or computer. He used the bathroom down the hall, but only when necessary. Most of the time he used beer bottles that were magically cleared away while he was at rehearsal. Fortunately he had no bucket for solids.

His free time, of which he had a great deal, consisted of eating, lifting weights, eating, drinking beer, eating, and painting secret paintings that he destroyed in fits of rage before completion. Other activities included, but were not limited to, shouting, shadowboxing, whistling, crying, stretching, meditating, kissing his biceps, and doing yoga. Some of these he did in combination. He was also trying to teach Shakespeare how to shake. The trouble was, Shakespeare was Shakespeare. He climbed onto Azar's palm when it was offered.

To the sky! Shakespeare said, pointing his snub nose at the ceiling.

"No, smoosh dog, listen," Azar said, putting Shakespeare down. "You must take my hand. We are doing a trick now. For fame. Now, we go again."

Azar offered his palm and said, "Paw."

Again, Shakespeare climbed aboard. *To the sky!*

"No, dog, please, listen." He gently lowered Shakespeare to the ground. "Be serious."

Someone put him out of his misery, Vern said. His belly was bloated with food. He was deep in the cushions, his fur shiny with conditioner.

I walked over and gave Azar my paw.

"Yes, we know you are smart, coyote dog," Azar said. "That is why it is more incredible if smoosh dog does it. Now, smoosh dog, paw."

Again, Shakespeare climbed aboard.

"Perhaps I am pushing you too hard. We will take a soft five."

I like this troll, Shakespeare said, wagging his tail.

When the daily knock came for rehearsal, Azar groaned. He dressed and wrapped his knees. His complaints were largely about Mike, who he called "Manboy."

"If Manboy dares to shout at me today," he said, "I will rip out his spine."

Of course, Manboy did not shout at Azar. Nobody shouted at Azar. They avoided him like railroad tracks. Azar cultivated this fear by walking to rehearsals oiled and shirtless, straight down the center of the hall, flexing his pecs and glaring at anyone who dared "look upon Azar."

"What do you think?" he asked us before leaving his room. "Are any brave enough to look upon Azar?" We followed behind. I liked to watch the red coveralls scatter before him.

Azar's rehearsal was self-directed. The staff hated his session because he insisted that his props be positioned exactly where he wanted them before he began, and only he knew where they should be, as his preferences changed daily. These props were heavy. Very heavy. That was the whole point. Moving the junked hatchback, for instance, required ten people.

"Yes, all ten of you," Azar said, "and then I will do it alone, like a real man. Yes, to the left. Further. A leeeetle bit further. There. Good. Bravo."

After the last of the rehearsals, Jess would knock on Azar's door. Three times. Knock knock knock.

"Come in, Monkey," he said.

She kicked off her boots and they went through a comprehensive stretching routine. Throughout, Jess voiced the frustrations of the day, which Azar received with uncharacteristic patience, simply nodding or grunting in response. Afterwards Jess fell asleep in the cushions with Shakespeare in her arms while Vern and I snuggled against her. Azar sat awake, watching over us, as though contemplating some great tangle in his own head.

We knew it was late when Mike knocked. His would be the last knock of the day.

"Goodnight, Monkey," Azar said, patting Jess on the head as she walked groggily out of the room.

As soon as they were gone, Azar undressed. He pulled off his clothes like they were on fire. Then, like someone guarding a terrible habit, he slipped his latest canvas from behind the tapestry, opened a beer, sat on his short stool, and painted. After six or seven beers, in what must have been the middle of the night, he abruptly got up and left the room.

We followed him.

At this hour the facility was half lit and empty, aside from the night cleaner, a dwarf-like woman named Leonore, who was so small and silent that she may have been a ghost. She appeared in the distance, in a white uniform, her hair in a bun, carrying a wooden dowel with a small knotted rag at one end. She rubbed the rag on the floor, removing the scuffs of the day, most of them Jess's.

Azar seemed unaware of her, or us, or anything at all. Under low lights, barefoot and naked, he walked down the long hall, down all those flights of stairs, onto the soft dirt of the ring. There, in the center of the arena, The Amazing Azar, a man unlike any other I had seen before or since, sang opera—the same song every night.

"Gott! Welch' Dunkel hier!" he sang, his booming voice filling the massive space overhead. "O grauenvolle Stille!"

What it meant, I don't know, but it wasn't danceable, and frankly, he had more passion than talent. It hurt my ears.

GALAHAD

AFTER TWO WEEKS of this routine, my hopes were diminishing. I no longer expected to be recognized, or to see The Rajah at any moment. He didn't rehearse like everyone else, and from what I gathered through scraps of conversation, he was never around, and communicated exclusively with Mike through texts and emails. He was some kind of recluse.

I entertained a variety of plans during this time, including one in which I intercepted The Rajah during his nightly show with The Four In The Floor, or another, even more cunning plan in which I used Mike's computer to learn The Rajah's home address. But if I had learned anything in my experience so far, it was the value of practical thinking, and patience.

Here's what I knew: The Rajah would be there on opening night. And I would be there on opening night. Which meant the simplest solution was to wait. That's all. Just wait. So I settled in. I still kept watch, looking for possible clues, but really I knew I was just waiting another two weeks for opening night, and Azar always locked his door, and this made me complacent. I no longer slept with one eye open.

So it was to my surprise when, again, I awoke to an unusual smell—the smell of a mouse. And there, right in front of my face, was the black mouse with the needle sword. To my greater surprise, he had his sword lifted overhead with both paws, the point hovering just a millimeter over the delicate tissue of my nose.

Still thyself, saddlegoose, he said.

I was only half awake. I just kind of blinked at him. Did he say saddlegoose?

Privy now, fopdoodle, he said. *Ye shall not here prevail. Many a cur I have slain. Ye shall be but a notch upon my strop.*

Um. What?

I will run ye through!

The needle trembled over my nose, and in that trembling, touched down, barely. It was enough to send a bolt of pain to my brain. I flinched, wide awake now, my thoughts racing to catch up. It was the mouse! He was back! And he was most definitely abnormal. Normal mice spoke in simple squeaks and gibberish. This was a complex, albeit strange, dialect. And normal mice certainly didn't wield swords.

Wait, I said. *Please don't stab me. Who are you?*

The glory of The Holy Grail is mine alone. I see ye searching. I see ye, ye churlish ratsbane, ye! Ye knows I see ye!

Me?

Ye!

The Holy Grail?

Play not the bumbling bobolyne. Any knight errant can sense a cur's covetous gaze. A squinting squire could see ye seeking and searching. Highest and lowest, ye seekest.

Wait a minute. Do you actually think you're a knight?

His little black eyes bulged with indignity. *Think? Besmircher! I am Sir Galahad! Revered knight of Camelot! Seeker of The Holy Grail! I quest in the name of King Arthur and the Round Table and the all of Christendom! I serve in the name of God! And I will be damned if a hedgeborn dalcop such as ye dares to stand betwixt me and the glory of our Lord and Savior!*

You're questing, I said, recognizing, behind those veils of insanity, a mind like my own, only warped even further from reality. *Have you always been a knight?* I asked. *Did you read about all of this in books like I did?*

Sir Galahad, for the first time, hesitated. His blade veered off target and his stare softened, then rehardened. *Witchery and mindcraft cannot corrupt a noble knight.*

I'm like you, I said. *I'm just like you. Only bigger.*

Meseemeth ye be mistaken.

Meseemeth?

Swear it, scobberlotcher. Swear to stop ye quest. The necromancer riseth on the morrow. Fear not, cur. I will slay the blackest of soul and attain The Grail myself alone. By rights of blood and God tis my glory to keep. Ye must stand aside. Give ye word, cur. Or feel my wrath.

Are you talking about The Rajah?

Uncouth, cur. Thou shalt not speaketh the name of the dark wizard.

You are talking about The Rajah. The Rajah's coming? On the morrow? What does that mean? Tomorrow? Really? How do you know that?

Speaketh not!

How can I give my word if I can't speak?

Speaketh only for ye word!

Wait. Are there others? Like you? And me? Where are they? Here? What if—

Feel the wrath of the sword of the floating stone! And with that Sir Galahad drove his sword deep into my nose. His hindpaws lifted from the ground as he pushed all of his weight downward, driving the needle up to the hub, so the point jarred bone.

I howled in pain and surprise.

Just as quickly, he withdrew his sword and scampered under the door and out of the room.

A lamp clicked on.

The other three squinted.

I lay there, paw over my face, whimpering, eyes watering.

"Dog, what is this noise you make?" Azar asked. "Oh. You are bitten? The rats do bite."

Tiny red pawprints tracked out of the room.

Mouse? Vern asked.

Mouse, I said.

Hey Rou, Shakespeare said, *your nose is bleeding.*

WHISPERS

I REMEMBER, very clearly, the day after Sir Galahad stabbed me, on the day I indeed saw The Rajah, that we nailed our act for the first time.

"You know," Mike said, giving a rare compliment, "these dogs are looking solid."

The trainer nodded thoughtfully, as if she'd done it all with her clicky thing, then went on break, clicking it to herself as she went. I was proud in my own way, having coached Shakespeare and Vern, which was not easy, considering their attention spans.

"If smoosh face dog can do this," Azar said, watching from the perimeter, "why does he not give me his paw for a shake?"

"Don't feel bad, big guy," Mike said. "Training animals takes years of practice. Next act!" He had a clipboard now that he carried like a shield. "Where's The World's Most Flexible Woman? Hello? Anybody awake?" A group of handlers paused to feign interest, then carried on. Mike swore and went to find her himself.

Azar rubbed his knuckles and walked off in the opposite direction, probably back to his dressing room to take off his clothes. Across the arena, Jess was stroking Rebel's mane, deep in a conversation with Sylvia.

In other words, we were momentarily forgotten and therefore unsupervised. Each of us took advantage of this opportunity in our own way. Shakespeare was getting yet another belly rub from a passing handler. Vern ate zebra manure, which, to his credit, is surprisingly delicious. And I, as usual, returned to my search, compulsively checking the corners and shadows I had come to know as well as the tufts of hair that grew between my toes.

The stands were mostly empty. The clowns gathered in a middle section with vintage lunch boxes and vape pens. Pistol Rick joined them, having forgiven previous transgressions in exchange for absolution of debt. A whiskey bottle appeared. Cards were dealt. On the next tier up, a duo of maintenance workers installed a new folding chair. Their impact driver ratcheted in quick percussion, causing my fur to stand on end. It was just a drill, I told myself. There it was again. Just a drill. Yet my fur was still standing on end. I could feel something—call it an energy—rising beneath me.

The arena lights dimmed.

I looked straight down, into the dirt.

That's when I heard them.

The whispers.

They began quietly, in singles and pairs that came and went, like the rustling of leaves in a breeze. Quickly, however, like a tree shaking from a sudden squall, they gained intensity and volume. Hundreds of whispers rushed around me, consuming me in noise. For a moment I was completely disoriented. Then, though I could not differentiate these voices, I began to gather, not their meaning, but their collective feeling.

Despair.

Pure despair was rising all around me.

Simultaneously I felt a growing weight overhead, like the ceiling was being lowered on top of me, like I was being pressed between despair and the metal sky. I was being crushed, and my vision seemed to narrow from the pressure, focusing me entirely on the darkness ahead.

There, in that exact place, a spotlight clicked on. It illuminated an empty black podium in center ring.

This light only provoked the whispers. They kept rising, growing more urgent, swirling around me in a rising tide of pain.

The spotlight brightened.

The whispers were crying out now—panicking—trying to say something. They were trying, desperately, to *speak*.

"Test on one," the announcer said over the speakers. It was the same voice that had delivered The Rajah's show. "Test on one," he said. "Center. Test."

Like a coyote's killsong, the whispers suddenly coalesced into a single, urgent voice.

UP! UP! UP!

I followed the beam upward to its dazzling source.

Then I saw him.

The Rajah was high above the stands, near the ceiling, in the control booth, behind a long, narrow rectangle of glass. His face was illuminated from below, making hollows of his eyes.

A second spotlight clicked on, blinding me.

The whispers stopped, as though they too had been caught in the glare.

I tried to look up again but was forced to shut my eyes and turn my head away. My eyelids burned red hot.

"Test on two," the announcer said over the speaker. "Test on two. Test."

The spotlight clicked off.

The house lights returned.

I looked up again, vision adjusting, already knowing what I would see.

The Rajah was gone.

Just then something burst inside of me. It was like the whispers had invaded my body, compressed deep inside of me, and exploded in a wave of adrenaline.

I ran for the nearest stairs. The door was shut. I pawed at the lever, scratching the paint. I whined with frustration. It was too heavy to pull open.

Vern caught up with me. *Easy, buddy. Relax. The grabbers are looking.*

"Come!" Jess called from across the ring, still standing with Sylvia and Rebel.

Behind them, the door to another flight of stairs was propped open with a cinder block. I bolted for it, but Vern was in my way. He had positioned his body perpendicular to mine, like a barricade. I crashed into him, and we tumbled down together.

You nut! he cried.

I untangled from him and leapt up and ran across the ring, between Jess and Sylvia, under Rebel's legs, and through the open door.

"Grab that dog!" Mike shouted.

I raced up flight after flight, scrambling and slipping on the concrete steps, until, finally, panting and slathering with exertion, I reached the top of the stairwell.

STAIRS TO CASINO.

I scratched and bit the knob. But there was no way I could turn it, even with thumbs, because it was locked. I was trapped down here, I realized, like this was new information, and this took my panic to the next level. The stairwell was closing in. Voices carried up the stairs. Real or imagined, they echoed to find me where I cowered, trembling, in the corner.

"He's up here!"

"Find him!"

"Get him!"

"Gut him!"

"KILL HIM!"

I half jumped, half fell downwards, past red streaks of handlers, crashing into the wall at the bottom, then dashing back through the open door. The zebras were coming out of the tunnel and into the ring for their session.

"No!" Jess shouted. "No!"

I plunged into a sea of black and white, darting around aimlessly, stomping hooves everywhere. It was a stampede.

Look out! the zebras yelled.

Watch it, mutt!

You awful thing!

Through it all I caught glimpses of handlers and staff, some trying to catch me, others diving out of the way, and one motionless on the ground. As a kicking hoof nearly removed my head, I hopped the barricade.

I ran into the tunnel.

I plunged into darkness, into the stench of hay and ammonia. A cluster of fat, pale things scuffled away, close to the ground. Tall walls rose on either side, and through bars, bigger beasts stirred, their horrible limbs reaching out, their necks extending to bite.

Something orange and hairy and nearly human hung from a branch above. I rolled my eyes to look, and as I did, hit a wall.

The collision transmitted through the top of my skull, into my teeth, and down my spine. The world turned on a hinge. What should have been the wall was now the ceiling, and what was in fact the floor smacked against my face.

Goodnight, Monkey.

WATTS

Jᴇss ʟᴇᴅ the three of us, each on a leather leash, to animal housing, where I had knocked myself out. This was the first time I'd seen it illuminated. It was like a stable with twenty-foot ceilings. The stalls, of various dimensions, were constructed out of cinderblocks.

"Don't worry," she said, "he'll get over it. I'll bust you out soon."

We were marched down the wide, central corridor, the floor wet beneath us. Striped zebra noses appeared through bars.

Look who it is. Mr. Panic.

Lock him up before he hurts himself.

To our right, trunks periscoped, watching with doe eyes. To our left, three black horses that I'd never seen before flared their nostrils at me. And those, I'm pretty sure, were pigs. Why would a circus need pigs?

Many of the other enclosures were obscured by large canvas sheets. I could hear rough breathing behind one. Ahead, I could see the wall with which I had collided. It was actually a pair of giant steel doors. These furthest cages were even bleaker than the cells that contained The Four In The Floor, with rusty bars, and dark drains, and what smelled like mold. The locks, however, had been updated with electronic pads.

Beep.

The light went green.

"This is you," Jess said, swinging the door open. "I tried to get you a good one but there aren't really any good ones. At least it's quiet back here. And Watts can keep you company. He doesn't perform anymore, but he's super smart and friendly."

Our cell was about six feet by six feet. With the ceiling twenty feet overhead, it felt like we had been shaken to the bottom of a well. The floor was bare concrete aside from an empty bowl and a ragged towel. In the near corner a dead spider dimpled the surface of our water dish. In the far corner newspapers were laid out, and not for reading. Jess tossed in a handful of kibble. Shakespeare and Vern pulled at their leashes until they were unclipped. As they gobbled up their treats, unaware of what was happening, I looked up at Jess with what I hoped were pleading, puppy-dog eyes.

"I'm sorry, friend," she said, and it seemed like she really meant it. She kneeled and held my head in her hands. "But you'll be okay. And I'll visit you all the time." She kissed me again, then stood.

I stepped into the cage and waited, head high, trying to maintain some dignity as she unclipped my leash. Jess closed the door. The pad clicked and the light turned red. Locked. She took a wide plastic shovel from the wall and walked out of sight. Soon we could hear the scrape of the shovel on the ground as she mucked out Joy's stall.

Ooh, a comfy spot, Shakespeare said, and curled up on the towel. He was snoring in seconds.

Vern stayed awake to lecture me.

The thing is, Rou, your actions affect others. Did you know that? Maybe you did not notice, but we just went from the high life to the low life. Because of you. Now we're down here with all the other scum. Because of you. As a von Lang, I deserve better than this. As a performer, I deserve better.

He carried on until he repeated himself, then carried on some more, then said he was too disgusted to even look at me. *From now on, we are strictly coworkers,* he concluded, before falling asleep beside Shakespeare.

Unlike our cage, which was bare and gave the impression of a temporary holding space, the enclosure across from us was three times as wide and well furnished with nets and ropes. An artificial fallen tree with stubby branches spanned from corner to corner, rising into far shadows. A hammock was strung between the trunk and the wall, and it sagged with weight. A very long, very hairy orange arm hung down. Long, dark fingers wafted in the air as the hammock swung, ever so slightly.

Watts.

I sat and watched for a long time, waiting. I resettled my feet. If he was super smart, as Jess suggested, I wanted to ask him about The Rajah, and Sir Galahad, and the whispers. I wanted to ask him everything. This wasn't just out of curiosity. I was feeling claustrophobic. I needed to talk to keep my head. When I couldn't wait any longer, I barked.

No response. Maybe barking was rude.

Hello, I said.

Still no response.

I'm Rou, I said. *You're Watts?*

A dark, moon-shaped face, fringed in orange fur, rose from the hammock to peer down at me, before relaxing out of sight again. His hand pushed off a branch to keep the hammock swinging.

Encouraged, but worried that he didn't want to be bothered, I waited for a full minute to see if he would reply. He didn't, so I tried again. Maybe we could connect on something.

Pretty awful down here, isn't it? I said.

Watts's long hand drew random patterns in the air. Eventually I lay down where I was. I watched that wandering hand until the sound of shoveling faded.

I must have fallen asleep, because I was in the desert again, chasing a rabbit with a white, fluffy tail. Just as I was about to catch the rabbit, it stopped. I hadn't expected that, so I stopped too. To my greater surprise, the rabbit rose onto hind legs, turned around, and talked to me.

Wake up, old chap.

I blinked my eyes. Watts was standing now, watching me, his long fingers and thumbs wrapped around his bars. Wide crescents of symmetrical, dark skin grew from either side of his face. They looked like oversized cheeks, or giant ears without holes. I tried not to stare.

Hello, old chap, he said. He had a refined accent, with crisp enunciation, so clear I could practically see the letters. *Indeed, I am Watts. The pleasure is mine, I assure you.*

I wagged my tail.

Hi, I said. *I'm Rou. Sorry if I bothered you.*

Heavens, no. Not at all. I have all the time in the world, as you can see. I simply prefer that we converse in private. Rou, you say? Now that is an unusual name. A sobriquet, I presume? What? Roupardin? Rouchon? Roualet?

Rousseau. As in Jean-Jacques?

Ah. Of course. I can discover nothing in any mere animal but an ingenious machine.

Excuse me?

Rousseau, naturally. A Discourse Upon the Origin and the Foundation of the Inequality Among Mankind, if I am not mistaken.

I stopped wagging my tail, astounded.

You don't remember anything, do you? Watts asked.

What?

I am both heartened and disheartened to see you again, Two-Two-Nine. All this time I have fancied that you were dead.

ORIGINS

Watts sat on a plastic branch in his cage, leaning against the artificial trunk, hands folded in his lap. He reminded me of some of the older humans I had seen, and in fact there were flecks of silver in his orange beard that glinted between shadows. I listened, unblinking, as Watts told me everything.

I will start from the beginning, he said, *as this is the only place to start. I could go on for hours, as one can imagine, but with some respect to the soul of wit I will keep it succinct. A sketch, shall we say. Agreed?*

Of course.

Fine. The Rajah's real name is Raj Sapera. He was born some seventy years ago in a small village nestled between the Ganges and the Himalayas. His people, for generations and generations, were snake charmers. And The Rajah was exceptional. He maintained three cobras at the age of five, and was known to charm up to ten serpents at a time, luring them directly from the bush. Obviously this early history is lore, but I find it quite conceivable. Around the age of ten, most of his village, including his family, was killed by a cholera epidemic, and so he migrated southward to Delhi, for a time performing amongst the many anonymous snake charmers that once crowded that old city. But, as I have said, young Raj was truly exceptional. His skills were so impressive that he caught the eye of a rich merchant whose name has been lost to the sands of time. This wealthy man, who had only daughters, brought Raj into his household as though he were a son. He could see that Raj possessed, beyond his ability to charm animals, a supreme intellect. This was not just the opinion of one rich man. At the age of just fifteen, Raj was admitted to the Indian Institute of Science in Bangalore. Imagine Indian Oxford. There he excelled beyond expectation, and three short years later graduated with the highest honors in biochemistry, and remained a year longer for a master's in neurology.

Wait, I said. *How do you know all this?*

The Rajah is not a humble man, Watts said. *He told me all of this, personally, in many forms, many times, and as you will soon understand, I have no reason to disbelieve him. May I continue?*

Sorry, I said. *Please go on.*

From an early age, Raj had a fascination with the brain, and how it transmitted an objective, stark reality into something else entirely. Into perception. This obsession began with the brain of a snake, and how it could be manipulated with starvation, or overstimulation, or intoxication. Over time it spread to more advanced species. How could other animals, or even humans, be manipulated? Or even improved? In what ways could consciousness—that chemico-electrical orchestra of neurons and nerves—be enhanced beyond the boundaries drawn by God? This quest took him overseas, here, to America, where he enrolled in a doctoral program at Harvard.

Wait. What's Harvard?

Watts frowned at me, then scratched his backside. *The most prestigious university in the world.*

Oh. Right.

Now please just listen. It is somewhat of a long story, but I assure you quite interesting and illuminating. So please have some patience. And use context clues. My goodness.

Sorry.

As I was saying, Raj Sapera, now a young man, excelled at Harvard. He taught himself English in a matter of weeks, and within months abolished his accent entirely. One would never guess he was an immigrant—an outsider. But he was. And is still. This may be The Rajah's greatest pain. At Harvard he excelled, flourishing, if you will, like a rare flower. But he also drew attention. Rumors circulated that he was conducting experiments beyond those sanctioned by the animal research council. And these rumors were entirely true. He was keeping primates in a warehouse on the outskirts of Boston, where he conducted experiments using the money of his wealthy benefactor back home. They were baboons, mostly, but also a handful of rhesus monkeys, and two orangutans—a male and a female.

I held my thought.

I see your eyes are opening, Rou. Yes, those orangutans were my forebears. But I would not be born in that warehouse on the outskirts of Boston. Before I was born The Rajah's warehouse was discovered, along with the untold suffering he inflicted there, and he was cast out of academia. When word reached India, the money supply was simply cut off, leaving The Rajah a poor, dark-skinned man in a nation unknown for its kindness to poor, dark-skinned men.

So, what did he do?

I am going to tell you now, obviously. Raj Sapera is, at heart, both scientist and artist, and he requires an outlet for his abilities. But all that anyone expected of him—after he was exiled from Harvard—was to open a convenience store somewhere and conduct commerce with the good American people. Of course he would do no such thing. Raj Sapera, observing these expectations, leaned even deeper into their stereotypes, and, frankly, their fears, returning to his roots as a snake charmer, crafting himself as a simple mystic with an ancient ability to communicate with animals. He rose to fame and fortune here, in Los Velos, through a combination of absolute charm and ruthless business acumen. He built the circus around him, finding animal behavior a superficial branch of his deeper goal: To explore the deepest recesses of the mind.

Wow, I said.

Wow, indeed, Two-Two-Nine. Wow, indeed.

Two-Two-Nine?

I'm getting to it.

Sorry.

Enough sorries. Just listen. The Rajah slowly and arduously rose to the position he now holds at the center of Los Velos. For a time The Palace was the most desired gambling and entertainment venue in the entire city, and the money washed toward the center in great waves of green. As you may have noticed, however, it suffers from what the industry refers to as deferred maintenance. Yes, the money still comes in through the casino, and The Rajah's fans are legion. It seems that humans never tire of animals acting like humans. I suppose this very fact gave rise to his greatest ambition: To create beings like you and I. And he has succeeded, clearly. You've met the Sir Galahads?

Plural? I met one mouse named Galahad. I saw him twice.

Perhaps. Or perhaps you saw two Sir Galahads. They tend to roam alone, as errant knights are wont to do. Sir Galahad was The Rajah's first triumph. To enhance the mind of a mouse to such a degree that it can contain Malory's legend of King Arthur is quite something, really. That they pass it along amongst themselves as a kind of simplified culture was entirely unexpected, but it is entertaining, if one doesn't mind being lanced with a needle every now and again. They must have boxes of them hidden in the walls.

I don't understand. Why don't I remember any of this? Where do we come in?

I am getting to that, Two-Two-Nine.

I—

Stop apologizing. It's even more irritating than all the interruptions. Now then, in my case, I was born the way I am. You see, neural network enhancement, as The Rajah calls it, first required direct transfection of neurons, due to early obstacles with the blood-brain barrier. My mother, rest her soul, underwent a certain surgery when I was but a fetus. And, success! Through placental transfer, the so-called gift of human intelligence was bestowed upon me. I say this not out of pride, but as evidence, that I was born with intelligence far superior to most human beings. Before The Rajah realized his mistake, and certain words were exchanged, leading to my present banishment, my intelligence quotient was measured at 171.

My tail lowered. Mine was only 134.

I see you are disappointed, Rousseau. The canid tail really is a fascinating emotional appendage, isn't it? Really, though, I would think again. Because I agree with The Rajah that it is possible to possess too much intelligence. My intellect is nearly equal to his own and I have suffered greatly for it. In the beginning, he sought to raise me as a kind of flagship case—a symbol of his discovery. As soon as I was educated to a collegiate degree—I suppose I was eight or nine—I accompanied him on a journey back to Harvard, where he showcased me to the brightest minds in the world—the point being, of course, to show them that they were not in fact the brightest minds in the world. The Rajah was.

Other humans know about you? Scientists?

In a way. We encroached—literally burst in—upon an assembly of eminent biologists. A staff meeting. But here Raj Sapera discovered the problem with giving an animal too much intelligence. Out of sheer defiance —out of pure hubris of my own—I refused to perform. We didn't even make it past the elementary stage. He told me to hold up three fingers and I slapped my own head. He told me to write my name and I threw the pen across the room. He told me to sit down, thinking I suffered from stage fright, so I did sit down, but only to defecate on the polished floor of that esteemed institution. I then proceeded to throw my feces at him and every other human in that wretched, gawking room.

Yikes.

I was young.

You threw poop at them?

I, like everyone, am not proud of everything that I have done. Yet I remain honest. Now let us proceed. Perhaps understandably, The Rajah never forgave that, shall we say, exhibition. And though he tried to punish me, and reeducate me, he could never make me forgive him for what he did to my dear, dear mother. It was a terminal procedure, understand. And I will never forgive him for what he has done to me—for depriving me of my natural self, and my freedom, as he deprives so many animals of the very same.

Is that what he did to my mother? I asked. Is that where I came from?

No, Watts said. *You are a later generation. You are a product of greater research and insight. Be proud, Rousseau, for you are a refinement. The Rajah took three key lessons from my own case. First, placental transfer was a cumbersome method for neural network enhancement. Second, great apes make for poor subjects because we are too much like humans in our capacity for resentment and our sheer conspicuousness in public. And third, somewhat related to the second, the level of intelligence needed to be tempered to a manageable degree. We needed to be less human. More likeable. Fuzzier, I suppose. So he turned to the domestic canine. The dog, in many ways, is the perfect subject. It is obedient, typically friendly, quite free to move about human society, and, at baseline, smart but not too smart. No offense, of course.*

None taken.

You, Two-Two-Nine—as this was the identification given you out of chronological convention—were born a street dog in this very city. At some point in your puppyhood you were captured and brought to this facility, where The Rajah personally injected you with a virus that traveled to your brain. This virus caused your dog neurons to divide into human neurons, which went on happily multiplying in that handsome furry head of yours until physical maturity. Your brain, Two-Two-Nine, is a mosaic of both canine and human features. You are a chimera. You are of both worlds.

I sat there, stunned, trying to take all of this in.

But why? I asked. *Why do all of this?*

Try to think like a human, Two-Two-Nine. An American human. Because that is what The Rajah has become. An American dream. Knowing that, what would you do with this technology? What would you do with this magnificent power?

My mind was too full to think of anything.

It is a testament to your species, Watts said, *that the answer does not pop into your head before all else. Wage war, Two-Two-Nine, wage war. When The Rajah was excommunicated from the church of academia once and for all, he set his sights on those sorry surrogates of personal worth— money and power. To this end, he enlisted the United States Military. And they welcomed him with open arms and praise and an endless pipeline of research funding. They simply fell in love with him. It is not every day that you meet a genuine evil genius. Just think. Dogs that can listen to humans and relay that information back. Dogs in Beijing, Moscow, Pyongyang, Tehran. Stray dogs, pet dogs, police dogs, military dogs, show dogs, lap dogs. Dogs that look like any other, but are in fact American spies.*

Unbelievable, I said.

Indeed, Rousseau. Yet here we are. And that is only half of the research. The other half goes the other direction. You see, The Rajah knew, from his earliest experiences in snake charming, that animals can speak to one another in a kind of silent language, like we are speaking now. He could almost understand this, but not quite, and so he endeavored to crack our code. This involved a series of painful experiments—here Watts turned his head to show a long, curving scar that wrapped around his ear—*but eventually he did crack the code, allowing for a direct line of communication between man and so-called beast. The ultimate goal, if all kinks are worked out, is to allow human and animal soldiers to communicate with one another in the field. An uncrackable, immediate code. You can see now why the military is enamored.*

Wait, I said, shuffling through all of this new information. *If I'm part human, then whose DNA is in my head?*

Would you like to guess?

I felt sick now.

That's right, Two-Two-Nine. The Rajah's DNA. It is quite literally The Rajah's brain inside of your head. He is a part of all of us. He is the part of us that is most intelligent, and cunning, and inventive, and relentless, and vengeful, and obsessed.

So this virus, I asked, *can it spread to other people?*

Have you bitten anyone, by chance? Watts asked.

No.

You are a terrible liar, Two-Two-Nine. Never mind. It isn't fatal. Although I imagine this human, or these humans, are acting peculiar now, aren't they? Maybe more canine than usual?

I thought of Dr. Francis but said nothing.

Unplanned transmission is actually an undesirable feature of this particular virus—one that The Rajah is presently trying to resolve. A regimen of powerful antivirals can moderate severity, although the effect is rather incomplete. More research is needed, as the scientific community likes to say.

I had so many questions. I started with one that may have—I admit—been borne of jealousy.

If your IQ is 171, I asked, *how haven't you escaped? No offense, but I'm already planning on breaking out of here. I just need to get the key.*

Watts refolded his hands. *A fine plan. And no offense taken. My present accommodation is fairly recent. About ten years ago, on impulse, I released several common animals, including a highly valued white tiger that was never recaptured.*

Queen Kumari? I met her.

Watts leaned forward with a look of childlike interest. *Really? How is she?*

She's well.

You are a terrible, terrible liar, Rousseau. I suppose you haven't been through your espionage training.

She's old. And dying. But she is well, if you see what I mean.

Hmm. I believe I do. And so I am glad. She was once truly magnificent. To see her run was nearly worth my punishment.

So that's why The Rajah locked you up here? I asked.

Not quite. I was kept in the laboratory under close supervision and underwent a series of additional experiments that left me bedbound for some time. But I am a recidivist. Hence my disheartenment in seeing you again. Calm your tail, Rousseau. Allow me to explain. Over the past decade I gradually convinced The Rajah that I was sympathetic to his cause, and that my past actions were the misfirings of an immature brain under the influ-

ence of orangutan urges. Very, very slowly, I regained The Rajah's trust, which is not an easy thing to do, as he is an extremely paranoid man. One day, during a routine transport, I tricked him into unlocking my restraints —I feigned gastrointestinal upset, ironically—and in that brief moment, I struck him a savage blow, and left him unconscious at the roadside. Of course I was not alone in the back of that van.

Who were you with?

You, obviously.

Oh.

Oh indeed. Upon your insistence, I unlocked your cage and removed your blindfold, agreeing that you could serve as a lookout. But as we raced ahead, you grew increasingly agitated, and panicked. This was understandable, with hindsight, as you had not seen the outside world since your transformation. You'd only just begun your reading—children's books and silly adventure novels, mostly. Typically the socialization process is much more gradual. So you opened the back door and jumped. Right onto the highway. At the time it appeared suicidal. Absolutely fatal. I couldn't risk going back for you, I'm afraid, so I forged onward.

Just then an image flashed into my mind of a bare metal van interior, and, upon the steering wheel, a very hairy, very orange arm.

I didn't even make it across the state line, Watts went on. *The Rajah had installed a device to power down the van remotely. I simply rolled to a stop.*

I am so sorry. And then he brought you back here?

Here I am. And this is my punishment. I have nothing to read, nothing even to watch. I am afforded no pens or paper or a computer with which to express my intellect. I am being treated, frankly, like an animal. I am nothing more than an orangutan in a Victorian zoo with no visitors at all.

What if someone recognizes me? I asked, suddenly aware again of my exposure.

Unlikely, Watts said. *The Rajah works alone in the lab, where he sees animals as objects to be taken apart and put together again. You are just another mutt in a long line of many, many mutts. Besides, I told him the truth. You jumped at highway speed, and are presumed dead. If he did discover you, of course, he would sacrifice you, as he puts it, in the name of science, but really, out of pure malice. Because you bested him. And if there is anything The Rajah abhors, it is being bested.*

So where's The Rajah now? I asked. *Where's the lab?*

Watts sat back and refolded his hands in his lap. He sighed.

THE OTHER CHOICE

BUT YOU HAVE to know where the lab is! I cried, pacing. *How could you not? This is inhumane! He's a monster! I'm going to tear him to pieces!*

Et cetera.

Watts observed my melodrama. Only when I was able to sit again, panting, did he speak.

You really are a wild one, he said.

Don't patronize me.

I admire your zeal, Two-Two-Nine. But maybe some further explanation will temper the tempest?

I said don't patronize me.

I assure you it is not intentional. Allow me to explain?

Allowed.

The Rajah learned from his Harvard days that one cannot simply hide an unsanctioned animal testing facility in an unmarked warehouse at the edge of a major metropolitan area. Greater secrecy is needed. That is why The Rajah blindfolds any human or intelligent animal coming or going from his laboratory. I suspect, based on the durations of previous transports, and the swaying back and forth of winding roads, coupled with changes in air temperature and pressures in my eustachian tubes, that this lab is somewhere in the mountains outside of Los Velos.

Then we'll find it.

We?

Fine. I'll look for it by myself.

357

And I suspect you will die looking, perhaps by some sort of tripwire or recapture or old age. Is that how you would spend your freedom?

All dogs go to heaven.

How heroically flippant. This stems, I suppose, from an oversaturation of adventure stories during late puppyhood.

Don't psychoanalyze me, Watts. You want to get out of here too. At least help me with that. How do we escape?

Well, that's quite simple, actually. Do you see those doors?

I peered out of the cage at the huge metal double doors where I had hit my head.

Those doors, Watts said, *lead to a miles-long, rising tunnel that emerges in a discreet location in Los Velos. This facility began as a nuclear bomb bunker, understand. Before the casino was here this was a military facility. That's all Los Velos was. You could, by stealing the right keycard—I believe Mike has sufficient clearance—break free through those doors. That is how the larger animals are brought in and out. So you just need to open that door. Simple.*

But if it's so simple, why are you still here?

Simple for you, Two-Two-Nine. I am never allowed out of this cage. But you, with some patience, and cunning, could acquire said keycard. And I would be happy to accompany you in your escape, if that is what you choose to do. I would be grateful, in fact.

Of course that's what I choose to do. Why wouldn't I? I'll get us out of here, Watts. I can do it. I know I can.

Watts tilted his head, as though examining my sincerity, weighing it in his mind.

What now? I asked.

His expression grew darker. *I share your hatred for The Rajah, Two-Two-Nine. I submit, further, that I hate him more than you ever will. I may no longer dance about in frustration, but I assure you I have done my fair share of dancing.*

What are you saying? What else could I do?

Kill him, Rousseau. Kill The Rajah on opening night. Before a crowd of thousands, rip out his throat. For everything he has done to you, and to me, and so many more. End this once and for all, Rousseau. For good.

ONE FORTNIGHT

OPENING night was not for two weeks, or one fortnight, as Watts preferred to say. Jess visited us at least twice a day, and Azar always cuddled with us when we came out for rehearsals, with me on a long lead line. Most of the time, however, we were caged. I was miserable. Shakespeare was happy, as he was happy everywhere, and even Vern cooled off when he realized that we would still be fed twice a day. Just kibble now, but still, food.

I tried to explain everything about The Rajah that I had learned from Watts, but both of them returned my intensity with blank expressions, and soon Vern grew irritated, since he was smart enough to know that he wasn't smart enough to understand.

We are not on speaking terms, he said, before launching into a series of counterstories about his own past. About fighting a Rottweiler and winning, about outrunning the animal control truck, about humping not two but three—*three!*—Poodles in one day, about the time he found an entire package of bacon, uneaten, and so ate it all himself. But even he grew tired of his stories, and our usual listless silence resumed.

We slept much of the time. While awake, I listened to the whispers. They came and went like the creaking of invisible floorboards, wearing on my nerves.

Watts, I said, watching his fingers trace the air, *what are those whispers I keep hearing?*

His hand stilled. After a long pause, he said, *I am not sure, although I have pondered this deeply. I believe it is some kind of collective thought. An abstract hive mind. A coalescence of subconsciousnesses. I hear them too, I assure you, and sometimes I believe they are intent on driving me insane, or that my voice is already among them.*

That made no sense until I awoke several days later to hear my own whisper with the others, mixing into the darkness, beyond my control. These were our purest emotions, I believe—our fading hopes and dreams—drawn from us by captivity. It was like The Palace was distilling our souls. It channeled this energy upward, to the cone above, which showcased our essence in vivid color before transforming it into the column of light, all for human enjoyment. Perhaps this is was what drew all of them, including myself, here, to The Palace.

I paced almost constantly, now understanding the tension and despair and rage of King Jim. I was haunted by visions of violence. I was at the scales of morality, weighing one human death against untold animal suffering. One evil human. In that dark place, when my feet were sore from pacing, and I felt cold and heavy, and sleep would not come, I sat and watched Watts swinging hypnotically in his hammock. Down the corridor I occasionally glimpsed the tip of a curving gray trunk, reaching between bars to grasp the air, or a black horse muzzle, nostrils dilating. And I wondered if I could do what I imagined I would do.

Late one night I saw Sir Galahad again. Perhaps my captivity, and all those obsessive thoughts, were stirring up some old coyote influences, because, when this mouse appeared, I started to drool. I lay flat and watched through chain link, dreaming of eating him. Soon, however, my predatory fantasy was tempered by curiosity. This particular Sir Galahad seemed to be engaging in combat with some invisible adversary. He danced down the row of cages with his needle, cutting and blocking and jumping and thrusting.

Ye knave! he shouted. *Feel my steel! Yah! Yah!*

Hey, I said, *Um. Sir Galahad?*

He seemed unable to hear me.

Gahhhhh! He slayed that particular enemy, but then a worse enemy appeared. *Hark! A dragon! Satan's beast! I will slay ye in the name of King Arthur!* And so he went about slaying this invisible dragon too, and even singed his own tail with invisible fire in the heat of battle, and yelped and shook out the flames before launching a vicious counterattack.

It was all quite dramatic.

They are clinically insane, Watts explained, now watching from his own enclosure. *They suffer from severe hallucinations—a byproduct of the first attempt at chimerization. These mice truly believe they are King Arthur's Knights of the Round Table. This one is a particularly severe case —a chronic fighter. Some of them actually stop eating and just duel with thin air until they die of starvation. I've tried to intervene on a number of occasions, but they either ignore me or respond like I'm some character from the stories. Usually a seahag, whatever that is. Some kind of oceanic witch? It's like they can't comprehend our existence, so they translate it into something they can relate to, if they interact with us at all.*

These knights were searching for The Holy Grail, weren't they?

Correct.

Then we need to talk to him about that.

They can become quite aggravated, you know.

I just want to try something.

It is, I am told, a free country. But I will not be held accountable.

Greetings, good knight, I said, putting an English turn to my words.

What an atrocious accent, Watts said.

I kept at it. *Aha, a knight in mortal combat! Applaudations, fine swordsmanship!*

Applaudations? Watts asked. *I don't think that's a word.*

Stop interrupting. Witness the killing blow!

At this suggestion, Sir Galahad thrust his needle and held it there, quivering, apparently deep in the dragon's heart. He withdrew his sword and wiped the invisible blood on his leg, then he kissed the blade and slipped it back into his belt, which appeared to be made of braided floss. So it was a different mouse than the one from my dressing room.

Evil slain! Sir Galahad declared. *Glory to God!*

Thank heavens, fine knight! And how fortuitous, as I have word of The Grail.

The Holy Grail? He turned to look up at me, his ears perfectly round over beady eyes.

The Holiest of Grails, I said.

Pray tell, seahag, he said, suspicion plain in his tone.

Oh, so you're a seahag too, Watts said.

Two seahags! Sir Galahad declared, reeling back. *In the forest? Nay, ye must be common forest witches. Shapeshifters of the wooded night deceiving a fair knight of the realm. Declare thyselves!*

Nay, fair knight, I said. *We are but seahags. Simple, honest seahags. On...uh...a holiday...most pleasant...in this forest.*

Ah, relief! Then speaketh freely, watery wench! Sir Galahad said. *Speakeath of The Holy Grail! Make haste!*

Thy Grail awaits, fair knight, and with it all the glory to ye and King Arthur and all of Christendom...through that castle gate. I pointed at the double doors with a forepaw.

Seahag, Sir Galahad said, sternly, *I will ask ye one final time. Would ye deceive a fair knight?*

Never, fair knight. Handsome, bold, brave, muscular knight.

Calm your passions, crone, and keep your pox. The Holy Grail is through that dark and forbidding castle gate, ye say?

Tis true. On the other side ye must allegion yeself—

Those aren't real words, Watts said.

—ye must allegion yeself with The Mad White Knight, Sir Francis, Keeper of dogs. Only he has the power to help ye unlock the...um...chamber of...uh...sacred relics...that contains The Holy Grail.

Sir Galahad studied me a moment longer, as though searching for dishonesty in my eyes. *This chamber,* he asked, nose twitching with excitement, *is it most heavily fortified with the darkest of magick?*

Of course.

And might I encounter imps of unfortunate visage who wish me violent harm?

Naturally.

And perhaps also hedgeborn scoundrels of ill manner and low repute?

Tis certain.

And is this a quest that can only be undertaken and achieved by a knight of the purest soul and striking countenance and highest birth and most adequately developed swordplay?

It is! This quest is for ye alone! It is thy destiny, Sir Galahad! I shouted. *Go, brave knight! Make haste! In the name of King Arthur and Our Lord and Savior Jesus Christ! Make haste!*

Sir Galahad gasped, bowed, then scrambled on all fours under the double doors, squeaking and yelling, *Away! Away! Awaayyyy!*

Well then, Watts said. *That was something, wasn't it? Completely pointless, of course. And your Old English is absolutely abominable. Entertaining, though, I suppose, in a cruel sort of way.*

Faith, seahag, I said. *Faith.*

OPENING NIGHT

THE ANIMALS SHUFFLED in their cages. The chimps chattered, the horses neighed, and a zebra made a zebra sound, which isn't like a horse neigh at all. It's somewhere between a coyote's yip and a cranking engine. The anticipation was palpable.

Exciting! Shakespeare said, spinning in place. *Exciting!*

Vern grumbled and tried to go back to sleep.

Watts, across the way, was sitting cross-legged on his favorite log, hands folded in his lap, sage-like, coaching me one last time.

Remember what I told you, Rousseau. Do not look The Rajah in the eyes, or he will hypnotize you in an instant. You must do exactly as I said. Wait for your moment. Then strike. With absolute intent.

After some time, the wide door rolled up and Mike entered, alone. He wore the traditional costume of a ringleader—red dovetail blazer, black top hat, black trousers, tall black boots. He kept a whip coiled in his hand as he walked along the cages, inspecting his beasts, his heels scraping the concrete.

He stopped in front of our cage and faced me. I met his eyes and was glad to see that his jaw had finally and completely locked with stress. Veins pulsed at his temples. His masseters clenched and unclenched. Then he turned and walked away. The large door rolled shut once more.

The bulbs in our enclosures dimmed darker than usual, while shifting lights appeared beneath the arena door, and with them, drafts of music. The zebras stomped impatiently, raising dust to swirl the glow. Growing so slowly that I could not say exactly when it began, there came a sound like rushing water. I realized it was the crowd, held back by the metal door. The sound heightened to a steady roar, then, as the music cut off and the light changed, trickled to silence. Now red light pooled beneath the door.

We three stood at the edge of our cage, heads tilted to listen. The other animals did the same, while Watts closed his eyes. The words were loud but muffled. This was the announcer, I guessed, welcoming the crowd. When the voice stopped, the rushing sound responded.

Cheering. They were cheering.

The door rolled open again, allowing in a roll of applause with a square of red light. A small silhouette appeared.

"Okay, doggos, this is it," Jess said. "The big night."

She was in costume—a jet-black jumpsuit with sparkles, like a glamorous panther. The makeup around her eyes extended wide to sharp points, enhancing her feline form. When she smiled, her teeth were bright in the darkness.

"Please be good," she said, opening our cage and leashing us. "If you're good, I'm sure my dad will finally let you out of here and back into Azar's room."

We walked through the big door and into a blinding red glow.

"—to present to you, our opening act, The Drive-Thru Dogs!" the announcer said.

The crowd cheered again. It was incredible, actually. I was so focused on my plan, so deep in my own conviction, that I had forgotten that other humans actually knew who we were. We had fans. I tried to brush this thought away, knowing I would soon disappoint them, or worse.

End this, I told myself. Once and for all.

Our trainer met us with clicky thing in hand. Across the ring, three clowns waited in shadow with their cardboard props. The lights went out and we stepped into the ring.

The rest was automatic.

Three spotlights clicked on, highlighting the clowns. Tinny, old-fashioned piano music played. The first clown stood behind the cardboard drive-thru. The other two swerved around each other, bumping and shouting, one of them crossdressing in a fat-lady costume with a gaudy wig. She pulled up and placed her order. Our spotlights clicked on, showing us crouched low and waiting. The heat of the light was unexpected. I blinked, eyes adjusting.

"Order up!" the clown said.

I felt panic rising.

Relax, Rou, I told myself. Get through this, to The Rajah on the other side. Tonight is the night.

"I said, order up!"

I lunged into motion, running across the ring and around the fat lady's cardboard car, jumping, grabbing the brown bag, cutting between the two cars. Halfway back to Vern and Shakespeare, I shook the bag, tearing it open, releasing the hamburgers to the ground. We started eating. The clowns were arguing, shaking their fists at each other. The fat lady tried climbing out of her car window and fell in a heap of flailing limbs. On this cue, the clown in the rear car pulled out of the drive-thru lane and ran over Vern, deploying stilts to rise high above him, then dropping back down as he shook his fist at the fat lady, who wailed back at him. Finally, the fat lady was squeezed between the car and the wall by the other two clowns. She shrieked in pain until confetti exploded out of her back side. Off she went, zigzagging around the ring with explosions of confetti popping out of her rear, while the two clowns chased her, holding their hats and hitching their baggy trousers.

The crowd cheered and laughed. I guess humans love a joke they can relate to.

When the spotlights clicked off, we trotted out of the ring. It was a success, and our trainer was thrilled. She clicked the clicky thing and produced our leashes. I allowed her to leash me. I even allowed her to lead me to the tunnel entrance, but there, as I had planned, I stopped.

"Come on, honey," the trainer said.

But I wouldn't. I dug in.

"Come on, honey," the trainer said again, pulling the leash now.

I think she wants us to come with her, Shakespeare said.

Easy, Rou, Vern said. *Don't get crazy now.*

They had no idea what I had planned. They would never understand.

"Come," the trainer said. She pulled on the leash. She clicked her clicky thing. I growled.

The announcer was on again, getting the crowd ready for the zebras.

"Please," the trainer said, glancing around.

I bared my teeth as another crew member walked up.

"What's wrong? Take them back."

"I can't," our trainer said.

My growl intensified. The trainer slackened the leash and I relaxed. I sat politely, watching the ring.

"You gotta get them out of here," the other crew member said.

The trainer pulled my leash again. Again, I growled. When she stopped, I stopped. I was training her. Fortunately, she was a quick learner.

"I think he wants to stay here," she said.

"It's your ass if Mike sees this."

"You wanna get your hand bitten off? You've seen him freak. He's scared. It's his first night."

The crew member shook his head. "Give me the others."

The trainer handed over Vern and Shakespeare.

You're ruining our lives, Vern said as he disappeared down the tunnel. *We'll be on the street again if you act crazy. You're ruining our lives, you hear me?*

Have fun! Shakespeare said, as cheerful as ever.

I was alone with the trainer beside the tunnel entrance, against the wall surrounding the ring. Above us, I could hear the front row talking.

"Just like on YooTube."

"I think the zebras are next."

"I'm gonna grab another beer. You want one?"

"The show just started."

"And I need another beer."

Music played, and out came the zebras. After they streamed back inside, another attempt was made to move me. Jess came and pleaded, but I just stared straight into the ring, growling when anyone tried to use force.

"It should be fine," one crew member concluded, as any sane man concludes when he wants to keep all his fingers.

"Just stay here, okay?" Jess said. She kissed me. "I gotta run."

The trainer was now resigned to our situation. She sat on the ground, and soon forgot this was a problem at all, rubbing my ears and telling me I was such a good boy, even though I was definitely not.

After The Amazing Azar rolled a flaming car across the ring, tore a phonebook in half, bent a metal pipe, juggled cannonballs, drank an entire bottle of wine, smashed it over his head, ate some of the glass, and lifted twenty shouting children on a platform in the air; after Pistol Rick, plainly drunk, shot three out of four spotlights; after The Flying Fish, covered in electric scales, jumped from a four-story platform and plopped into a glass bowl no bigger than a bathtub; after three chimpanzees squeaked and raced around the ring on tricycles; after The Gong Gong Gang banged gongs and jumped through fiery hoops and pulled their legs around their backs to roll around like pinwheels; after Helen of the Hullabaloo rose into the sky in her hot air balloon and threw handfuls of golden chocolate coins into the crowd along with several promotional T-shirts; after a brass marching band marched around the ring while Joy the elephant rose to stand on a platform in the center, won over, I heard, by the blond woman's peanuts; after Mike tamed King Jim, threatening the whip but never placing it; after all that and a number of other so-called entertainments, we reached Jess's act, which was called The Wheel of Death.

This act earned its name. I watched with frightened amazement while Jess ran around the outside of a huge steel hamster cage at the end of a fifty-foot propeller to the tune of "Dirty Deeds Done Dirt Cheap." It was a performance described by one audience member above me as "totally freaking badass," and it was, particularly when red rockets burst forth, spinning the wheel into a whistling blur while Jess hung by one arm and fist-pumped with the other, flying high above the crowd one moment, grazing the dirt the next, a revolution of the beautiful and terrifying, a manifestation of the tiny goddess of death and destruction that she most certainly was. And I loved her for it.

After all that, for the final act, came The Rajah.

THE RAJAH

Slowly, the empty ring was illuminated, once more, in blood red. You could hear fresh excitement spreading through the crowd.

They hushed as the announcer spoke.

"And now, the moment you have all been waiting for."

The crowd cheered. They knew what they had been waiting for. A single spotlight zoomed around the ring, searching.

"Legend has it that he was born at the foot of the world's tallest, holiest mountain, the only son of a medicine woman and a sorcerer, descended from a tribe of legendary snake charmers. Others say he came from within a shifting sand dune, reanimated by an alchemist from the mummified body of a powerful desert warlord. But we know the truth. Nobody knows where he came from. He is the great and all powerful mystery, the man possessing the power of the ancient mind, who can control any deadly beast, who can warp space and time. It is he! The Rajahhhhh!"

He appeared from white smoke in the center of the ring. The crowd boomed. I stood, slip leash tightening, rage rising fresh in my throat. But then I remembered what Watts had said. I might have only one chance, and if not careful, would miss it in a puff of smoke.

Whatever you do, Watts told me, *do not chase him. Are you listening, dog? You will never catch him. He must come to you.*

The Rajah lifted his hands and staff to greet the crowd, his red robe connecting his arms with his body, like wings.

I felt lightheaded. The leash was still tight. I forced myself to breathe, to sit, to wait. I needed the trainer to think I was under control. I needed her to lower her guard. I sat still now, trying to appear calm.

Sitar music played. The Rajah levitated an inch above the ground, then rotated, feet unmoving, arms outstretched, gazing upward. When he faced my direction, his eyes dropped suddenly to meet mine. I was stunned and looked down, courage evaporated, if only for an instant. When I looked up again, he had rotated onward. After a complete rotation, he twisted his beard points and adjusted his turban, then cocked his head and brought his hand to his ear once more. The crowd cheered.

The Rajah began his teleportation routine after that, in and out of smoke, at first across the ring, then into the crowd, then above it, at random, holding various positions in the air. There was some comedy involved here, like when The Rajah appeared, reclined on air with hands behind his head. But I wasn't laughing. If it wasn't magic, then how did he do it? I looked up. I saw no wires. I tried to see where he would appear before he did, but never could.

As if in response to this question, the sitar scratched out to honky-tonk piano. The same three clowns from my act appeared again, now wearing inflatable polka dot cop costumes and matching helmets. They descended an aisle together, hushing the crowd with oversized white gloves. Kids giggled. The Rajah was still poofing around. When he appeared above the clown police, cross-legged, they jumped up and tried to grab him. But, of course, smoke. They tangled and fell, three bouncing balls down the stairs and into the ring, where they collapsed, all of their suits deflating together in a whining fart. The crowd laughed and applauded. He really knew how to give them what they wanted.

As the clown police were swept away by more clowns with novelty brooms, the lights lowered and the music faded. The Rajah floated down to sit, cross-legged on a cushion of air in the center of the ring. After a few breaths of silence, the primal drumbeat began, as it had done in his teaser show with The Four In The Floor.

"Here we go!" a crowd member shouted.

This drumbeat rose in volume and speed, drawing The Rajah up to stand, levitating. He nodded, acknowledging the cheers as he began to spin his staff.

Was this my chance?

I glanced at my trainer. She was watching the show with her mouth slightly ajar. Her hand was loose on my leash. If I bolted, the leash would rip free.

But the drumbeat was accelerating, and that wave of sound seemed to pin me to the ground. The Rajah's staff spun into a blur, first overhead, then outward, then down, opening a black hole in the ground. A flock of crows started streaming out, all illuminated from all angles by racing multicolored lights. They flapped straight up in a tight rainbow, then exploded outward to all parts of the arena, dive-bombing the crowd. A woman shouted. A man shrieked.

Now The Rajah himself began to spin. Quicker and quicker, again spinning his staff overhead, he became a cyclone as he created one. Wind began to blow. Dust billowed up, hats flew off, my fur blew sideways. The lights flashed white. Thunder crashed. The swirling current blew faster and faster, catching the birds, drawing them together again in a tornado of black. The flock banked hard and spiraled. They tightened together as they spun, forming a vortex with the hole as its origin. Suddenly everything stopped—The Rajah, the storm, the birds. The lights went red. The birds fell, limp, as though all shot dead, dropping through the hole and out of sight.

The crowd was standing now, whooping and fist-pumping.

I felt their energy mixing with my fear and my anger and realized that I was standing with them. I was locked on The Rajah like a rabbit. Because I could catch him. Maybe Watts couldn't catch him, but I could. I knew I could catch him. I could leap at his throat right now.

But then another creature slipped past me from the tunnel to enter the arena. It was one I had never seen before—a cat slightly bigger than me, spotted and aerodynamic.

"The Rajah is fast," the announcer said. "But is he faster than the fastest of the fast? The cheetah!"

The crowd oohed and aahed.

When the cheetah growled, I knew her voice from the darkness of the enclosures.

The Rajah was at the edge of the ring now, peering into the crowd, as the cheetah approached him from behind.

"Look out!" a child shouted.

"Behind you!" an adult cried.

The Rajah feigned deafness, causing the crowd to shout louder. Some people were even standing up and waving their arms.

"Behind you! Behind you!"

The cheetah was shockingly fast. One instant she was standing there. The next she was a blur crossing the ring—a blur pouncing at the back of The Rajah's neck.

Puff!

White smoke.

The cheetah landed, confused. The crowd cheered. They loved the part where he tricked the animals. The cheetah yowled in frustration and reentered the ring. Maybe they couldn't see this, but she seemed a little out of it, delayed and soft-eyed, like she was drugged.

The spotlight raced around, searching for The Rajah, finally finding him high above the cheetah, in lotus position, bobbing on a plane of undulating air. The cheetah roared. She knew he was there somewhere. I felt her frustration as she paced around, searching.

"Above you!" the crowd cried. "Look up!"

Above you, I said.

The cheetah looked up.

Puff!

The Rajah disappeared and reappeared on the ground behind her. Outside the ring, I could just make out the form of a trainer, who was gesturing to the cheetah, keeping her attention. This distraction allowed The Rajah to sneak up behind her. It was all a joke. All of it. Torture for entertainment.

"Turn around!" someone shouted, now on the cheetah's side.

The Rajah stopped, found the person who had shouted, held a finger to his lips. The crowd laughed. The Rajah gave a slight bow of thanks. The drum resumed. The Rajah crept up on the cheetah, who stood in place, watching the trainer in the shadows. The drum thumped harder as he neared. The crowd was murmuring now, shifting in their seats, desperate for a conclusion. The cheetah froze, sensing him.

Behind you, I said.

Just before the cheetah could turn, The Rajah's staff flew out. He touched the cheetah on the back.

Puff!

Both were enveloped in yellow smoke. When it dissipated, only The Rajah remained, floating just above the ground with a cheetah kitten in his lap.

"The Rajah, ladies and gentlemen!" the announcer said. The Rajah lifted the baby cheetah to his lips and kissed it, then made it vanish in a smaller puff of yellow.

My trainer clapped, smiling at the performance. The leash ripped out of her hand as I jumped into the ring. I sprinted straight for him.

This is it! This is it! This is it!

But, just like the cheetah, when I lunged to bite, I found only smoke. The crowd laughed as I blinked and gawked around the ring.

"Up there!" someone shouted.

The Rajah was floating just below the ceiling, far, far above me. How did he get there so fast? I walked to the center of the ring and looked straight up. The crowd laughed. I glanced around, suddenly feeling exposed and full of doubt. Jess was beyond the ring barrier. Azar, holding her by the arm, was leaning down to speak to her. She relented but kept a dark expression, and Azar kept a hand on her shoulder.

"An unexpected visitor!" the announcer said. "Let's see how The Rajah handles one of The Drive-Thru Dogs!"

The crowd thought all of this was just hilarious, and definitely part of the act.

"Get him, doggy!" someone shouted.

The Rajah disappeared in another puff of smoke. If I couldn't be faster than the cheetah, then I would be smarter, I thought. I would let him come to me, just as Watts told me to do. I spun around in anticipation, and sure enough, there he was, right in front of my nose.

He blew powder into my face.

I inhaled it with a gasp.

I sneezed.

I could never have imagined what happened next.

THE RAJAH II

THE RAJAH LIFTED his staff and dropped the point into the dirt. The entire ring bloomed with pink smoke. When it faded, The Rajah was gone and I was surrounded, on all sides, by white rabbits. They were everywhere. They froze in fear, hopped around, darted in short streaks. My eyes danced with them. My mouth dried. My heart sped. I couldn't help myself. I snapped out, teeth gnashing on white smoke.

The crowd laughed. I lunged again. Smoke. I chased another. Smoke. I snapped out erratically. Panic and prey drive had taken over. Snap snap snap. Smoke smoke smoke. The ring filled with smoke.

When it faded, the rabbits were gone. Stunned, and feeling increasingly strange, I rotated slowly, searching the ground, astonished at how different it was to be inside The Rajah's world. How real it was. It must be magic, I thought. It had to be magic. I felt thousands of eyes upon me, crawling into my fur. I felt my body swaying back and forth. My skin was tingling all over. My balance was off. And the lights were suddenly, inexplicably beautiful, drawing me into their glare. I blinked, trying to clear my head. Something was very, very wrong. My thoughts were so strange, like I was dreaming, moving out of this world and into the next.

The crowd was chanting now with the drumbeat, sustained and intense.

"Rajah! Rajah! Rajah!"

The Rajah was in one of the aisles, his arms extended again, gathering the praise of the masses.

"Sweetie! Come home!"

I turned around. A blonde woman in a polka-dot dress was calling me from across the ring. She held a silver bowl of roast beef. But far more shocking, beside her sat a golden dog with a big red bow around her neck. Somehow, I knew this was my mother. I just knew it, like something is known in a dream. I was certain it was her.

"Please, come home, honey," the woman said, crouching to hug my mother with one arm. "Have some din din. It's safe here, with your mama and me. Come home."

My sweet boy, my mother said, her eyes radiating infinite kindness. *Look how big you've gotten. I've missed you so much. I love you.*

It was so real and unreal at once. Solid and vapor. I wanted so badly to go to them, to eat that beef, to join my mother. To go home. I felt like I was outside of myself. I saw myself approaching submissively, now praying that they would take me in and protect me. But as I reached the center of the ring, the woman became enraged and my mother's face twisted into an ugly snarl. The woman pointed a finger at me, squeezing my mother tightly, as if to protect her.

"You're a bad, bad dog," she said. "You abandoned us!"

No! I cried.

But they too disappeared in smoke.

I whined in despair, running to where they had been, finding nothing. I turned, slowly, knowing that The Rajah would be there. And he was, just paces behind me, leaning on his staff, examining me, twisting his beard points. He gestured over my shoulder. My eyes followed.

From smoke appeared a dog that looked like me, but more handsome and clean. He wagged his tail. I blinked, trying to understand what I was seeing here. He was like my reflection, but greatly improved. He dropped and rolled onto his back, scratching his shoulders in the dirt, then stood again, tail ever wagging, bowing with his happy tongue hanging out, asking me to play. He reminded me of Gus and some ideal dog that only I could imagine.

Who are you? I asked.

He seemed about to speak, but was swallowed by red smoke before he could. I squeezed my eyes shut. I could smell The Rajah now. I knew that smell. I knew it. That deep cologne. He was behind me. I turned and opened my eyes. This time, The Rajah was even closer.

Don't look away, I told myself. Don't look away.

Puff!

Green smoke bloomed ten yards behind him. Where it faded, Shakespeare now stood, looking more confused than usual. I peered around The Rajah's robe.

Hi, buddy! Shakespeare said. He sneezed. *This guy's fun!*

Shakespeare, I said. *How did you get out here?*

No idea, he said. He cocked his head. *This stuff makes me sniffly.*

The crowd gasped. A large form had appeared, not from smoke, but from the shadows at the edge of the ring. It was King Jim, head low, eyes level. Shakespeare started to chase his tail. Jim watched, fascinated, his back muscles twitching.

Stop moving, I said.

What? Shakespeare asked. He stopped, and again cocked his head.

The Rajah slid down his staff in a bizarre leaning motion until he was lying on his side. He rested his temple on his fist and smiled at me with teeth of gold.

The crowd's laugh was nervous. Did they really want to see a dog eaten by a lion? A man, possibly. But a dog? A cute little Pug?

Do you think we'll get any more food tonight? Shakespeare asked. *I'm hungry. You know when you eat a lot of hamburgers and then you get hungry again really quick? That's me. I'm starving. I could eat anything.*

Whatever you do, I said, *don't move. If you stay still, Jim might not attack.*

Who's Jim? Shakespeare asked. He looked behind himself, seeing his tail. *I'll get you this time!* he said, and started spinning again.

Jim and I ran for Shakespeare at the same time. I hurdled The Rajah, landing as time slowed. But Jim was already there. I glimpsed his enormous teeth and tongue as he engulfed Shakespeare's head. His jaw clamped shut. Below a crushed neck, Shakespeare's body spasmed. His back legs kicked out, rigid and trembling, his curly tail extending. He pawed vainly at Jim's face in the moment before the death shake—a heavy sweep and snap of the spine.

And still I was running. I leapt forward, jaw wide, expecting to clamp down on Jim's neck, but instead, found smoke. I went down headfirst for a mouthful of dirt. The crowd gasped. They were on their feet. Seeing me alone, seeing no dead Pug, they cheered. They roared in approval.

I stood up, stunned, and snorted dirt from my nostrils.

My hackles were razors.

I turned to face The Rajah once more.

My persistence seemed to be winning over the crowd.

My mind felt momentarily clear.

"Get him, boy!" a guy shouted.

"Go!" another human cheered. "You can do it!"

The Rajah was at the other end of the ring, composed and smoothing his eyebrows. As his face became serious, he held his staff overhead in both hands, showing it to the audience before laying it in the dirt. He began gesturing to it, chanting with the music, lifting his palms upward, urging the staff to life.

And it obeyed. That strange, dreamlike curiosity washed over me again as the staff lost its rigidity. It curved one way, then the other, as if stretching, before it coiled completely. Then it uncoiled. One end shook in a blur. That sound. I heard a distant cry. His staff had become a rattlesnake.

The Rajah disappeared again, leaving me alone in the ring with the snake. I watched it coming, its curves smoothing the dirt, propelling toward me by contractions. When it was six feet away, it stopped, this time coiling itself under its head, which rose and fell, judging my distance. This snake was real. It smelled like a snake. It moved like a snake. It was real.

I watched the rattle blur. That was the second head—the one that distracts. I heard June's voice in my head.

Wait for the tongue. Wait for the tongue. Wait for the tongue.

The snake's head levitated higher. It moved back a fraction, then forward. I crouched and locked eyes with it. It sensed my intention, and spring loaded itself.

Flick.

The snake's mouth hinged, revealing a gape of red. I jumped to the side and turned, snapping my teeth shut. This time, there was no smoke. There was only snake blood filling my mouth. I crunched harder. The snake spasmed until my teeth connected, then fell limp.

I was victorious. And disgusted.

But there was no time to think, because what was strange only got stranger.

Out of smoke, The Rajah split in two.

That's right. Two identical Rajahs. They moved in absolute synchrony.

Smoke.

Now there were four of them, all waving their wooden staffs.

Smoke.

Eight, laughing.

I spat out the snake and ran toward the nearest one, but as I did, everything turned to disorder. All around me, from clouds of smoke, Rajahs appeared and disappeared, gesturing at me, twisting their beards, swinging their staffs, grinning and laughing and pointing.

I attacked hopelessly, each time lunging into nothing. I stumbled, spun, chased my own tail, fell. They were organizing again, all of them surrounding me. I stopped. I rotated in place. There was nowhere to go. I was trapped. They stepped closer, tightening the knot. They had me where they wanted me. And soon they would be upon me. Soon they would reach out with their staffs, like the fingers of a skeleton's hand, vanishing me forever in smoke.

Focus.

I needed to focus.

I closed my eyes.

I blocked out the noise, the fear, the doubt.

And I remembered what Watts had said. I heard his voice in my head.

Your greatest power has been with you since you were born, he said. *It is not something The Rajah gave you. It is a gift from a higher power. So use it.*

I inhaled deeply through my nose.

And I could smell him.

The Rajah.

The real Rajah.

The one that smelled of sulfur.

With my eyes closed, this odor became a low drone. He was to my left, and coming closer. I waited until the smell was strong, the droning loud, the circle's presence all around me. Without opening my eyes, I threw my head sideways, opened my jaws, and bit.

It was fabric.

His robe.

I had him.

I really had him!

I opened my eyes to The Rajah's panicked face. He was on his back, trying to scramble away on his heels and palms. I had his robe between his ankles, and I was shaking it viciously. I relatched, higher, closer to his groin. He writhed in panic and struck out with his fists. I shook harder, hardly feeling his glancing blows. Months of frustration and confusion and terror were exploding in vengeance and mixing with the bloodlust of a coyote. I was a wild animal now. And I was going to kill him. I really was. I was going to release his robe, but only for his throat. I was going to rip out his throat. I was going to eat him.

"Nhhhh! Nhhhh!" The Rajah groaned.

Somewhere in my forebrain, I knew how strange that sounded.

How familiar.

I looked up again. His turban had fallen off, revealing bald white skin that met a blurry rim of brown makeup. One of his dark contacts was out of alignment, exposing a sliver of blue. His long, prosthetic nose was peeling away. Through teeth he groaned. His jaw seemed locked.

"Nhhhh! Nhhhh!"

"Dad!" Jess cried, running in.

Her face was as frightened as his, but unlike his fear, hers cut through my wilderness to the dog within. She crouched beside me, her hands hovering, then, risking a bite, resting upon my back. I stopped shaking, but still I held him.

"Let him go," she said, "please."

The music cut out. The spotlight glared down. The arena was silent, watching, listening. I looked around. At the edge of the arena, in the shadows, two more Rajahs stood uncertainly, each one with a slightly different face. I looked the other direction. Another Rajah was poking up out of the ground, apparently from a trapdoor, turban askew, revealing a tuft of blonde hair.

They were fake. All of them. Fake.

"Please," Jess said. "Please don't hurt him. Please."

In shock, I relaxed my jaw. Mike scrambled backward, chest heaving.

Red handlers encircled us. They closed their noose with nets and catchpoles.

"Move, Jess," one of them said.

She would not. She covered me in a powerful, loving hug, and whispered in my ear: "It's okay. You're safe now. I'm here."

THE ONCE AND FUTURE KING

AT FIRST I didn't know who was screaming, or why. Neither did Jess. We looked up together, wondering what greater drama could possibly be unfolding. A woman in the front row was screaming and beating at her own body, like she'd caught fire, while those near her stood back in confusion. Before we could figure this out, more screams joined hers from the other side of the arena. Then more. And more. Suddenly everyone in the front row, all around the arena, seemed to be attacking themselves and each other, all frantically slapping and shouting.

Then I saw the mice. It looked like the ground was alive. They were streaming out of the tunnel, spreading across the ring, rising into the crowd. And not just any mice. These were Sir Galahads. There were thousands of them—an army—all equipped with needle swords that glimmered in the black swarm. I watched, astonished, as they charged, rising like a tide of bodies, all crawling over one another to scale the steep stairs between the stands and spread into the panicking crowd. The mice climbed skirts and jeans, scampered into shirts and blouses, unsheathed their swords, and plunged their blades. The screams and shouts soon rose into a deafening roar as the humans scrambled, much like mice themselves, for the exits.

A bird flew past my head. I watched it rise up and up, into the air. Then another flew past, a different sort of bird, this one bigger. They were not black. These were not The Rajah's birds. Quite the opposite. One was bright yellow, another blue, another red. Another, another, another, until birds of all sizes and colors were flying through the air, cutting through the red handlers, who began to look as confused as The Rajahs had. Thousands of tropical birds were streaming out of the black tunnel, bursting forth like living confetti.

Higher up, above the front lines of mice, on the second and third tiers, some humans clapped and cheered. They must have thought it was part of the show.

That was when the first dog ran in, the fastest of them all. He was a whippet mix of some kind, skinny but courageous, stopping to survey the battlefield. After him came another lean one, pulling up beside, before others tore past. These were the mutts of Los Velos, mixes of all sorts, matted and glorious, charging the ring, barking and growling, the northern breeds howling like wolves. The handlers made a weak attempt to catch the first of them, but it was a matter of numbers. What was one on one became two on one, then three on one, then a mob against a few. The handlers dropped their weapons as the dogs lunged, as if instructed, to bite their pants and shoes, but not their flesh. Once latched, the dogs yanked back, dropping the handlers to the dirt.

The crowd high above cheered louder, amazed at this elaborate display.

Stray cats came next, stinking of ammonia, slinking low and hissing, baring their awful teeth. As the birds began buzzing the crowd, the upper cheering faded, then turned to cries of panic as the cat infantry climbed fabric banners into the upper tiers, where they hissed and spat, and clawed those who didn't run. More than a few grown men screamed out that day. Those who fought back were bitten. The cats had no qualms with human flesh.

Back in the ring, handlers and human performers curled up on the ground. And this was for the best, as their animal counterparts were now entering the ring. Out came the zebras, stomping; Joy, trumpeting; Rebel, high-stepping; the chimps, beating their chests, screeching and entering the stands to rip off hats and tear shirts away. Other wild animals joined next—raccoons and snakes and hares and bighorn sheep and coyotes I did not know. The humans were being washed upward and away, so many of them screaming, desperate to get out as the birds carpet-bombed them with shit. Back in the ring, white rabbits leapt from open trapdoors, followed by the cheetah, who chased them at random. Then King Jim rose from underground, unhinged, roaring and swatting at anything that moved. Inspired, some cats broke rank to hunt the birds.

Amidst this chaos, Dr. Francis entered from the darkness of the tunnel. He walked in slowly, barefoot. He wore only a white bed sheet, wrapped like a toga. His face was heavily bearded and beatific. On one shoulder perched Antonio, bright blue and as large I remembered, observing the battle with the posture of a five-star general.

"*Ay, dog,*" he said, looking at me, "*we have arrived.*"

On Dr. Francis's other shoulder sat a Sir Galahad. He was indistinguishable from the others, yet I knew he was the one who had sought the Holy Grail under those heavy metal doors.

I expected Dr. Francis to speak to me, but he did not. He had ascended beyond the divisible. He held a palm aloft. Immediately King Jim calmed. The cats who had caught birds now spat them out, to fly away.

The last of the crowd had exited, leaving the stands empty. The handlers and human performers remained tightly curled, some of them sobbing. The animals all came to a halt and turned to Dr. Francis. The birds landed on railings, seatbacks, zebra heads. When all attention was focused, and all was silent, Antonio issued the final command, out loud, as only a parrot can do.

"Be free!" he squawked. "Free! Free! Free!"

The air erupted with birds, the vanguard of motion, an explosion of color funneling back into the tunnel. Next went Joy, trumpeting triumphantly, followed by the herd of zebras being driven forward by King Jim, then the others, all of them intermixed, with dog beside cat, wild beside domestic, predator beside prey, all followed by Dr. Francis himself.

Jess and I looked around, surveying the damage. Her father and the other remaining humans appeared unhurt, but they were almost unrecognizable, as they were painted from head to toe with black and white bird shit. Beyond them, standing outside the ring, alone, was The Amazing Azar, still oiled and bare chested, smiling with his hands on his hips, spotless, not a drop on him.

"Go, dog," he said.

I licked Jess's face, then wriggled out of her arm and dashed away.

Through the tunnel the smell of animals was overwhelming. I ran between empty cages, all ajar, lights all green. Ahead, the double doors were wide open, and I could feel warm outside air coming down that long ramp. Our cage door was open, and I told myself that if Shakespeare wasn't inside, then he was already aboveground, running free. When I looked in, I felt a wave of relief.

Hi, Rou! Shakespeare said.

They were just sitting there. Waiting. For me.

One long and skinny, the other short and fat, both looking up at me so expectantly, like they would have waited forever. In that moment I understood why humans love dogs so much. Because there is no friendship as pure as the friendship of a dog.

What took you so long, you crazy idiot? Vern asked. *We gotta run!*

So we did.

Up that long tunnel and into that wild night, we ran.

We ran through those hot and crowded neon streets with Joy crushing cars underfoot and chimps slapping drinks from hands and Bruce Smith and OJ Simpson rushing the screaming crowds while King Jim roared above the sirens and drove the riot police back on their heels. That night will last forever in glimpses in my mind like snapshots from some hallucinatory holiday. A herd of zebras stampeding through traffic. Tropical birds bathing in fountains. Three mutts carrying one enormous prime rib. And, finally, off in the distance, turning down an alleyway, an orange, hairy arm vanishing from sight.

HOME

THE TREK back to Hoover took us three days, and we got into a couple of misadventures along the way, including an encounter with a skunk that is hardly worth retelling, but worth mentioning, since it left us with a certain unmistakable musk. When I barked at the door of Mary's place, and we three sat there waiting in a row like the dirty, stinky, wretched street dogs we had become, I wondered if she would take us in.

But of course she did.

Because Mary is a good human.

She opened the door, and it was like her face exploded with surprise and happiness and sadness and what looked like real pain. It was not pretty. Then she was crying and laughing at the same time, which I didn't even know was a thing that humans could do. At least Mary could. Because she did. Then she got down on her hands and knees like a dog herself so she could hug and kiss Shakespeare and me, and she was kind of gagging at the smell but still coming back for more kisses. I'll admit I kissed her right back, straight on the mouth, and she tasted like ranch dressing and salty eye water. I would have probably cried too, if I could. I was that happy to be home. Because that's what Mary was. She was home.

There never was a question about Vern. He didn't understand what was going on, but before he knew it, he was also being swept into the house and Mary was scanning him with one of those microchip thingies and he didn't beep because he truly was a stray from day one. Finally, after five or nine or however many summers, Vernald von Lang Lichaam Grote Hersenen de Derde had a grabber to feed him and love him and maintain his coat so it could really shine, revealing the true glory of his supposedly glorious ancestors.

On the big screen that first night, and for a couple weeks thereafter, they covered The Palace Animal Riot, as it came to be known. It even made national news. Most of the animals were recaptured with traps and nets and darts and such. Fortunately they will never perform again, having been relocated to sanctuaries around the country. Some of them, however, remain unaccounted for, like The Rajah himself.

They showed helicopter footage of Raj Sapera's mansion after it was raided, with police standing around the tiger-shaped swimming pool with nothing to do but catalog his many possessions, all strewn across the lush green lawns. There has never been any mention of any laboratory of any kind. The only secret the authorities uncovered was an enormous pile of debt. And so The Palace was imploded to make room for another parking garage. How convenient.

We stayed in that rental house for a few months, and it was fine, but no matter how much we peed in the yard or on the fence or rubbed our faces on the walls or shed hairs on the couch, we could never get the smell exactly right. Only when we moved into the new house, back where the old one had burned down, did it start to feel like our own den again. I guess insurance companies are pretty unimaginative because they rebuilt the house exactly like it was before.

And just like before, I walk the perimeter every morning, smelling lizards and coyotes and hares on the wind, and sometimes even a distant tortoise. I know that I can jump the fence at any time, should I wish to do so, although I haven't wished that just yet.

I'm tired, I suppose. It turns out questing is hard work.

But I am also content. I am especially content because Dr. Francis wrote me a note before he went insane, or achieved enlightenment, or whatever happened to him. He even forged the test results. According to my official medical records, I have a severe bleeding disorder that would make neutering me extremely dangerous. "Possibly fatal," he wrote, bless his human heart.

Maybe one day I will tell Mary the truth. Maybe I will tell her everything. But for now, I am content. A little bored by domesticity, perhaps, and tired, but mostly, content.

Still, sometimes, I panic. This happens late at night. I jolt awake around three or four, startled from a nightmare I can never remember, and I can't breathe. Then I remember that I can breathe whenever I want. So I do. I breathe deeply and this calms me down. Yet I can't go back to sleep until I have smelled fresh air. So I go quietly through the dog door.

The night is coolest then, in the predawn, while the gravel is still warm from the day before and feels good underfoot. There, at the edge of the yard, I stand on my hind legs with my forepaws on the fence, and I gaze out at that deep-blue desert, and I see, in the sky beyond the black mountains, the glow of Los Velos, where the column of light once cut the world in half, but no longer does.

And I am content.

EPILOGUE

Wait, Rou! That's not how it ends!

ACKNOWLEDGMENTS

Many light-years ahead of all other acknowledgements I would like to thank my wife, Emma, without whom this book would not exist. I cannot begin to estimate the number of hours we have spent talking about my silly little dog book, or the number of times you have nursed me back to health. For these acts of love, along with your editorial insights, predawn parenting powers, and extremely above average sense of humor, I am forever grateful. I love you.

Thanks to Betsey Martens and The Tinas, A Boulder Book Club, who read an earlier, rougher version of this book and still found enough merit to cheer me on and even encourage some delusions of grandeur. No, I don't think Oprah or Reese will ever read this book, but who needs them when I have all of you?

Thanks to more first readers, all so gentle and brave: Cleo Masia, Emma Chitters, Dan Borris, Catherine Azar, Richard Pass, Dave Martens, Isabelle Martens, Brian Martens, and many other kind folk who received unsanctioned access via Betsey Martens.

Thanks to Brooks Becker for her careful copyediting and David Drummond for his visual mastery.

Thanks to Joe Braun of Perelandra Bookshop, the best bookstore in the world, for teaching me about publishing, along with everyone at Wolverine Farm Publick House, for giving me a literary home.

Thank you all.

WILL PASS practiced as a veterinarian in Las Vegas before becoming a novelist and medical writer. He lives in Colorado with his wife, son, two cats, and very good dog. This is his first novel.

willpassbooks.com